EOIN COLFER

ARTEMIS FOWL

THE ARCTIC INCIDENT

THE GRAPHIC NOVEL

Adapted by **Michael Moreci**
Art by **Stephen Gilpin**

DISNEP · HYPERION

Los Angeles   New York

Adapted from the novel *The Arctic Incident*

Text copyright © 2021 by Eoin Colfer

Illustrations copyright © 2021 Disney Enterprises, Inc.

First Hardcover Edition, March 2021
First Paperback Edition, March 2021

10 9 8 7 6 5 4 3 2 1

FAC-038091-21015
Printed in the United States of America

This book is set in Colleen Doran/Fontspring; DIN Next LT Pro, ITC Novarese Pro,
Neutraface Condensed/Monotype

Designed by Stephen Gilpin and Tyler Nevins

Library of Congress Cataloging-in-Publication Data

Names: Moreci, Michael, adapter. • Gilpin, Stephen, artist. • Colfer, Eoin, author.
Artemis Fowl.
Title: Artemis Fowl, the arctic incident : the graphic novel / adapted by
Michael Moreci ; art by Stephen Gilpin.
Other titles: Arctic incident
Description: Los Angeles ; New York : Disney-Hyperion, 2021. • Series: Artemis Fowl ;
2 • Sequel to: *Artemis Fowl.* • Audience: Ages 8–12 • Audience: Grades
4–6 • Summary: "A full-color graphic novel adaptation of the
internationally best-selling book about a twelve-year-old criminal
mastermind and the world of fairies"—Provided by publisher.
Identifiers: LCCN 2019056129 (print) • LCCN 2019056130 (ebook) •
ISBN 9781368064705 (hardcover) • ISBN 9781368065306 (paperback) •
ISBN 9781368065368 (ebook) •
Subjects: LCSH: Graphic novels. • CYAC: Graphic novels. • Fairies—Fiction.
• Kidnapping—Fiction. • Magic—Fiction.
Classification: LCC PZ7.7.M658 Ar 2021 (print) • LCC PZ7.7.M658 (ebook) •
DDC 741.5/942—dc23
LC record available at https://lccn.loc.gov/2019056129
LC ebook record available at https://lccn.loc.gov/2019056130

Visit www.DisneyBooks.com

To Ferdia and Lara for all their
hard work and talent.
—E.C.

For my family, who remind me every
day why I love telling stories.
—M.M.

For Jen
—S.G.

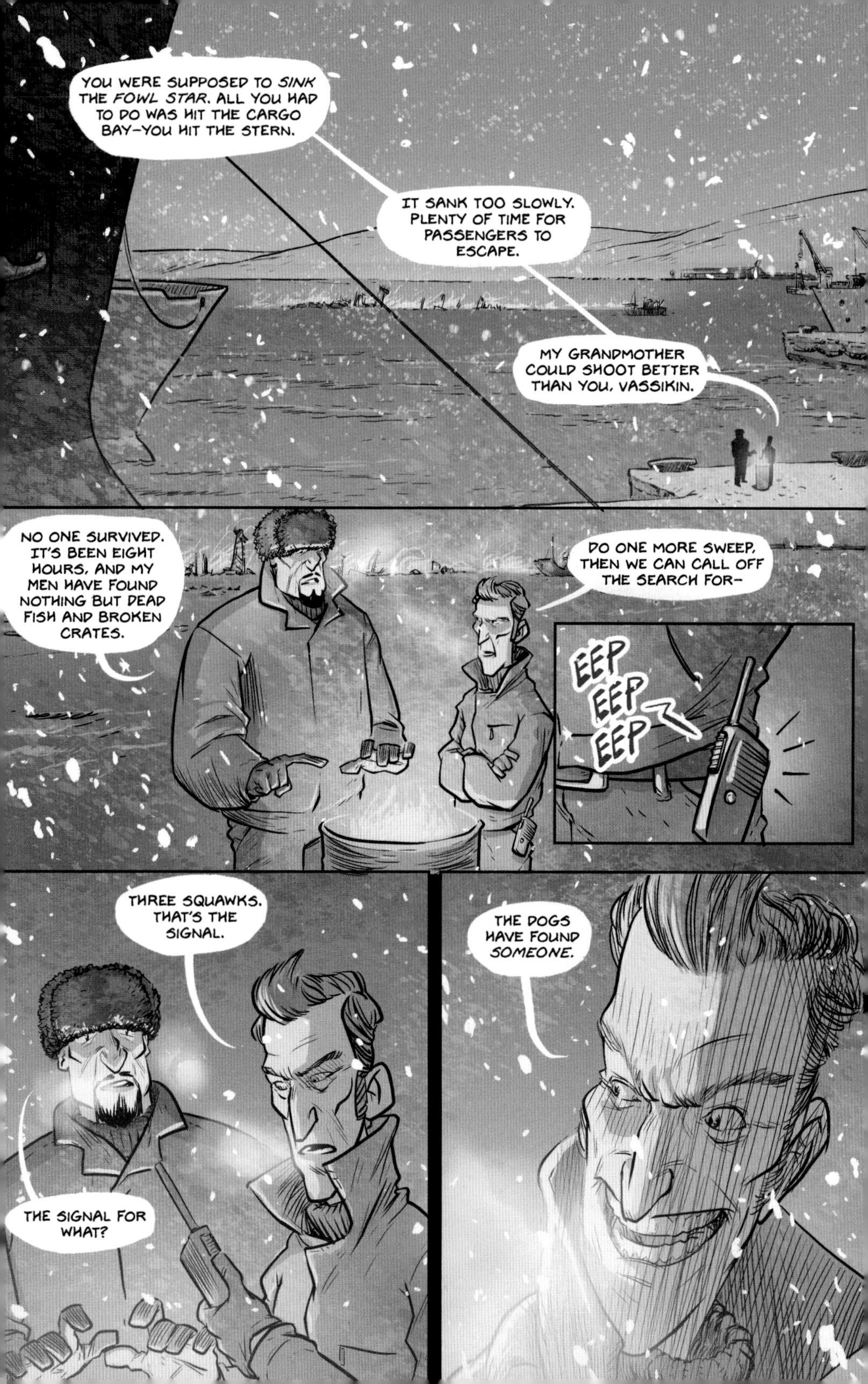
YOU WERE SUPPOSED TO SINK THE FOWL STAR. ALL YOU HAD TO DO WAS HIT THE CARGO BAY–YOU HIT THE STERN.
IT SANK TOO SLOWLY. PLENTY OF TIME FOR PASSENGERS TO ESCAPE.
MY GRANDMOTHER COULD SHOOT BETTER THAN YOU, VASSIKIN.
NO ONE SURVIVED. IT'S BEEN EIGHT HOURS, AND MY MEN HAVE FOUND NOTHING BUT DEAD FISH AND BROKEN CRATES.
DO ONE MORE SWEEP, THEN WE CAN CALL OFF THE SEARCH FOR–
EEP EEP EEP
THREE SQUAWKS. THAT'S THE SIGNAL.
THE SIGNAL FOR WHAT?
THE DOGS HAVE FOUND SOMEONE.

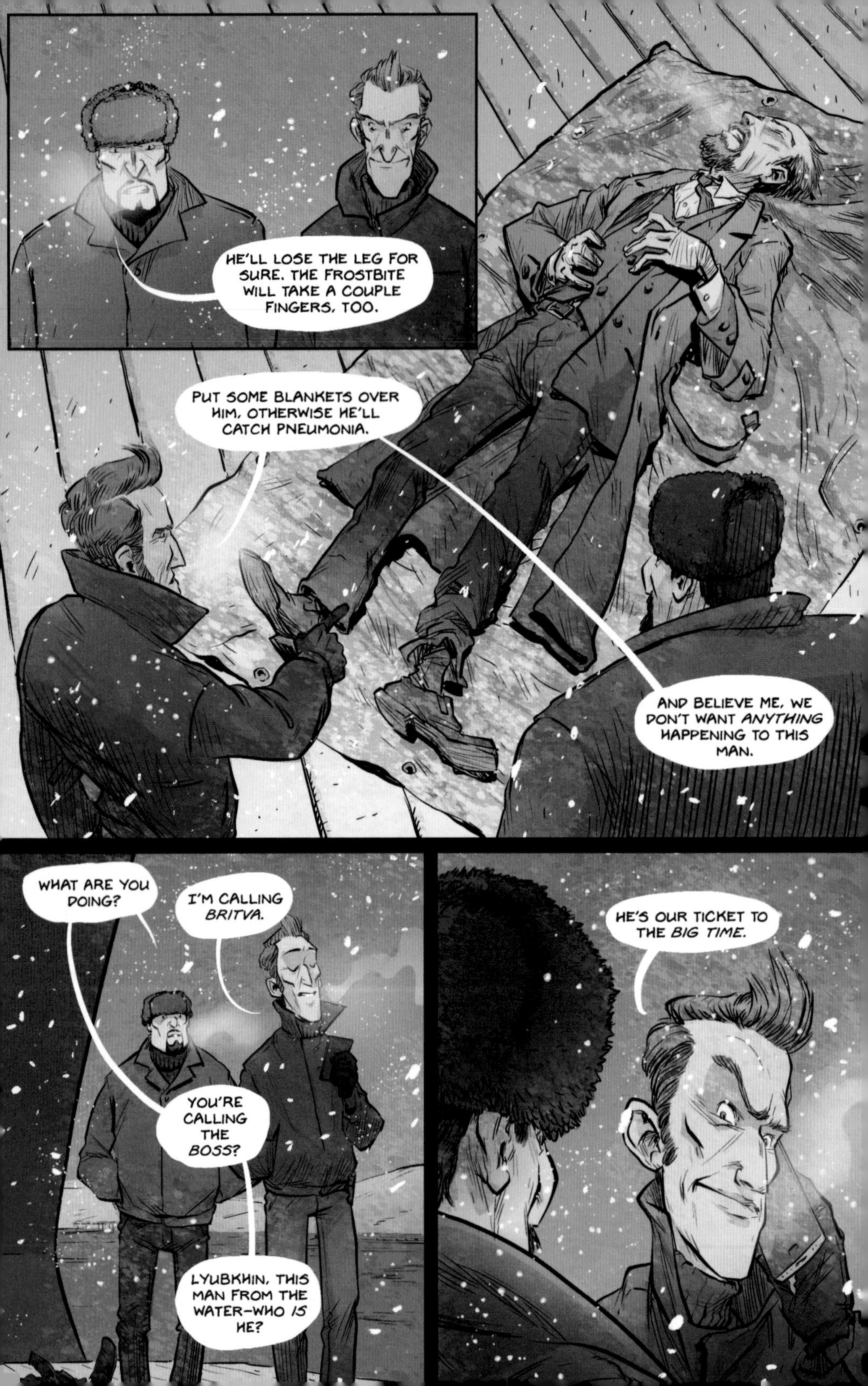
HE'LL LOSE THE LEG FOR SURE. THE FROSTBITE WILL TAKE A COUPLE FINGERS, TOO.
PUT SOME BLANKETS OVER HIM, OTHERWISE HE'LL CATCH PNEUMONIA.
AND BELIEVE ME, WE DON'T WANT *ANYTHING* HAPPENING TO THIS MAN.
WHAT ARE YOU DOING?
I'M CALLING *BRITVA*.
YOU'RE CALLING THE *BOSS*?
LYUBKHIN, THIS MAN FROM THE WATER–WHO *IS* HE?
HE'S OUR TICKET TO THE *BIG TIME*.

CHAPTER ONE

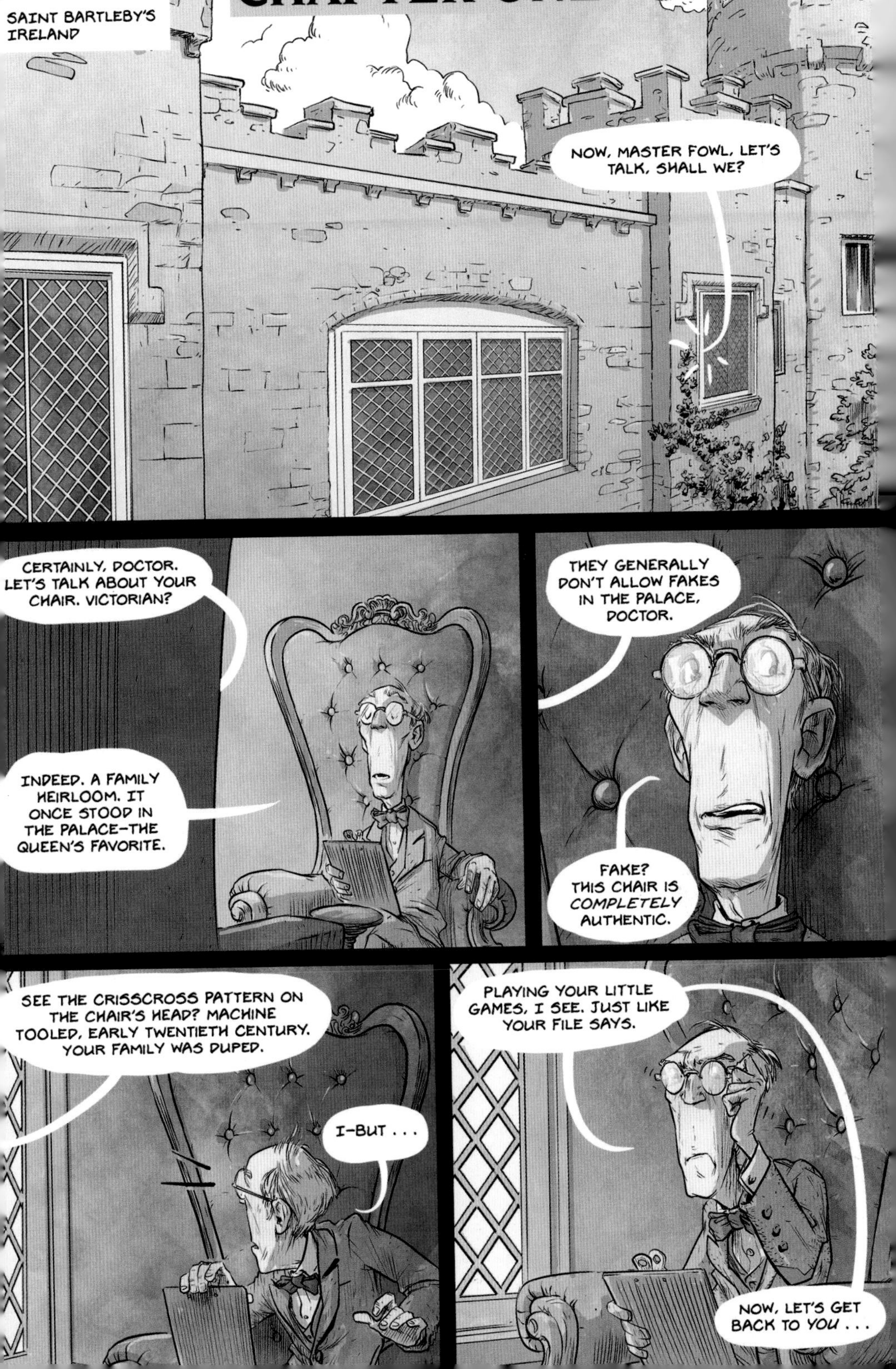
SAINT BARTLEBY'S
IRELAND
NOW, MASTER FOWL, LET'S TALK, SHALL WE?
CERTAINLY, DOCTOR. LET'S TALK ABOUT YOUR CHAIR. VICTORIAN?
INDEED. A FAMILY HEIRLOOM. IT ONCE STOOD IN THE PALACE—THE QUEEN'S FAVORITE.
THEY GENERALLY DON'T ALLOW FAKES IN THE PALACE, DOCTOR.
FAKE? THIS CHAIR IS *COMPLETELY* AUTHENTIC.
SEE THE CRISSCROSS PATTERN ON THE CHAIR'S HEAD? MACHINE TOOLED, EARLY TWENTIETH CENTURY. YOUR FAMILY WAS DUPED.
I—BUT . . .
PLAYING YOUR LITTLE GAMES, I SEE. JUST LIKE YOUR FILE SAYS.
NOW, LET'S GET BACK TO *YOU* . . .

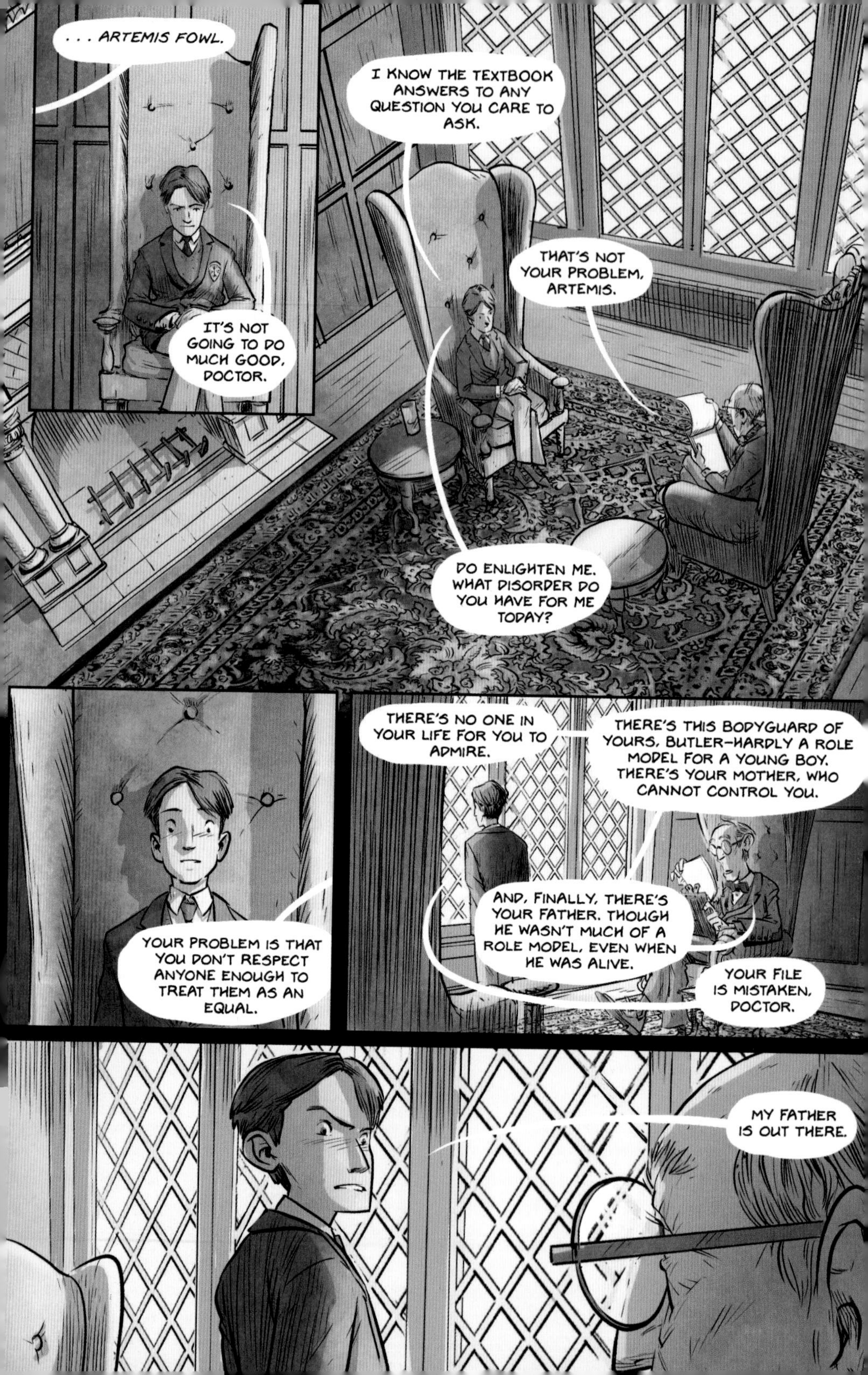
. . . ARTEMIS FOWL.
IT'S NOT GOING TO DO MUCH GOOD, DOCTOR.
I KNOW THE TEXTBOOK ANSWERS TO ANY QUESTION YOU CARE TO ASK.
THAT'S NOT YOUR PROBLEM, ARTEMIS.
DO ENLIGHTEN ME. WHAT DISORDER DO YOU HAVE FOR ME TODAY?
YOUR PROBLEM IS THAT YOU DON'T RESPECT ANYONE ENOUGH TO TREAT THEM AS AN EQUAL.
THERE'S NO ONE IN YOUR LIFE FOR YOU TO ADMIRE.
THERE'S THIS BODYGUARD OF YOURS, BUTLER—HARDLY A ROLE MODEL FOR A YOUNG BOY. THERE'S YOUR MOTHER, WHO CANNOT CONTROL YOU.
AND, FINALLY, THERE'S YOUR FATHER. THOUGH HE WASN'T MUCH OF A ROLE MODEL, EVEN WHEN HE WAS ALIVE.
YOUR FILE IS MISTAKEN, DOCTOR.
MY FATHER IS OUT THERE.

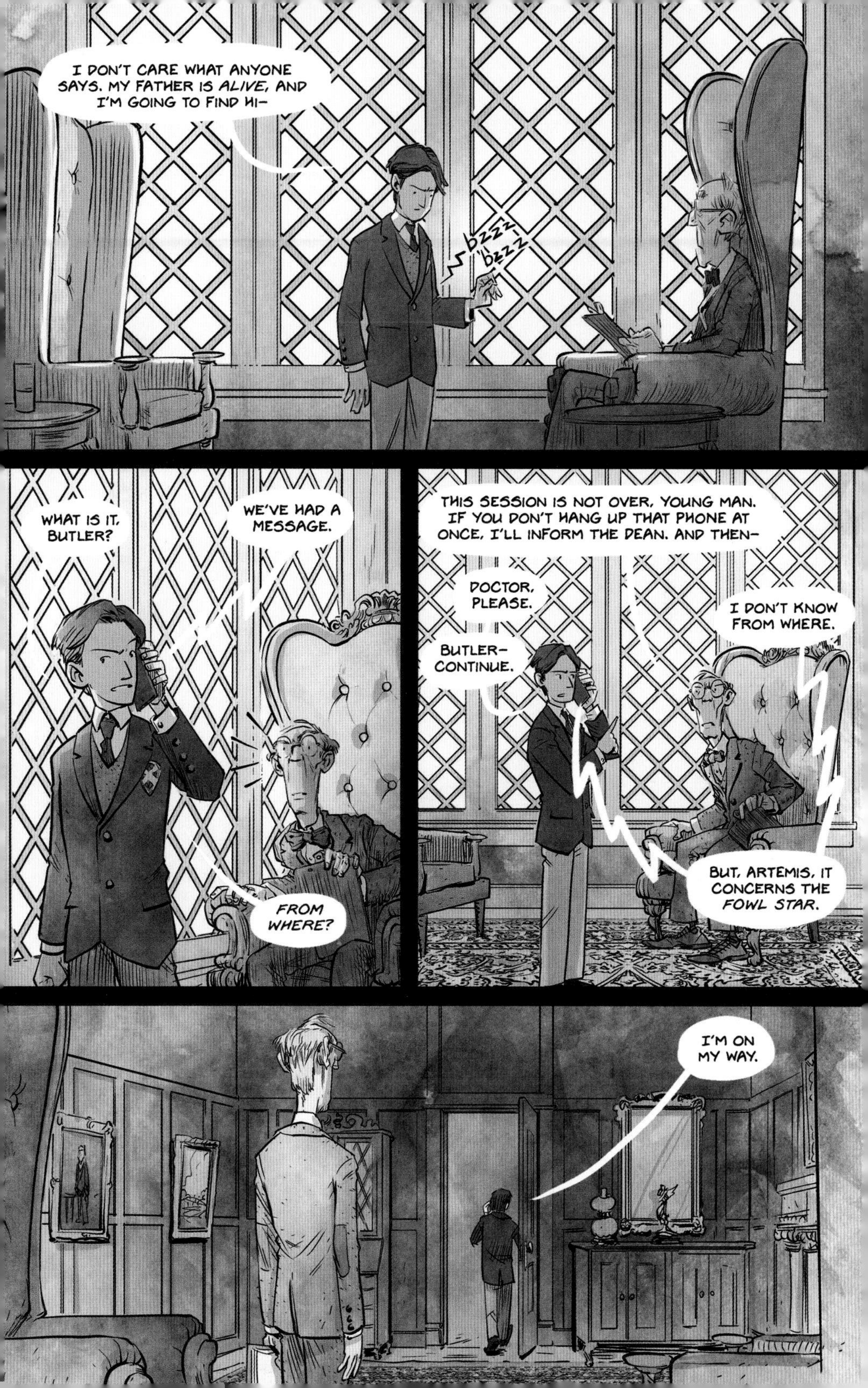
I DON'T CARE WHAT ANYONE SAYS. MY FATHER IS *ALIVE*, AND I'M GOING TO FIND HI–
BZZZ BZZZ
WHAT IS IT, BUTLER?
WE'VE HAD A MESSAGE.
FROM WHERE?
THIS SESSION IS NOT OVER, YOUNG MAN. IF YOU DON'T HANG UP THAT PHONE AT ONCE, I'LL INFORM THE DEAN. AND THEN–
DOCTOR, PLEASE.
BUTLER– CONTINUE.
I DON'T KNOW FROM WHERE.
BUT, ARTEMIS, IT CONCERNS THE *FOWL STAR*.
I'M ON MY WAY.

CHAPTER TWO

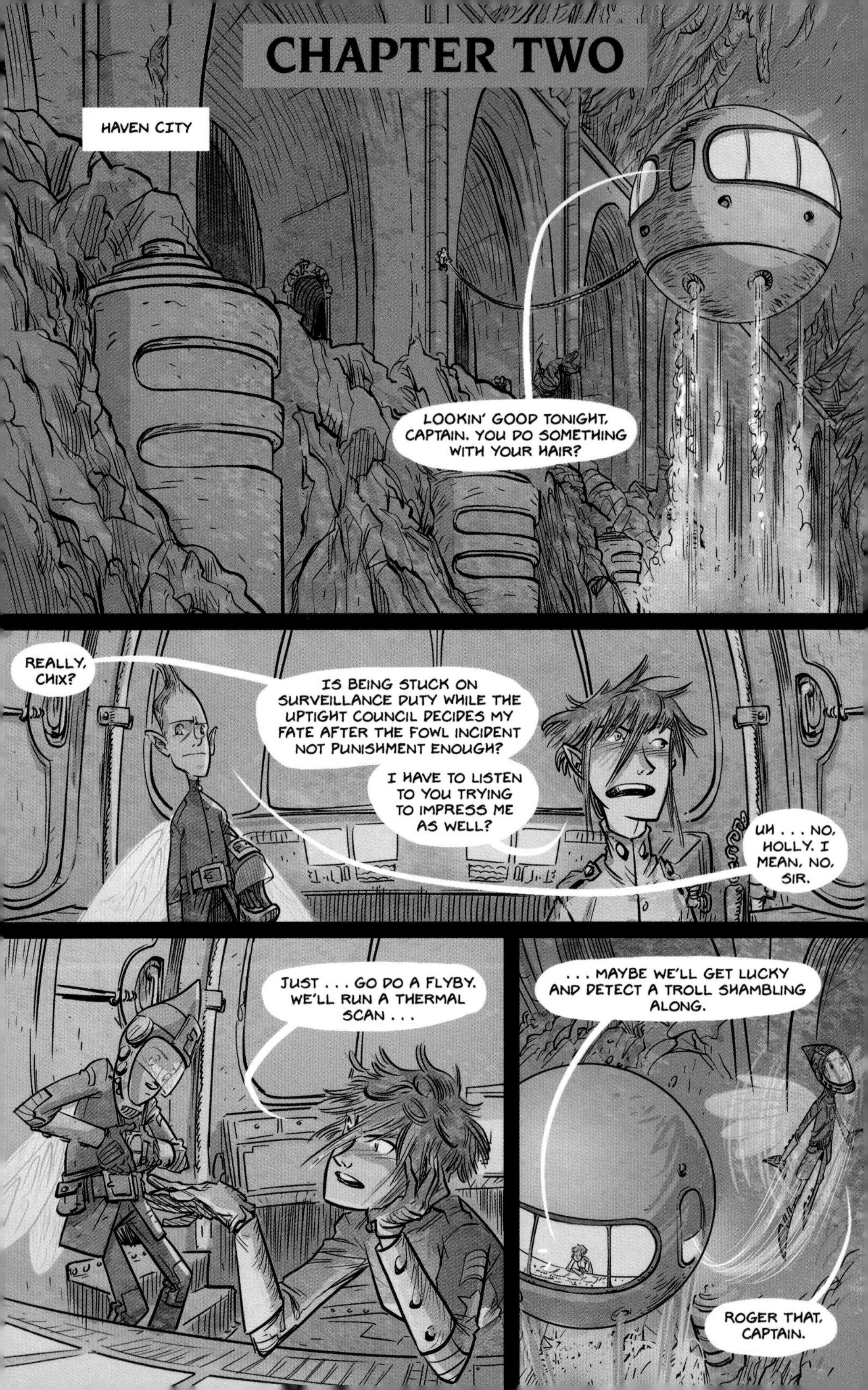
HAVEN CITY
LOOKIN' GOOD TONIGHT, CAPTAIN. YOU DO SOMETHING WITH YOUR HAIR?
REALLY, CHIX?
IS BEING STUCK ON SURVEILLANCE DUTY WHILE THE UPTIGHT COUNCIL DECIDES MY FATE AFTER THE FOWL INCIDENT NOT PUNISHMENT ENOUGH?
I HAVE TO LISTEN TO YOU TRYING TO IMPRESS ME AS WELL?
UH . . . NO, HOLLY. I MEAN, NO, SIR.
JUST . . . GO DO A FLYBY. WE'LL RUN A THERMAL SCAN . . .
. . . MAYBE WE'LL GET LUCKY AND DETECT A TROLL SHAMBLING ALONG.
ROGER THAT, CAPTAIN.

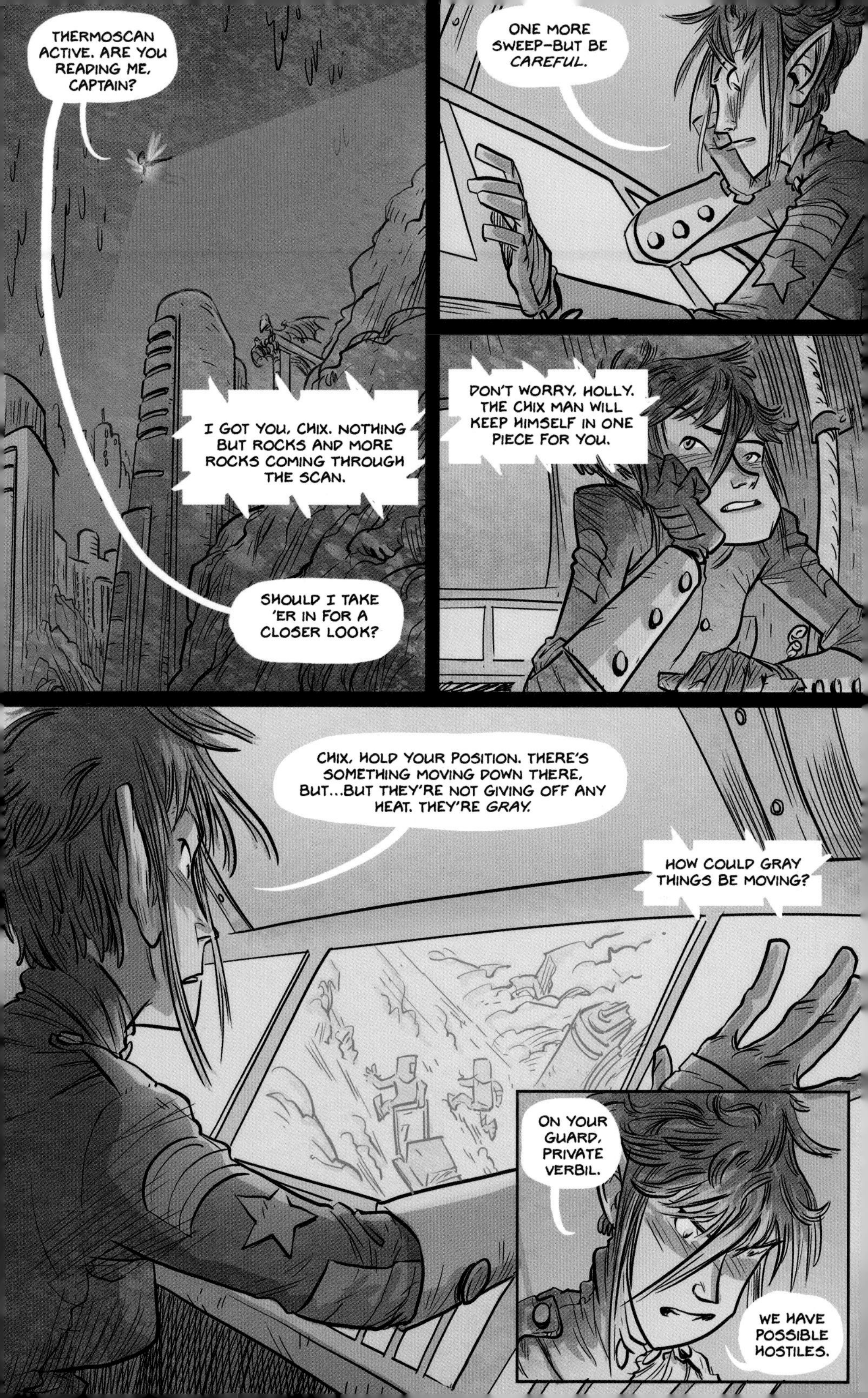
THERMOSCAN ACTIVE. ARE YOU READING ME, CAPTAIN?
I GOT YOU, CHIX. NOTHING BUT ROCKS AND MORE ROCKS COMING THROUGH THE SCAN.
SHOULD I TAKE 'ER IN FOR A CLOSER LOOK?
ONE MORE SWEEP—BUT BE *CAREFUL*.
DON'T WORRY, HOLLY. THE CHIX MAN WILL KEEP HIMSELF IN ONE PIECE FOR YOU.
CHIX, HOLD YOUR POSITION. THERE'S SOMETHING MOVING DOWN THERE, BUT...BUT THEY'RE NOT GIVING OFF ANY HEAT. THEY'RE *GRAY*.
HOW COULD GRAY THINGS BE MOVING?
ON YOUR GUARD, PRIVATE VERBIL.
WE HAVE POSSIBLE HOSTILES.

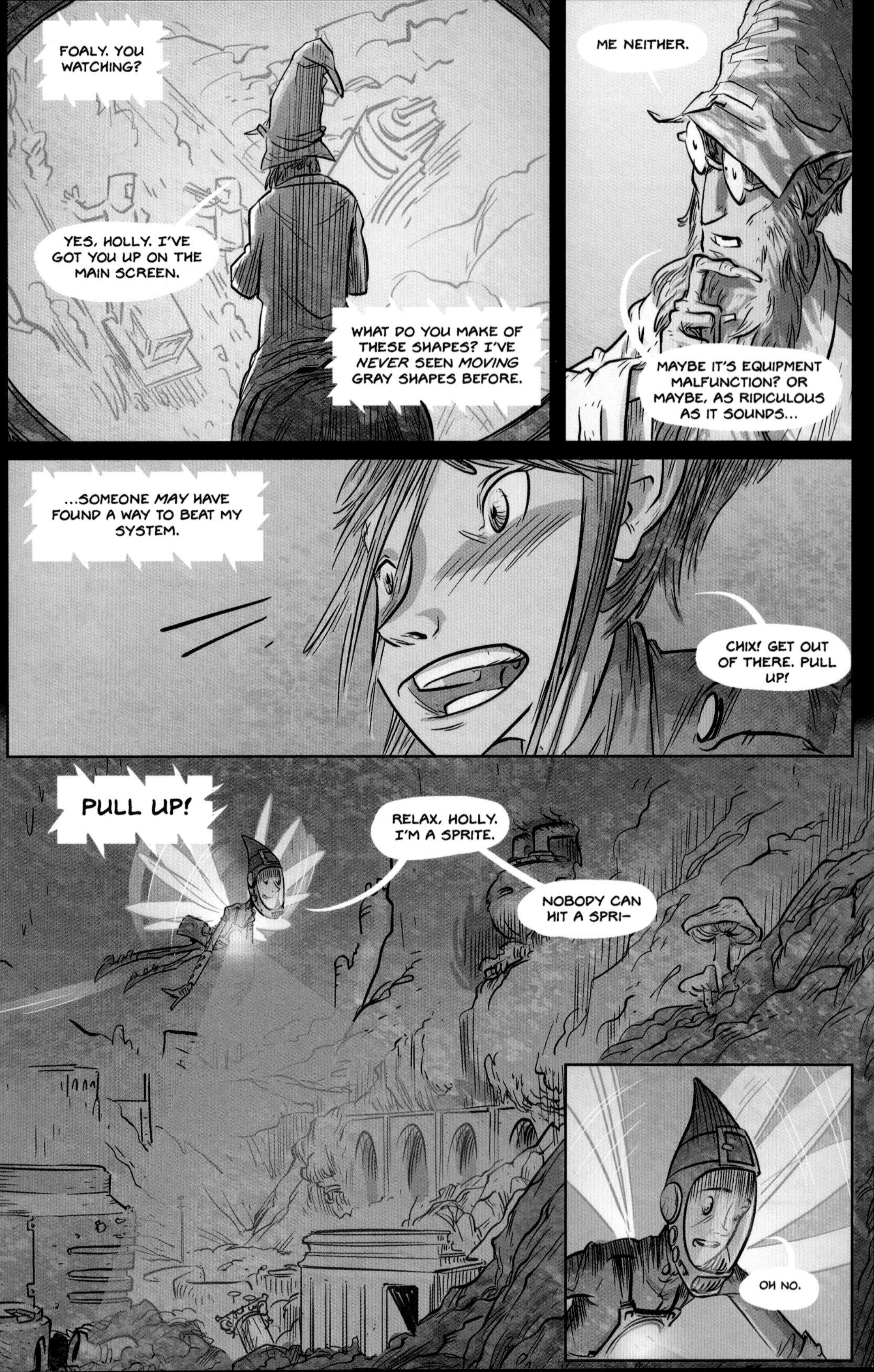
FOALY. YOU WATCHING?
YES, HOLLY. I'VE GOT YOU UP ON THE MAIN SCREEN.
WHAT DO YOU MAKE OF THESE SHAPES? I'VE *NEVER* SEEN *MOVING* GRAY SHAPES BEFORE.
ME NEITHER.
MAYBE IT'S EQUIPMENT MALFUNCTION? OR MAYBE, AS RIDICULOUS AS IT SOUNDS...
...SOMEONE *MAY* HAVE FOUND A WAY TO BEAT MY SYSTEM.
CHIX! GET OUT OF THERE. PULL UP!
PULL UP!
RELAX, HOLLY. I'M A SPRITE.
NOBODY CAN HIT A SPRI–
OH NO.

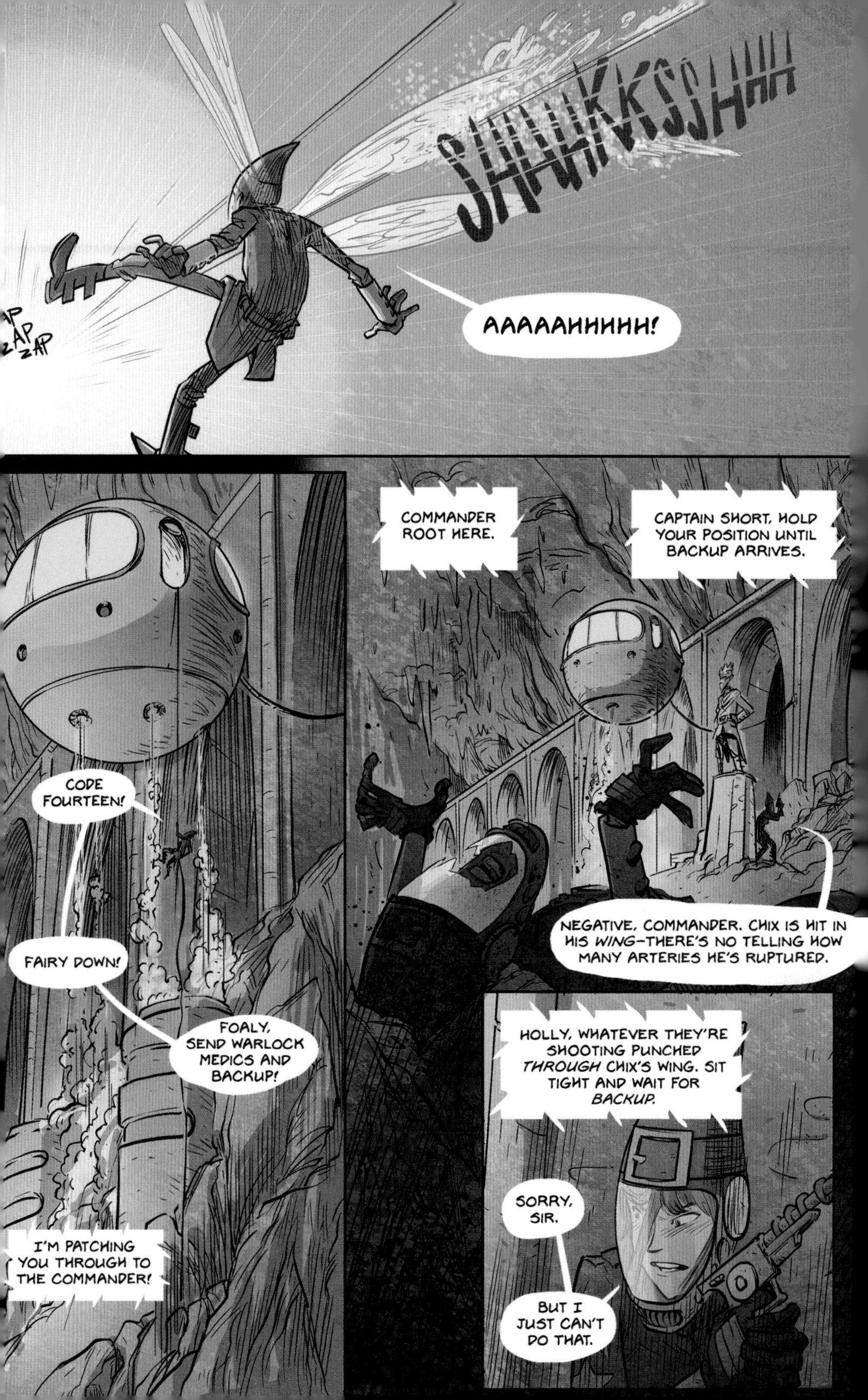
SHHUKSSHHHH
ZAP
ZAP
AAAAAHHHHH!
CODE FOURTEEN!
FAIRY DOWN!
FOALY, SEND WARLOCK MEDICS AND BACKUP!
I'M PATCHING YOU THROUGH TO THE COMMANDER!
COMMANDER ROOT HERE.
CAPTAIN SHORT, HOLD YOUR POSITION UNTIL BACKUP ARRIVES.
NEGATIVE, COMMANDER. CHIX IS HIT IN HIS *WING*—THERE'S NO TELLING HOW MANY ARTERIES HE'S RUPTURED.
HOLLY, WHATEVER THEY'RE SHOOTING PUNCHED *THROUGH* CHIX'S WING. SIT TIGHT AND WAIT FOR *BACKUP*.
SORRY, SIR.
BUT I JUST CAN'T DO THAT.

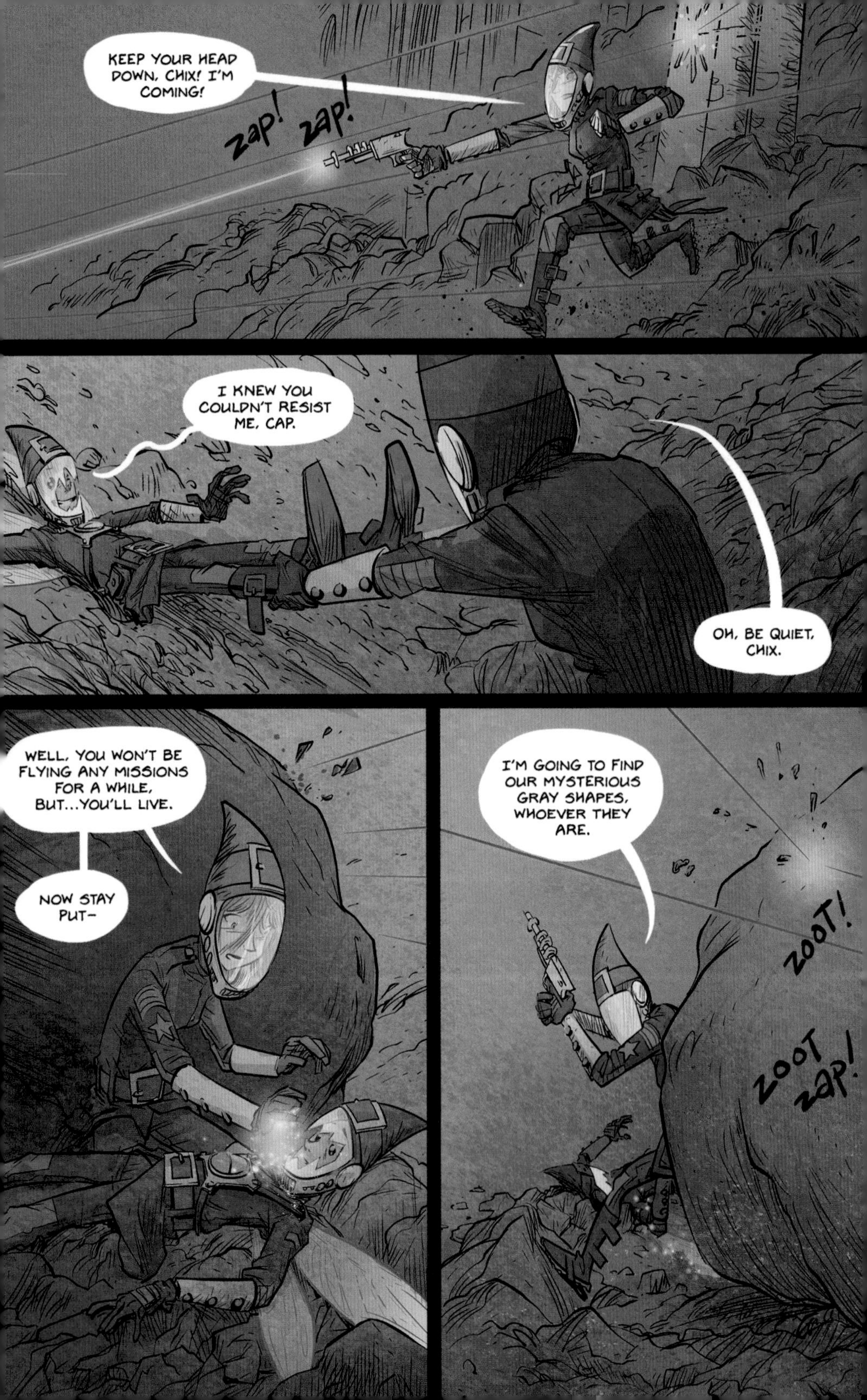
KEEP YOUR HEAD DOWN, CHIX! I'M COMING!
ZAP! ZAP!
I KNEW YOU COULDN'T RESIST ME, CAP.
OH, BE QUIET, CHIX.
WELL, YOU WON'T BE FLYING ANY MISSIONS FOR A WHILE, BUT...YOU'LL LIVE.
NOW STAY PUT–
I'M GOING TO FIND OUR MYSTERIOUS GRAY SHAPES, WHOEVER THEY ARE.
ZOOT!
ZOOT ZAP!

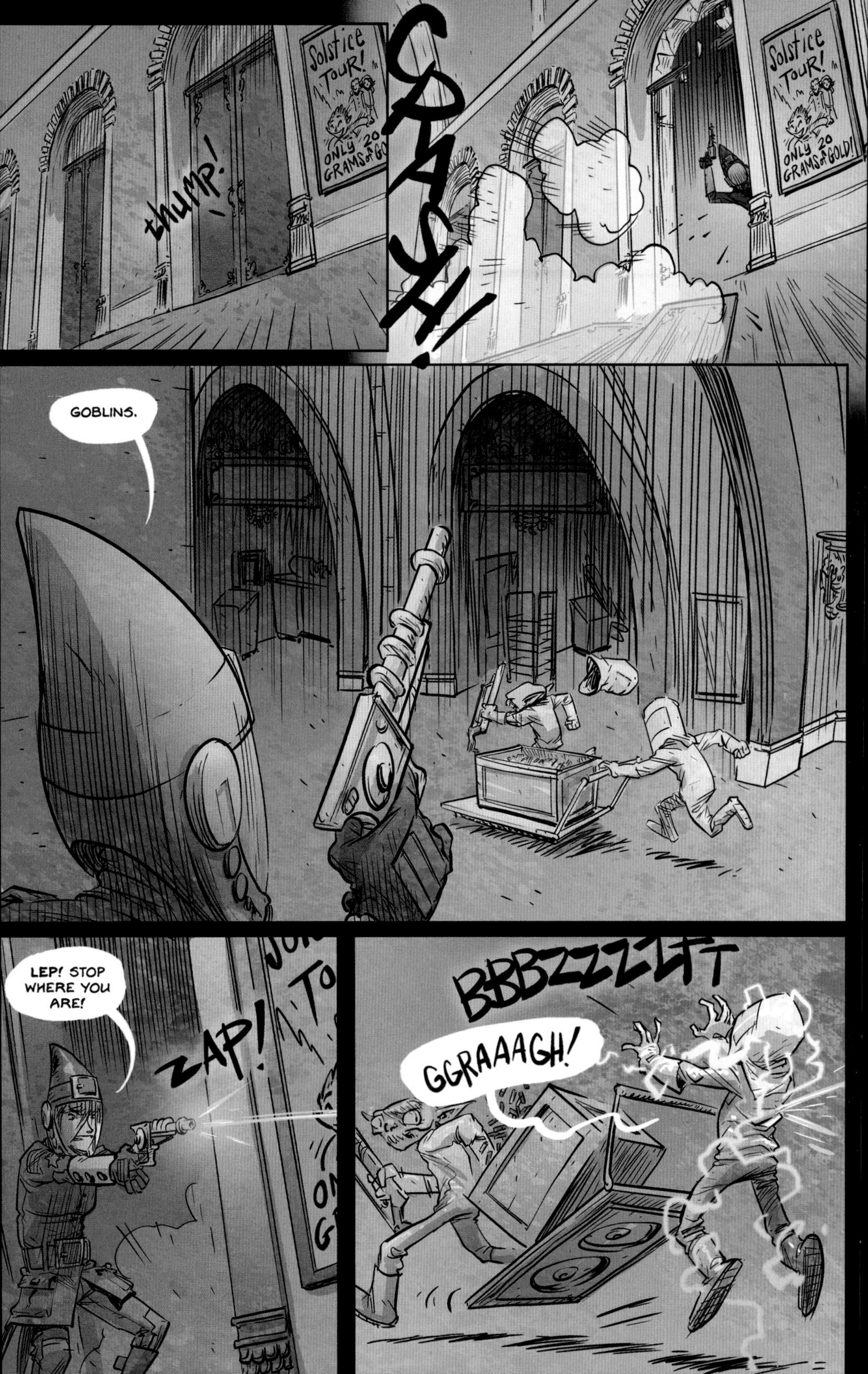
Solstice TOUR!
ONLY 20 GRAMS of GOLD!
thump!
CRASH!
Solstice TOUR!
ONLY 20 GRAMS of GOLD!
GOBLINS.
LEP! STOP WHERE YOU ARE!
ZAP!
BBBZZZZZZZT
GGRAAAGH!

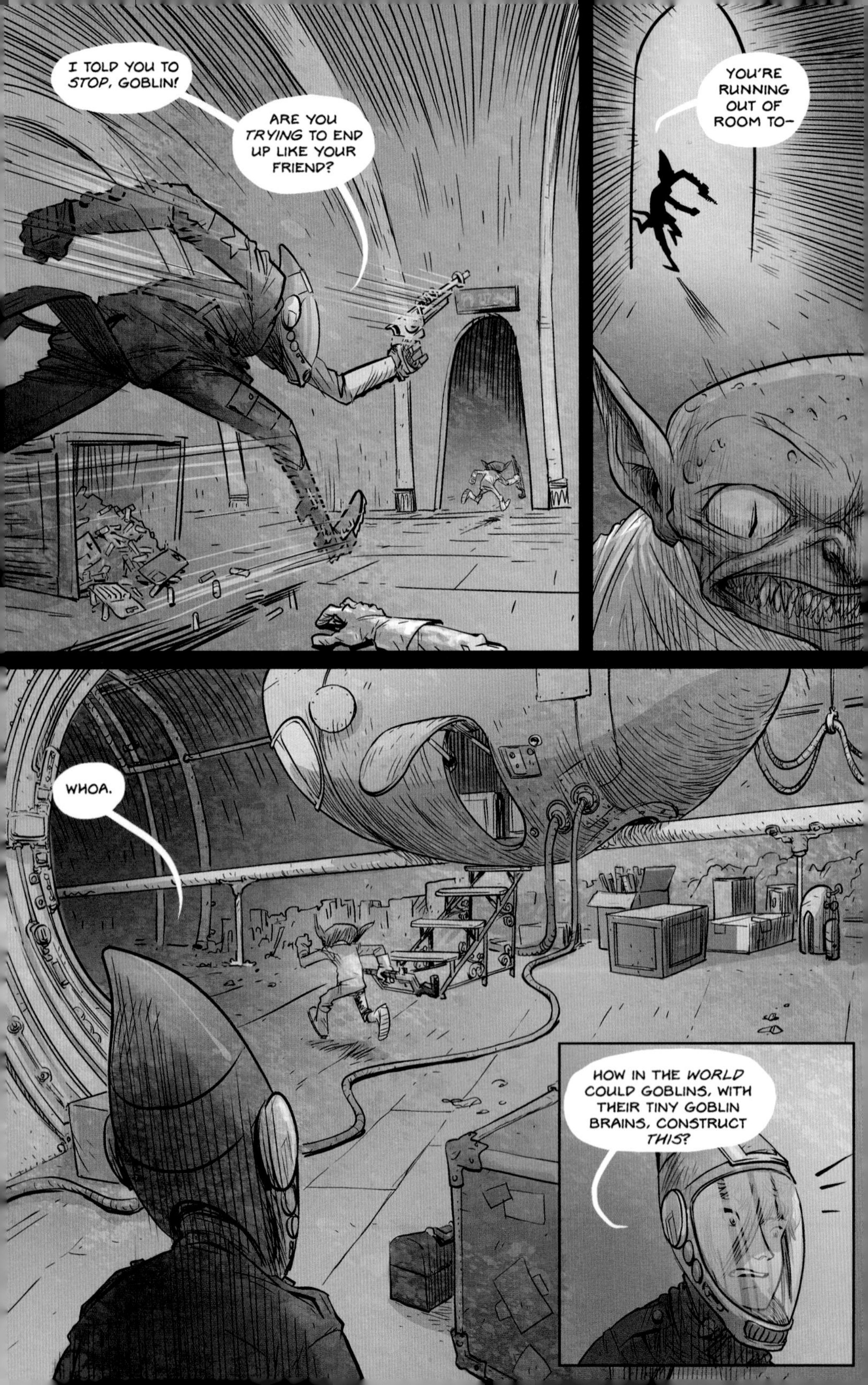

I TOLD YOU TO *STOP*, GOBLIN!
ARE YOU *TRYING* TO END UP LIKE YOUR FRIEND?
YOU'RE RUNNING OUT OF ROOM TO–
WHOA.
HOW IN THE *WORLD* COULD GOBLINS, WITH THEIR TINY GOBLIN BRAINS, CONSTRUCT *THIS*?

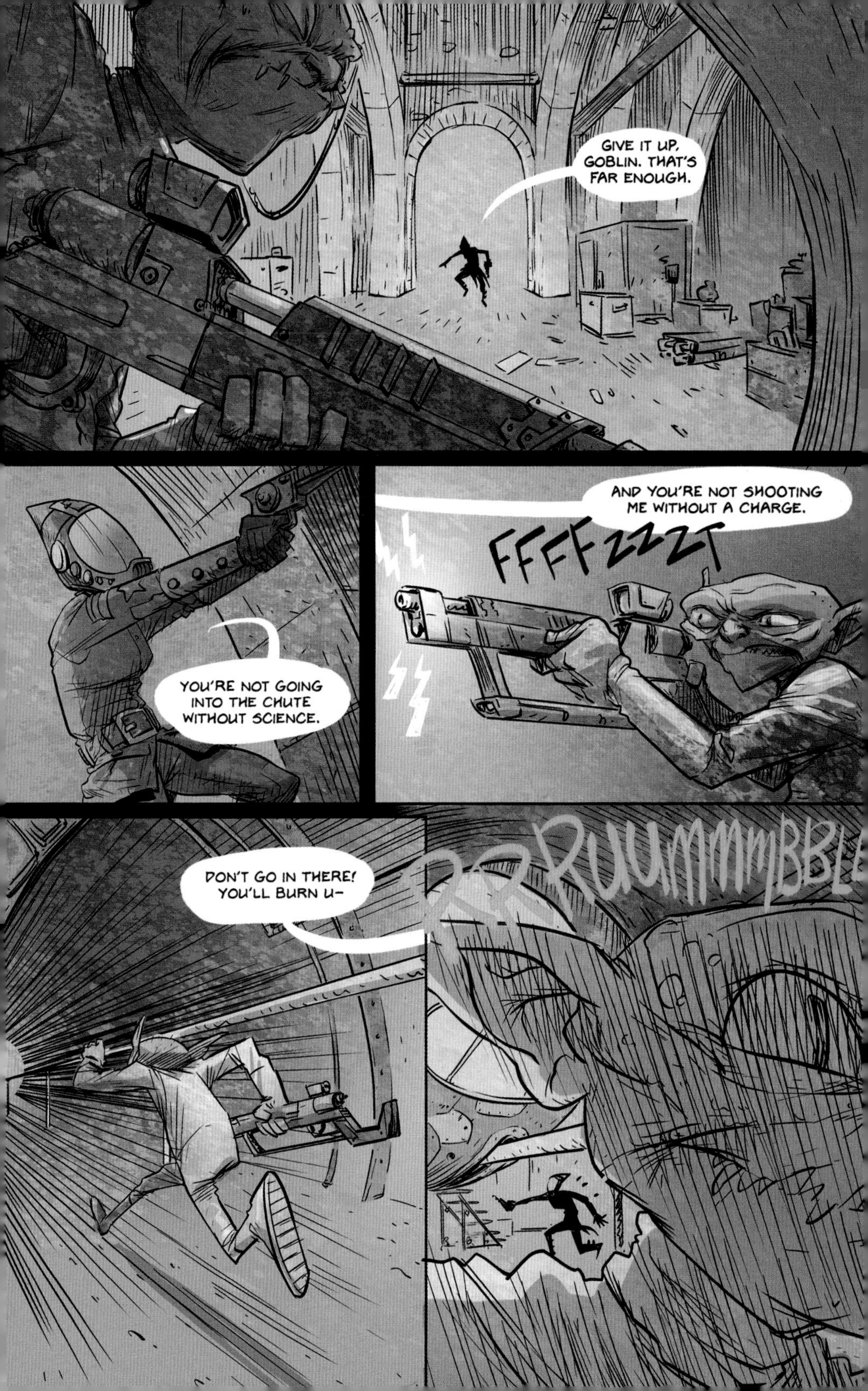
GIVE IT UP, GOBLIN. THAT'S FAR ENOUGH.
YOU'RE NOT GOING INTO THE CHUTE WITHOUT SCIENCE.
AND YOU'RE NOT SHOOTING ME WITHOUT A CHARGE.
FFFFZZZT
DON'T GO IN THERE! YOU'LL BURN U-
RRRUUMMMBBLE

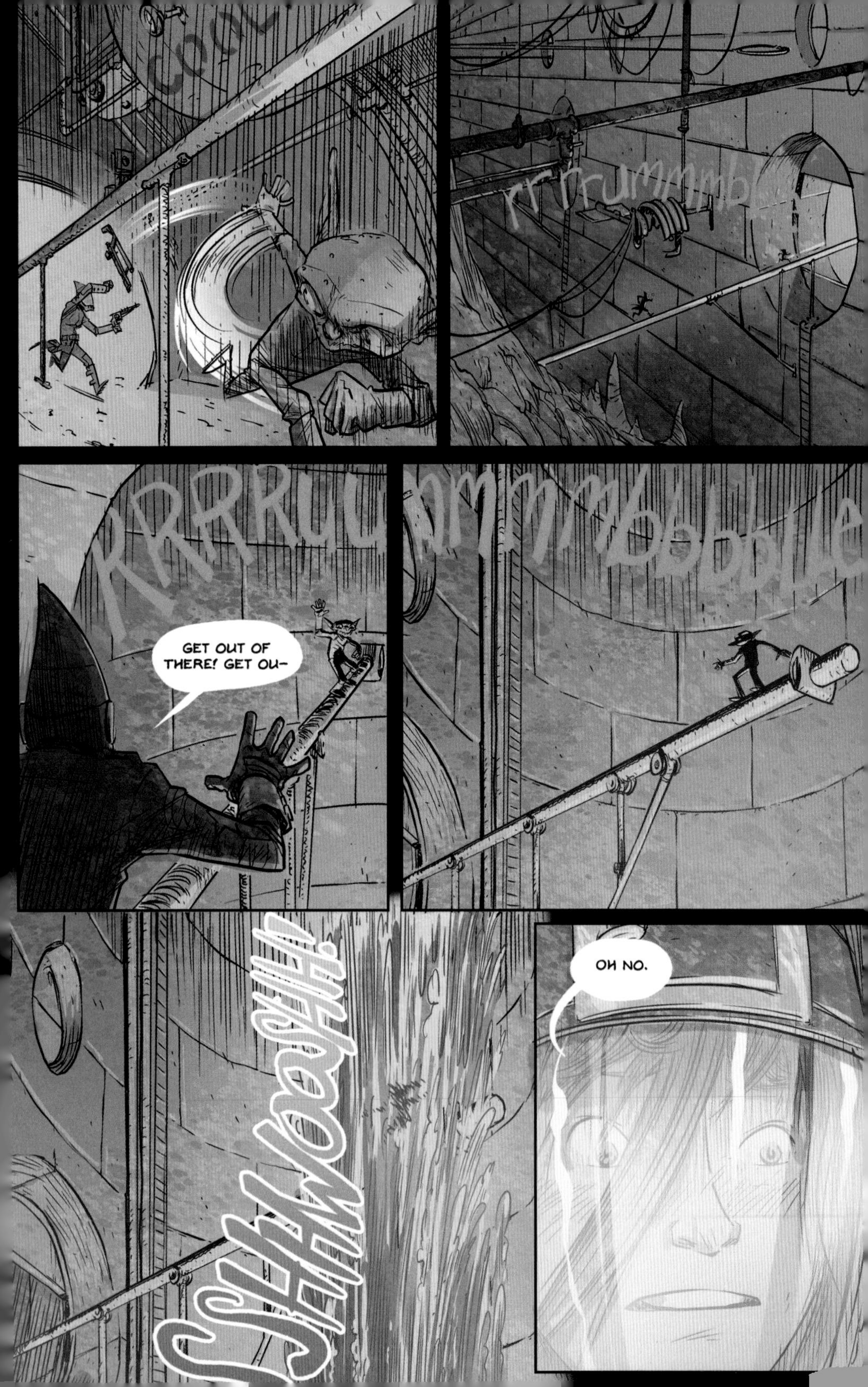

rrrrummmbl
RRRRuummmmbbblle
GET OUT OF THERE! GET OU-
SHHWOOSH!!
OH NO.

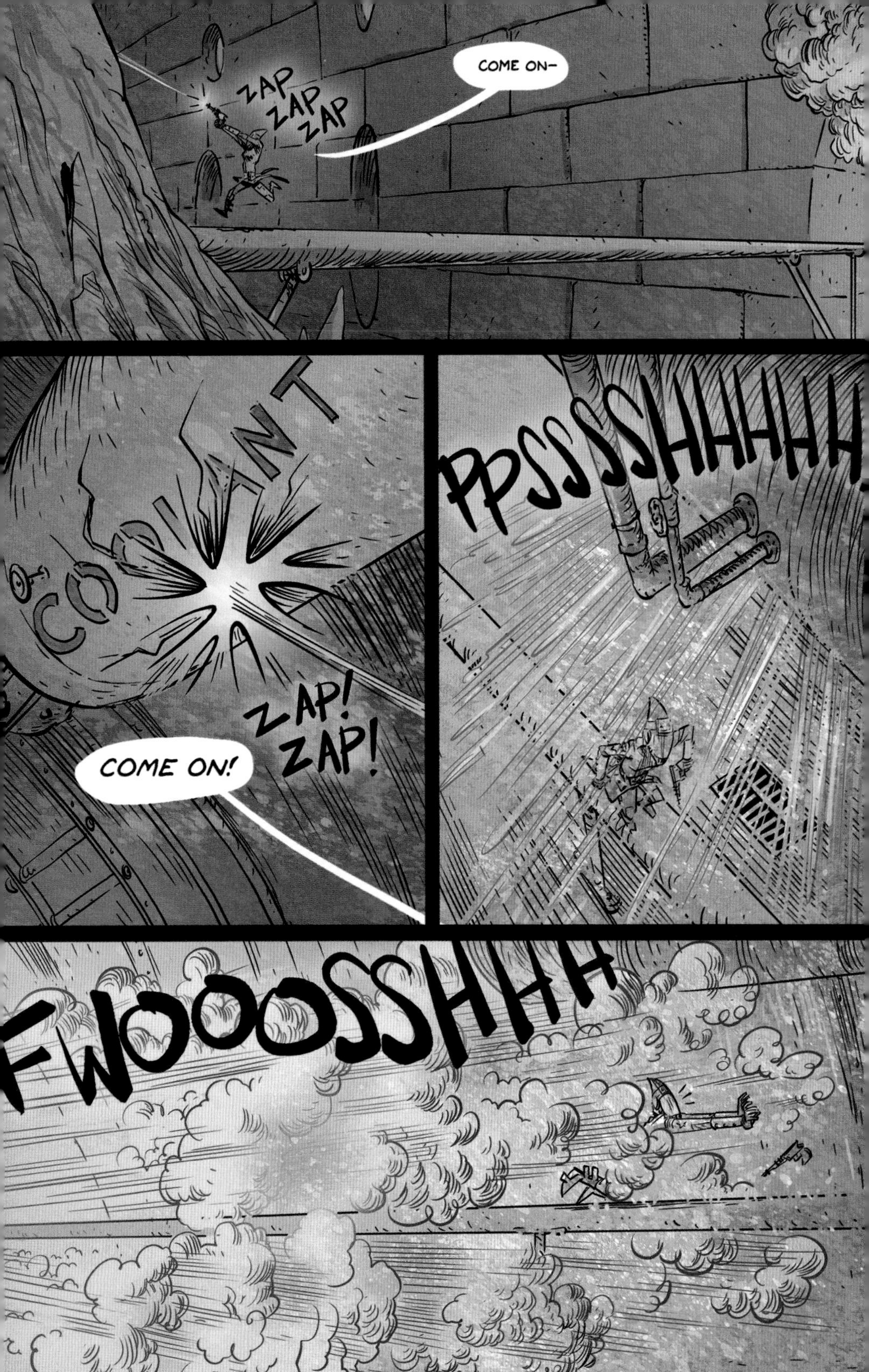
ZAP
ZAP
ZAP
COME ON–
COOLANT
ZAP!
ZAP!
COME ON!
PPSSSSHHHHH
FWOOOSSHHH

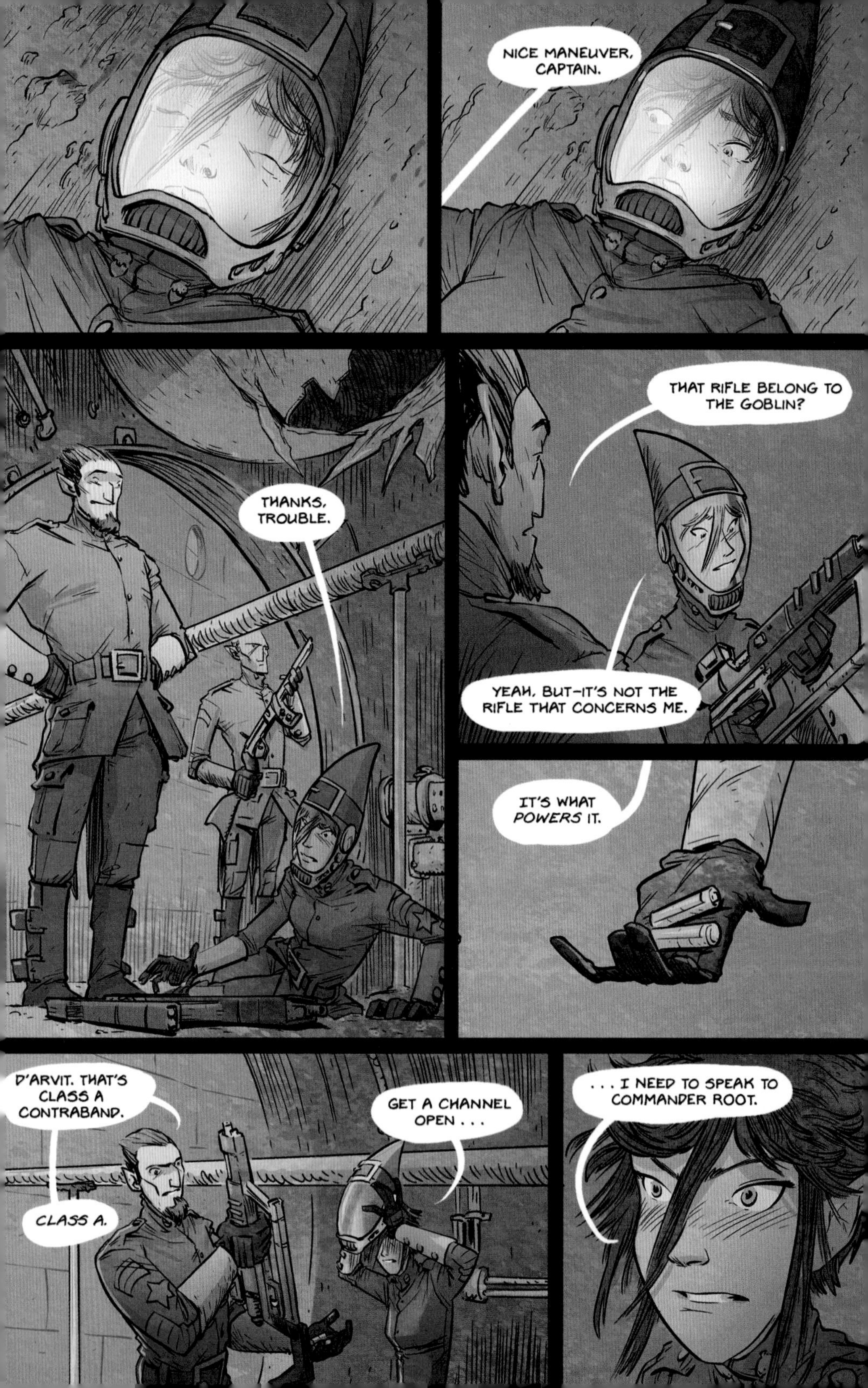
NICE MANEUVER, CAPTAIN.
THANKS, TROUBLE.
THAT RIFLE BELONG TO THE GOBLIN?
YEAH, BUT–IT'S NOT THE RIFLE THAT CONCERNS ME.
IT'S WHAT *POWERS* IT.
D'ARVIT. THAT'S CLASS A CONTRABAND.
CLASS A.
GET A CHANNEL OPEN . . .
. . . I NEED TO SPEAK TO COMMANDER ROOT.

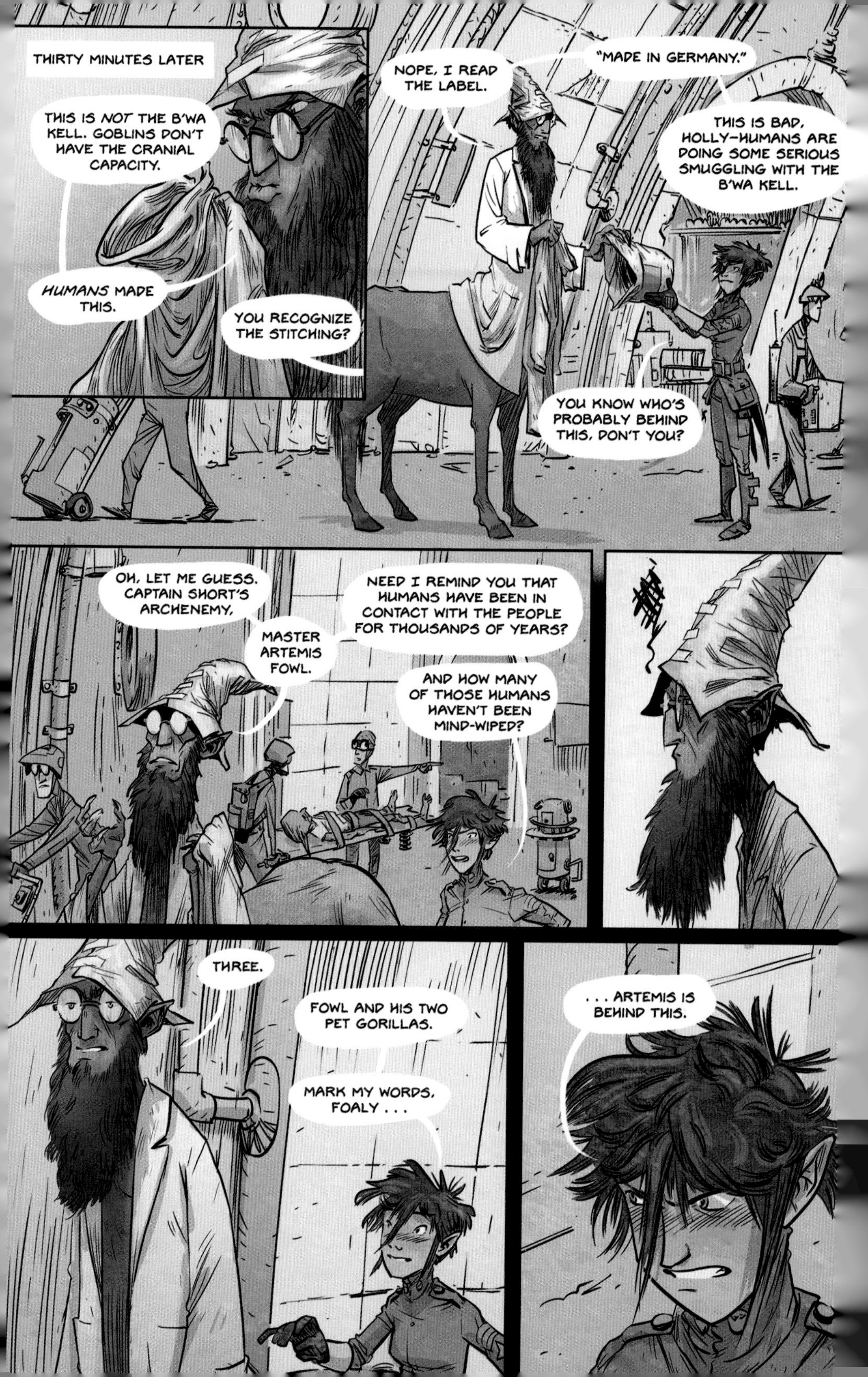
THIRTY MINUTES LATER
THIS IS *NOT* THE B'WA KELL. GOBLINS DON'T HAVE THE CRANIAL CAPACITY.
HUMANS MADE THIS.
YOU RECOGNIZE THE STITCHING?
NOPE, I READ THE LABEL.
"MADE IN GERMANY."
THIS IS BAD, HOLLY—HUMANS ARE DOING SOME SERIOUS SMUGGLING WITH THE B'WA KELL.
YOU KNOW WHO'S PROBABLY BEHIND THIS, DON'T YOU?
OH, LET ME GUESS. CAPTAIN SHORT'S ARCHENEMY,
MASTER ARTEMIS FOWL.
NEED I REMIND YOU THAT HUMANS HAVE BEEN IN CONTACT WITH THE PEOPLE FOR THOUSANDS OF YEARS?
AND HOW MANY OF THOSE HUMANS HAVEN'T BEEN MIND-WIPED?
THREE.
FOWL AND HIS TWO PET GORILLAS.
MARK MY WORDS, FOALY . . .
. . . ARTEMIS IS BEHIND THIS.

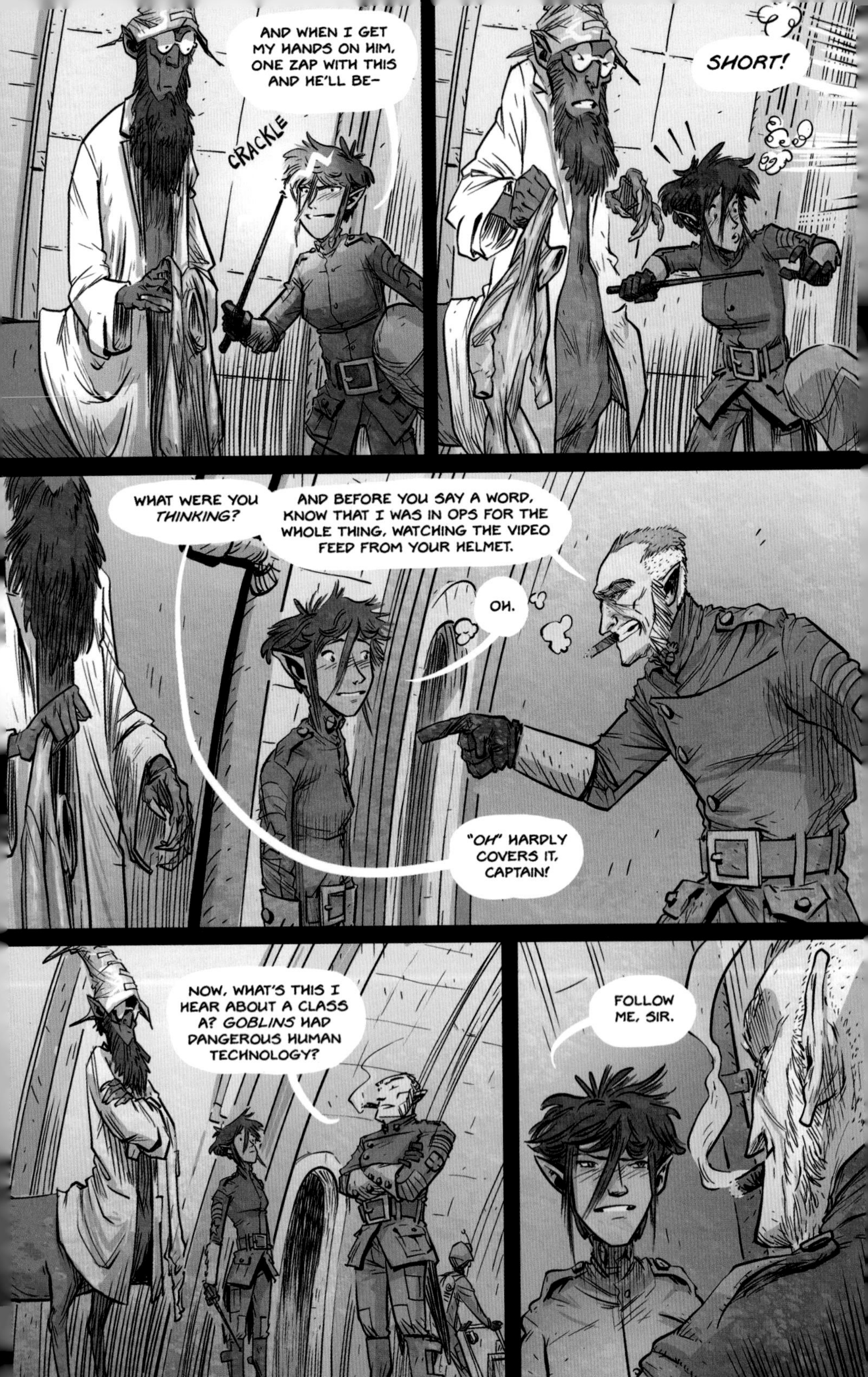
AND WHEN I GET MY HANDS ON HIM, ONE ZAP WITH THIS AND HE'LL BE-
CRACKLE
SHORT!
WHAT WERE YOU *THINKING*?
AND BEFORE YOU SAY A WORD, KNOW THAT I WAS IN OPS FOR THE WHOLE THING, WATCHING THE VIDEO FEED FROM YOUR HELMET.
OH.
"*OH*" HARDLY COVERS IT, CAPTAIN!
NOW, WHAT'S THIS I HEAR ABOUT A CLASS A? *GOBLINS* HAD DANGEROUS HUMAN TECHNOLOGY?
FOLLOW ME, SIR.

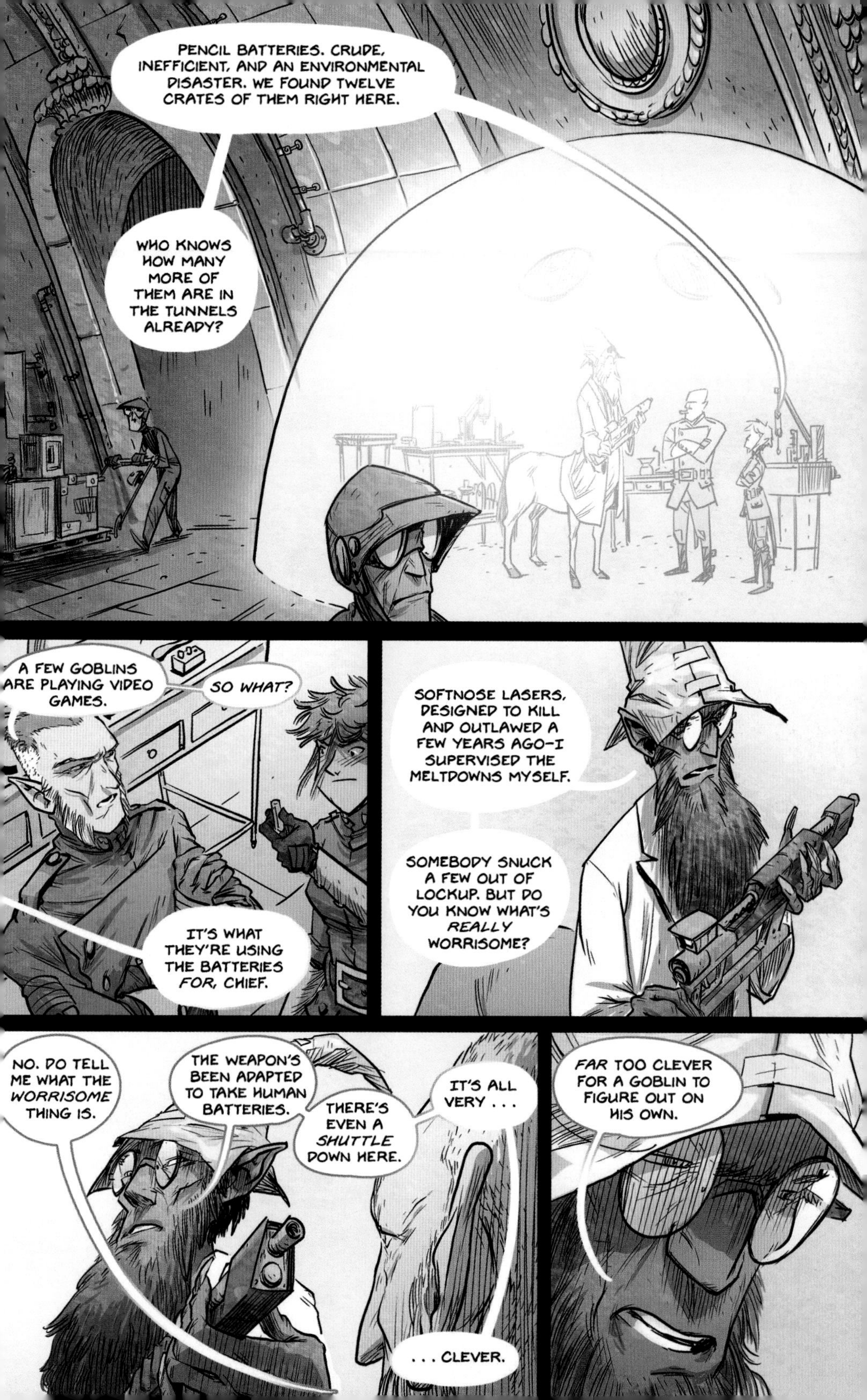
PENCIL BATTERIES. CRUDE, INEFFICIENT, AND AN ENVIRONMENTAL DISASTER. WE FOUND TWELVE CRATES OF THEM RIGHT HERE.
WHO KNOWS HOW MANY MORE OF THEM ARE IN THE TUNNELS ALREADY?
A FEW GOBLINS ARE PLAYING VIDEO GAMES.
SO WHAT?
IT'S WHAT THEY'RE USING THE BATTERIES *FOR*, CHIEF.
SOFTNOSE LASERS, DESIGNED TO KILL AND OUTLAWED A FEW YEARS AGO—I SUPERVISED THE MELTDOWNS MYSELF.
SOMEBODY SNUCK A FEW OUT OF LOCKUP. BUT DO YOU KNOW WHAT'S *REALLY* WORRISOME?
NO. DO TELL ME WHAT THE *WORRISOME* THING IS.
THE WEAPON'S BEEN ADAPTED TO TAKE HUMAN BATTERIES.
THERE'S EVEN A *SHUTTLE* DOWN HERE.
IT'S ALL VERY . . .
. . . CLEVER.
FAR TOO CLEVER FOR A GOBLIN TO FIGURE OUT ON HIS OWN.

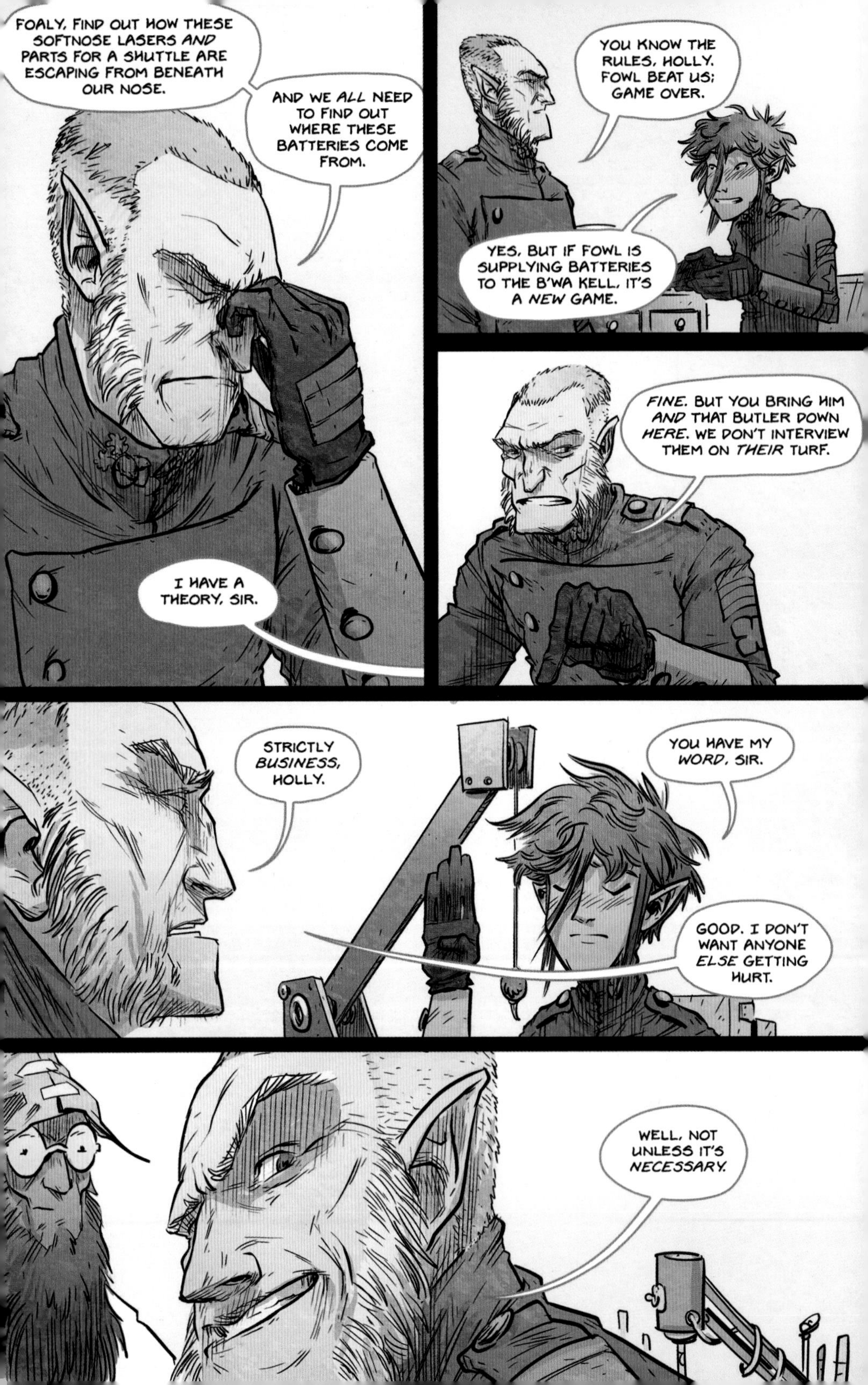
FOALY, FIND OUT HOW THESE SOFTNOSE LASERS *AND* PARTS FOR A SHUTTLE ARE ESCAPING FROM BENEATH OUR NOSE.
AND WE *ALL* NEED TO FIND OUT WHERE THESE BATTERIES COME FROM.
I HAVE A THEORY, SIR.
YOU KNOW THE RULES, HOLLY. FOWL BEAT US; GAME OVER.
YES, BUT IF FOWL IS SUPPLYING BATTERIES TO THE B'WA KELL, IT'S A *NEW* GAME.
FINE. BUT YOU BRING HIM *AND* THAT BUTLER DOWN *HERE*. WE DON'T INTERVIEW THEM ON *THEIR* TURF.
STRICTLY *BUSINESS*, HOLLY.
YOU HAVE MY *WORD*, SIR.
GOOD. I DON'T WANT ANYONE *ELSE* GETTING HURT.
WELL, NOT UNLESS IT'S *NECESSARY*.

CHAPTER THREE

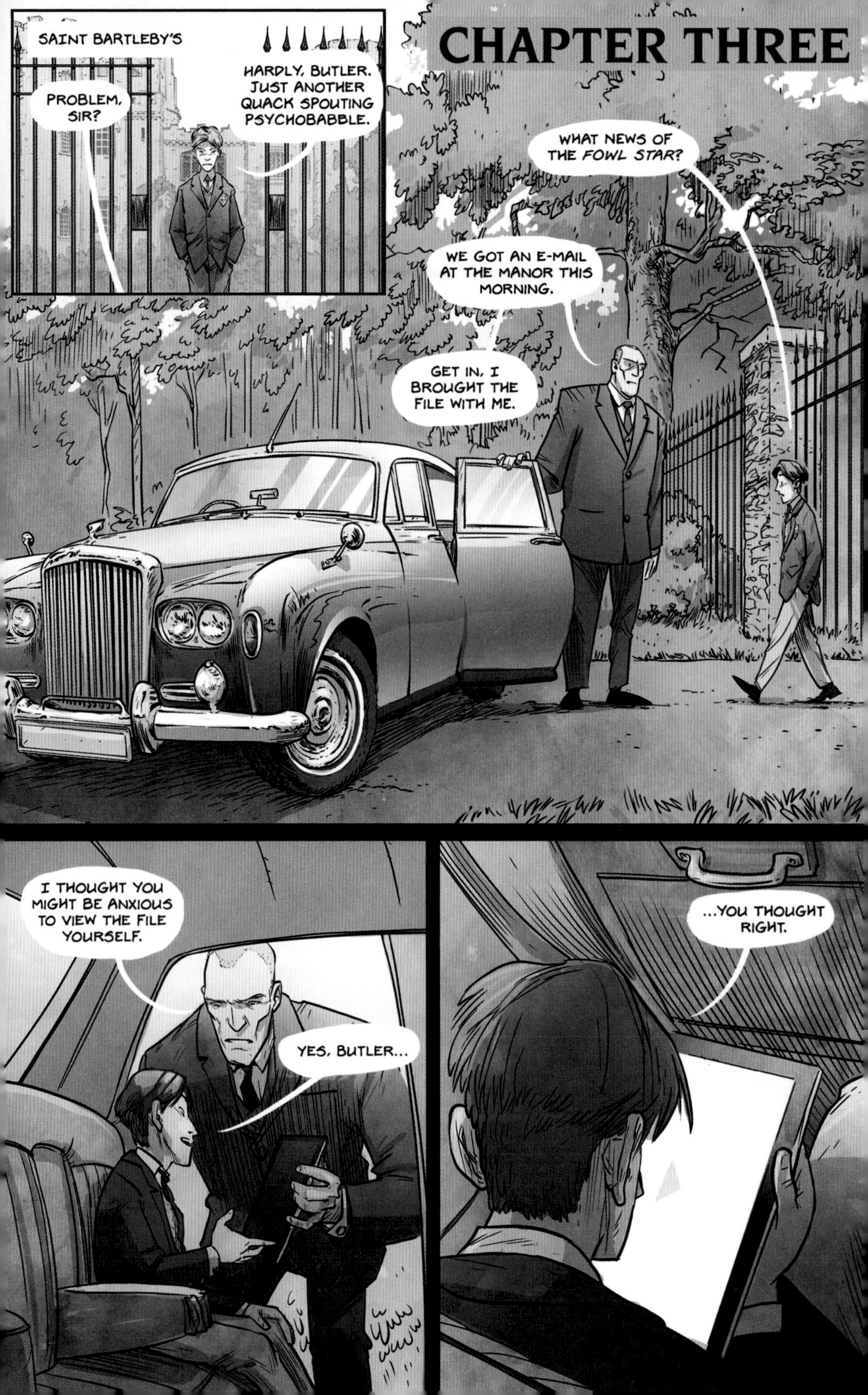
SAINT BARTLEBY'S
PROBLEM, SIR?
HARDLY, BUTLER. JUST ANOTHER QUACK SPOUTING PSYCHOBABBLE.
WHAT NEWS OF THE *FOWL STAR*?
WE GOT AN E-MAIL AT THE MANOR THIS MORNING.
GET IN, I BROUGHT THE FILE WITH ME.
I THOUGHT YOU MIGHT BE ANXIOUS TO VIEW THE FILE YOURSELF.
YES, BUTLER...
...YOU THOUGHT RIGHT.

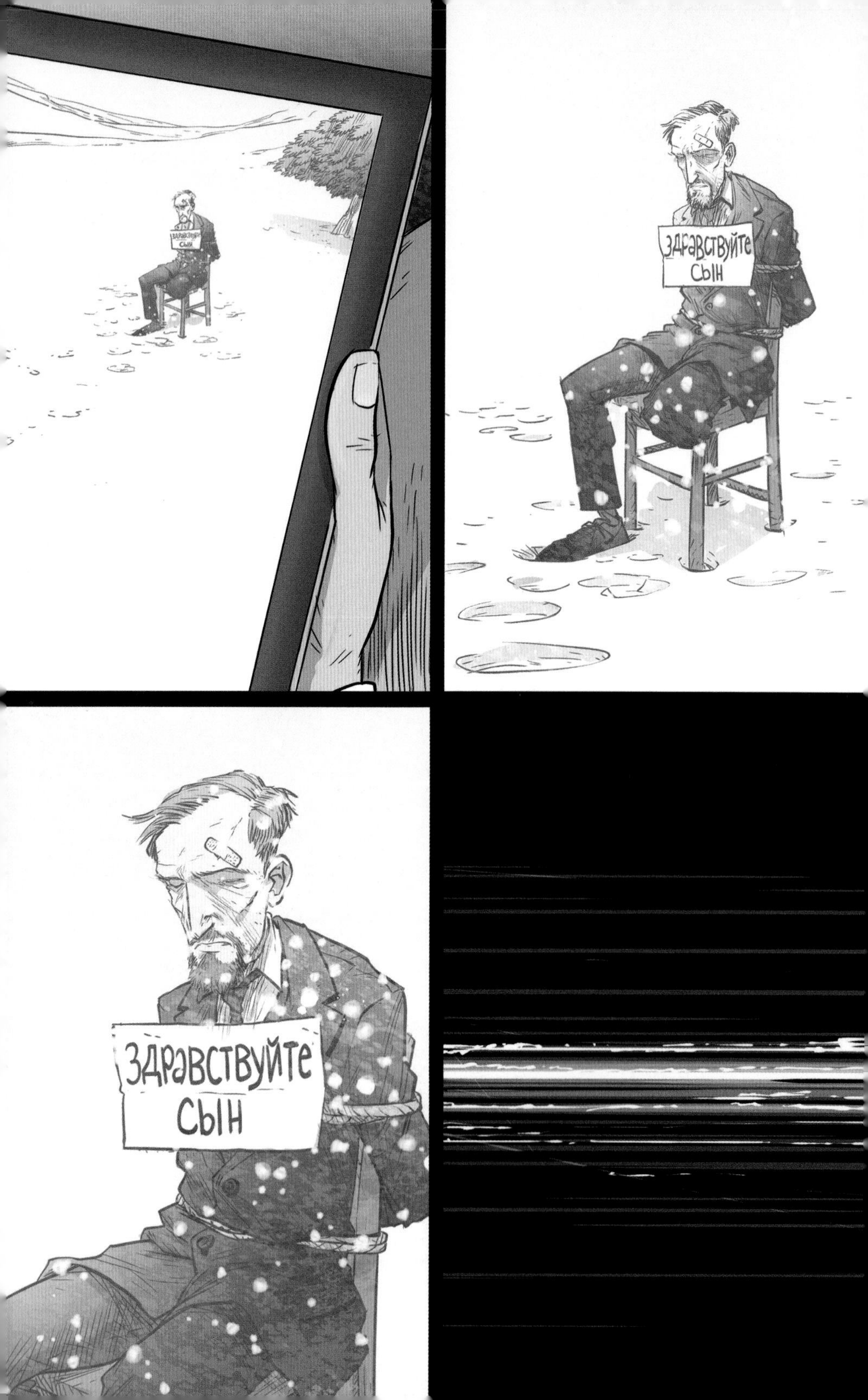
ЗДРАВСТВУЙТЕ СЫН
ЗДРАВСТВУЙТЕ СЫН
ЗДРАВСТВУЙТЕ СЫН

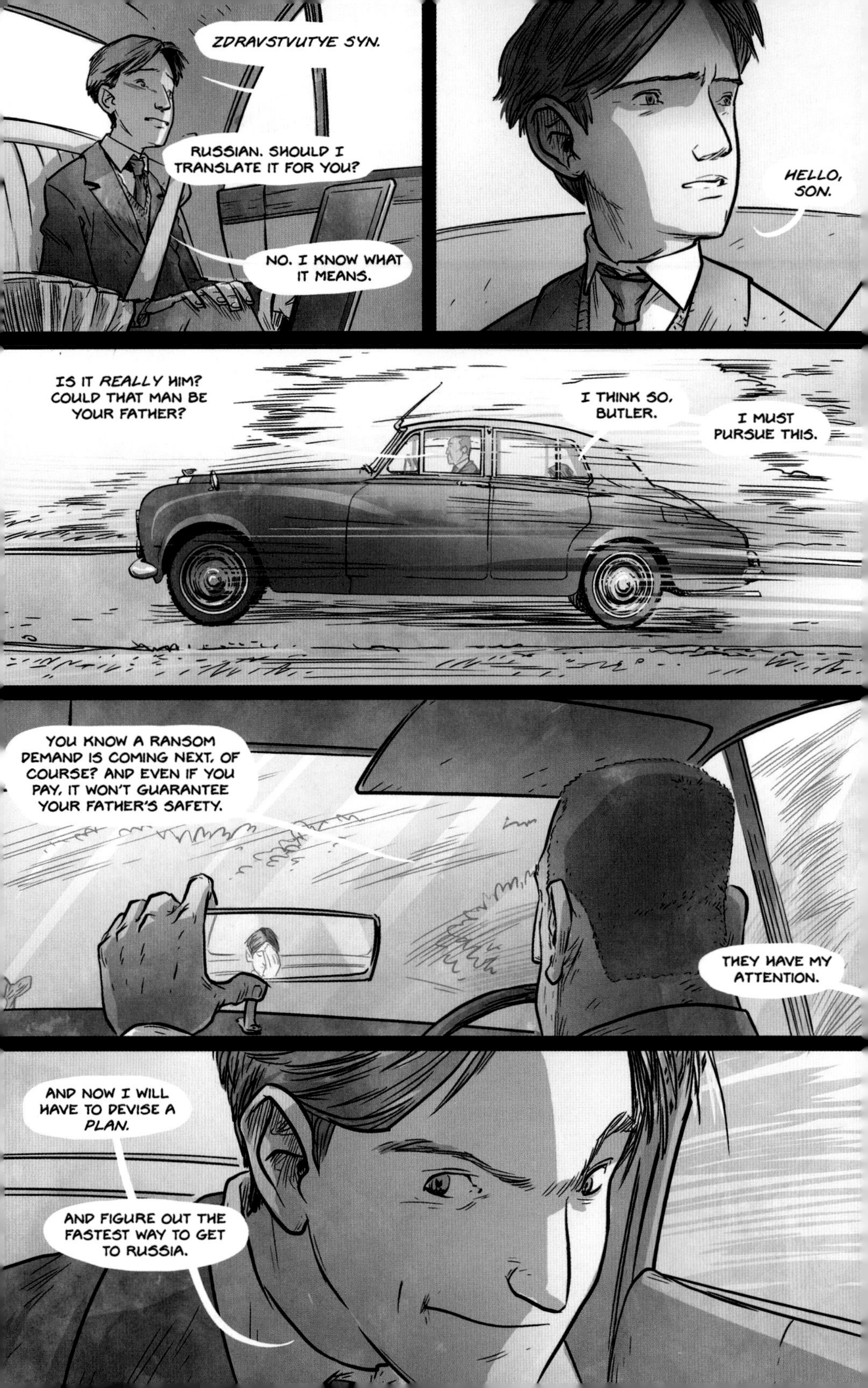
ZDRAVSTVUTYE SYN.
RUSSIAN. SHOULD I TRANSLATE IT FOR YOU?
NO. I KNOW WHAT IT MEANS.
HELLO, SON.
IS IT *REALLY* HIM? COULD THAT MAN BE YOUR FATHER?
I THINK SO, BUTLER.
I MUST PURSUE THIS.
YOU KNOW A RANSOM DEMAND IS COMING NEXT, OF COURSE? AND EVEN IF YOU PAY, IT WON'T GUARANTEE YOUR FATHER'S SAFETY.
THEY HAVE MY ATTENTION.
AND NOW I WILL HAVE TO DEVISE A *PLAN*.
AND FIGURE OUT THE FASTEST WAY TO GET TO RUSSIA.

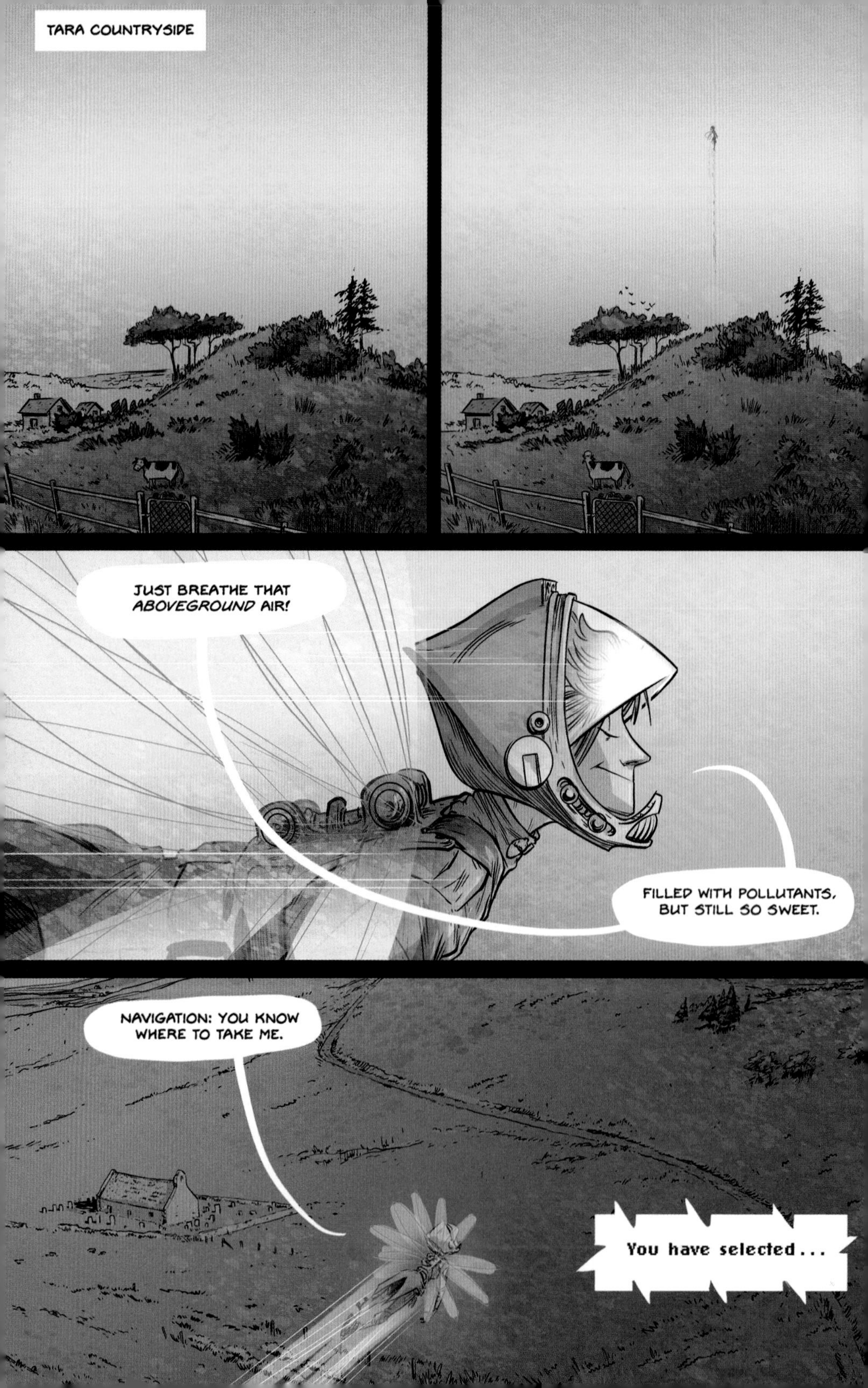
TARA COUNTRYSIDE
JUST BREATHE THAT *ABOVEGROUND* AIR!
FILLED WITH POLLUTANTS, BUT STILL SO SWEET.
NAVIGATION: YOU KNOW WHERE TO TAKE ME.
You have selected . . .

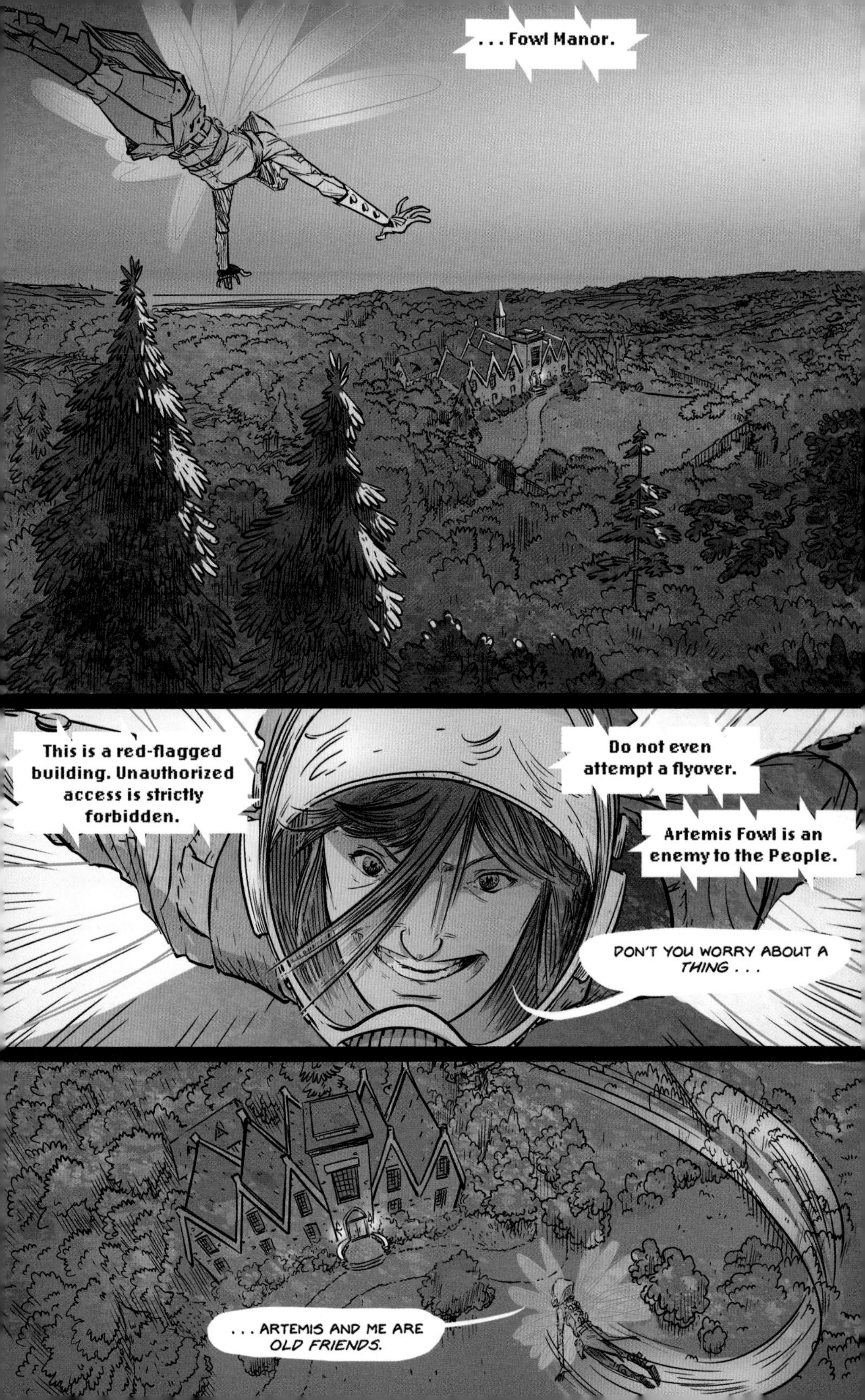
. . . Fowl Manor.
This is a red-flagged building. Unauthorized access is strictly forbidden.
Do not even attempt a flyover.
Artemis Fowl is an enemy to the People.
DON'T YOU WORRY ABOUT A *THING* . . .
. . . ARTEMIS AND ME ARE *OLD FRIENDS.*

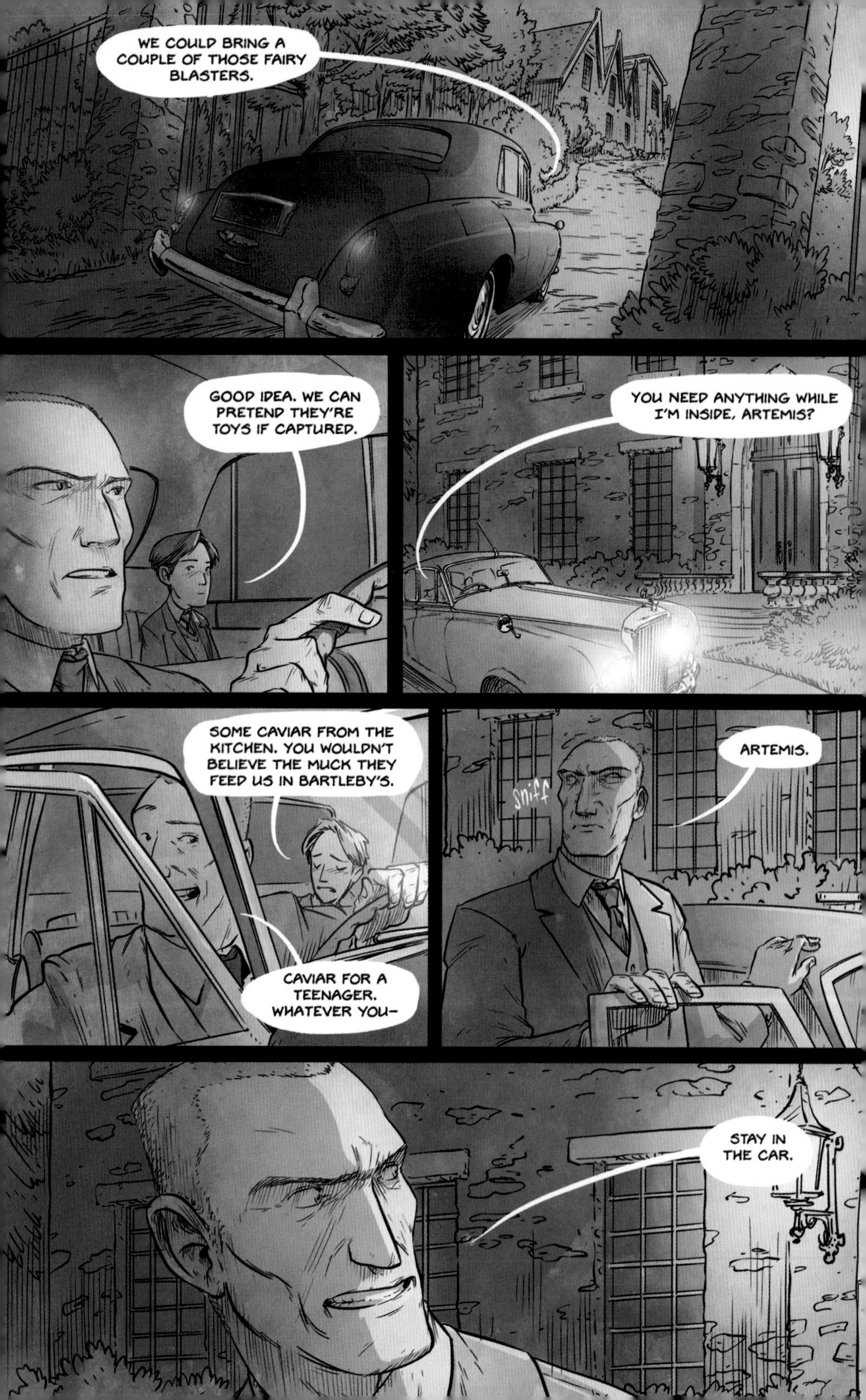
WE COULD BRING A COUPLE OF THOSE FAIRY BLASTERS.
GOOD IDEA. WE CAN PRETEND THEY'RE TOYS IF CAPTURED.
YOU NEED ANYTHING WHILE I'M INSIDE, ARTEMIS?
SOME CAVIAR FROM THE KITCHEN. YOU WOULDN'T BELIEVE THE MUCK THEY FEED US IN BARTLEBY'S.
CAVIAR FOR A TEENAGER. WHATEVER YOU-
sniff
ARTEMIS.
STAY IN THE CAR.

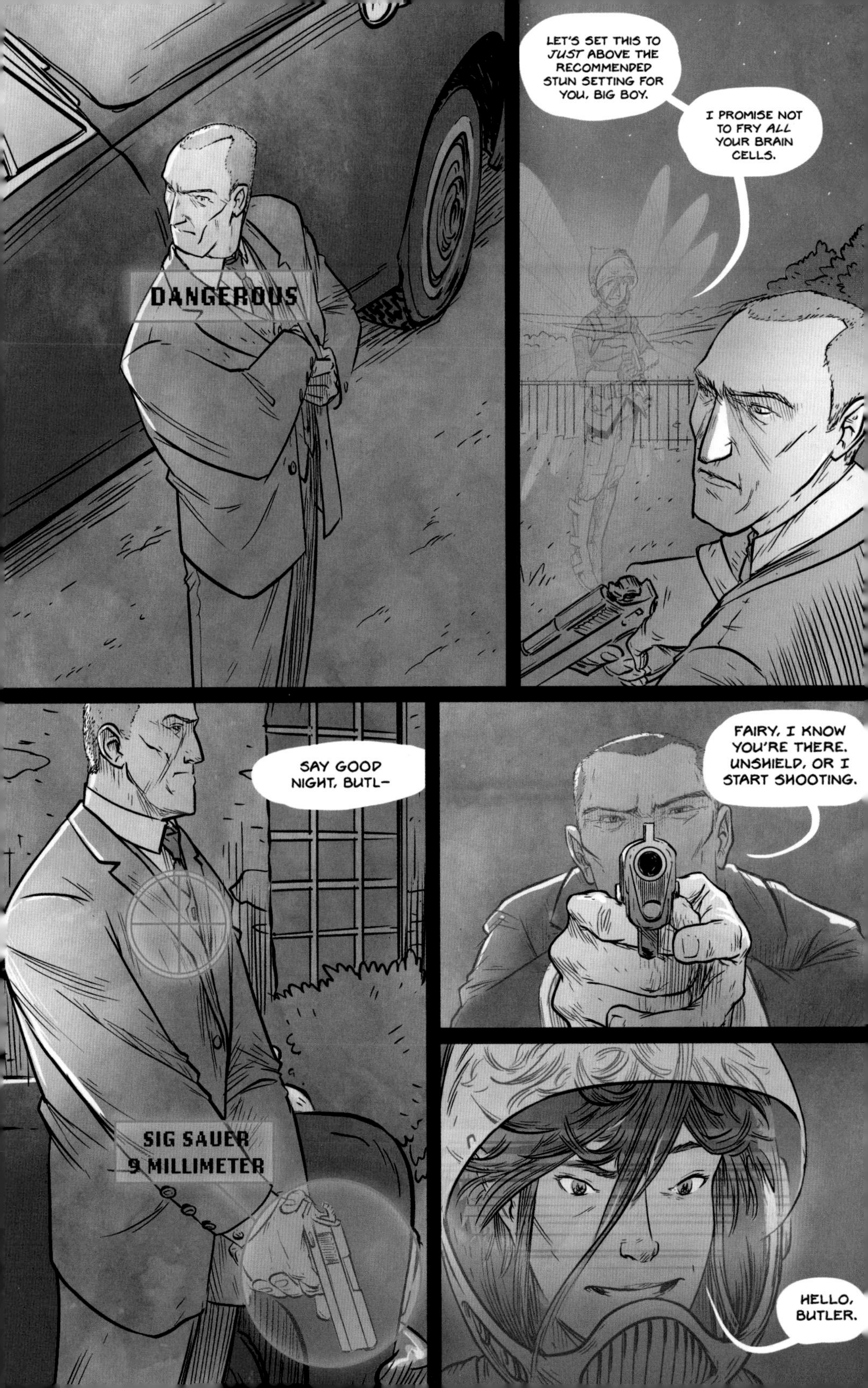
DANGEROUS
LET'S SET THIS TO JUST ABOVE THE RECOMMENDED STUN SETTING FOR YOU, BIG BOY.
I PROMISE NOT TO FRY ALL YOUR BRAIN CELLS.
SIG SAUER 9 MILLIMETER
SAY GOOD NIGHT, BUTL-
FAIRY, I KNOW YOU'RE THERE. UNSHIELD, OR I START SHOOTING.
HELLO, BUTLER.

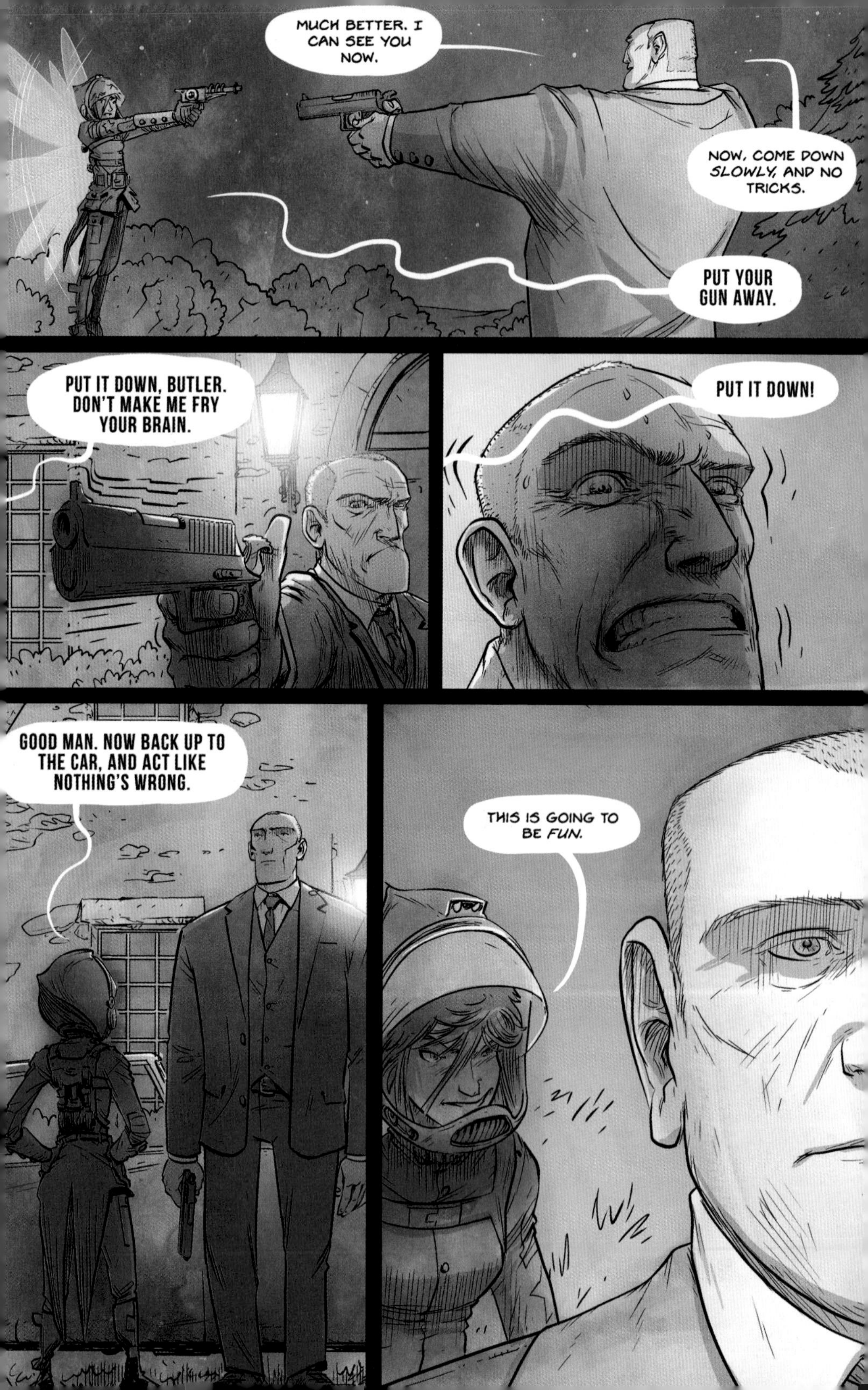
MUCH BETTER. I CAN SEE YOU NOW.
NOW, COME DOWN *SLOWLY,* AND NO TRICKS.
PUT YOUR GUN AWAY.
PUT IT DOWN, BUTLER. DON'T MAKE ME FRY YOUR BRAIN.
PUT IT DOWN!
GOOD MAN. NOW BACK UP TO THE CAR, AND ACT LIKE NOTHING'S WRONG.
THIS IS GOING TO BE *FUN.*

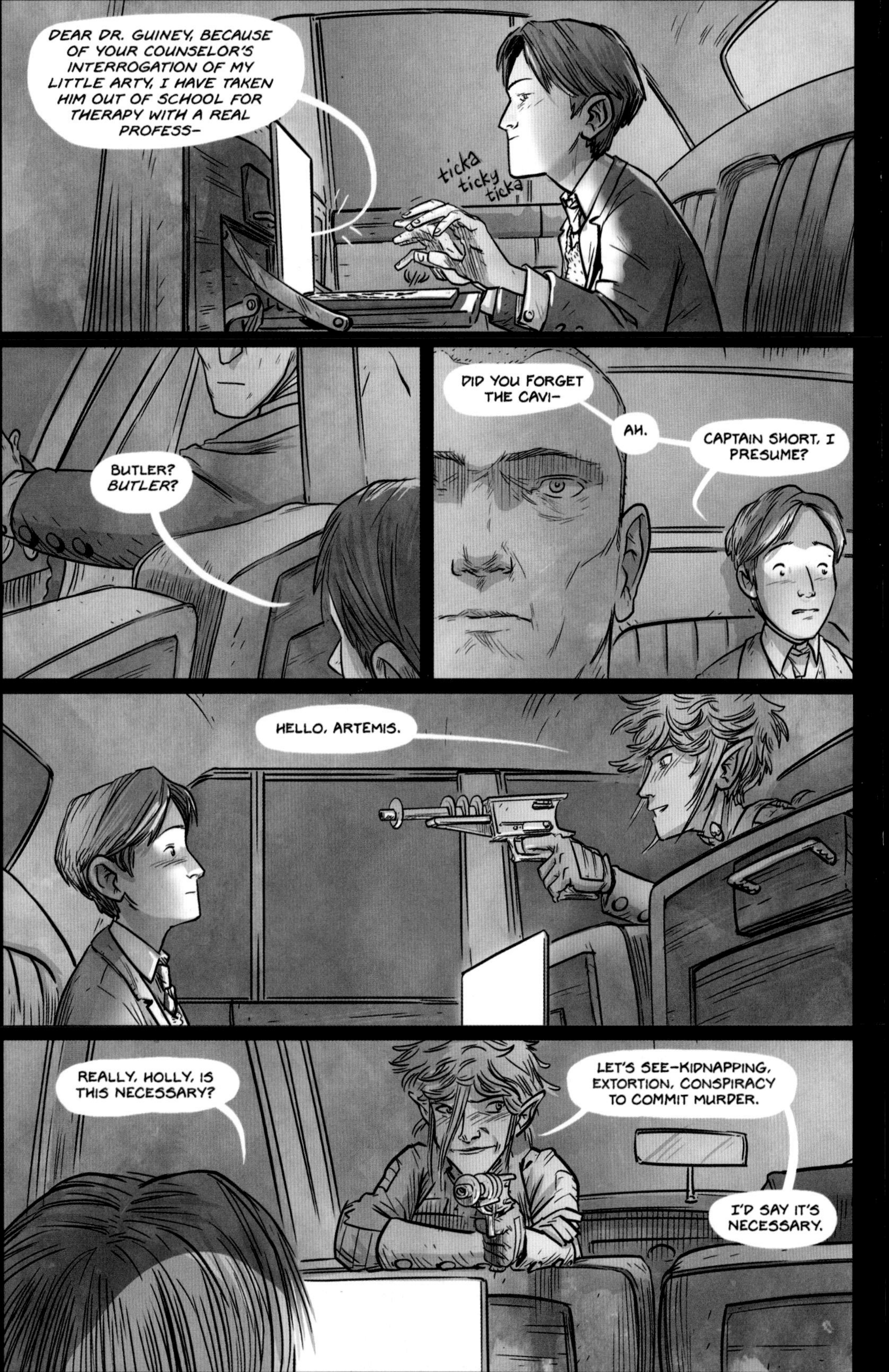
DEAR DR. GUINEY, BECAUSE OF YOUR COUNSELOR'S INTERROGATION OF MY LITTLE ARTY, I HAVE TAKEN HIM OUT OF SCHOOL FOR THERAPY WITH A REAL PROFESS–
ticka ticky ticka
BUTLER? BUTLER?
DID YOU FORGET THE CAVI–
AH.
CAPTAIN SHORT, I PRESUME?
HELLO, ARTEMIS.
REALLY, HOLLY, IS THIS NECESSARY?
LET'S SEE–KIDNAPPING, EXTORTION, CONSPIRACY TO COMMIT MURDER.
I'D SAY IT'S NECESSARY.

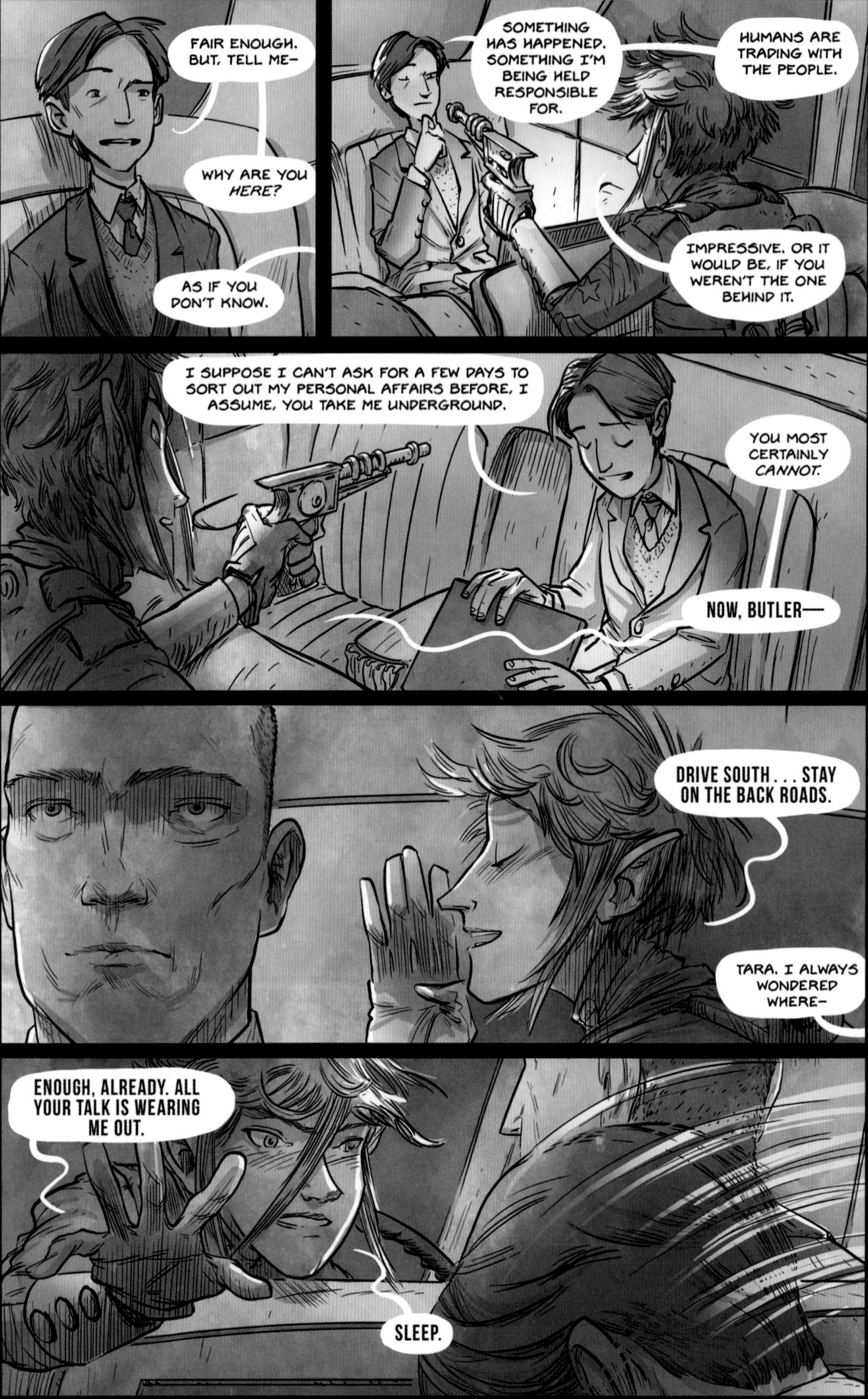
FAIR ENOUGH. BUT, TELL ME–
WHY ARE YOU *HERE?*
AS IF YOU DON'T KNOW.
SOMETHING HAS HAPPENED. SOMETHING I'M BEING HELD RESPONSIBLE FOR.
HUMANS ARE TRADING WITH THE PEOPLE.
IMPRESSIVE. OR IT WOULD BE, IF YOU WEREN'T THE ONE BEHIND IT.
I SUPPOSE I CAN'T ASK FOR A FEW DAYS TO SORT OUT MY PERSONAL AFFAIRS BEFORE, I ASSUME, YOU TAKE ME UNDERGROUND.
YOU MOST CERTAINLY *CANNOT.*
NOW, BUTLER—
DRIVE SOUTH . . . STAY ON THE BACK ROADS.
TARA. I ALWAYS WONDERED WHERE–
ENOUGH, ALREADY. ALL YOUR TALK IS WEARING ME OUT.
SLEEP.

CHAPTER FOUR

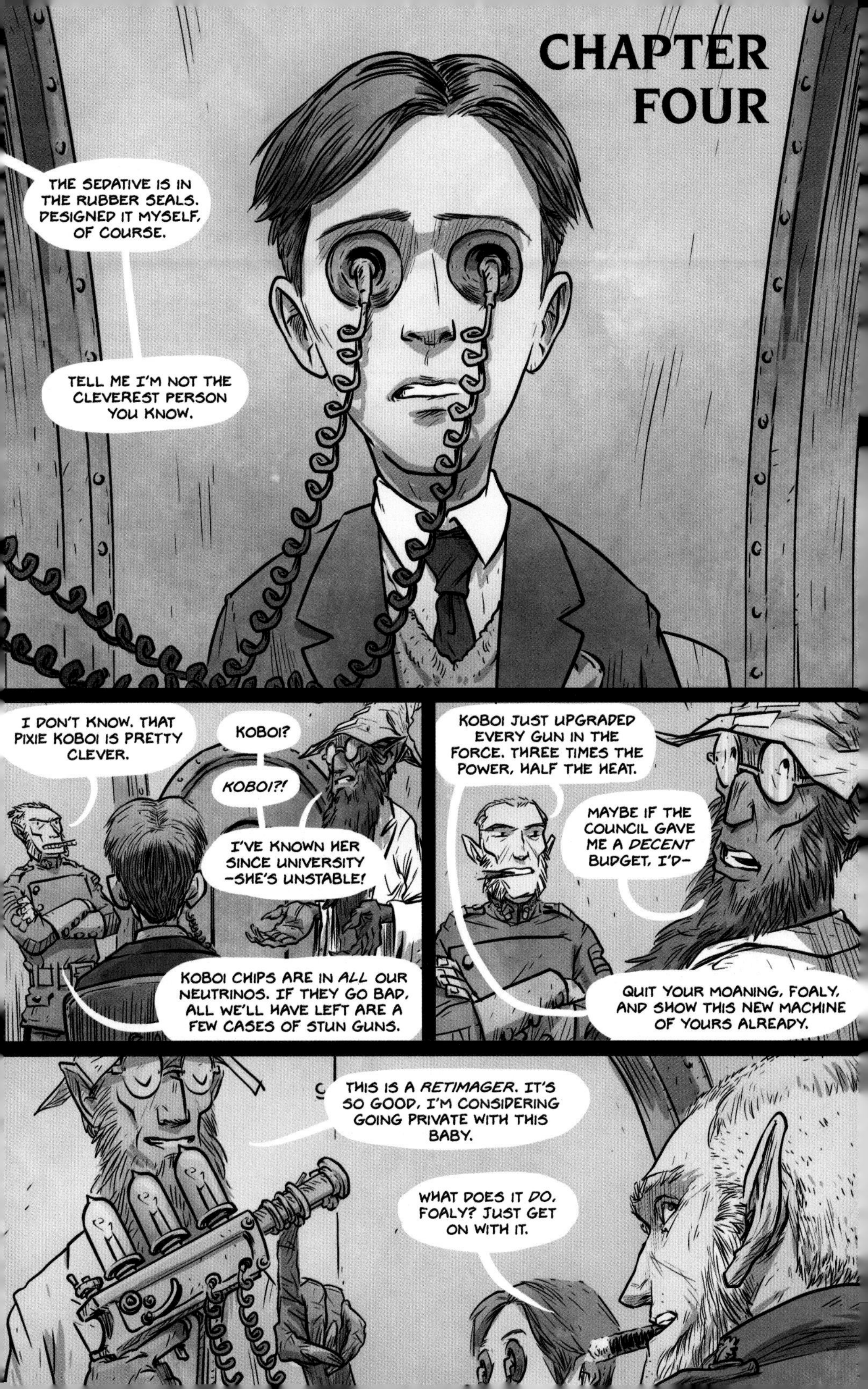
THE SEDATIVE IS IN THE RUBBER SEALS. DESIGNED IT MYSELF, OF COURSE.
TELL ME I'M NOT THE CLEVEREST PERSON YOU KNOW.
I DON'T KNOW. THAT PIXIE KOBOI IS PRETTY CLEVER.
KOBOI?
KOBOI?!
I'VE KNOWN HER SINCE UNIVERSITY —SHE'S UNSTABLE!
KOBOI CHIPS ARE IN *ALL* OUR NEUTRINOS. IF THEY GO BAD, ALL WE'LL HAVE LEFT ARE A FEW CASES OF STUN GUNS.
KOBOI JUST UPGRADED EVERY GUN IN THE FORCE. THREE TIMES THE POWER, HALF THE HEAT.
MAYBE IF THE COUNCIL GAVE ME A *DECENT* BUDGET, I'D—
QUIT YOUR MOANING, FOALY, AND SHOW THIS NEW MACHINE OF YOURS ALREADY.
THIS IS A *RETIMAGER*. IT'S SO GOOD, I'M CONSIDERING GOING PRIVATE WITH THIS BABY.
WHAT DOES IT *DO*, FOALY? JUST GET ON WITH IT.

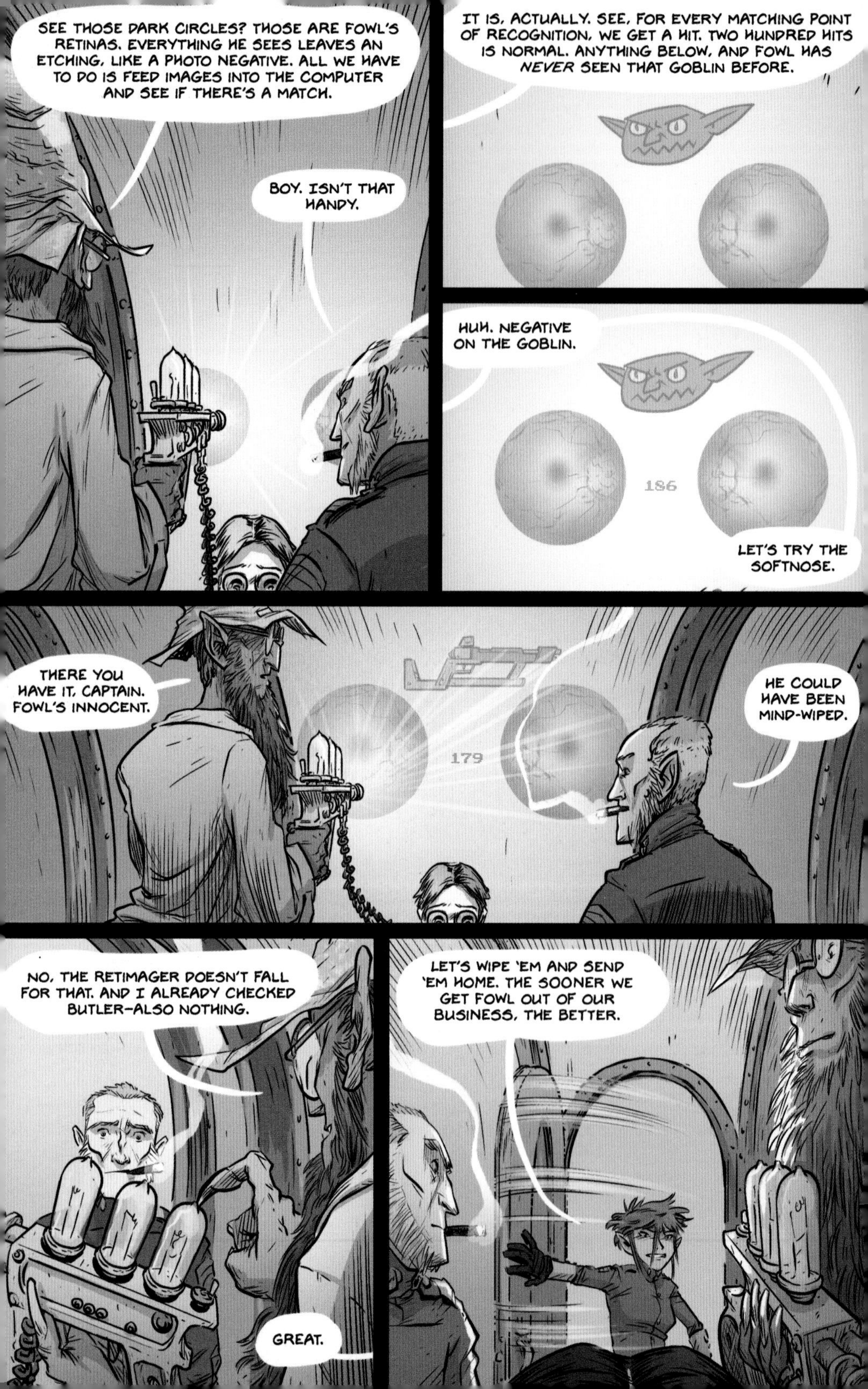
SEE THOSE DARK CIRCLES? THOSE ARE FOWL'S RETINAS. EVERYTHING HE SEES LEAVES AN ETCHING, LIKE A PHOTO NEGATIVE. ALL WE HAVE TO DO IS FEED IMAGES INTO THE COMPUTER AND SEE IF THERE'S A MATCH.
BOY. ISN'T THAT HANDY.
IT IS, ACTUALLY. SEE, FOR EVERY MATCHING POINT OF RECOGNITION, WE GET A HIT. TWO HUNDRED HITS IS NORMAL. ANYTHING BELOW, AND FOWL HAS *NEVER* SEEN THAT GOBLIN BEFORE.
HUH. NEGATIVE ON THE GOBLIN.
186
LET'S TRY THE SOFTNOSE.
THERE YOU HAVE IT, CAPTAIN. FOWL'S INNOCENT.
179
HE COULD HAVE BEEN MIND-WIPED.
NO, THE RETIMAGER DOESN'T FALL FOR THAT. AND I ALREADY CHECKED BUTLER—ALSO NOTHING.
GREAT.
LET'S WIPE 'EM AND SEND 'EM HOME. THE SOONER WE GET FOWL OUT OF OUR BUSINESS, THE BETTER.

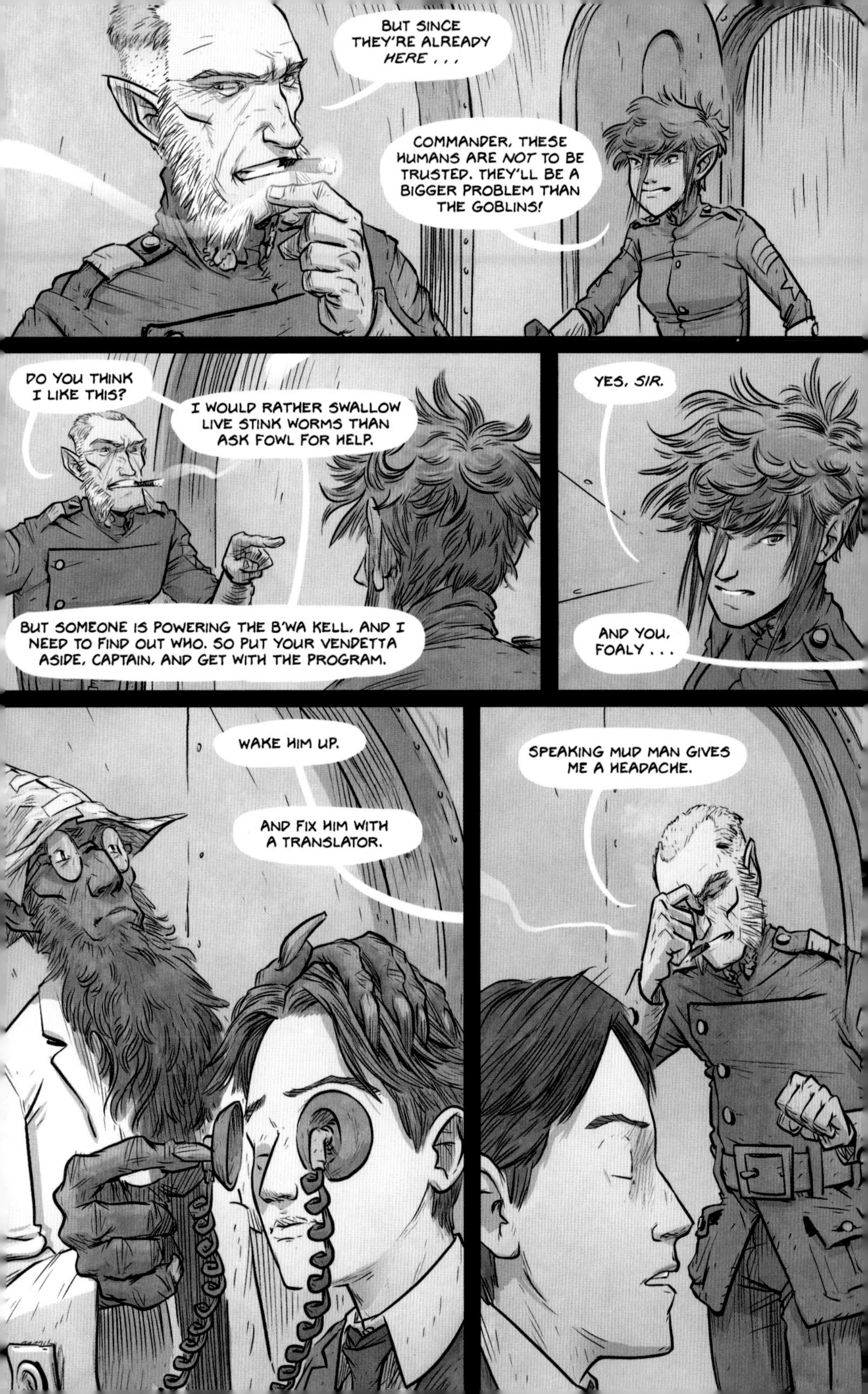
BUT SINCE THEY'RE ALREADY *HERE* . . .
COMMANDER, THESE HUMANS ARE *NOT* TO BE TRUSTED. THEY'LL BE A BIGGER PROBLEM THAN THE GOBLINS!
DO YOU THINK I LIKE THIS?
I WOULD RATHER SWALLOW LIVE STINK WORMS THAN ASK FOWL FOR HELP.
BUT SOMEONE IS POWERING THE B'WA KELL, AND I NEED TO FIND OUT WHO. SO PUT YOUR VENDETTA ASIDE, CAPTAIN, AND GET WITH THE PROGRAM.
YES, *SIR.*
AND YOU, FOALY . . .
WAKE HIM UP.
AND FIX HIM WITH A TRANSLATOR.
SPEAKING MUD MAN GIVES ME A HEADACHE.

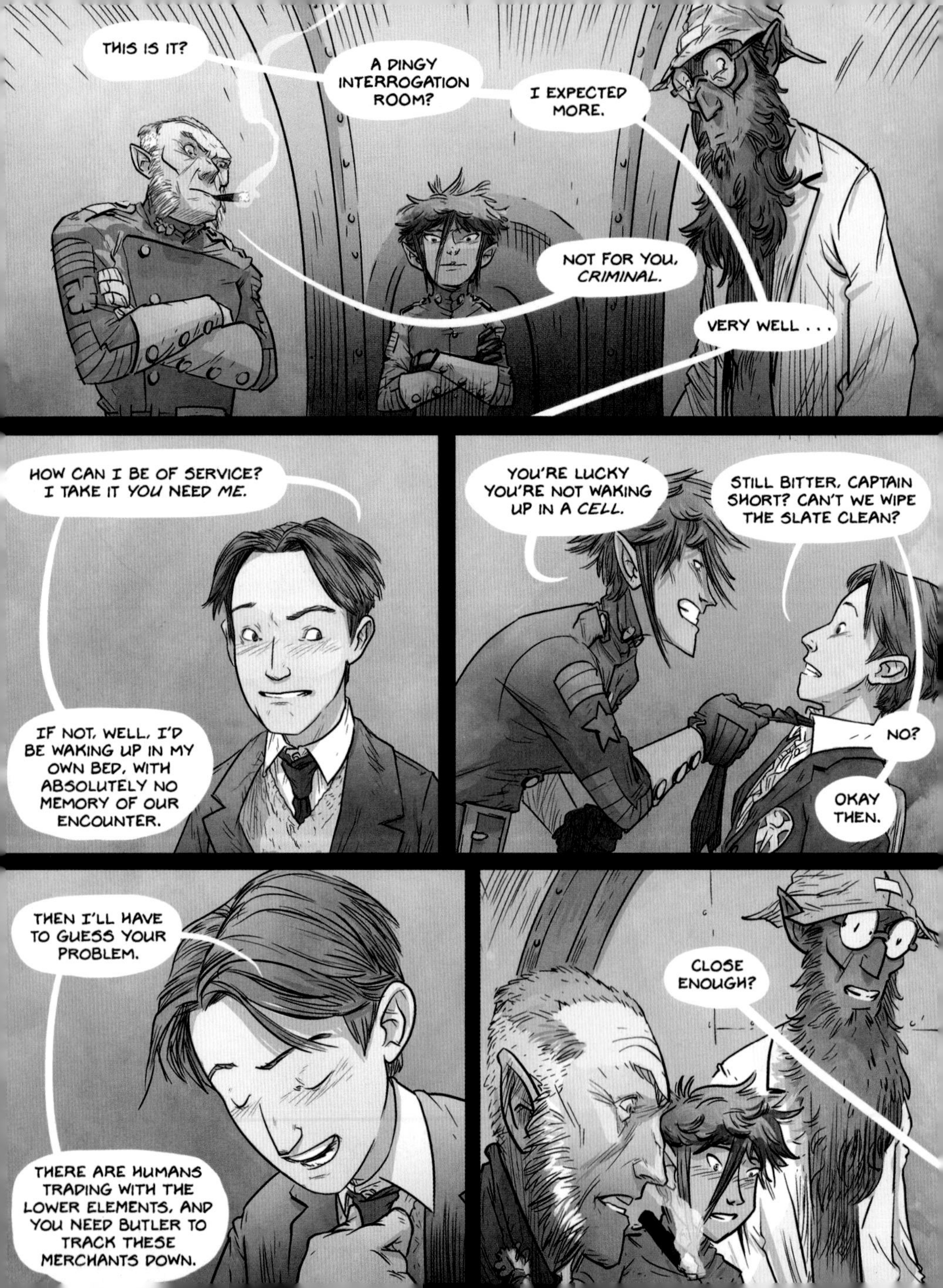
THIS IS IT?
A DINGY INTERROGATION ROOM?
I EXPECTED MORE.
NOT FOR YOU, *CRIMINAL.*
VERY WELL . . .
HOW CAN I BE OF SERVICE? I TAKE IT *YOU* NEED *ME.*
IF NOT, WELL, I'D BE WAKING UP IN MY OWN BED, WITH ABSOLUTELY NO MEMORY OF OUR ENCOUNTER.
YOU'RE LUCKY YOU'RE NOT WAKING UP IN A *CELL.*
STILL BITTER, CAPTAIN SHORT? CAN'T WE WIPE THE SLATE CLEAN?
NO?
OKAY THEN.
THEN I'LL HAVE TO GUESS YOUR PROBLEM.
THERE ARE HUMANS TRADING WITH THE LOWER ELEMENTS, AND YOU NEED BUTLER TO TRACK THESE MERCHANTS DOWN.
CLOSE ENOUGH?

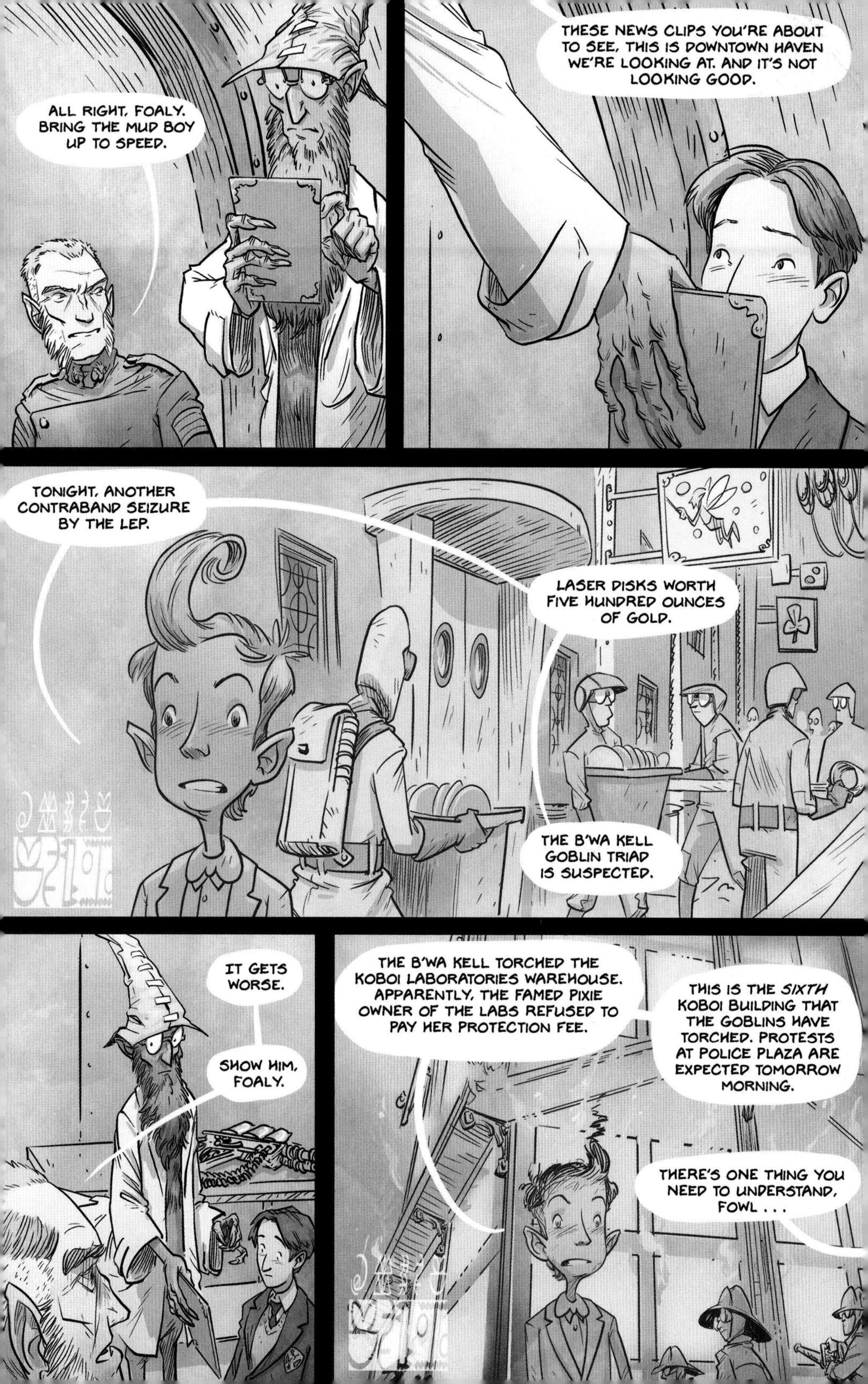
ALL RIGHT, FOALY. BRING THE MUD BOY UP TO SPEED.
THESE NEWS CLIPS YOU'RE ABOUT TO SEE, THIS IS DOWNTOWN HAVEN WE'RE LOOKING AT. AND IT'S NOT LOOKING GOOD.
TONIGHT, ANOTHER CONTRABAND SEIZURE BY THE LEP.
LASER DISKS WORTH FIVE HUNDRED OUNCES OF GOLD.
THE B'WA KELL GOBLIN TRIAD IS SUSPECTED.
IT GETS WORSE.
SHOW HIM, FOALY.
THE B'WA KELL TORCHED THE KOBOI LABORATORIES WAREHOUSE. APPARENTLY, THE FAMED PIXIE OWNER OF THE LABS REFUSED TO PAY HER PROTECTION FEE.
THIS IS THE *SIXTH* KOBOI BUILDING THAT THE GOBLINS HAVE TORCHED. PROTESTS AT POLICE PLAZA ARE EXPECTED TOMORROW MORNING.
THERE'S ONE THING YOU NEED TO UNDERSTAND, FOWL . . .

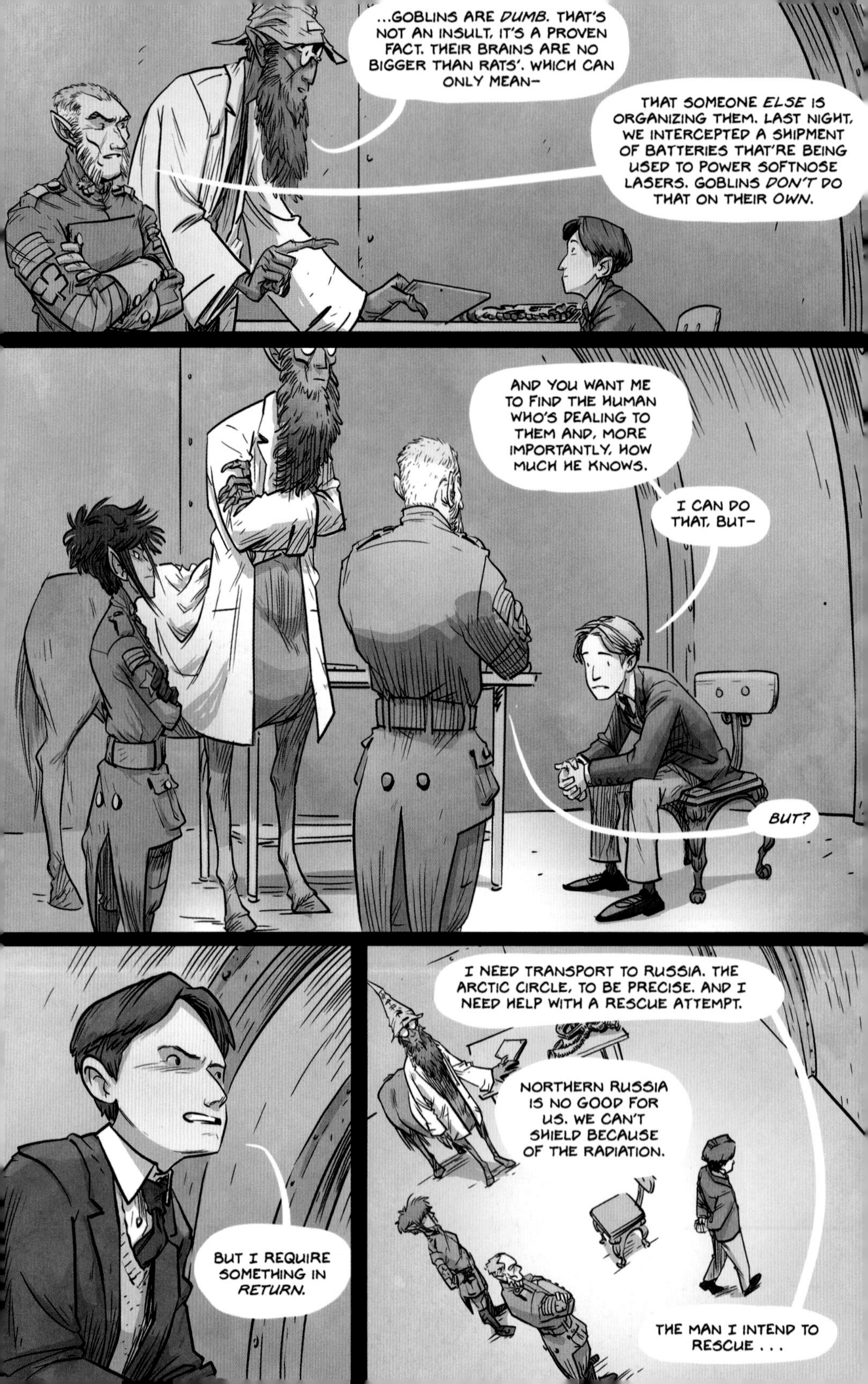
...GOBLINS ARE *DUMB*. THAT'S NOT AN INSULT, IT'S A PROVEN FACT. THEIR BRAINS ARE NO BIGGER THAN RATS'. WHICH CAN ONLY MEAN–
THAT SOMEONE *ELSE* IS ORGANIZING THEM. LAST NIGHT, WE INTERCEPTED A SHIPMENT OF BATTERIES THAT'RE BEING USED TO POWER SOFTNOSE LASERS. GOBLINS *DON'T* DO THAT ON THEIR *OWN*.
AND YOU WANT ME TO FIND THE HUMAN WHO'S DEALING TO THEM AND, MORE IMPORTANTLY, HOW MUCH HE KNOWS.
I CAN DO THAT, BUT–
BUT?
BUT I REQUIRE SOMETHING IN *RETURN*.
I NEED TRANSPORT TO RUSSIA. THE ARCTIC CIRCLE, TO BE PRECISE. AND I NEED HELP WITH A RESCUE ATTEMPT.
NORTHERN RUSSIA IS NO GOOD FOR US. WE CAN'T SHIELD BECAUSE OF THE RADIATION.
THE MAN I INTEND TO RESCUE . . .

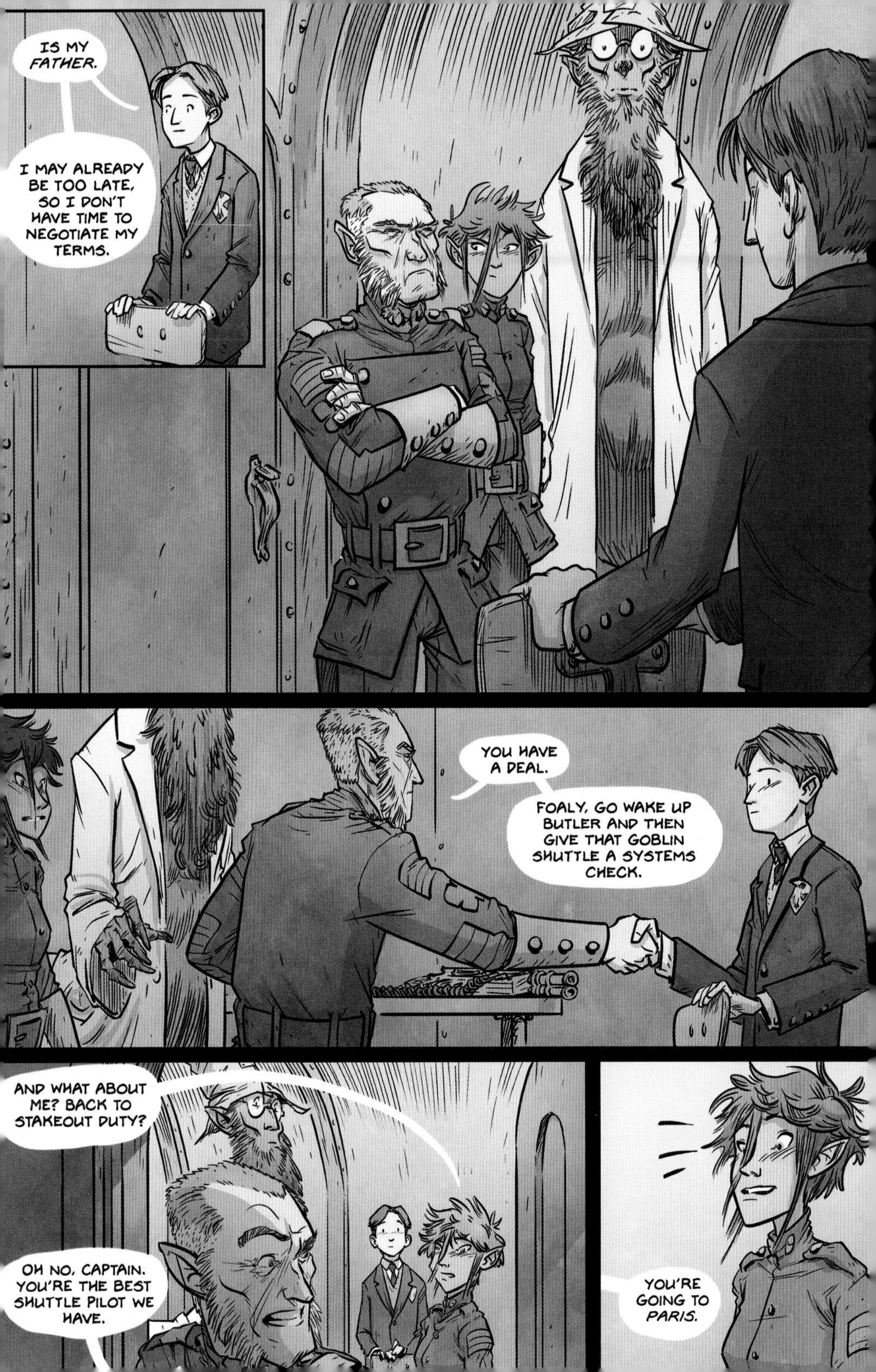

IS MY FATHER.
I MAY ALREADY BE TOO LATE, SO I DON'T HAVE TIME TO NEGOTIATE MY TERMS.
YOU HAVE A DEAL.
FOALY, GO WAKE UP BUTLER AND THEN GIVE THAT GOBLIN SHUTTLE A SYSTEMS CHECK.
AND WHAT ABOUT ME? BACK TO STAKEOUT DUTY?
OH NO, CAPTAIN. YOU'RE THE BEST SHUTTLE PILOT WE HAVE.
YOU'RE GOING TO *PARIS*.

CHAPTER FIVE

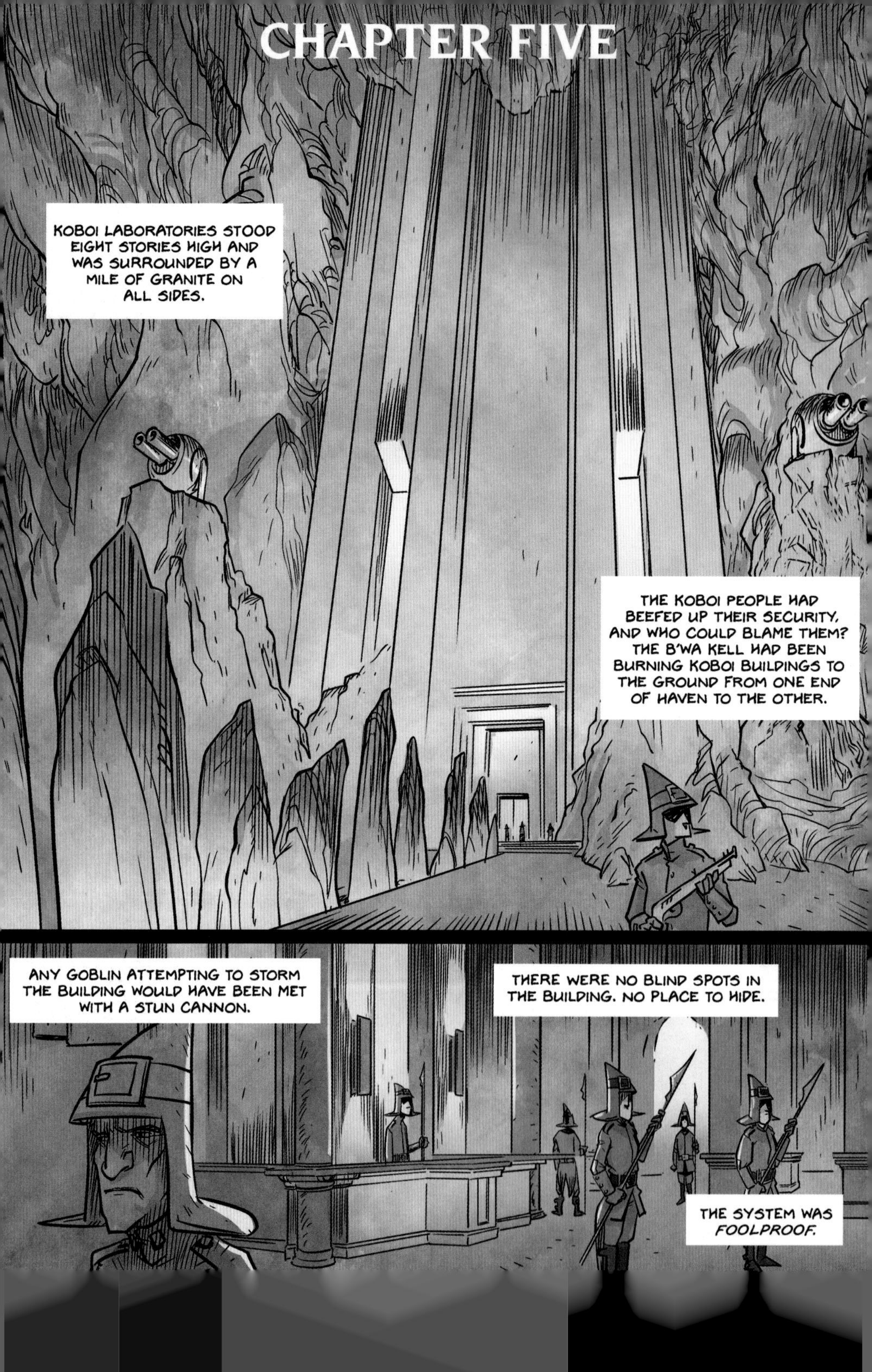
KOBOI LABORATORIES STOOD EIGHT STORIES HIGH AND WAS SURROUNDED BY A MILE OF GRANITE ON ALL SIDES.
THE KOBOI PEOPLE HAD BEEFED UP THEIR SECURITY, AND WHO COULD BLAME THEM? THE B'WA KELL HAD BEEN BURNING KOBOI BUILDINGS TO THE GROUND FROM ONE END OF HAVEN TO THE OTHER.
ANY GOBLIN ATTEMPTING TO STORM THE BUILDING WOULD HAVE BEEN MET WITH A STUN CANNON.
THERE WERE NO BLIND SPOTS IN THE BUILDING. NO PLACE TO HIDE.
THE SYSTEM WAS *FOOLPROOF.*

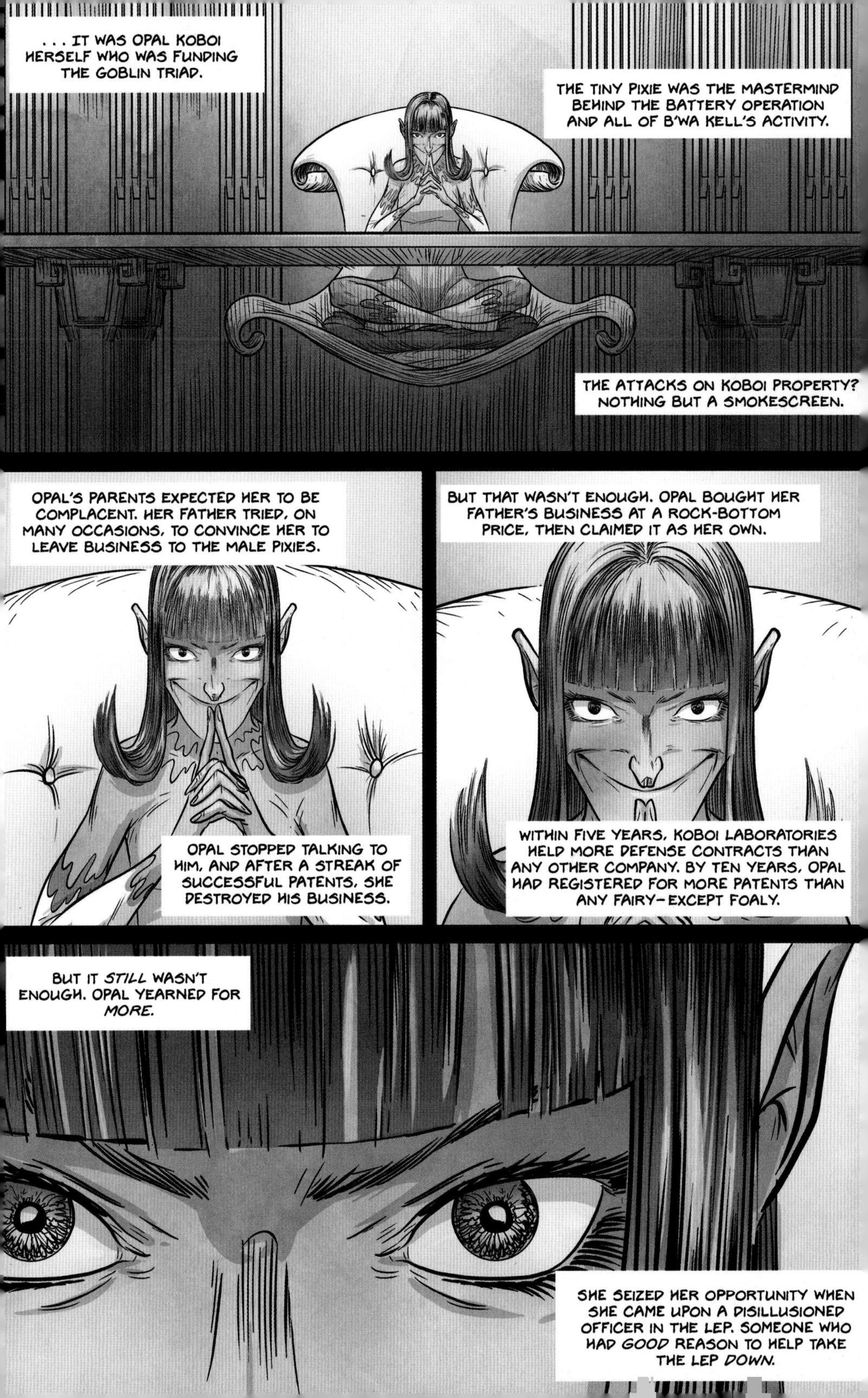
. . . IT WAS OPAL KOBOI HERSELF WHO WAS FUNDING THE GOBLIN TRIAD.
THE TINY PIXIE WAS THE MASTERMIND BEHIND THE BATTERY OPERATION AND ALL OF B'WA KELL'S ACTIVITY.
THE ATTACKS ON KOBOI PROPERTY? NOTHING BUT A SMOKESCREEN.
OPAL'S PARENTS EXPECTED HER TO BE COMPLACENT. HER FATHER TRIED, ON MANY OCCASIONS, TO CONVINCE HER TO LEAVE BUSINESS TO THE MALE PIXIES.
OPAL STOPPED TALKING TO HIM, AND AFTER A STREAK OF SUCCESSFUL PATENTS, SHE DESTROYED HIS BUSINESS.
BUT THAT WASN'T ENOUGH. OPAL BOUGHT HER FATHER'S BUSINESS AT A ROCK-BOTTOM PRICE, THEN CLAIMED IT AS HER OWN.
WITHIN FIVE YEARS, KOBOI LABORATORIES HELD MORE DEFENSE CONTRACTS THAN ANY OTHER COMPANY. BY TEN YEARS, OPAL HAD REGISTERED FOR MORE PATENTS THAN ANY FAIRY—EXCEPT FOALY.
BUT IT *STILL* WASN'T ENOUGH. OPAL YEARNED FOR *MORE*.
SHE SEIZED HER OPPORTUNITY WHEN SHE CAME UPON A DISILLUSIONED OFFICER IN THE LEP. SOMEONE WHO HAD *GOOD* REASON TO HELP TAKE THE LEP *DOWN*.

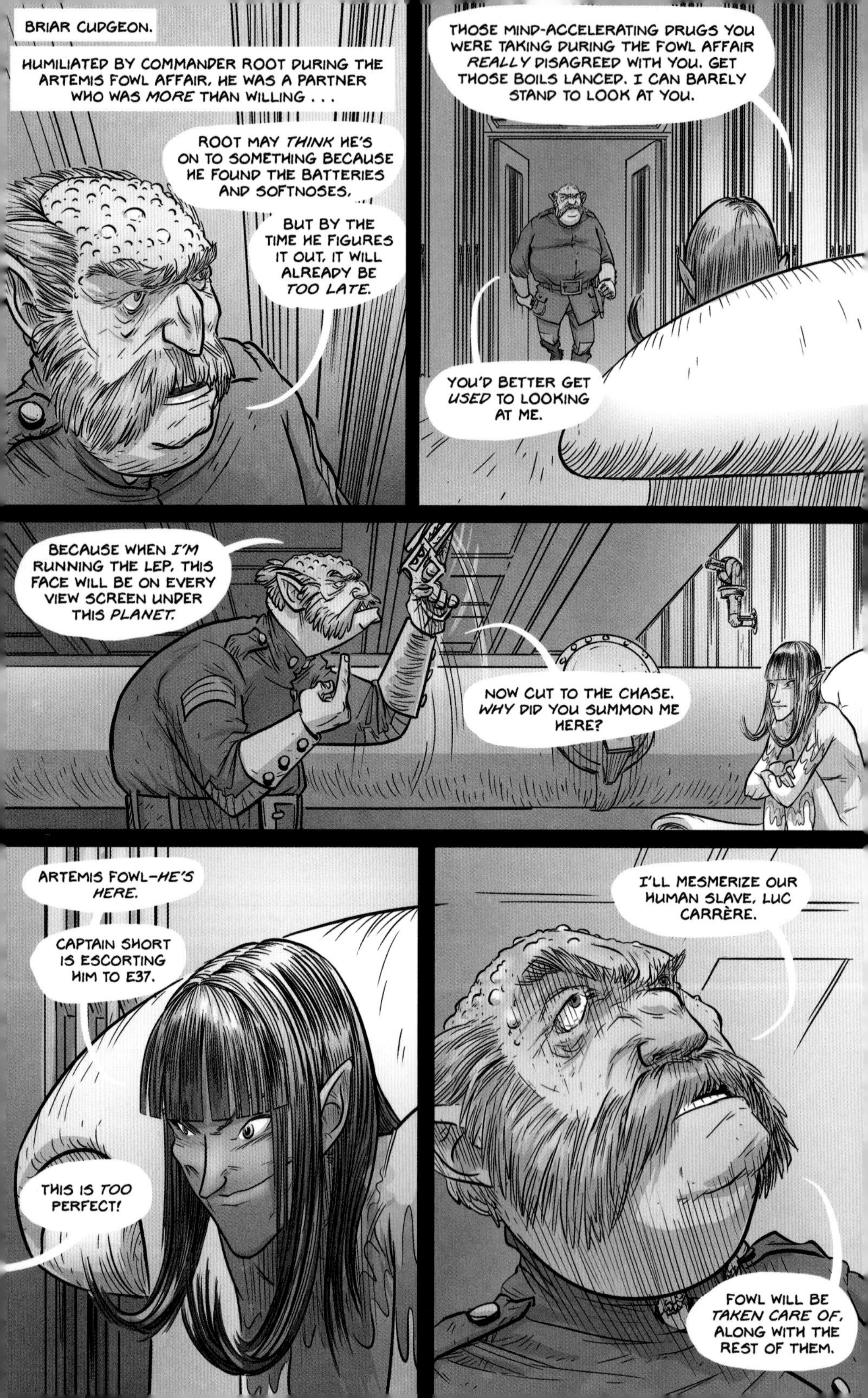

BRIAR CUDGEON.
HUMILIATED BY COMMANDER ROOT DURING THE ARTEMIS FOWL AFFAIR, HE WAS A PARTNER WHO WAS *MORE* THAN WILLING . . .
ROOT MAY *THINK* HE'S ON TO SOMETHING BECAUSE HE FOUND THE BATTERIES AND SOFTNOSES,
BUT BY THE TIME HE FIGURES IT OUT, IT WILL ALREADY BE *TOO LATE*.
THOSE MIND-ACCELERATING DRUGS YOU WERE TAKING DURING THE FOWL AFFAIR *REALLY* DISAGREED WITH YOU. GET THOSE BOILS LANCED. I CAN BARELY STAND TO LOOK AT YOU.
YOU'D BETTER GET *USED* TO LOOKING AT ME.
BECAUSE WHEN *I'M* RUNNING THE LEP, THIS FACE WILL BE ON EVERY VIEW SCREEN UNDER THIS *PLANET*.
NOW CUT TO THE CHASE. *WHY* DID YOU SUMMON ME HERE?
ARTEMIS FOWL—*HE'S HERE*.
CAPTAIN SHORT IS ESCORTING HIM TO E37.
THIS IS *TOO* PERFECT!
I'LL MESMERIZE OUR HUMAN SLAVE, LUC CARRÈRE.
FOWL WILL BE *TAKEN CARE OF*, ALONG WITH THE REST OF THEM.

CHAPTER SIX

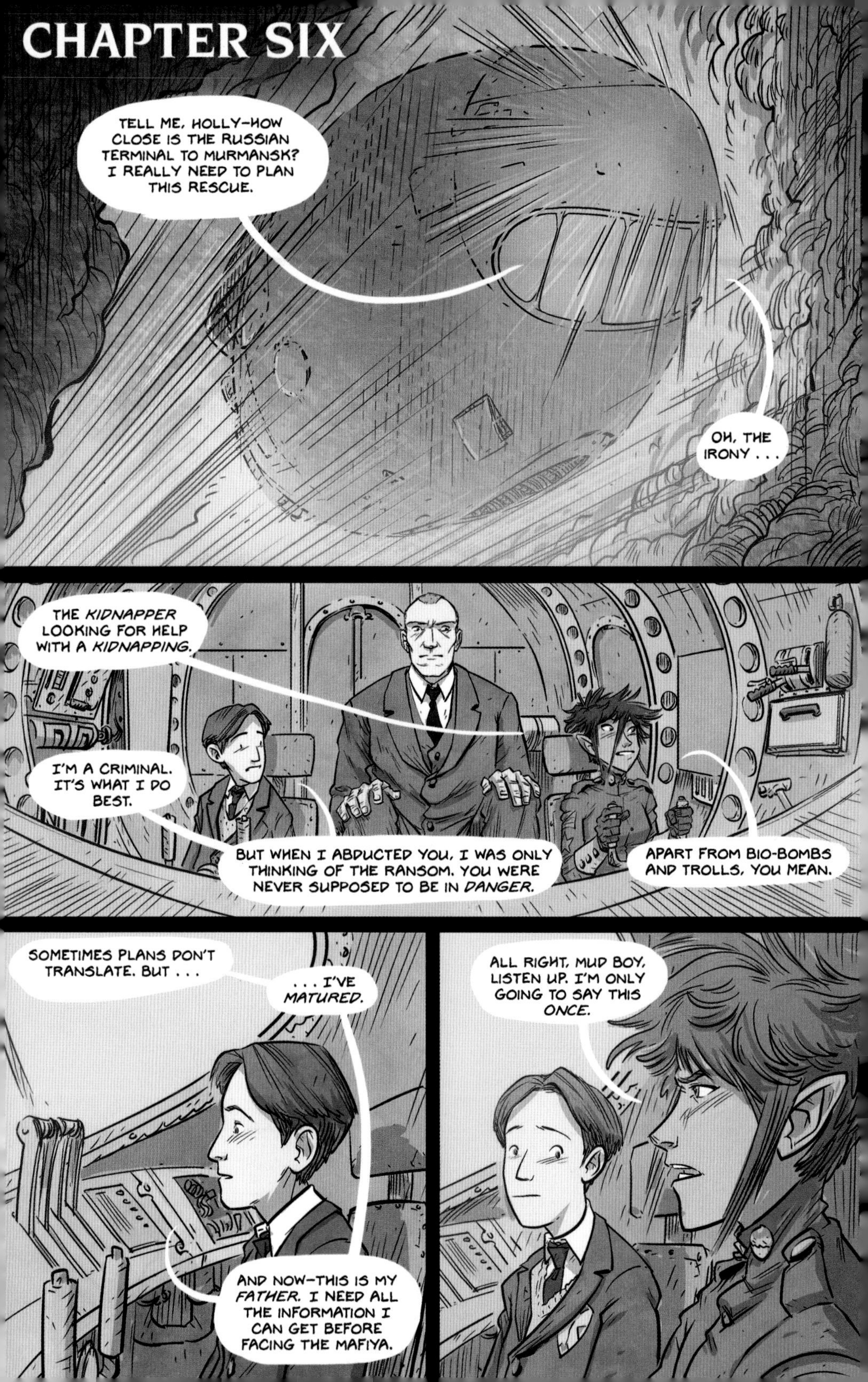
TELL ME, HOLLY—HOW CLOSE IS THE RUSSIAN TERMINAL TO MURMANSK? I REALLY NEED TO PLAN THIS RESCUE.
OH, THE IRONY . . .
THE *KIDNAPPER* LOOKING FOR HELP WITH A *KIDNAPPING*.
I'M A CRIMINAL. IT'S WHAT I DO BEST.
BUT WHEN I ABDUCTED YOU, I WAS ONLY THINKING OF THE RANSOM. YOU WERE NEVER SUPPOSED TO BE IN *DANGER*.
APART FROM BIO-BOMBS AND TROLLS, YOU MEAN.
SOMETIMES PLANS DON'T TRANSLATE. BUT . . .
. . . I'VE *MATURED*.
AND NOW—THIS IS MY *FATHER*. I NEED ALL THE INFORMATION I CAN GET BEFORE FACING THE MAFIYA.
ALL RIGHT, MUD BOY, LISTEN UP. I'M ONLY GOING TO SAY THIS *ONCE*.

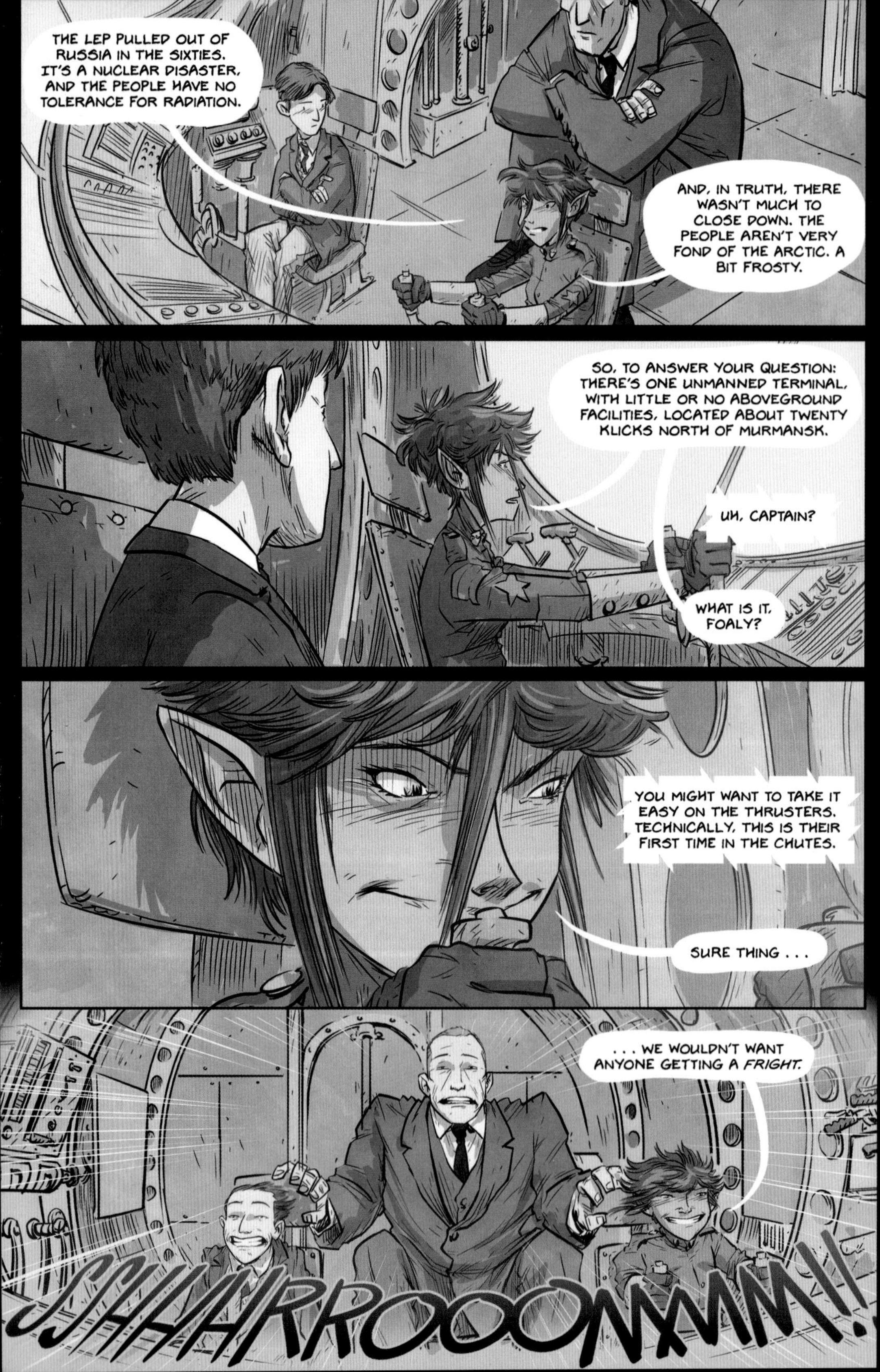
THE LEP PULLED OUT OF RUSSIA IN THE SIXTIES. IT'S A NUCLEAR DISASTER, AND THE PEOPLE HAVE NO TOLERANCE FOR RADIATION.
AND, IN TRUTH, THERE WASN'T MUCH TO CLOSE DOWN. THE PEOPLE AREN'T VERY FOND OF THE ARCTIC. A BIT FROSTY.
SO, TO ANSWER YOUR QUESTION: THERE'S ONE UNMANNED TERMINAL, WITH LITTLE OR NO ABOVEGROUND FACILITIES, LOCATED ABOUT TWENTY KLICKS NORTH OF MURMANSK.
UH, CAPTAIN?
WHAT IS IT, FOALY?
YOU MIGHT WANT TO TAKE IT EASY ON THE THRUSTERS. TECHNICALLY, THIS IS THEIR FIRST TIME IN THE CHUTES.
SURE THING . . .
. . . WE WOULDN'T WANT ANYONE GETTING A *FRIGHT*.
SHHHRROOOOMMM!

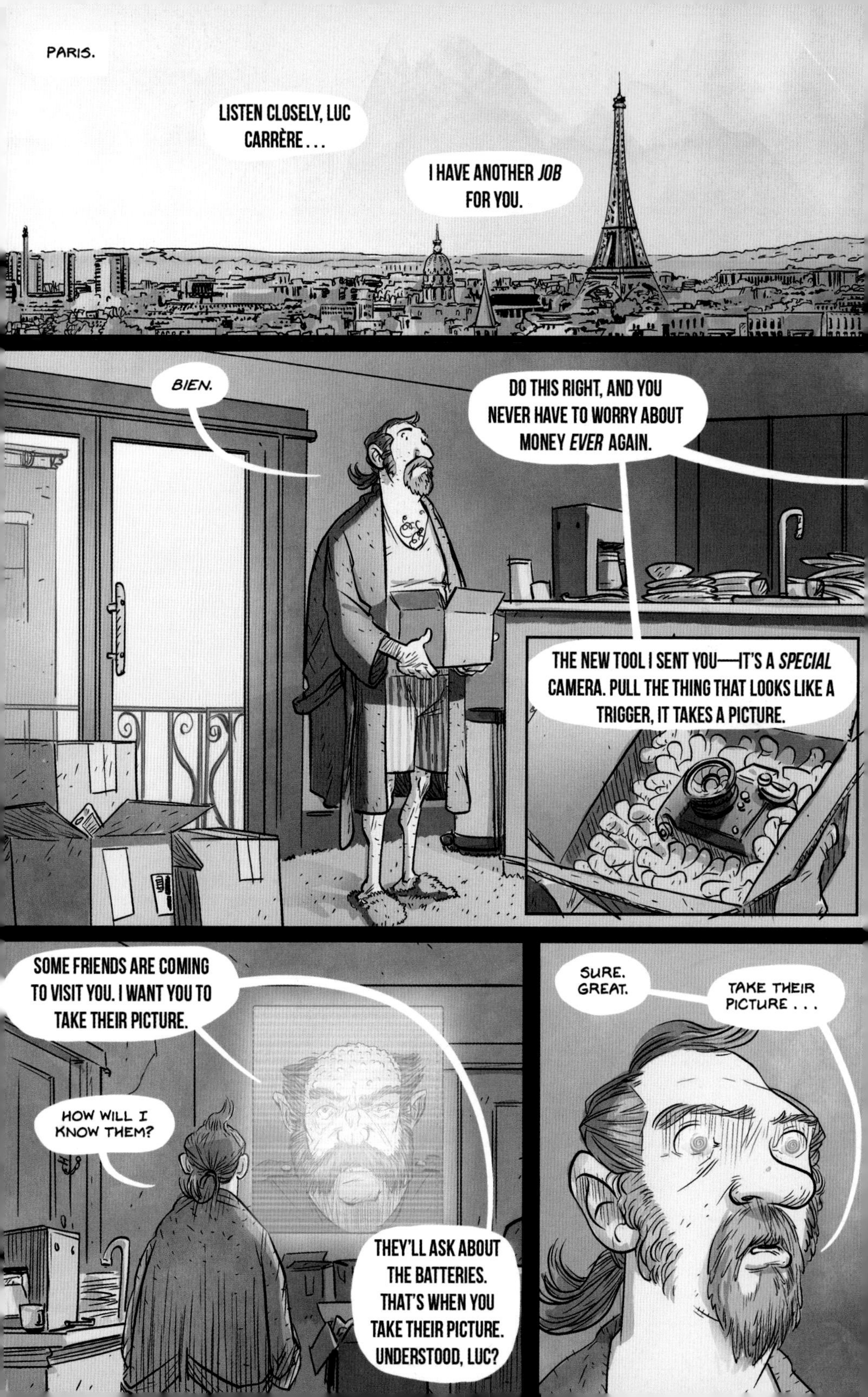
PARIS.
LISTEN CLOSELY, LUC CARRÈRE . . .
I HAVE ANOTHER *JOB* FOR YOU.
BIEN.
DO THIS RIGHT, AND YOU NEVER HAVE TO WORRY ABOUT MONEY *EVER* AGAIN.
THE NEW TOOL I SENT YOU—IT'S A *SPECIAL* CAMERA. PULL THE THING THAT LOOKS LIKE A TRIGGER, IT TAKES A PICTURE.
SOME FRIENDS ARE COMING TO VISIT YOU. I WANT YOU TO TAKE THEIR PICTURE.
HOW WILL I KNOW THEM?
THEY'LL ASK ABOUT THE BATTERIES. THAT'S WHEN YOU TAKE THEIR PICTURE. UNDERSTOOD, LUC?
SURE. GREAT.
TAKE THEIR PICTURE . . .

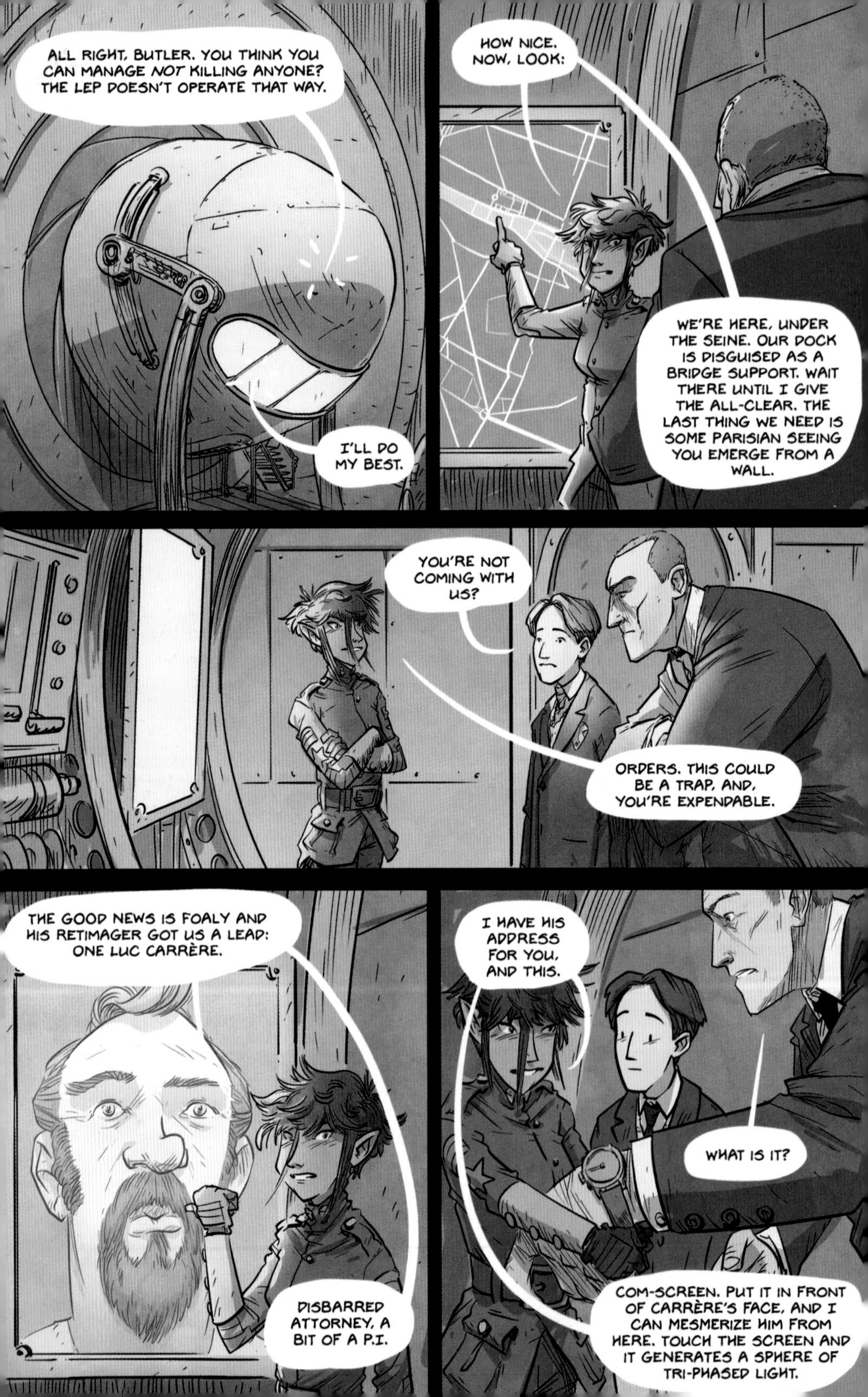
ALL RIGHT, BUTLER. YOU THINK YOU CAN MANAGE *NOT* KILLING ANYONE? THE LEP DOESN'T OPERATE THAT WAY.
I'LL DO MY BEST.
HOW NICE. NOW, LOOK:
WE'RE HERE, UNDER THE SEINE. OUR DOCK IS DISGUISED AS A BRIDGE SUPPORT. WAIT THERE UNTIL I GIVE THE ALL-CLEAR. THE LAST THING WE NEED IS SOME PARISIAN SEEING YOU EMERGE FROM A WALL.
YOU'RE NOT COMING WITH US?
ORDERS. THIS COULD BE A TRAP, AND, YOU'RE EXPENDABLE.
THE GOOD NEWS IS FOALY AND HIS RETIMAGER GOT US A LEAD: ONE LUC CARRÈRE.
DISBARRED ATTORNEY, A BIT OF A P.I.
I HAVE HIS ADDRESS FOR YOU, AND THIS.
WHAT IS IT?
COM-SCREEN. PUT IT IN FRONT OF CARRÈRE'S FACE, AND I CAN MESMERIZE HIM FROM HERE. TOUCH THE SCREEN AND IT GENERATES A SPHERE OF TRI-PHASED LIGHT.

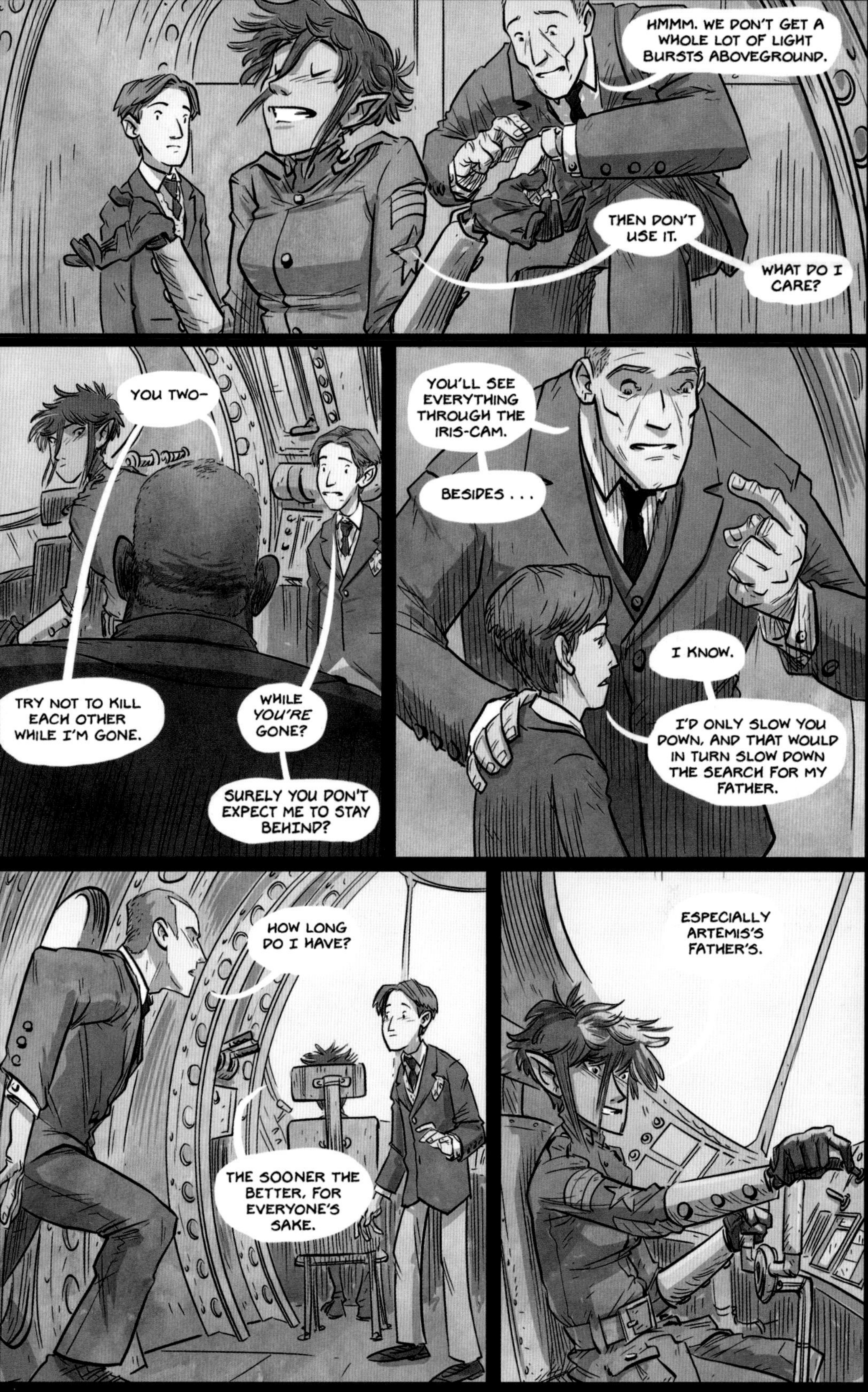
HMMM. WE DON'T GET A WHOLE LOT OF LIGHT BURSTS ABOVEGROUND.
THEN DON'T USE IT.
WHAT DO I CARE?
YOU TWO-
TRY NOT TO KILL EACH OTHER WHILE I'M GONE.
WHILE *YOU'RE* GONE?
SURELY YOU DON'T EXPECT ME TO STAY BEHIND?
YOU'LL SEE EVERYTHING THROUGH THE IRIS-CAM.
BESIDES . . .
I KNOW.
I'D ONLY SLOW YOU DOWN, AND THAT WOULD IN TURN SLOW DOWN THE SEARCH FOR MY FATHER.
HOW LONG DO I HAVE?
THE SOONER THE BETTER, FOR EVERYONE'S SAKE.
ESPECIALLY ARTEMIS'S FATHER'S.

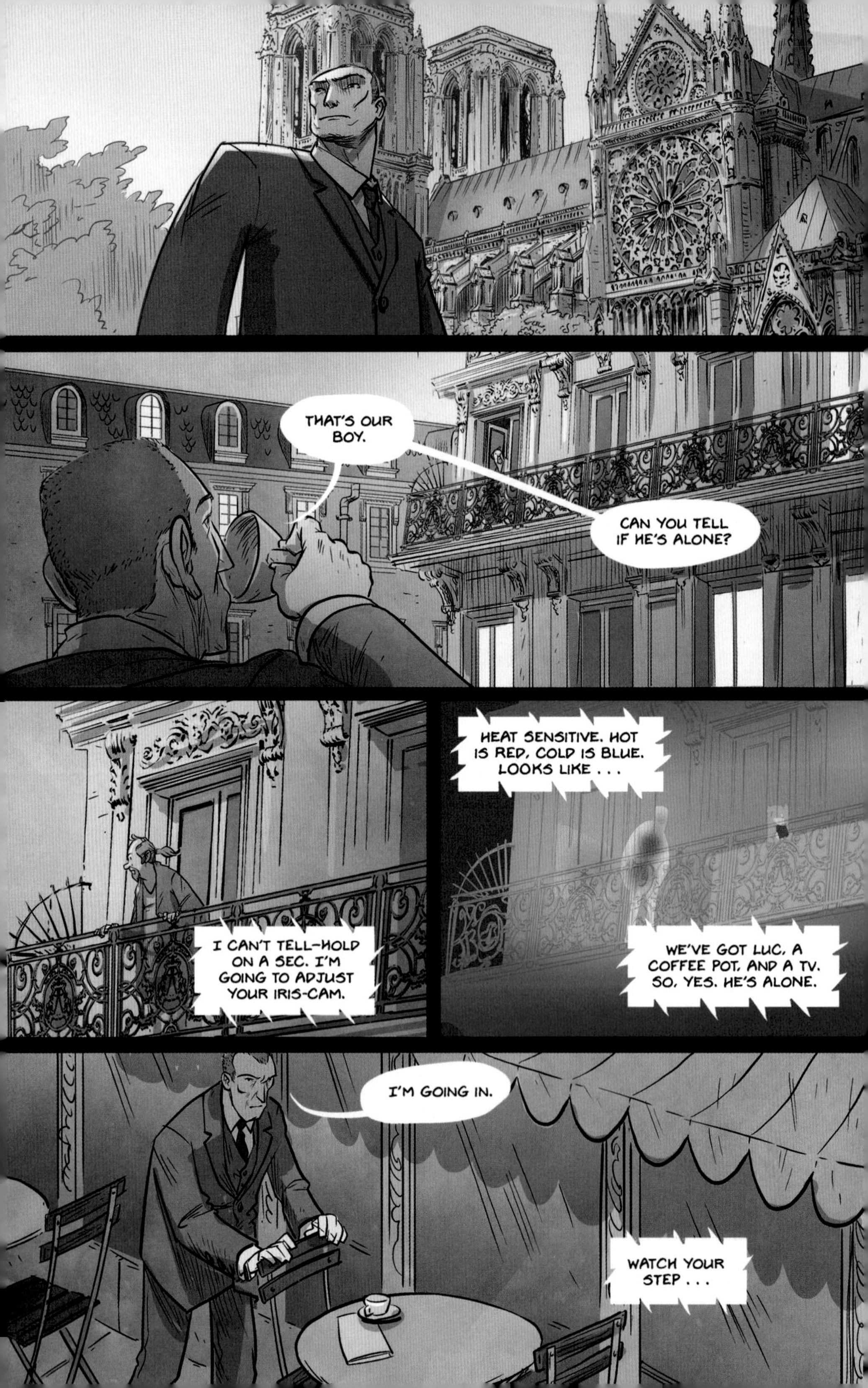
THAT'S OUR BOY.
CAN YOU TELL IF HE'S ALONE?
I CAN'T TELL—HOLD ON A SEC. I'M GOING TO ADJUST YOUR IRIS-CAM.
HEAT SENSITIVE. HOT IS RED, COLD IS BLUE. LOOKS LIKE . . .
WE'VE GOT LUC, A COFFEE POT, AND A TV. SO, YES. HE'S ALONE.
I'M GOING IN.
WATCH YOUR STEP . . .

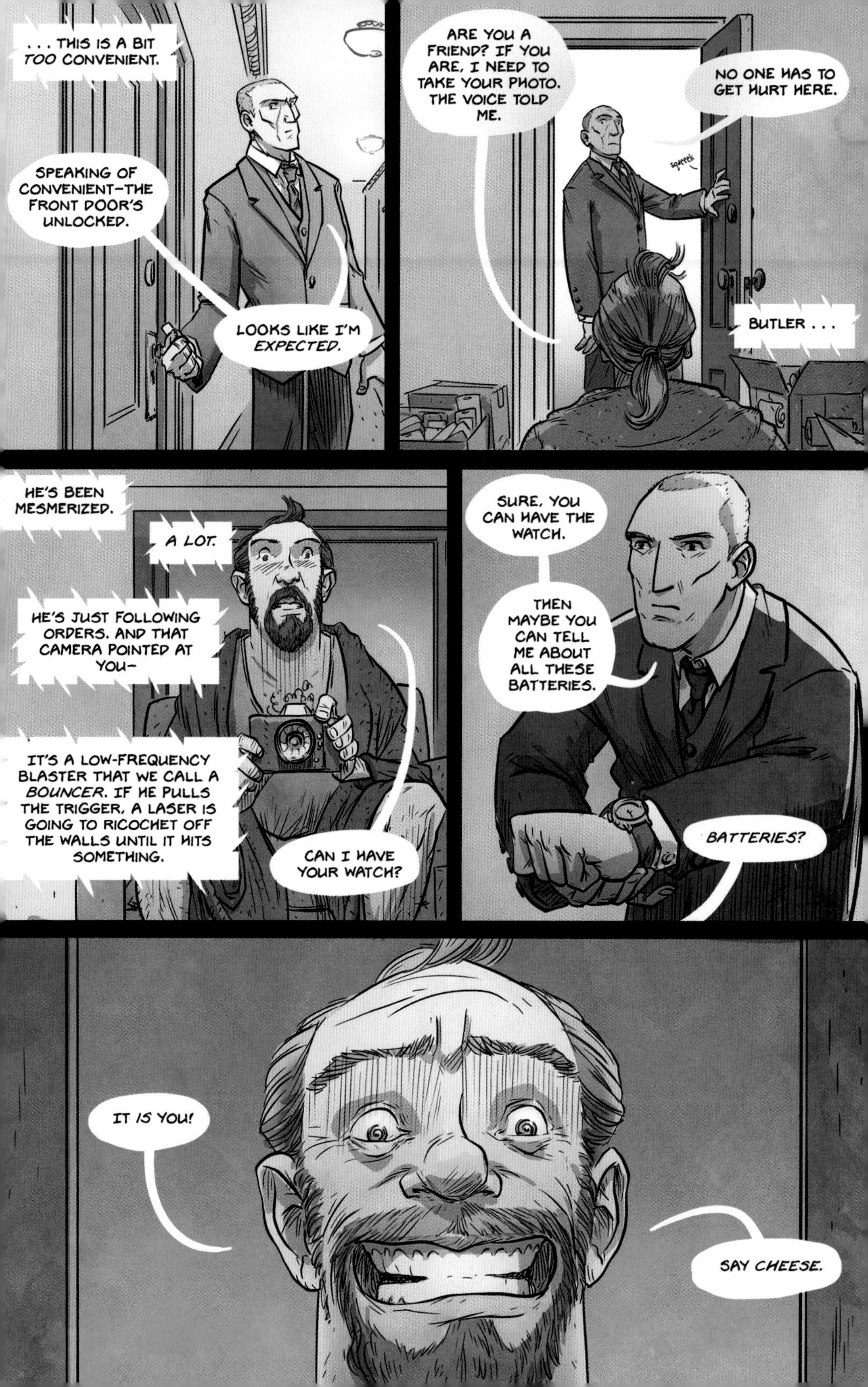
. . . THIS IS A BIT TOO CONVENIENT.
SPEAKING OF CONVENIENT—THE FRONT DOOR'S UNLOCKED.
LOOKS LIKE I'M EXPECTED.
ARE YOU A FRIEND? IF YOU ARE, I NEED TO TAKE YOUR PHOTO. THE VOICE TOLD ME.
NO ONE HAS TO GET HURT HERE.
squeeek
BUTLER . . .
HE'S BEEN MESMERIZED.
A LOT.
HE'S JUST FOLLOWING ORDERS. AND THAT CAMERA POINTED AT YOU—
IT'S A LOW-FREQUENCY BLASTER THAT WE CALL A BOUNCER. IF HE PULLS THE TRIGGER, A LASER IS GOING TO RICOCHET OFF THE WALLS UNTIL IT HITS SOMETHING.
CAN I HAVE YOUR WATCH?
SURE, YOU CAN HAVE THE WATCH.
THEN MAYBE YOU CAN TELL ME ABOUT ALL THESE BATTERIES.
BATTERIES?
IT IS YOU!
SAY CHEESE.

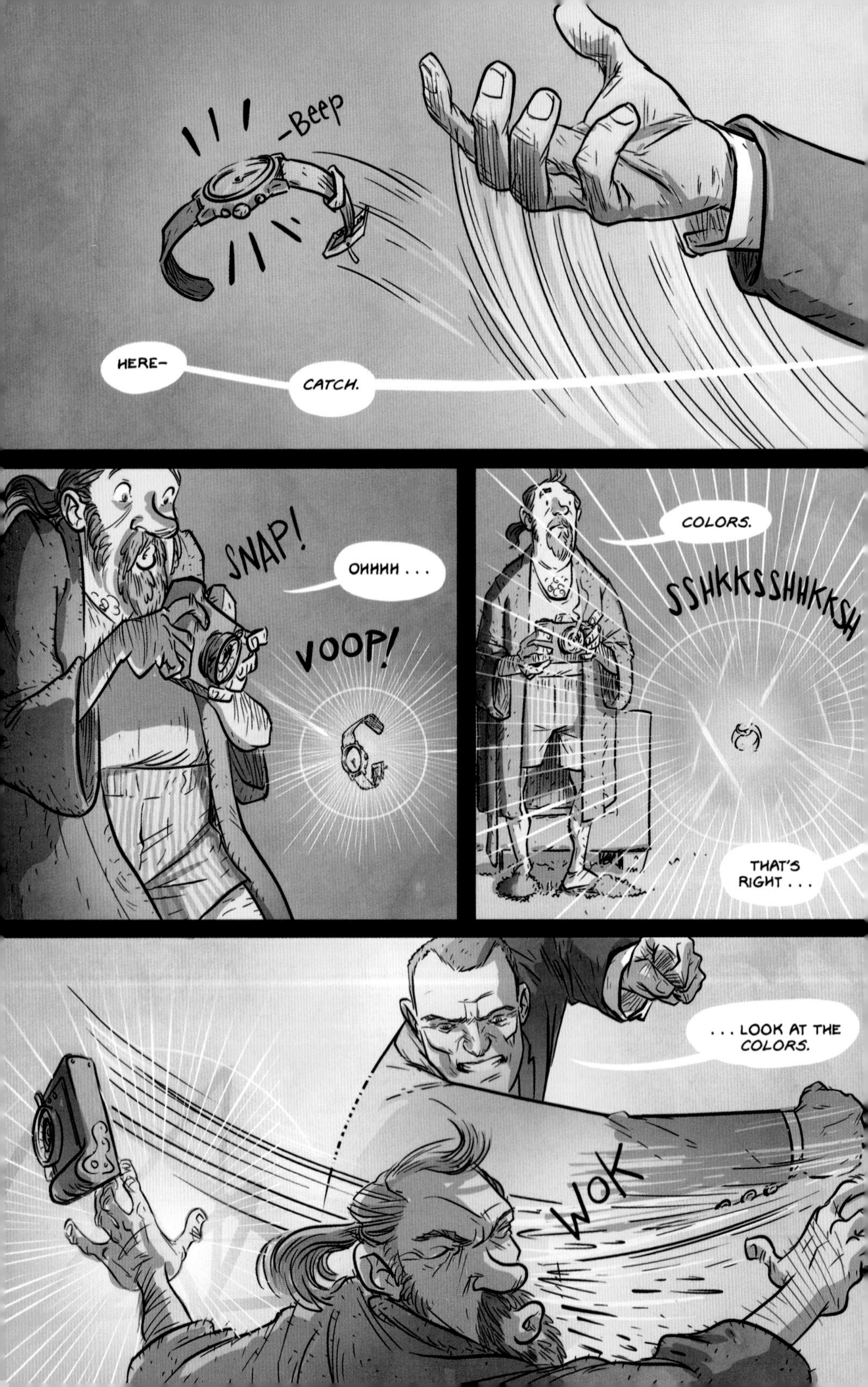
-Beep
HERE–
CATCH.
SNAP!
OHHHH . . .
VOOP!
COLORS.
SSHKKSSHHKKSH
THAT'S RIGHT . . .
. . . LOOK AT THE COLORS.
WOK

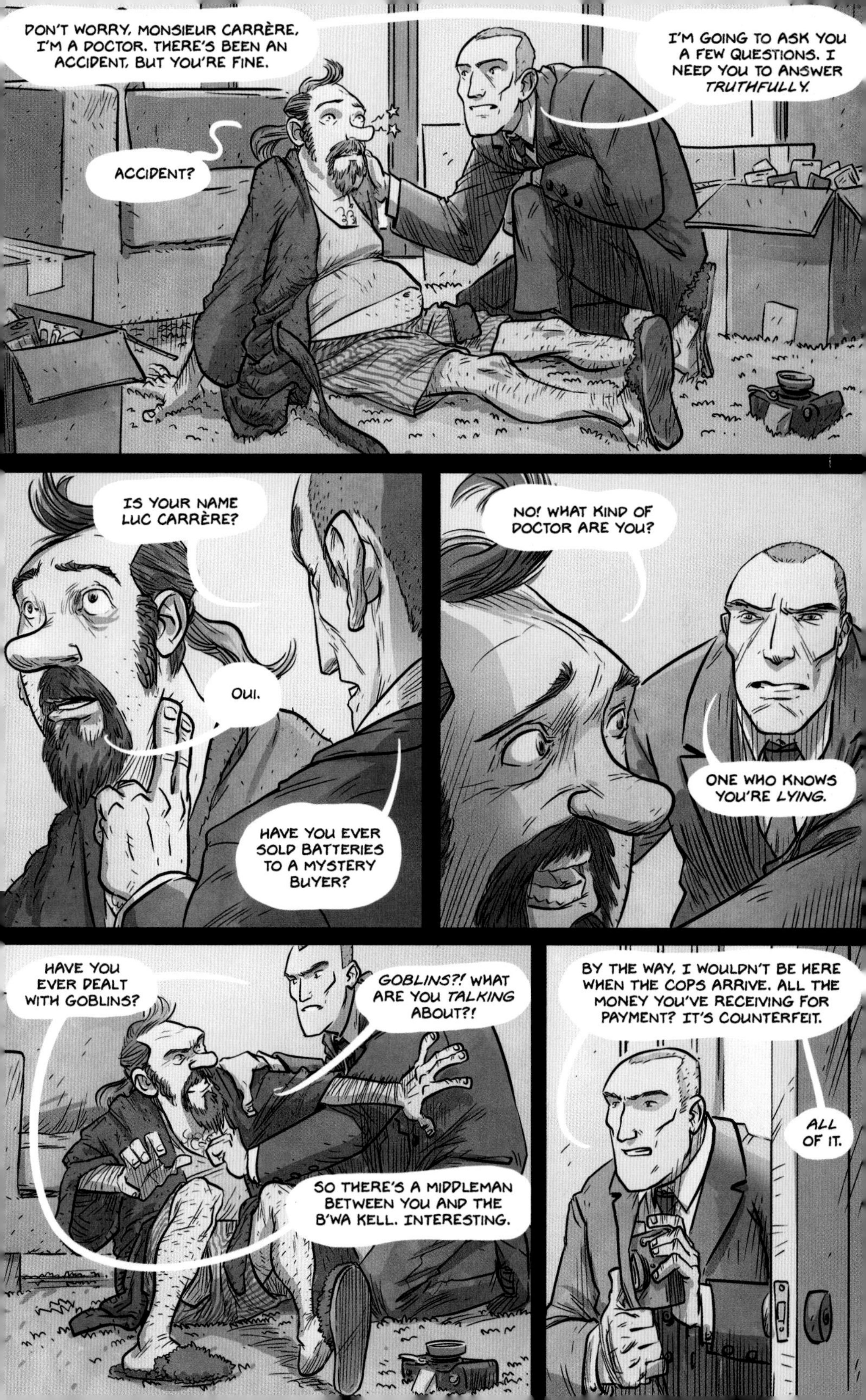
DON'T WORRY, MONSIEUR CARRÈRE, I'M A DOCTOR. THERE'S BEEN AN ACCIDENT, BUT YOU'RE FINE.
I'M GOING TO ASK YOU A FEW QUESTIONS. I NEED YOU TO ANSWER *TRUTHFULLY.*
ACCIDENT?
IS YOUR NAME LUC CARRÈRE?
OUI.
HAVE YOU EVER SOLD BATTERIES TO A MYSTERY BUYER?
NO! WHAT KIND OF DOCTOR ARE YOU?
ONE WHO KNOWS YOU'RE *LYING.*
HAVE YOU EVER DEALT WITH GOBLINS?
GOBLINS?! WHAT ARE YOU *TALKING* ABOUT?!
SO THERE'S A MIDDLEMAN BETWEEN YOU AND THE B'WA KELL. INTERESTING.
BY THE WAY, I WOULDN'T BE HERE WHEN THE COPS ARRIVE. ALL THE MONEY YOU'VE RECEIVING FOR PAYMENT? IT'S COUNTERFEIT.
ALL OF IT.

CHAPTER SEVEN

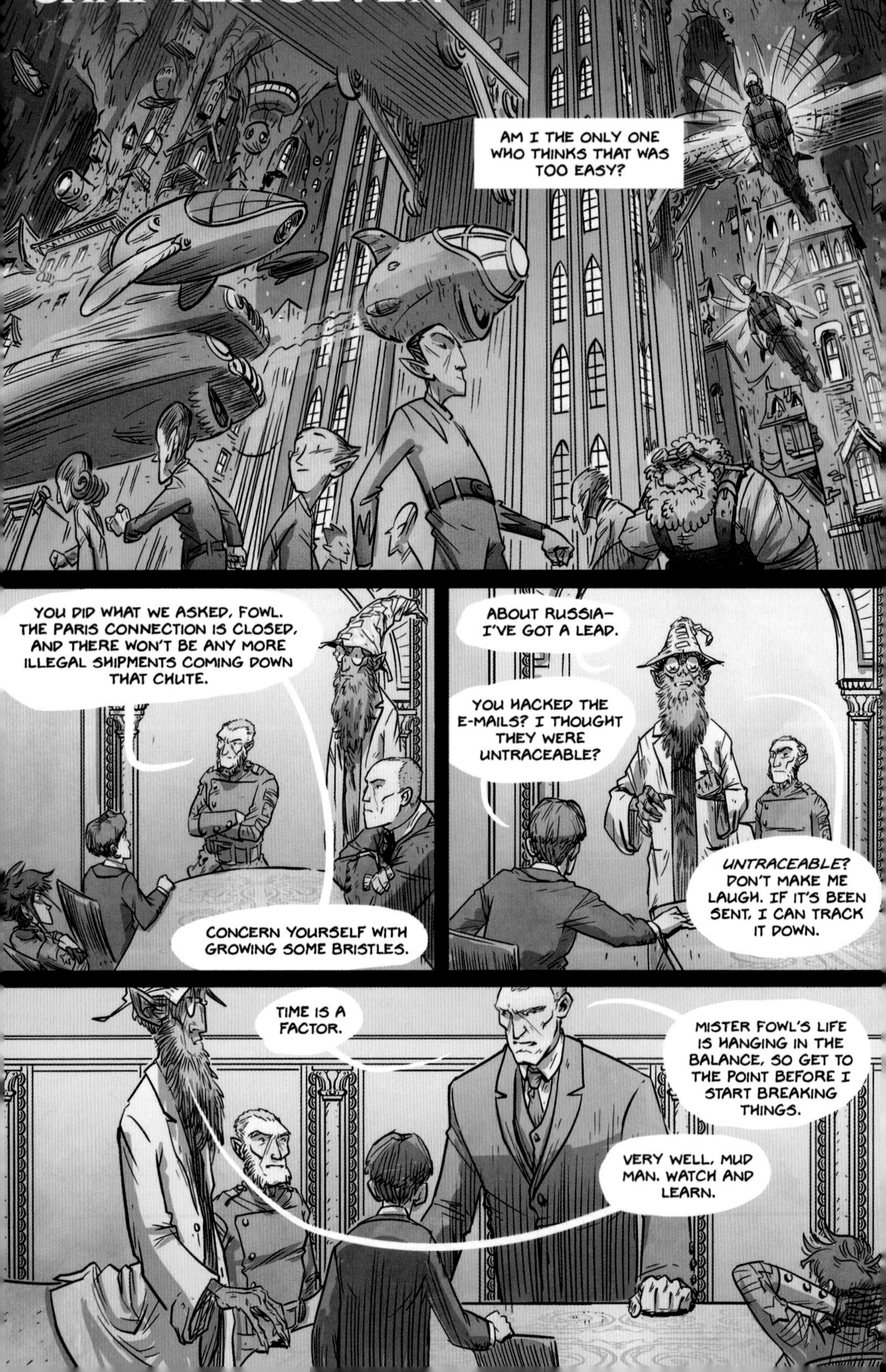

AM I THE ONLY ONE WHO THINKS THAT WAS TOO EASY?
YOU DID WHAT WE ASKED, FOWL. THE PARIS CONNECTION IS CLOSED, AND THERE WON'T BE ANY MORE ILLEGAL SHIPMENTS COMING DOWN THAT CHUTE.
CONCERN YOURSELF WITH GROWING SOME BRISTLES.
ABOUT RUSSIA– I'VE GOT A LEAD.
YOU HACKED THE E-MAILS? I THOUGHT THEY WERE UNTRACEABLE?
UNTRACEABLE? DON'T MAKE ME LAUGH. IF IT'S BEEN SENT, I CAN TRACK IT DOWN.
TIME IS A FACTOR.
MISTER FOWL'S LIFE IS HANGING IN THE BALANCE, SO GET TO THE POINT BEFORE I START BREAKING THINGS.
VERY WELL, MUD MAN. WATCH AND LEARN.

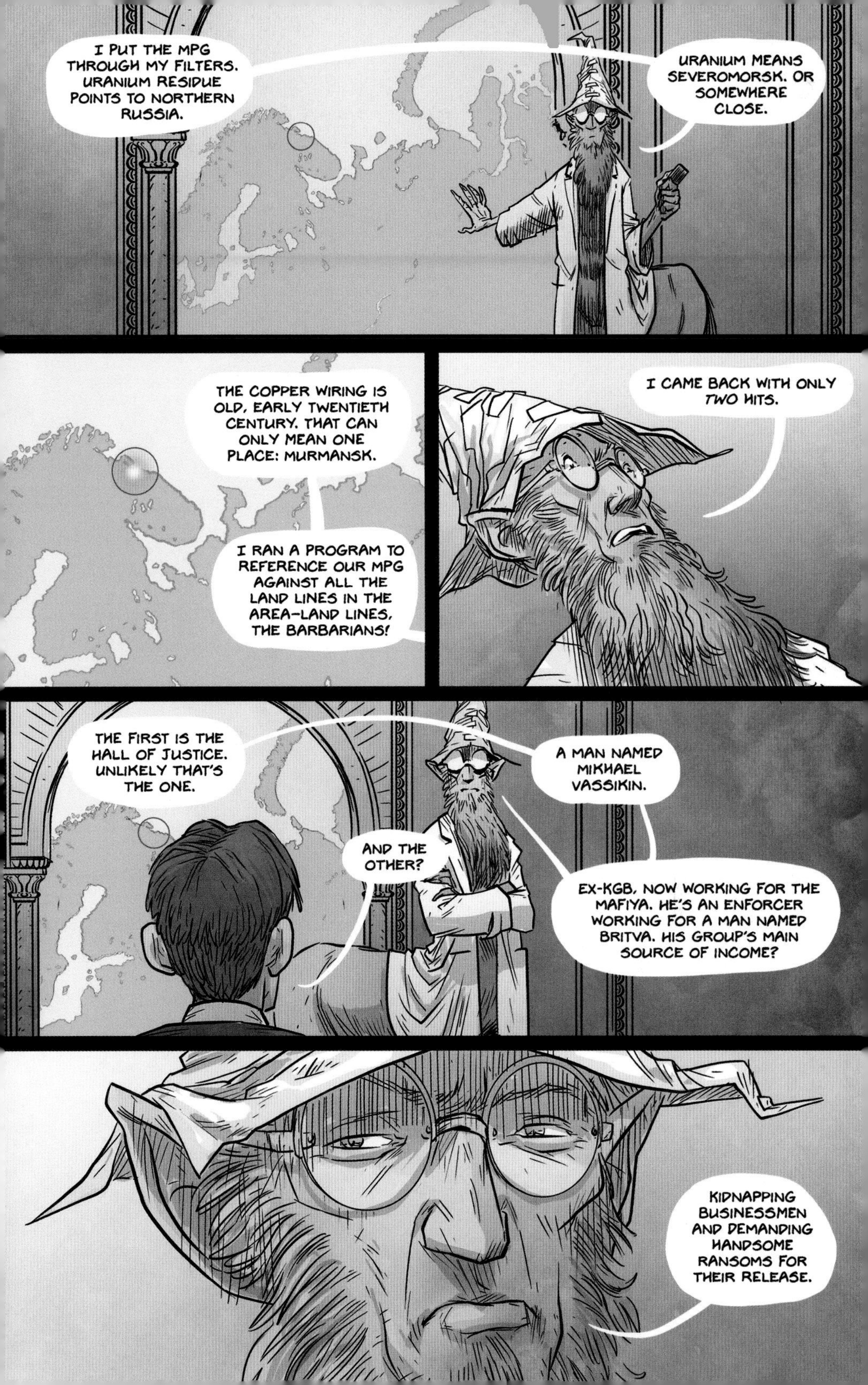
I PUT THE MPG THROUGH MY FILTERS. URANIUM RESIDUE POINTS TO NORTHERN RUSSIA.
URANIUM MEANS SEVEROMORSK. OR SOMEWHERE CLOSE.
THE COPPER WIRING IS OLD, EARLY TWENTIETH CENTURY. THAT CAN ONLY MEAN ONE PLACE: MURMANSK.
I RAN A PROGRAM TO REFERENCE OUR MPG AGAINST ALL THE LAND LINES IN THE AREA—LAND LINES, THE BARBARIANS!
I CAME BACK WITH ONLY *TWO* HITS.
THE FIRST IS THE HALL OF JUSTICE. UNLIKELY THAT'S THE ONE.
AND THE OTHER?
A MAN NAMED MIKHAEL VASSIKIN.
EX-KGB, NOW WORKING FOR THE MAFIYA. HE'S AN ENFORCER WORKING FOR A MAN NAMED BRITVA. HIS GROUP'S MAIN SOURCE OF INCOME?
KIDNAPPING BUSINESSMEN AND DEMANDING HANDSOME RANSOMS FOR THEIR RELEASE.

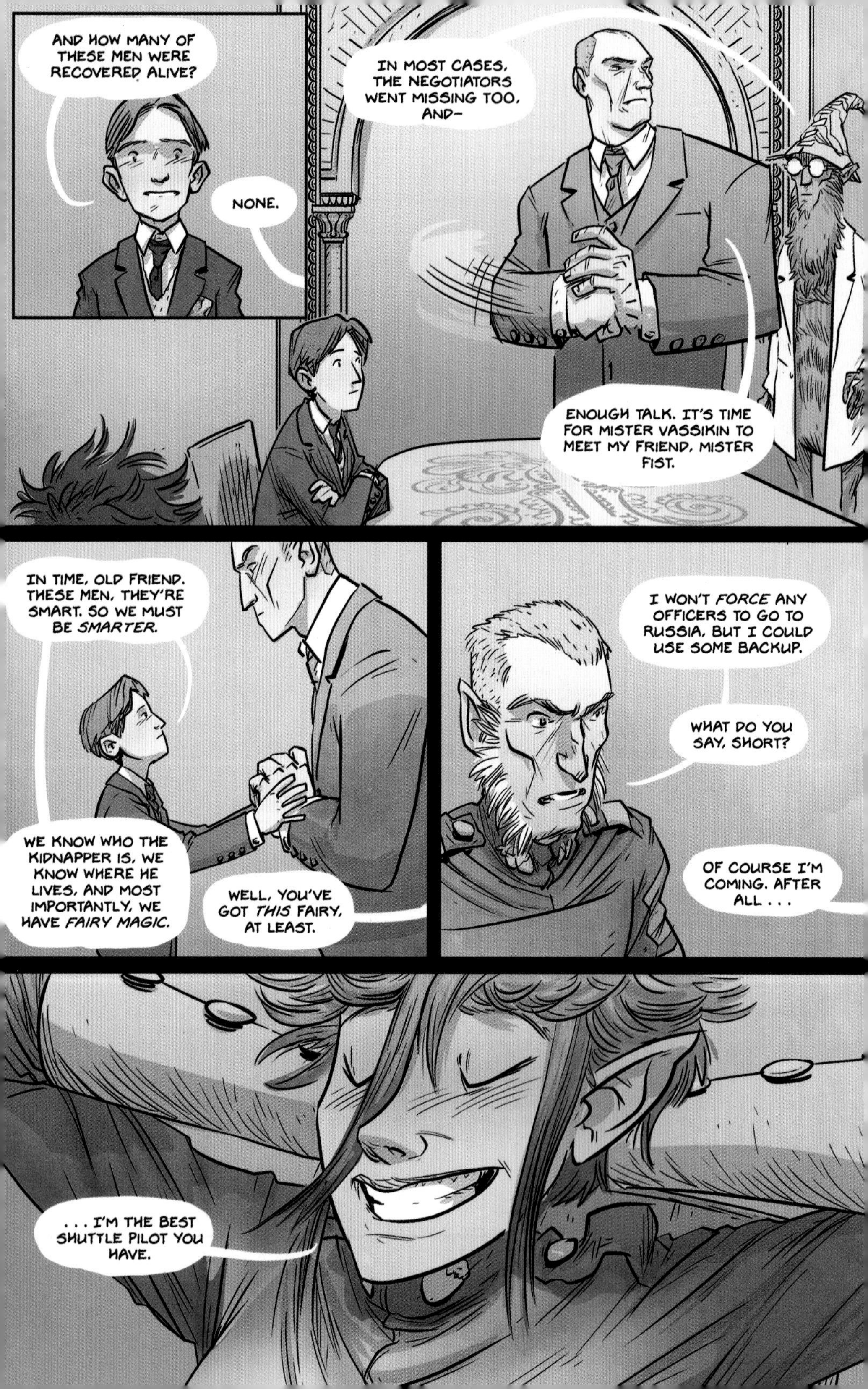
AND HOW MANY OF THESE MEN WERE RECOVERED ALIVE?
NONE.
IN MOST CASES, THE NEGOTIATORS WENT MISSING TOO, AND–
ENOUGH TALK. IT'S TIME FOR MISTER VASSIKIN TO MEET MY FRIEND, MISTER FIST.
IN TIME, OLD FRIEND. THESE MEN, THEY'RE SMART. SO WE MUST BE *SMARTER*.
WE KNOW WHO THE KIDNAPPER IS, WE KNOW WHERE HE LIVES, AND MOST IMPORTANTLY, WE HAVE *FAIRY MAGIC*.
WELL, YOU'VE GOT *THIS* FAIRY, AT LEAST.
I WON'T *FORCE* ANY OFFICERS TO GO TO RUSSIA, BUT I COULD USE SOME BACKUP.
WHAT DO YOU SAY, SHORT?
OF COURSE I'M COMING. AFTER ALL . . .
. . . I'M THE BEST SHUTTLE PILOT YOU HAVE.

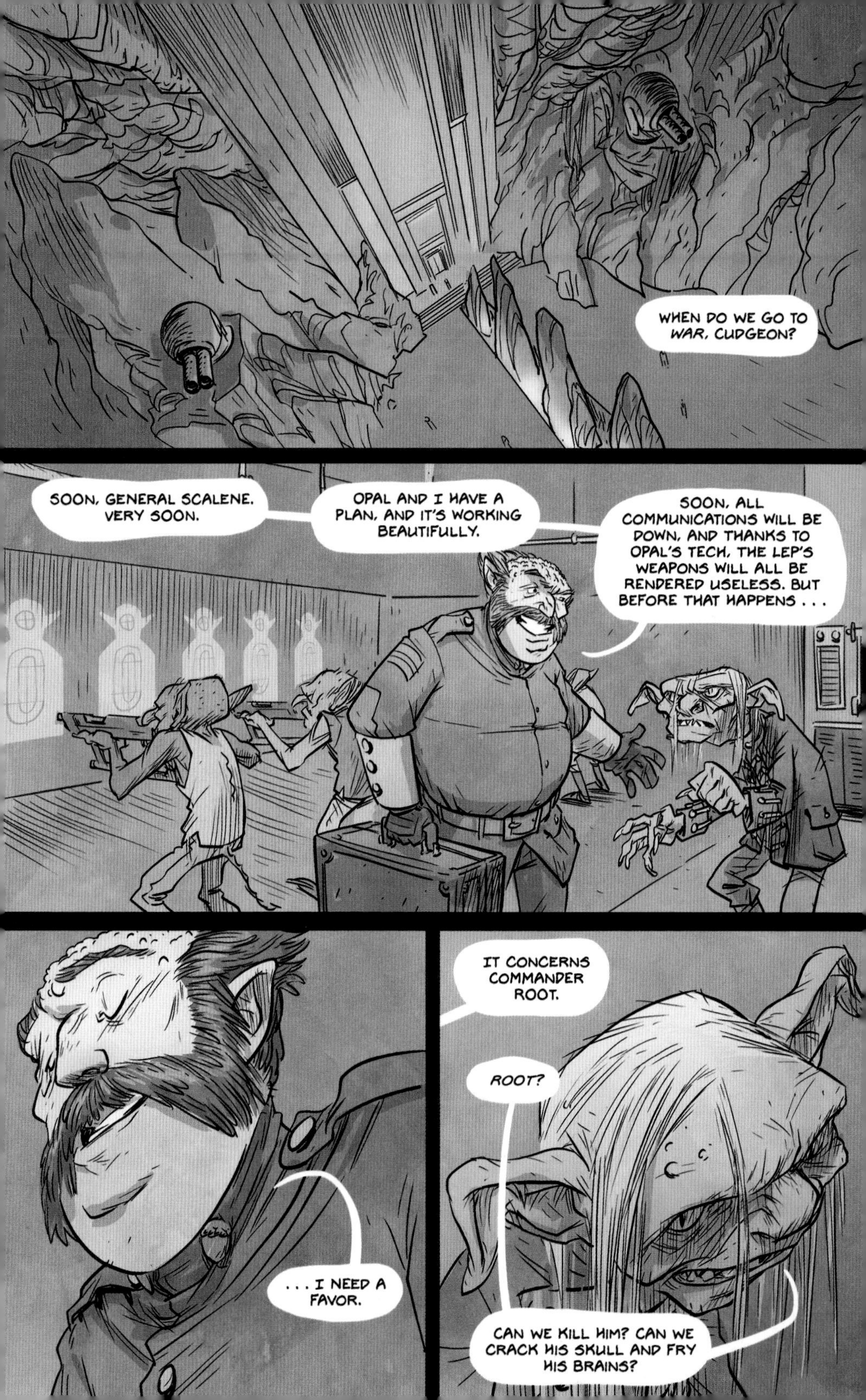
WHEN DO WE GO TO WAR, CUDGEON?
SOON, GENERAL SCALENE. VERY SOON.
OPAL AND I HAVE A PLAN, AND IT'S WORKING BEAUTIFULLY.
SOON, ALL COMMUNICATIONS WILL BE DOWN, AND THANKS TO OPAL'S TECH, THE LEP'S WEAPONS WILL ALL BE RENDERED USELESS. BUT BEFORE THAT HAPPENS . . .
. . . I NEED A FAVOR.
IT CONCERNS COMMANDER ROOT.
ROOT?
CAN WE KILL HIM? CAN WE CRACK HIS SKULL AND FRY HIS BRAINS?

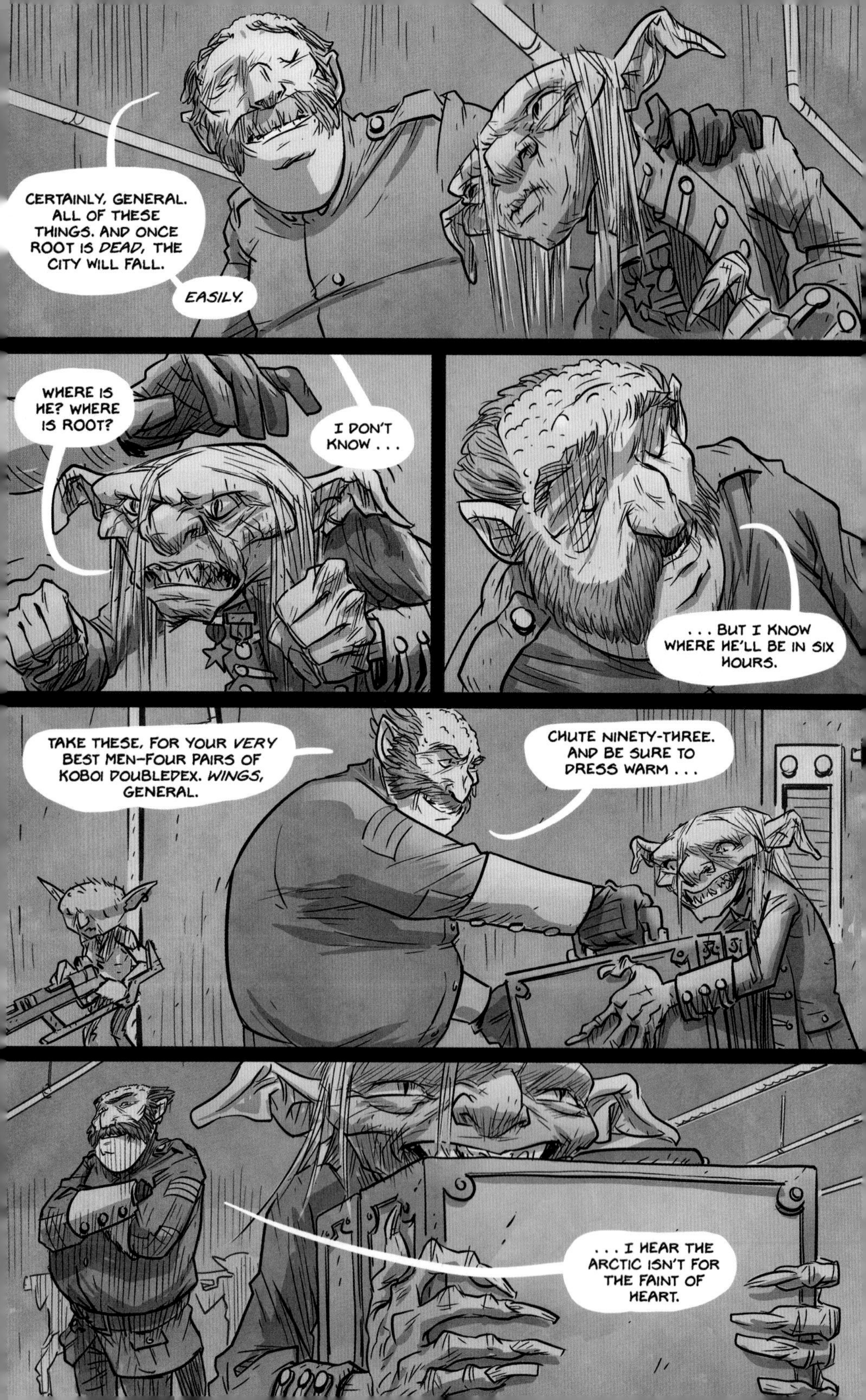
CERTAINLY, GENERAL. ALL OF THESE THINGS. AND ONCE ROOT IS *DEAD*, THE CITY WILL FALL.
EASILY.
WHERE IS HE? WHERE IS ROOT?
I DON'T KNOW . . .
. . . BUT I KNOW WHERE HE'LL BE IN SIX HOURS.
TAKE THESE, FOR YOUR *VERY* BEST MEN—FOUR PAIRS OF KOBOI DOUBLEDEX. *WINGS*, GENERAL.
CHUTE NINETY-THREE. AND BE SURE TO DRESS WARM . . .
. . . I HEAR THE ARCTIC ISN'T FOR THE FAINT OF HEART.

CHAPTER EIGHT

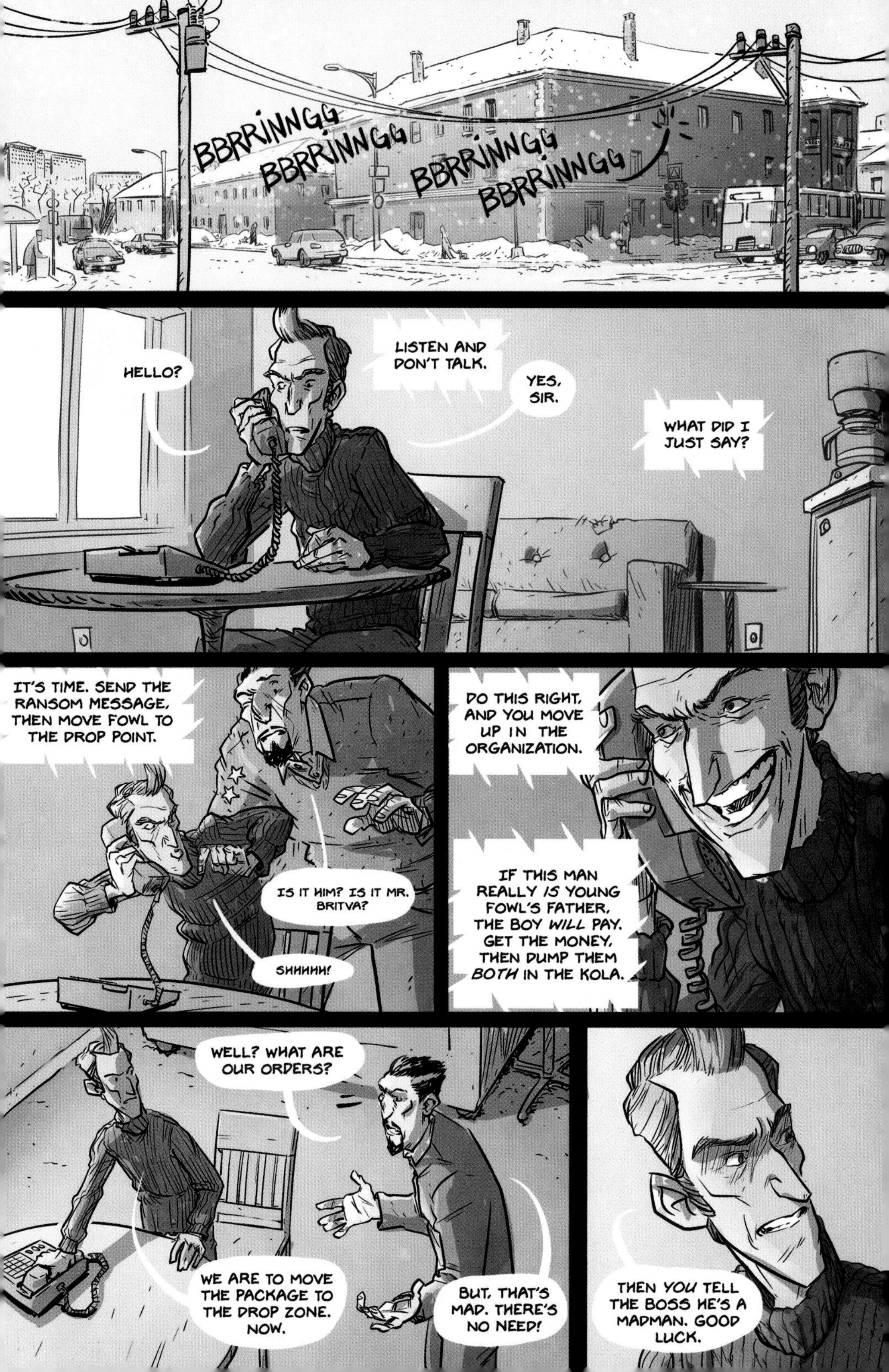

BBRRINNGG
BBRRINNGG
BBRRINNGG
BBRRINNGG
HELLO?
LISTEN AND DON'T TALK.
YES, SIR.
WHAT DID I JUST SAY?
IT'S TIME. SEND THE RANSOM MESSAGE, THEN MOVE FOWL TO THE DROP POINT.
IS IT HIM? IS IT MR. BRITVA?
SHHHHH!
DO THIS RIGHT, AND YOU MOVE UP IN THE ORGANIZATION.
IF THIS MAN REALLY *IS* YOUNG FOWL'S FATHER, THE BOY *WILL* PAY. GET THE MONEY, THEN DUMP THEM *BOTH* IN THE KOLA.
WELL? WHAT ARE OUR ORDERS?
WE ARE TO MOVE THE PACKAGE TO THE DROP ZONE. NOW.
BUT, THAT'S MAD. THERE'S NO NEED!
THEN *YOU* TELL THE BOSS HE'S A MADMAN. GOOD LUCK.

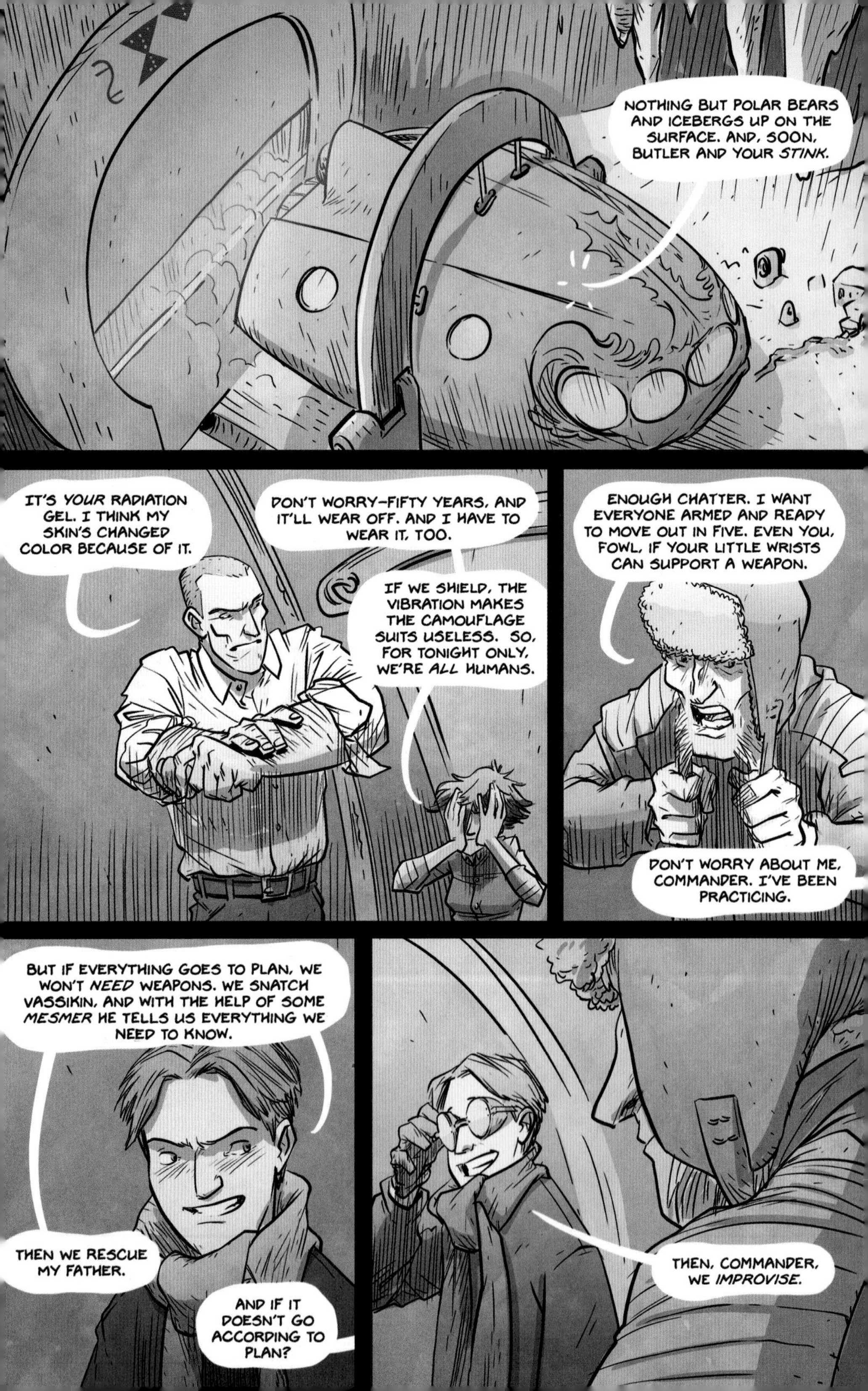
NOTHING BUT POLAR BEARS AND ICEBERGS UP ON THE SURFACE. AND, SOON, BUTLER AND YOUR *STINK*.
IT'S *YOUR* RADIATION GEL. I THINK MY SKIN'S CHANGED COLOR BECAUSE OF IT.
DON'T WORRY—FIFTY YEARS, AND IT'LL WEAR OFF. AND I HAVE TO WEAR IT, TOO.
IF WE SHIELD, THE VIBRATION MAKES THE CAMOUFLAGE SUITS USELESS. SO, FOR TONIGHT ONLY, WE'RE *ALL* HUMANS.
ENOUGH CHATTER. I WANT EVERYONE ARMED AND READY TO MOVE OUT IN FIVE. EVEN YOU, FOWL, IF YOUR LITTLE WRISTS CAN SUPPORT A WEAPON.
DON'T WORRY ABOUT ME, COMMANDER. I'VE BEEN PRACTICING.
BUT IF EVERYTHING GOES TO PLAN, WE WON'T *NEED* WEAPONS. WE SNATCH VASSIKIN, AND WITH THE HELP OF SOME *MESMER* HE TELLS US EVERYTHING WE NEED TO KNOW.
THEN WE RESCUE MY FATHER.
AND IF IT DOESN'T GO ACCORDING TO PLAN?
THEN, COMMANDER, WE *IMPROVISE*.

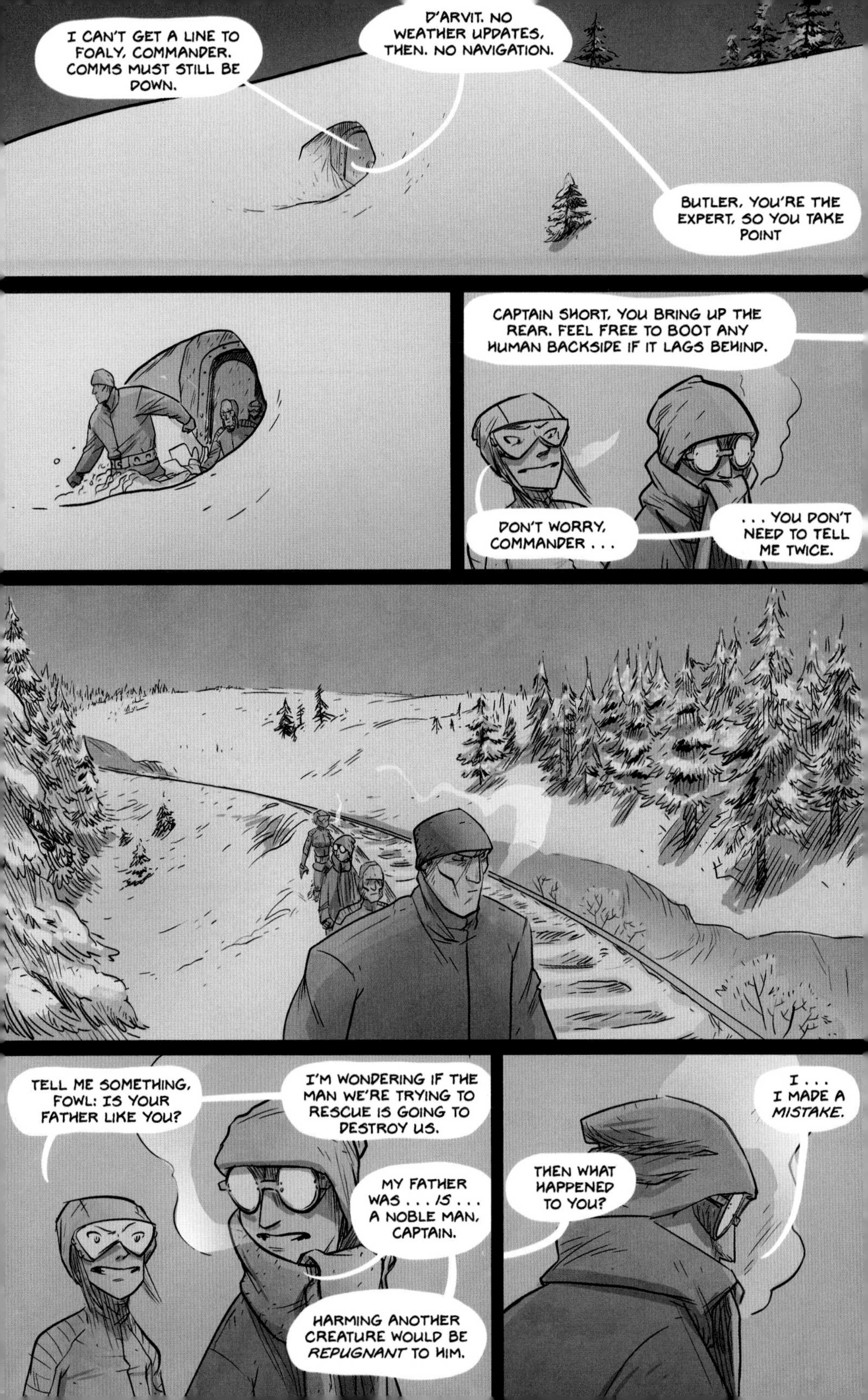
I CAN'T GET A LINE TO FOALY, COMMANDER. COMMS MUST STILL BE DOWN.
D'ARVIT. NO WEATHER UPDATES, THEN. NO NAVIGATION.
BUTLER, YOU'RE THE EXPERT, SO YOU TAKE POINT
CAPTAIN SHORT, YOU BRING UP THE REAR. FEEL FREE TO BOOT ANY HUMAN BACKSIDE IF IT LAGS BEHIND.
DON'T WORRY, COMMANDER . . .
. . . YOU DON'T NEED TO TELL ME TWICE.
TELL ME SOMETHING, FOWL: IS YOUR FATHER LIKE YOU?
I'M WONDERING IF THE MAN WE'RE TRYING TO RESCUE IS GOING TO DESTROY US.
MY FATHER WAS . . . *IS* . . . A NOBLE MAN, CAPTAIN.
HARMING ANOTHER CREATURE WOULD BE *REPUGNANT* TO HIM.
THEN WHAT HAPPENED TO YOU?
I . . . I MADE A *MISTAKE.*

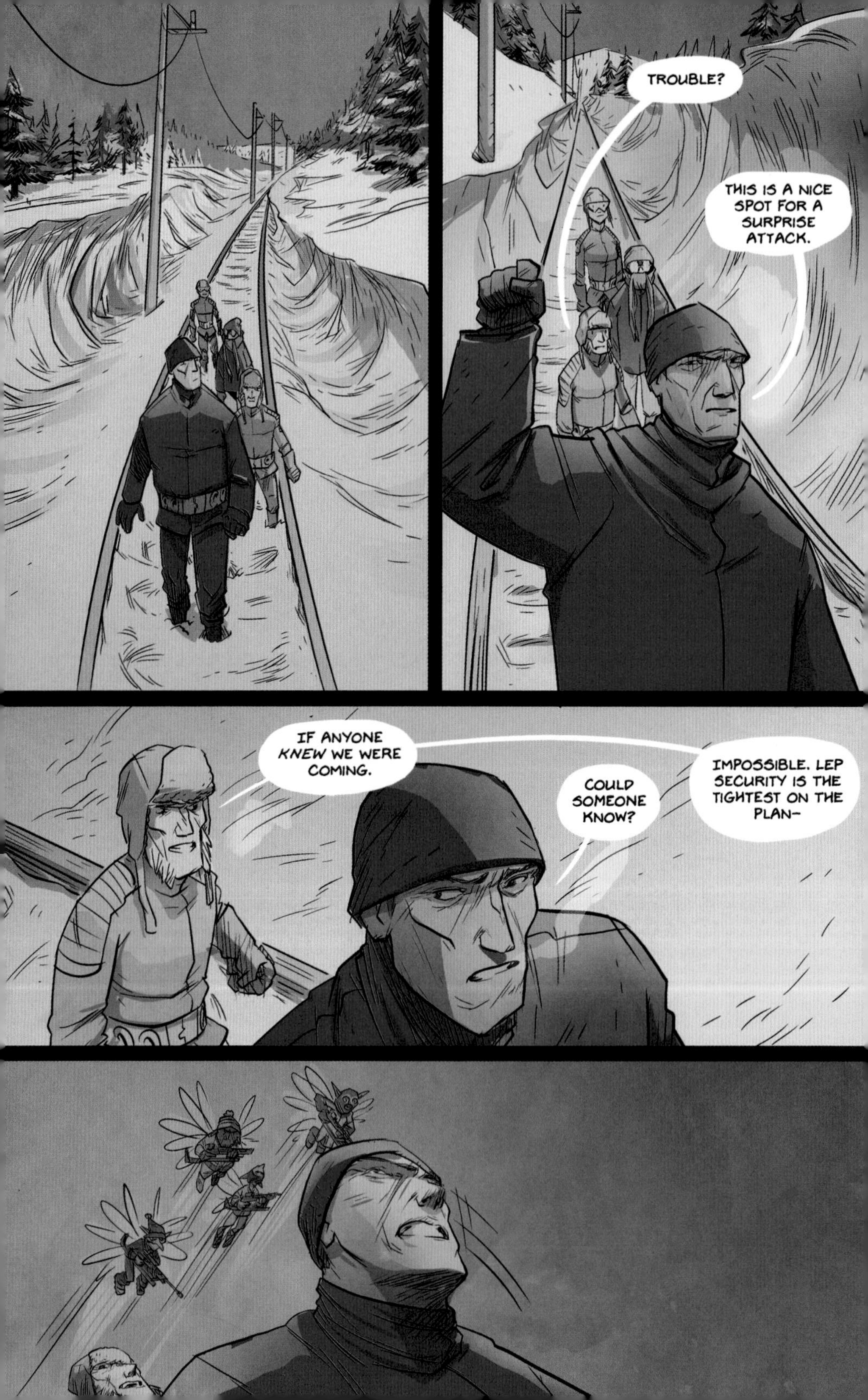
TROUBLE?
THIS IS A NICE SPOT FOR A SURPRISE ATTACK.
IF ANYONE KNEW WE WERE COMING.
COULD SOMEONE KNOW?
IMPOSSIBLE. LEP SECURITY IS THE TIGHTEST ON THE PLAN-

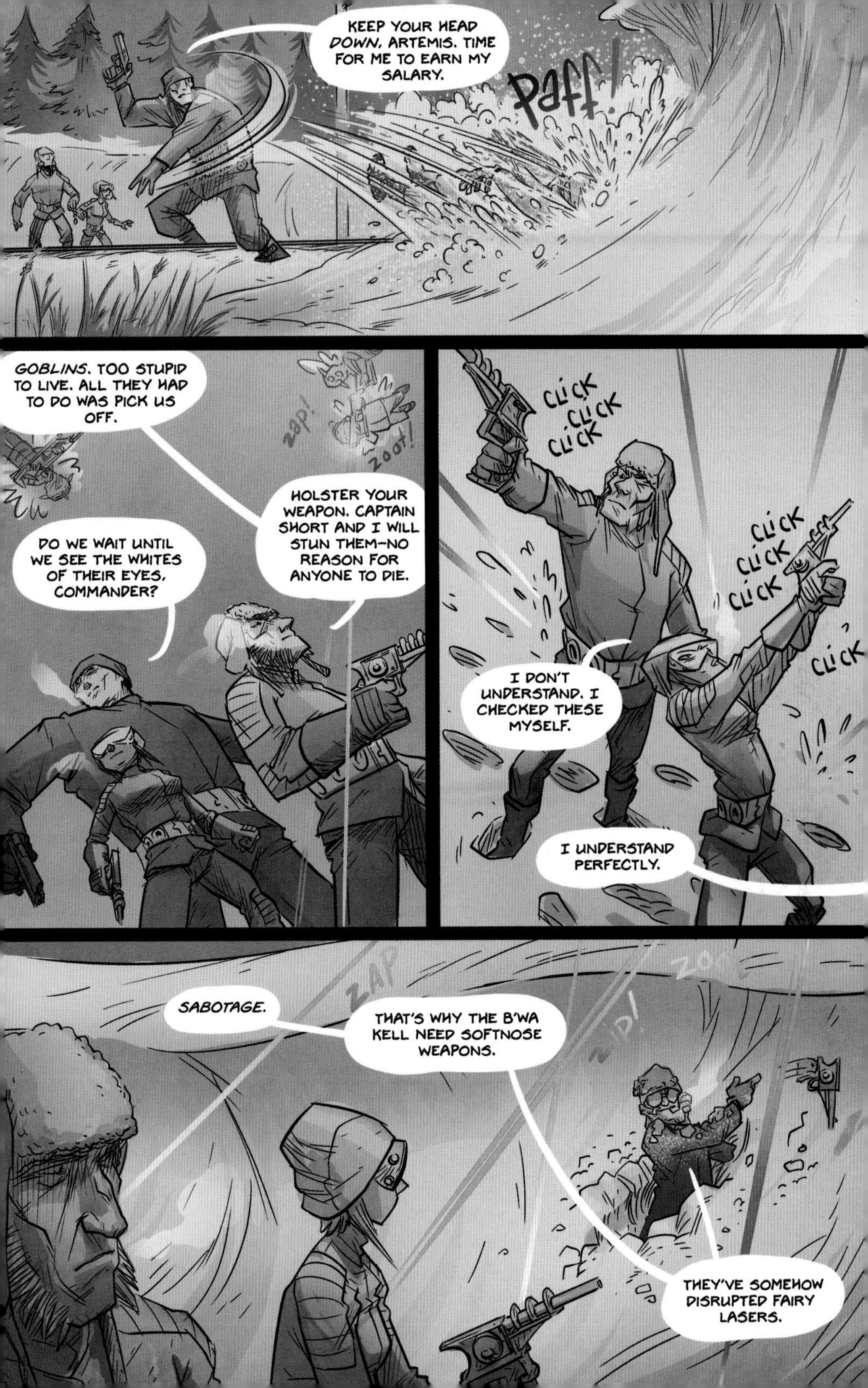
KEEP YOUR HEAD DOWN, ARTEMIS. TIME FOR ME TO EARN MY SALARY.
PAFF!
GOBLINS. TOO STUPID TO LIVE. ALL THEY HAD TO DO WAS PICK US OFF.
ZAP!
ZOOT!
DO WE WAIT UNTIL WE SEE THE WHITES OF THEIR EYES, COMMANDER?
HOLSTER YOUR WEAPON. CAPTAIN SHORT AND I WILL STUN THEM—NO REASON FOR ANYONE TO DIE.
CLICK CLICK CLICK
CLICK CLICK CLICK
CLICK
I DON'T UNDERSTAND. I CHECKED THESE MYSELF.
I UNDERSTAND PERFECTLY.
ZAP
SABOTAGE.
THAT'S WHY THE B'WA KELL NEED SOFTNOSE WEAPONS.
THEY'VE SOMEHOW DISRUPTED FAIRY LASERS.

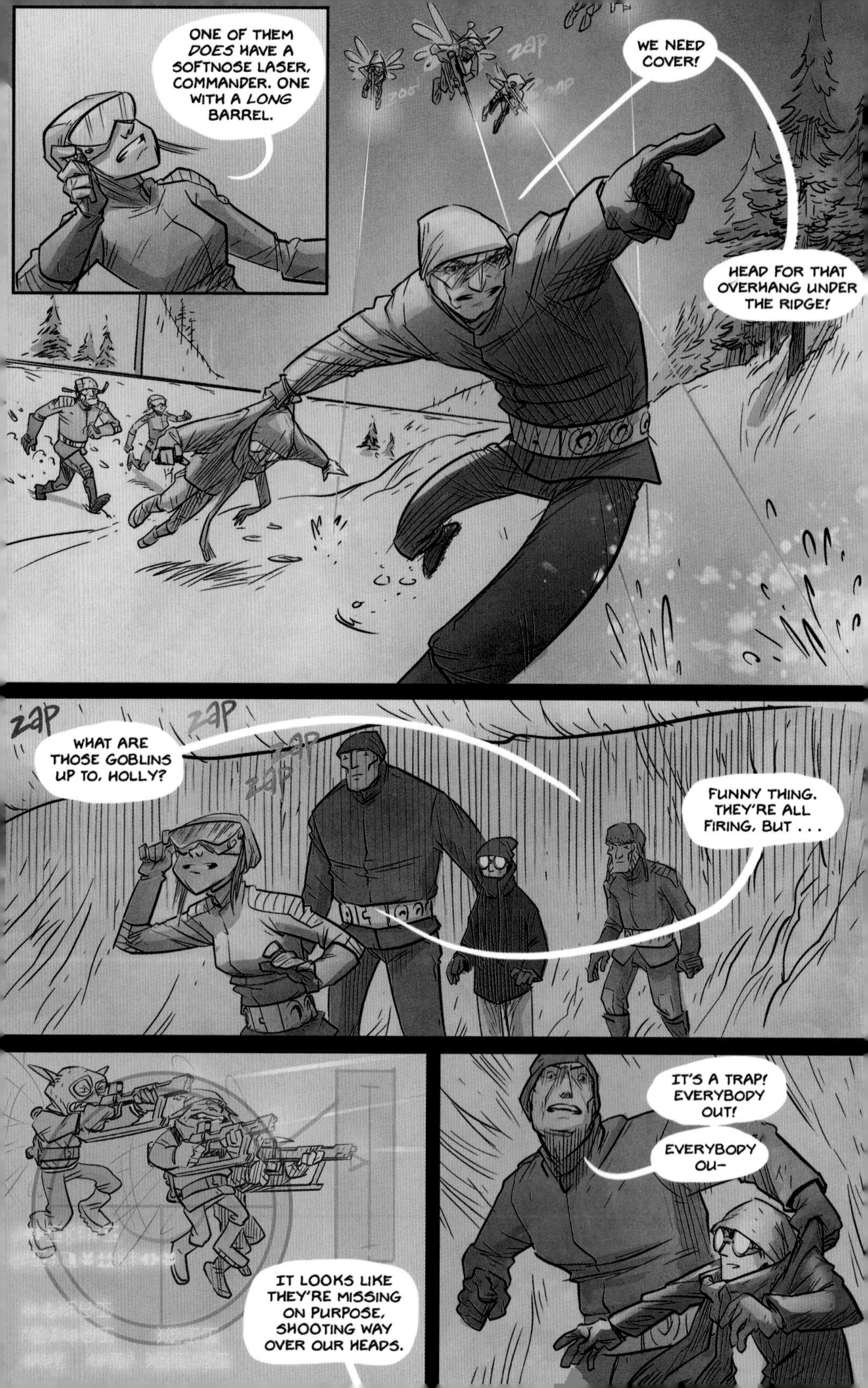
ONE OF THEM DOES HAVE A SOFTNOSE LASER, COMMANDER. ONE WITH A LONG BARREL.
zap
zap
WE NEED COVER!
HEAD FOR THAT OVERHANG UNDER THE RIDGE!
zap
zap
WHAT ARE THOSE GOBLINS UP TO, HOLLY?
zap
zap
FUNNY THING. THEY'RE ALL FIRING, BUT . . .
IT LOOKS LIKE THEY'RE MISSING ON PURPOSE, SHOOTING WAY OVER OUR HEADS.
IT'S A TRAP! EVERYBODY OUT!
EVERYBODY OU–

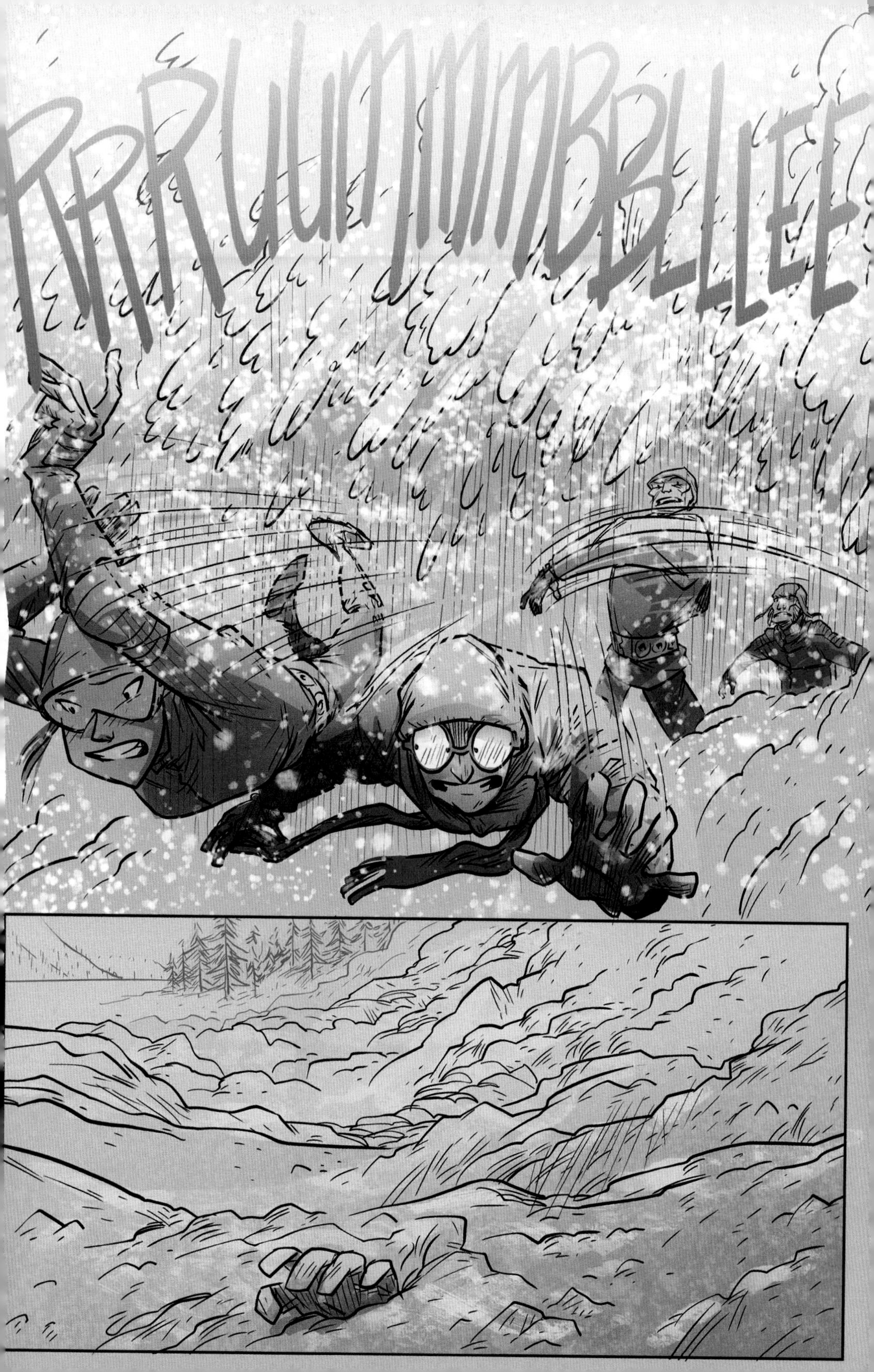
RRRUUMMMMBBLLEE

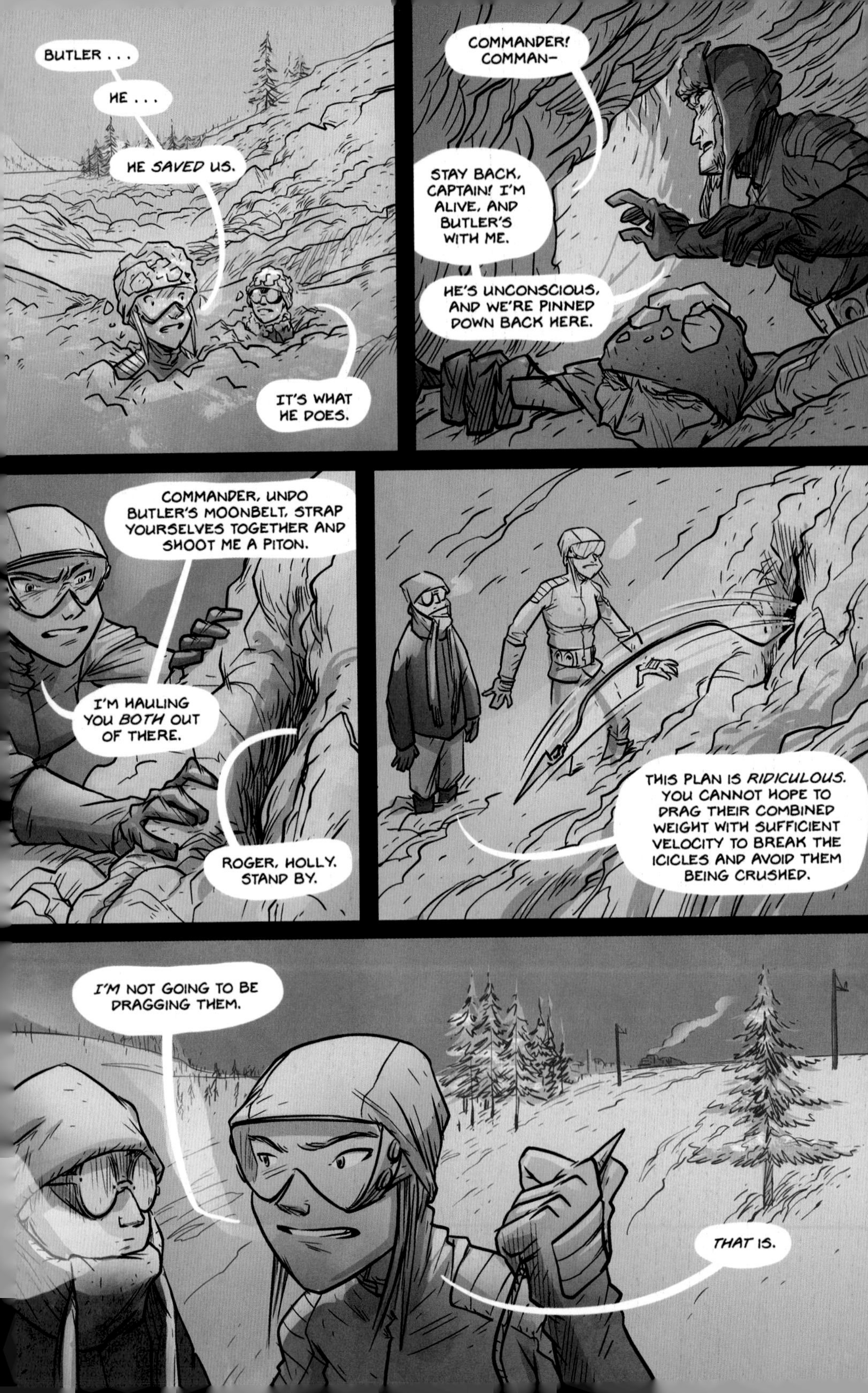
BUTLER . . .
HE . . .
HE *SAVED* US.
IT'S WHAT HE DOES.
COMMANDER! COMMAN-
STAY BACK, CAPTAIN! I'M ALIVE, AND BUTLER'S WITH ME.
HE'S UNCONSCIOUS, AND WE'RE PINNED DOWN BACK HERE.
COMMANDER, UNDO BUTLER'S MOONBELT, STRAP YOURSELVES TOGETHER AND SHOOT ME A PITON.
I'M HAULING YOU *BOTH* OUT OF THERE.
ROGER, HOLLY. STAND BY.
THIS PLAN IS *RIDICULOUS.* YOU CANNOT HOPE TO DRAG THEIR COMBINED WEIGHT WITH SUFFICIENT VELOCITY TO BREAK THE ICICLES AND AVOID THEM BEING CRUSHED.
I'M NOT GOING TO BE DRAGGING THEM.
THAT IS.

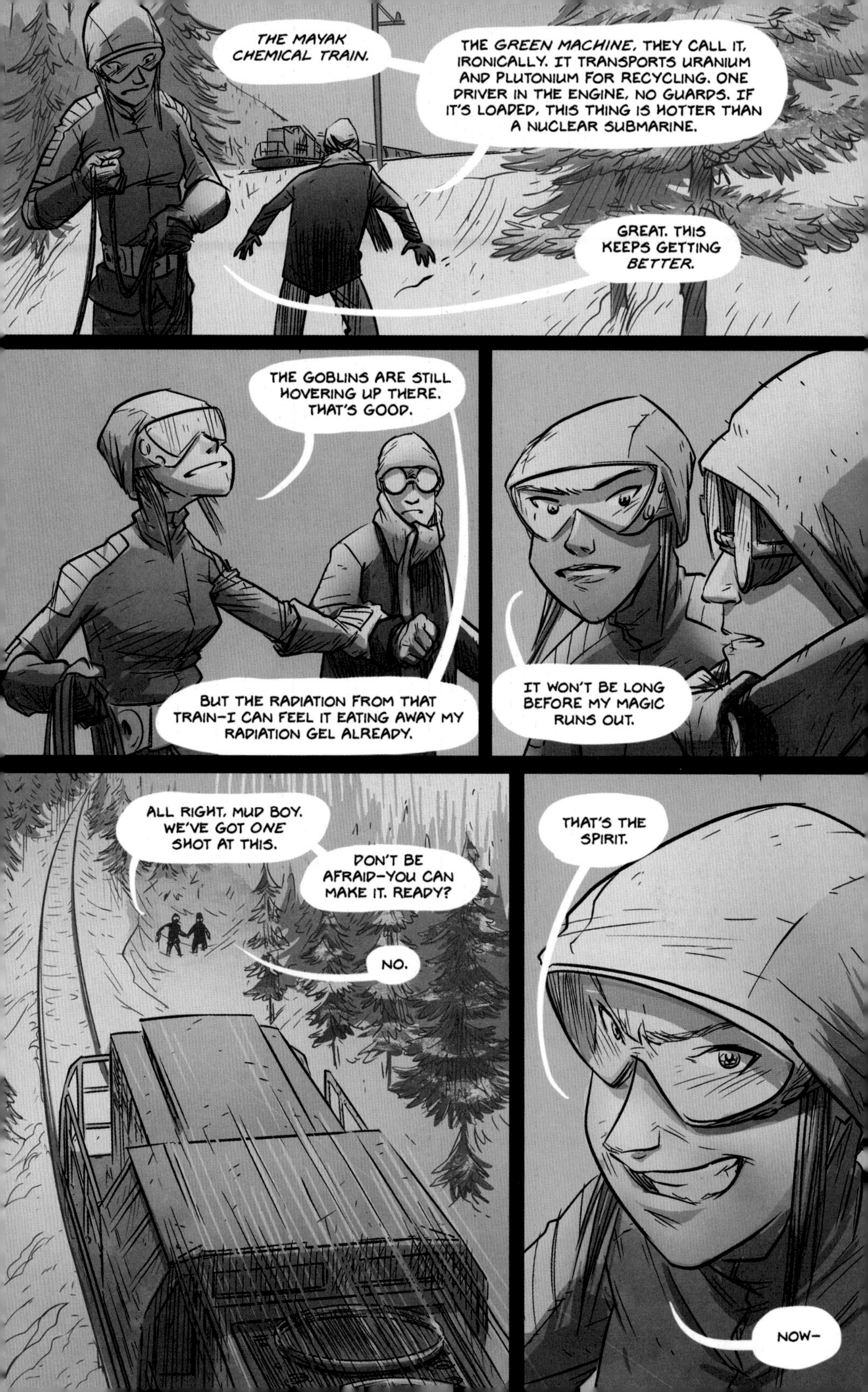
THE MAYAK CHEMICAL TRAIN.
THE GREEN MACHINE, THEY CALL IT, IRONICALLY. IT TRANSPORTS URANIUM AND PLUTONIUM FOR RECYCLING. ONE DRIVER IN THE ENGINE, NO GUARDS. IF IT'S LOADED, THIS THING IS HOTTER THAN A NUCLEAR SUBMARINE.
GREAT. THIS KEEPS GETTING BETTER.
THE GOBLINS ARE STILL HOVERING UP THERE. THAT'S GOOD.
BUT THE RADIATION FROM THAT TRAIN—I CAN FEEL IT EATING AWAY MY RADIATION GEL ALREADY.
IT WON'T BE LONG BEFORE MY MAGIC RUNS OUT.
ALL RIGHT, MUD BOY. WE'VE GOT ONE SHOT AT THIS.
DON'T BE AFRAID—YOU CAN MAKE IT. READY?
NO.
THAT'S THE SPIRIT.
NOW–

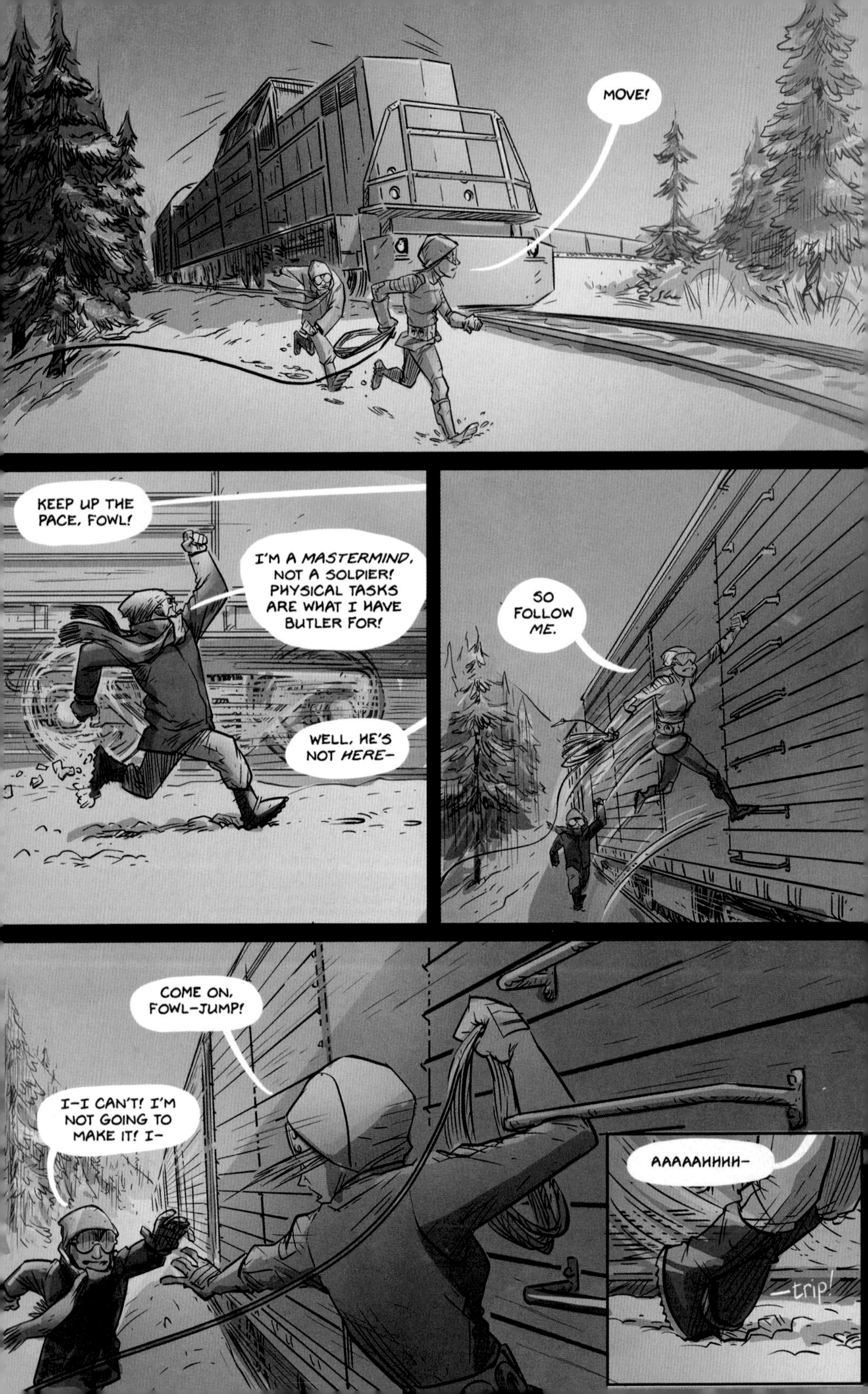
MOVE!
KEEP UP THE PACE, FOWL!
I'M A *MASTERMIND*, NOT A SOLDIER! PHYSICAL TASKS ARE WHAT I HAVE BUTLER FOR!
WELL, HE'S NOT *HERE*–
SO FOLLOW *ME*.
COME ON, FOWL–JUMP!
I–I CAN'T! I'M NOT GOING TO MAKE IT! I–
AAAAAHHHH–
–trip!

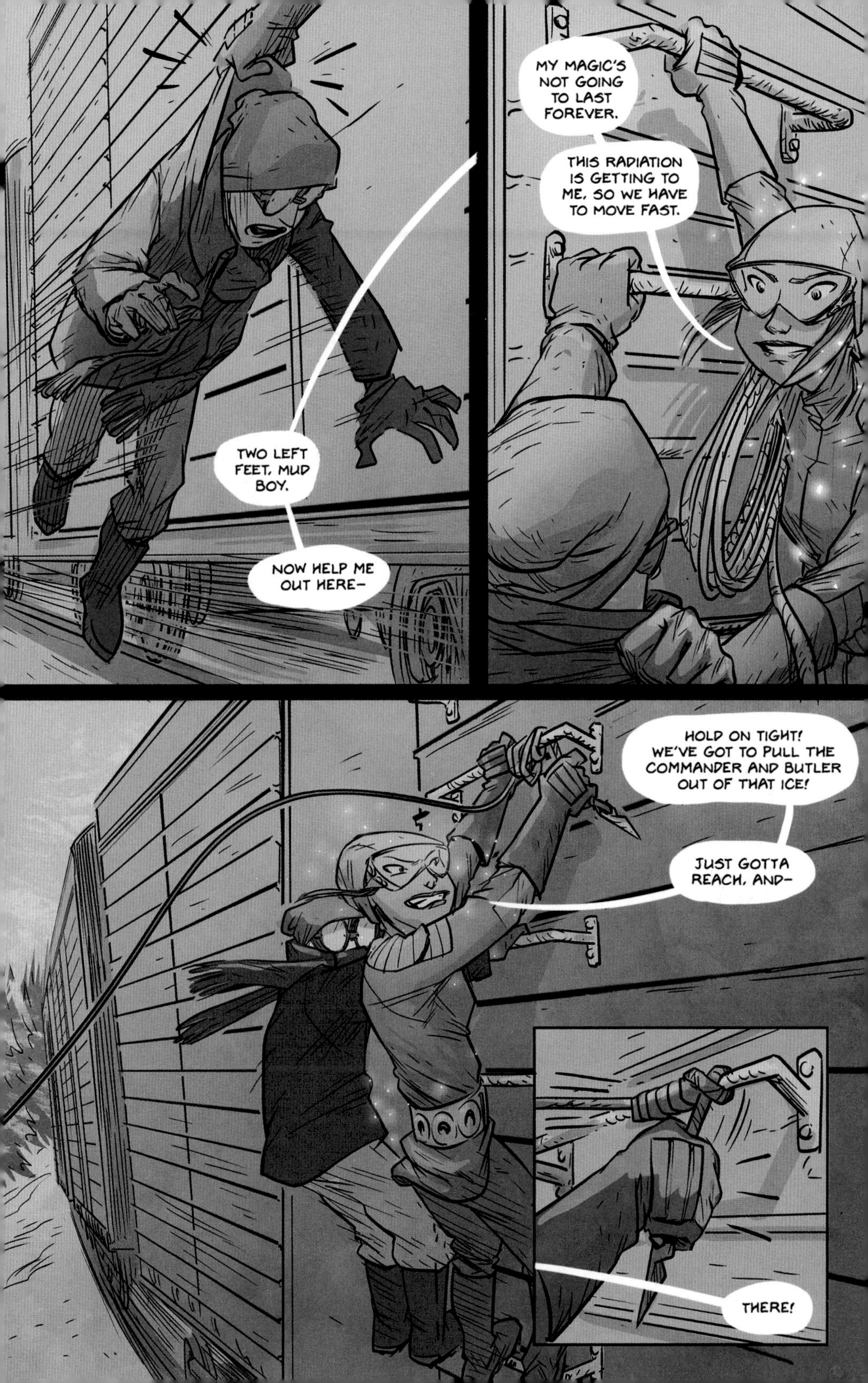
TWO LEFT FEET, MUD BOY.
NOW HELP ME OUT HERE-
MY MAGIC'S NOT GOING TO LAST FOREVER.
THIS RADIATION IS GETTING TO ME, SO WE HAVE TO MOVE FAST.
HOLD ON TIGHT! WE'VE GOT TO PULL THE COMMANDER AND BUTLER OUT OF THAT ICE!
JUST GOTTA REACH, AND-
THERE!

KKKSSSSSSHHHHH

ALL RIGHT, FOWL, YOU'RE UP. IN THE POCKET OF MY COAT, THERE'S A SMALL VIAL. TAKE IT.

AND DO WHAT WITH IT?

UP AND OVER YOU GO!

WHAT?!

YOU *HAVE* TO GET THAT DOOR OPEN SO I CAN REEL IN BUTLER AND THE COMMANDER. IF THIS TRAIN SLOWS DOWN, IF IT CURVES—THEY'RE *DONE FOR.*

THE VIAL'S ACID, FOWL. FOR THE DOOR'S LOCK—ON THE *INSIDE* OF THE CAR.

THIS IS OUR ONLY HOPE, MUD BOY. YOU CAN *DO THIS.*

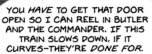

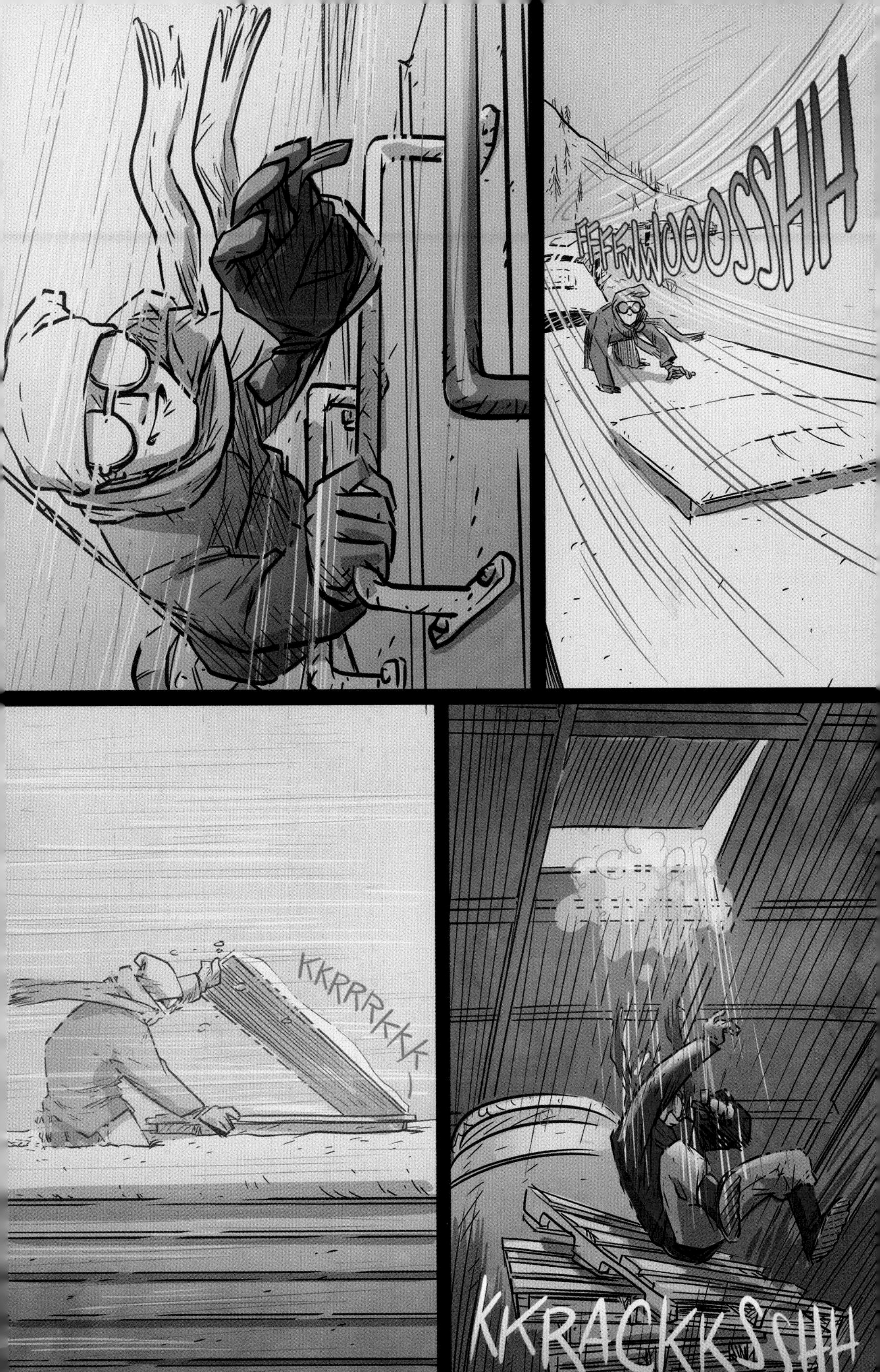
FFFFWWOOOSHH
KKRRRRKKK
KKRACKKSSHH

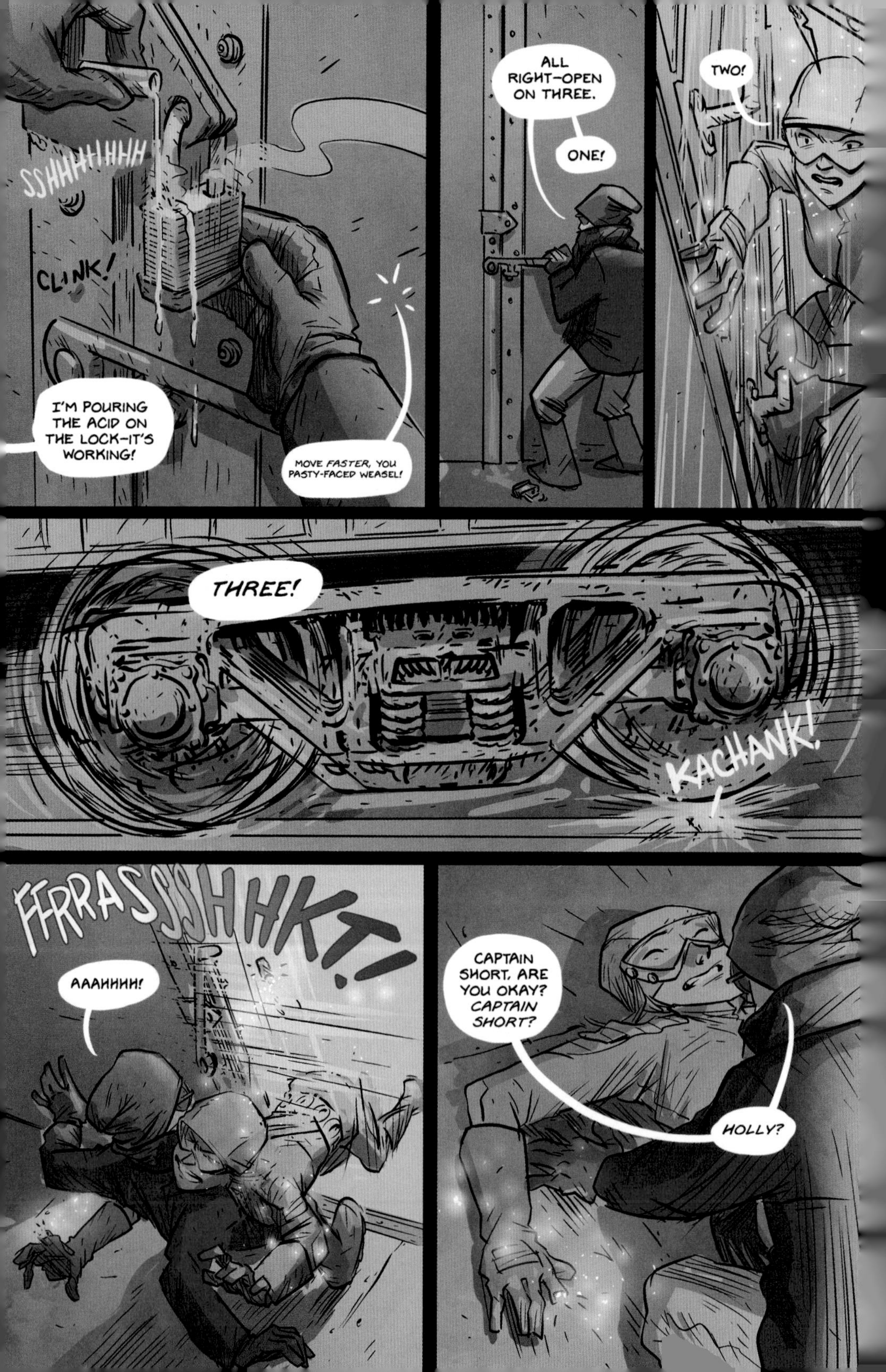
SSHHHHHHHH
CLINK!
I'M POURING THE ACID ON THE LOCK—IT'S WORKING!
MOVE FASTER, YOU PASTY-FACED WEASEL!
ALL RIGHT—OPEN ON THREE.
ONE!
TWO!
THREE!
KACHANK!
FFRRASSSHHKT!
AAAHHHH!
CAPTAIN SHORT, ARE YOU OKAY? CAPTAIN SHORT?
HOLLY?

CHAPTER NINE

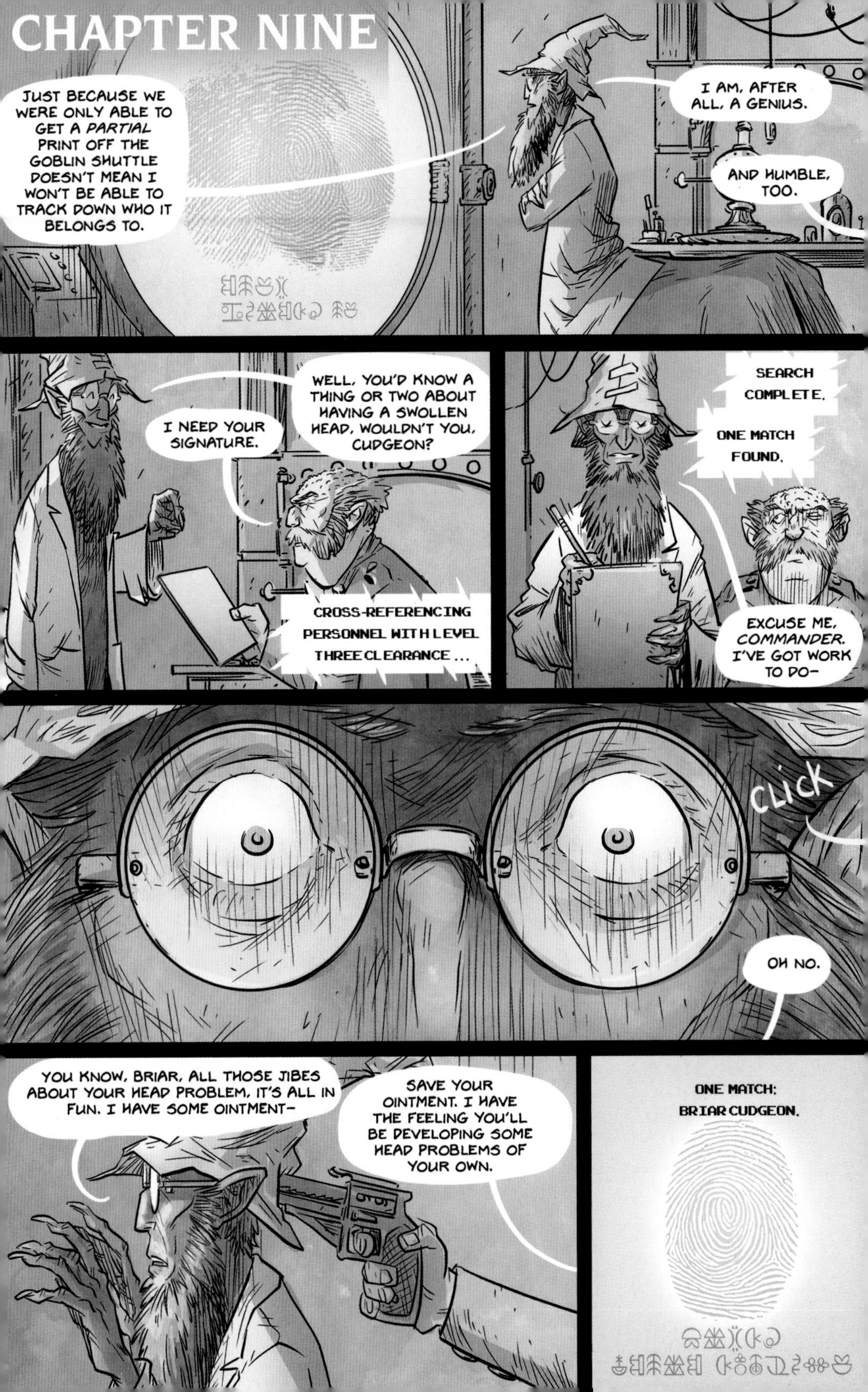
JUST BECAUSE WE WERE ONLY ABLE TO GET A *PARTIAL* PRINT OFF THE GOBLIN SHUTTLE DOESN'T MEAN I WON'T BE ABLE TO TRACK DOWN WHO IT BELONGS TO.
I AM, AFTER ALL, A GENIUS.
AND HUMBLE, TOO.
WELL, YOU'D KNOW A THING OR TWO ABOUT HAVING A SWOLLEN HEAD, WOULDN'T YOU, CUDGEON?
I NEED YOUR SIGNATURE.
CROSS-REFERENCING PERSONNEL WITH LEVEL THREE CLEARANCE ...
SEARCH COMPLETE.
ONE MATCH FOUND.
EXCUSE ME, COMMANDER. I'VE GOT WORK TO DO–
CLICK
OH NO.
YOU KNOW, BRIAR, ALL THOSE JIBES ABOUT YOUR HEAD PROBLEM, IT'S ALL IN FUN. I HAVE SOME OINTMENT–
SAVE YOUR OINTMENT. I HAVE THE FEELING YOU'LL BE DEVELOPING SOME HEAD PROBLEMS OF YOUR OWN.
ONE MATCH:
BRIAR CUDGEON.

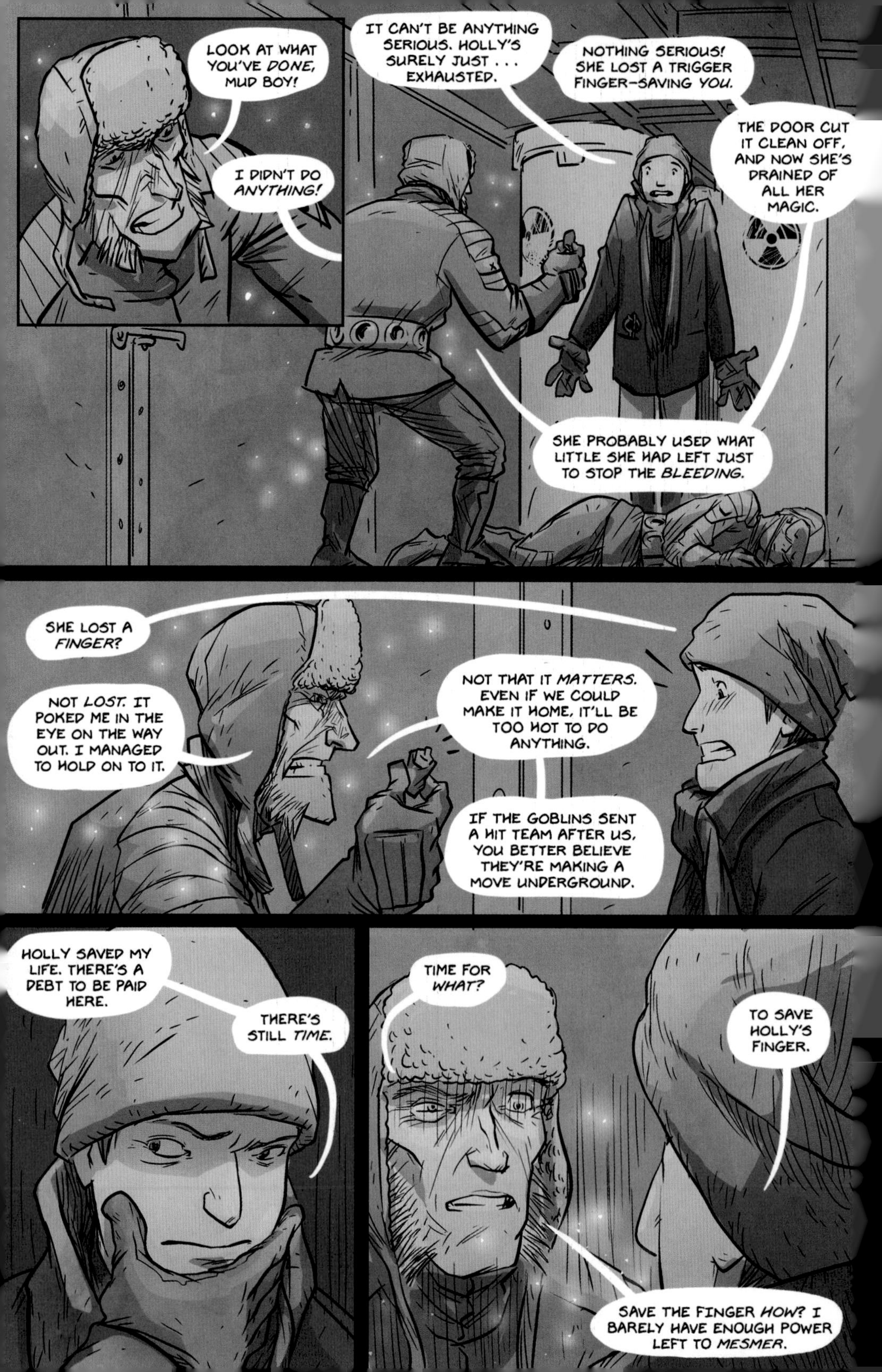
LOOK AT WHAT YOU'VE DONE, MUD BOY!
I DIDN'T DO ANYTHING!
IT CAN'T BE ANYTHING SERIOUS. HOLLY'S SURELY JUST . . . EXHAUSTED.
NOTHING SERIOUS! SHE LOST A TRIGGER FINGER—SAVING YOU.
THE DOOR CUT IT CLEAN OFF, AND NOW SHE'S DRAINED OF ALL HER MAGIC.
SHE PROBABLY USED WHAT LITTLE SHE HAD LEFT JUST TO STOP THE BLEEDING.
SHE LOST A FINGER?
NOT LOST. IT POKED ME IN THE EYE ON THE WAY OUT. I MANAGED TO HOLD ON TO IT.
NOT THAT IT MATTERS. EVEN IF WE COULD MAKE IT HOME, IT'LL BE TOO HOT TO DO ANYTHING.
IF THE GOBLINS SENT A HIT TEAM AFTER US, YOU BETTER BELIEVE THEY'RE MAKING A MOVE UNDERGROUND.
HOLLY SAVED MY LIFE. THERE'S A DEBT TO BE PAID HERE.
THERE'S STILL TIME.
TIME FOR WHAT?
TO SAVE HOLLY'S FINGER.
SAVE THE FINGER HOW? I BARELY HAVE ENOUGH POWER LEFT TO MESMER.

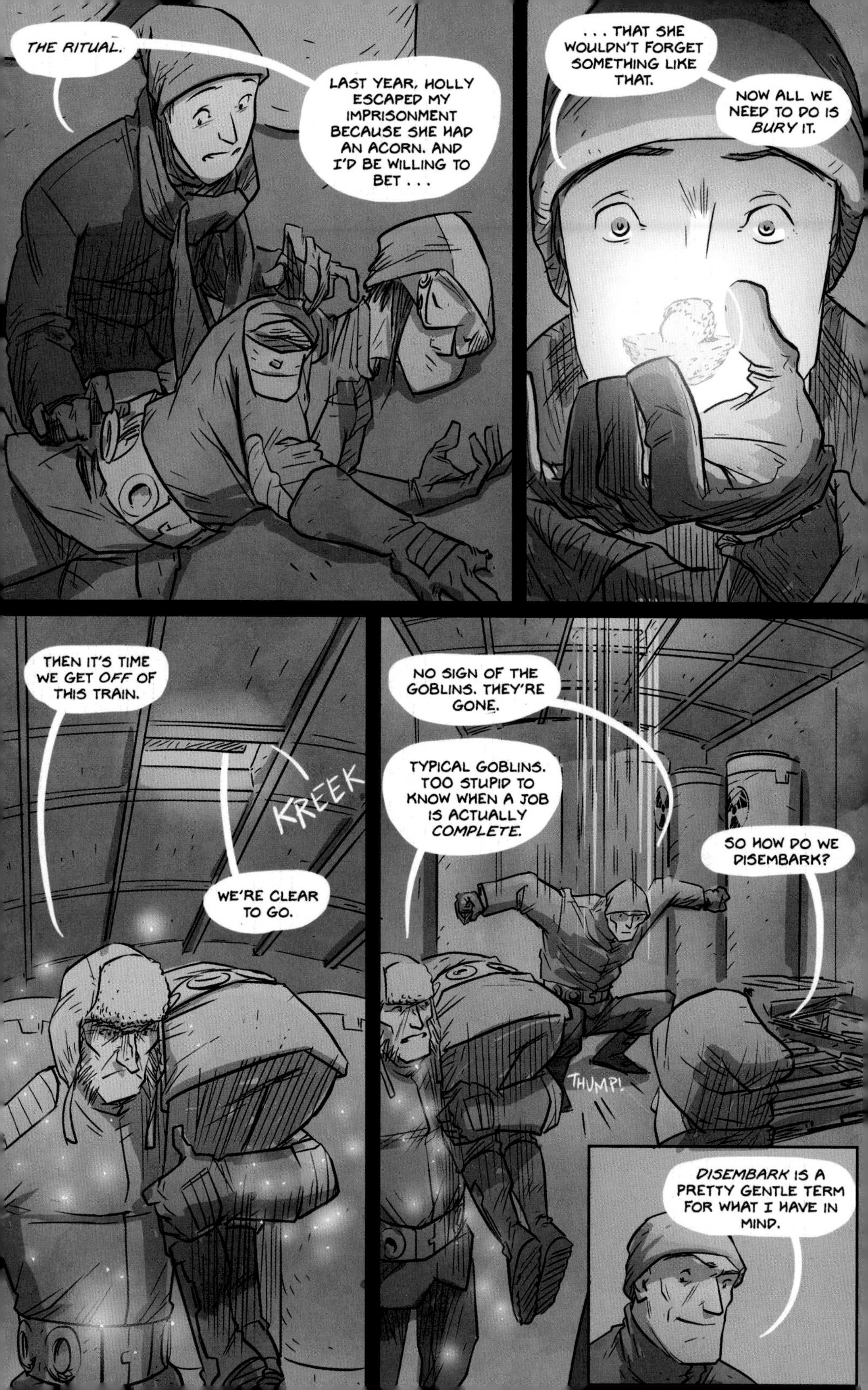
THE RITUAL.
LAST YEAR, HOLLY ESCAPED MY IMPRISONMENT BECAUSE SHE HAD AN ACORN. AND I'D BE WILLING TO BET . . .
. . . THAT SHE WOULDN'T FORGET SOMETHING LIKE THAT.
NOW ALL WE NEED TO DO IS *BURY* IT.
THEN IT'S TIME WE GET *OFF* OF THIS TRAIN.
KREEK
WE'RE CLEAR TO GO.
NO SIGN OF THE GOBLINS. THEY'RE GONE.
TYPICAL GOBLINS. TOO STUPID TO KNOW WHEN A JOB IS ACTUALLY *COMPLETE*.
SO HOW DO WE DISEMBARK?
THUMP!
DISEMBARK IS A PRETTY GENTLE TERM FOR WHAT I HAVE IN MIND.

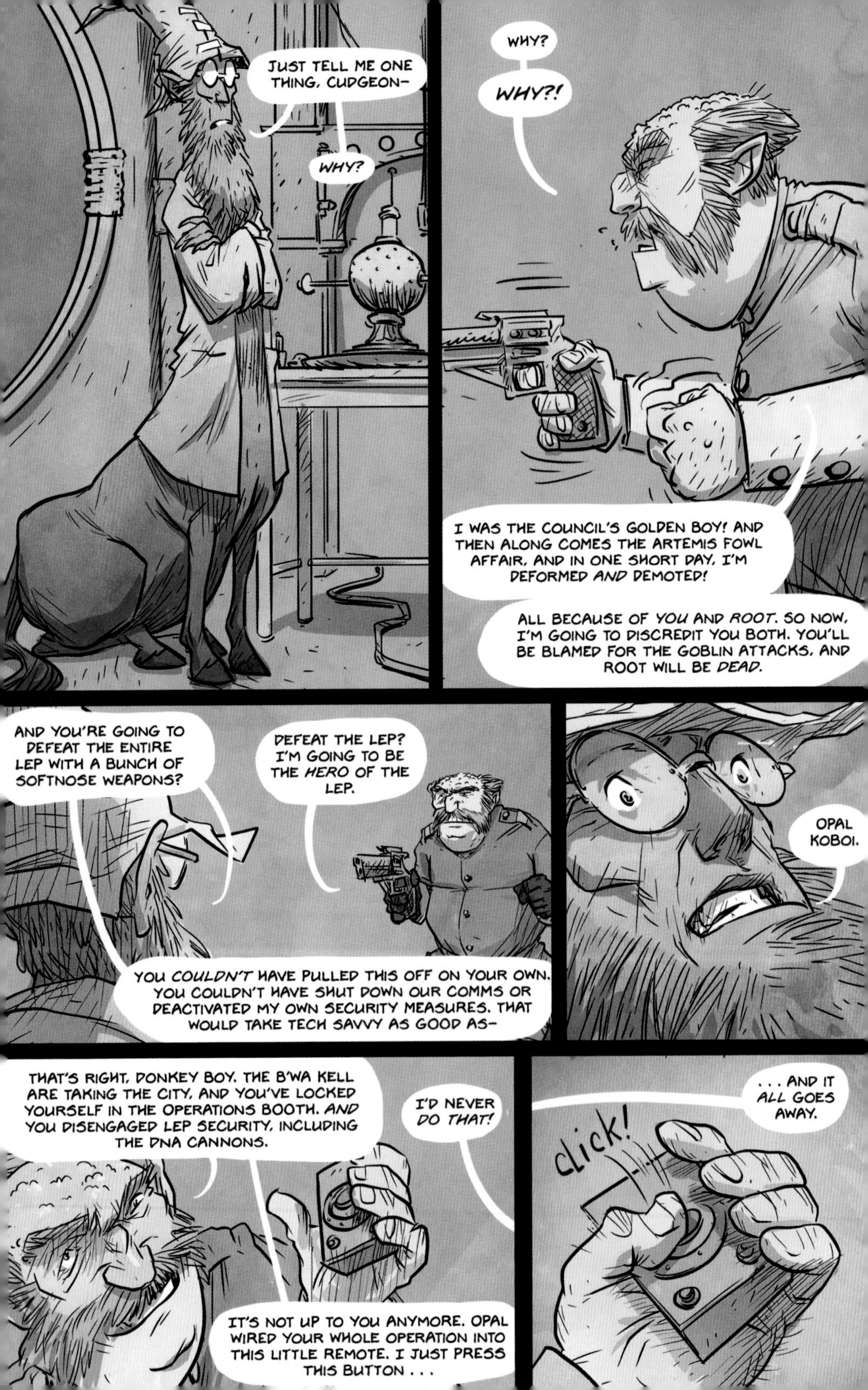
JUST TELL ME ONE THING, CUDGEON-
WHY?
WHY?
WHY?!
I WAS THE COUNCIL'S GOLDEN BOY! AND THEN ALONG COMES THE ARTEMIS FOWL AFFAIR, AND IN ONE SHORT DAY, I'M DEFORMED *AND* DEMOTED!
ALL BECAUSE OF *YOU* AND *ROOT*. SO NOW, I'M GOING TO DISCREDIT YOU BOTH. YOU'LL BE BLAMED FOR THE GOBLIN ATTACKS, AND ROOT WILL BE *DEAD*.
AND YOU'RE GOING TO DEFEAT THE ENTIRE LEP WITH A BUNCH OF SOFTNOSE WEAPONS?
DEFEAT THE LEP? I'M GOING TO BE THE *HERO* OF THE LEP.
YOU *COULDN'T* HAVE PULLED THIS OFF ON YOUR OWN. YOU COULDN'T HAVE SHUT DOWN OUR COMMS OR DEACTIVATED MY OWN SECURITY MEASURES. THAT WOULD TAKE TECH SAVVY AS GOOD AS-
OPAL KOBOI.
THAT'S RIGHT, DONKEY BOY. THE B'WA KELL ARE TAKING THE CITY, AND YOU'VE LOCKED YOURSELF IN THE OPERATIONS BOOTH. *AND* YOU DISENGAGED LEP SECURITY, INCLUDING THE DNA CANNONS.
I'D NEVER *DO THAT!*
IT'S NOT UP TO YOU ANYMORE. OPAL WIRED YOUR WHOLE OPERATION INTO THIS LITTLE REMOTE. I JUST PRESS THIS BUTTON . . .
click!
. . . AND IT *ALL* GOES AWAY.

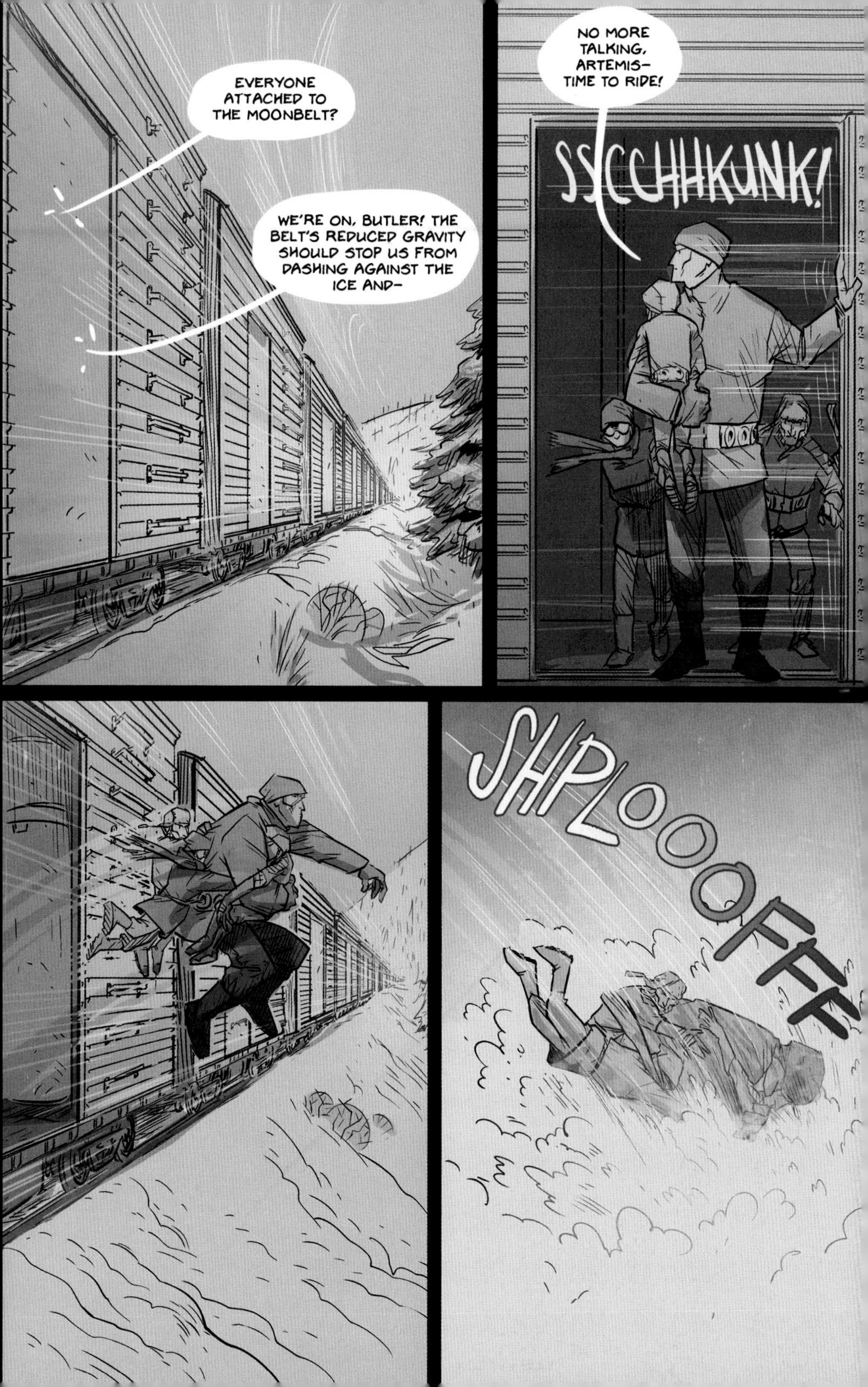
EVERYONE ATTACHED TO THE MOONBELT?
WE'RE ON, BUTLER! THE BELT'S REDUCED GRAVITY SHOULD STOP US FROM DASHING AGAINST THE ICE AND–
NO MORE TALKING, ARTEMIS– TIME TO RIDE!
SSCCHHKUNK!
SHPLOOOOFFF

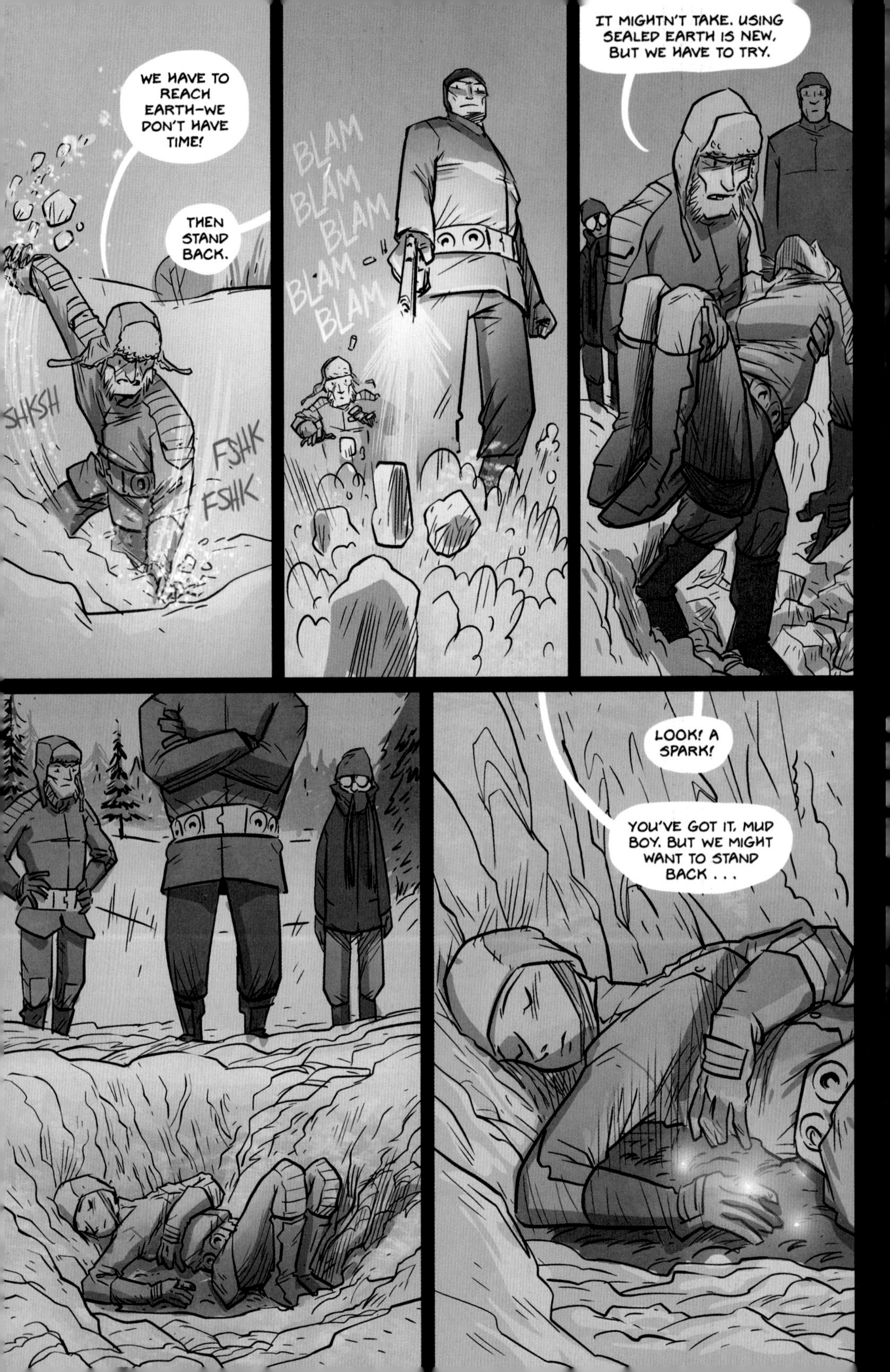
WE HAVE TO REACH EARTH—WE DON'T HAVE TIME!
THEN STAND BACK.
SHKSH
FSHK
FSHK
BLAM
BLAM
BLAM
BLAM
BLAM
IT MIGHTN'T TAKE. USING SEALED EARTH IS NEW, BUT WE HAVE TO TRY.
LOOK! A SPARK!
YOU'VE GOT IT, MUD BOY. BUT WE MIGHT WANT TO STAND BACK . . .

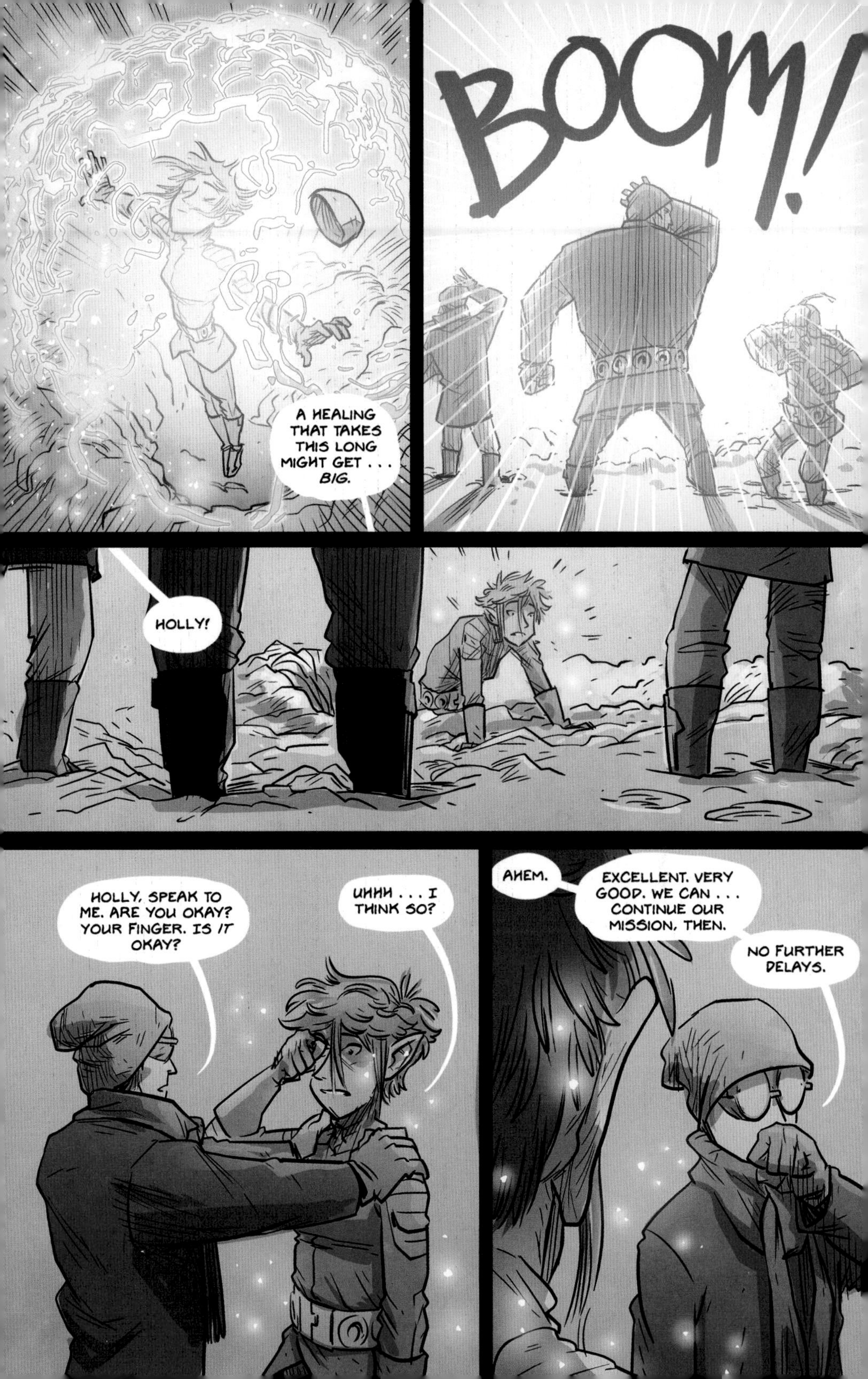
A HEALING THAT TAKES THIS LONG MIGHT GET . . . BIG.
BOOM!
HOLLY!
HOLLY, SPEAK TO ME. ARE YOU OKAY? YOUR FINGER. IS IT OKAY?
UHHH . . . I THINK SO?
AHEM.
EXCELLENT. VERY GOOD. WE CAN . . . CONTINUE OUR MISSION, THEN.
NO FURTHER DELAYS.

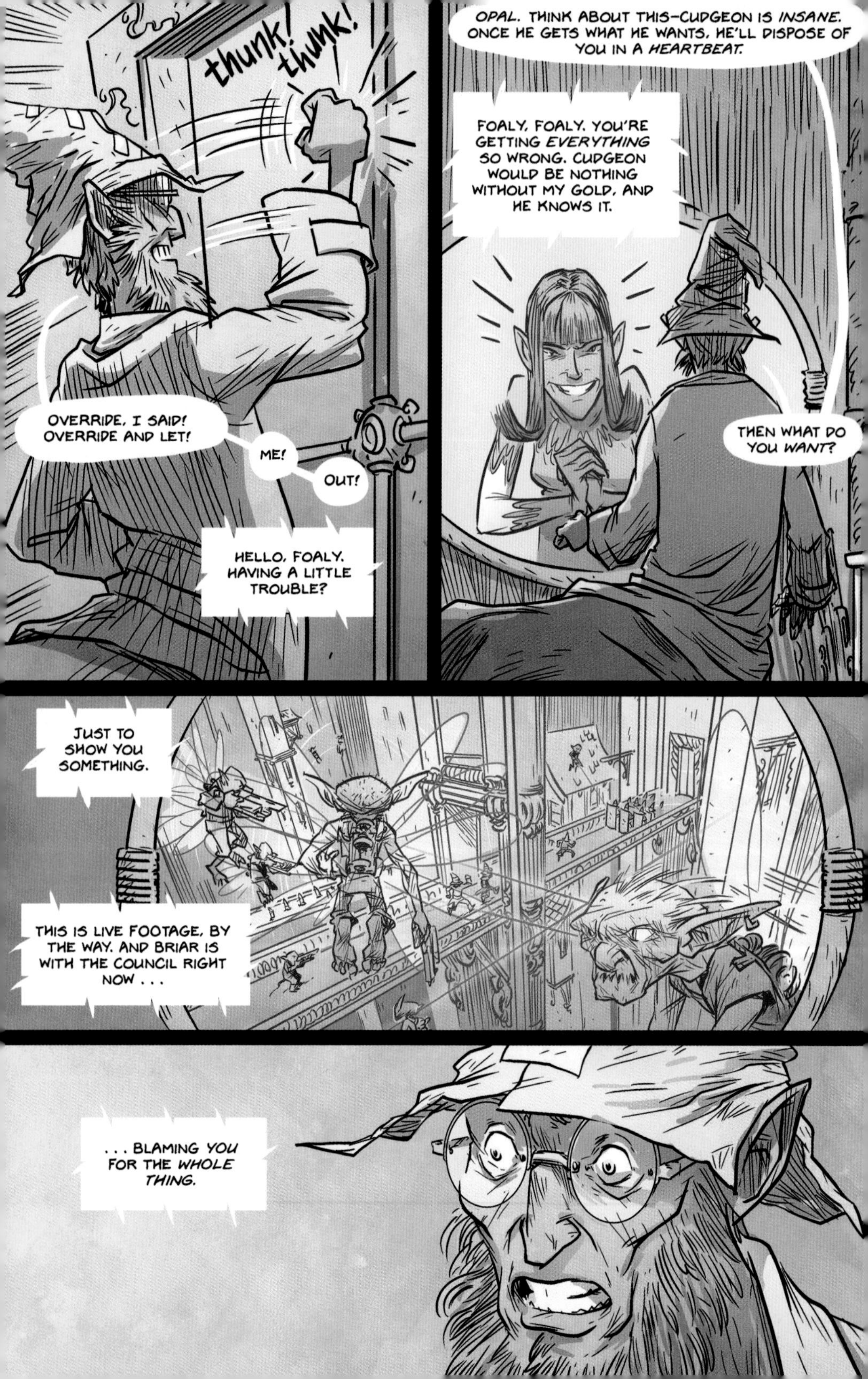
thunk! thunk!
OVERRIDE, I SAID! OVERRIDE AND LET!
ME!
OUT!
HELLO, FOALY. HAVING A LITTLE TROUBLE?
OPAL. THINK ABOUT THIS—CUDGEON IS *INSANE.* ONCE HE GETS WHAT HE WANTS, HE'LL DISPOSE OF YOU IN A *HEARTBEAT.*
FOALY, FOALY. YOU'RE GETTING *EVERYTHING* SO WRONG. CUDGEON WOULD BE NOTHING WITHOUT MY GOLD, AND HE KNOWS IT.
THEN WHAT DO YOU *WANT?*
JUST TO SHOW YOU SOMETHING.
THIS IS LIVE FOOTAGE, BY THE WAY. AND BRIAR IS WITH THE COUNCIL RIGHT NOW . . .
. . . BLAMING *YOU* FOR THE *WHOLE THING.*

CHAPTER TEN

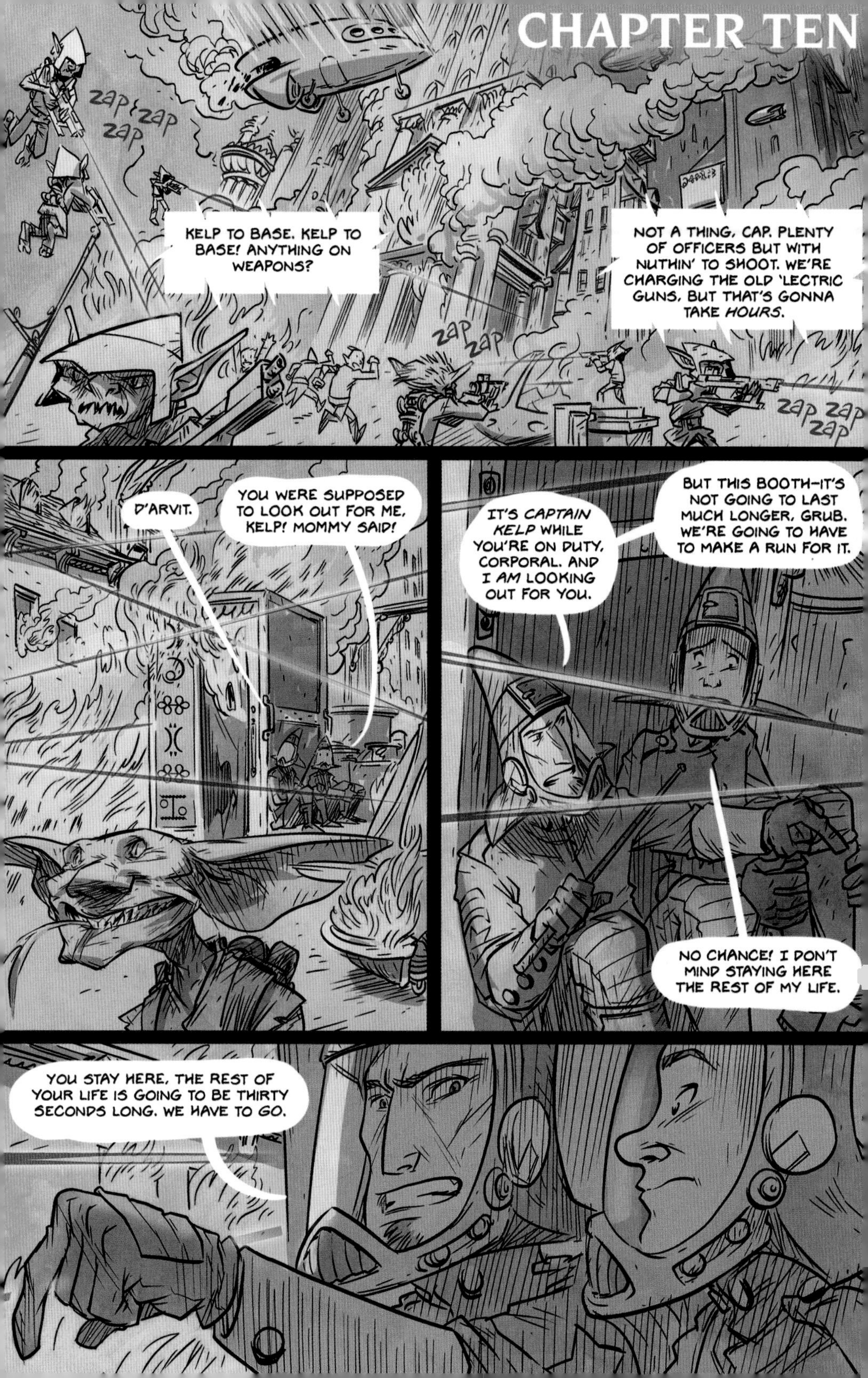
zap zap
zap
KELP TO BASE. KELP TO BASE! ANYTHING ON WEAPONS?
NOT A THING, CAP. PLENTY OF OFFICERS BUT WITH NUTHIN' TO SHOOT. WE'RE CHARGING THE OLD 'LECTRIC GUNS, BUT THAT'S GONNA TAKE *HOURS*.
zap zap
zap zap
zap
D'ARVIT.
YOU WERE SUPPOSED TO LOOK OUT FOR ME, KELP! MOMMY SAID!
IT'S *CAPTAIN KELP* WHILE YOU'RE ON DUTY, CORPORAL. AND I *AM* LOOKING OUT FOR YOU.
BUT THIS BOOTH—IT'S NOT GOING TO LAST MUCH LONGER, GRUB. WE'RE GOING TO HAVE TO MAKE A RUN FOR IT.
NO CHANCE! I DON'T MIND STAYING HERE THE REST OF MY LIFE.
YOU STAY HERE, THE REST OF YOUR LIFE IS GOING TO BE THIRTY SECONDS LONG. WE HAVE TO GO.

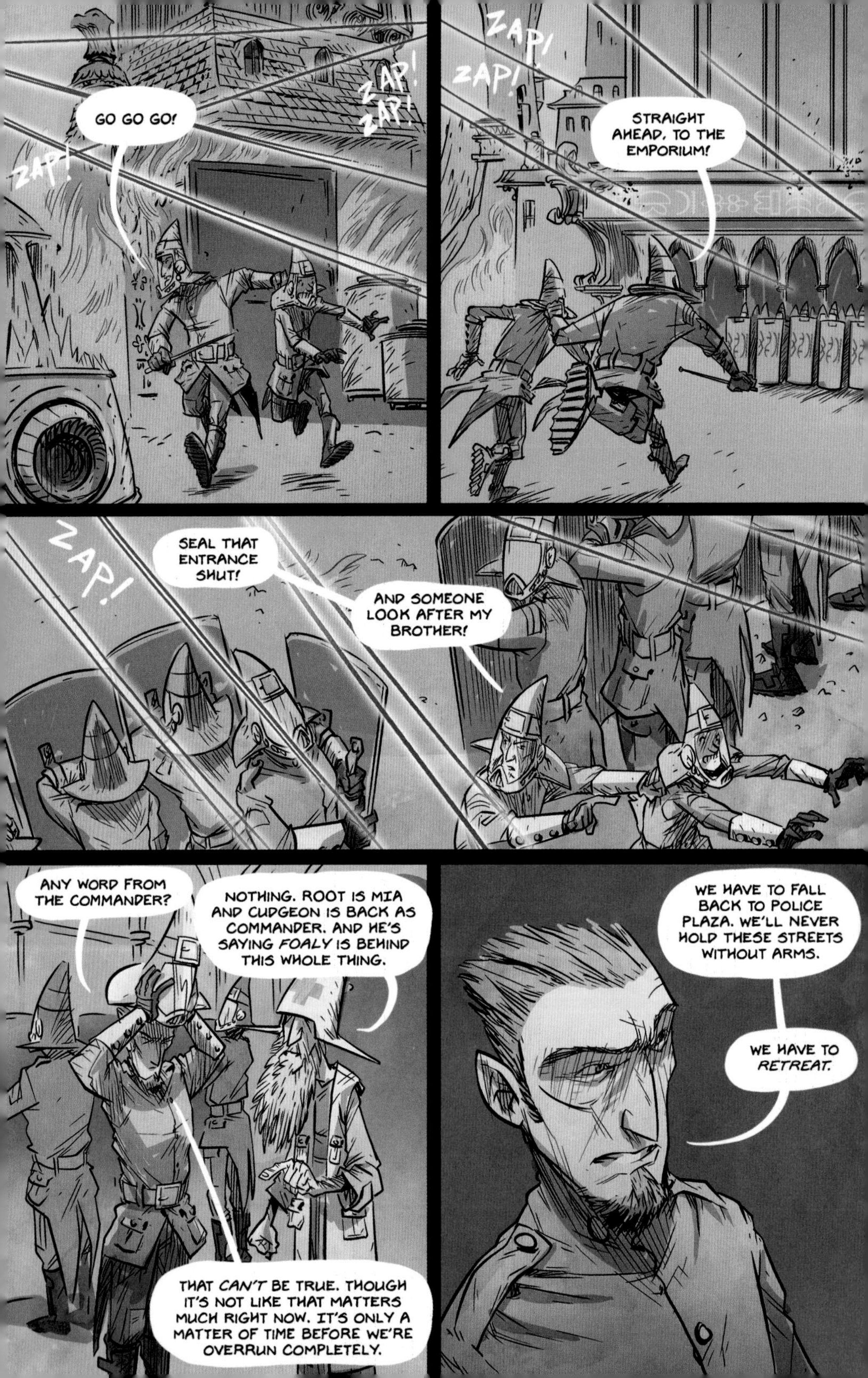
ZAP!
GO GO GO!
ZAP!
ZAP!
ZAP!
ZAP!
ZAP!
STRAIGHT AHEAD, TO THE EMPORIUM!
ZAP!
SEAL THAT ENTRANCE SHUT!
AND SOMEONE LOOK AFTER MY BROTHER!
ANY WORD FROM THE COMMANDER?
NOTHING. ROOT IS MIA AND CUDGEON IS BACK AS COMMANDER. AND HE'S SAYING *FOALY* IS BEHIND THIS WHOLE THING.
THAT *CAN'T* BE TRUE. THOUGH IT'S NOT LIKE THAT MATTERS MUCH RIGHT NOW. IT'S ONLY A MATTER OF TIME BEFORE WE'RE OVERRUN COMPLETELY.
WE HAVE TO FALL BACK TO POLICE PLAZA. WE'LL NEVER HOLD THESE STREETS WITHOUT ARMS.
WE HAVE TO *RETREAT.*

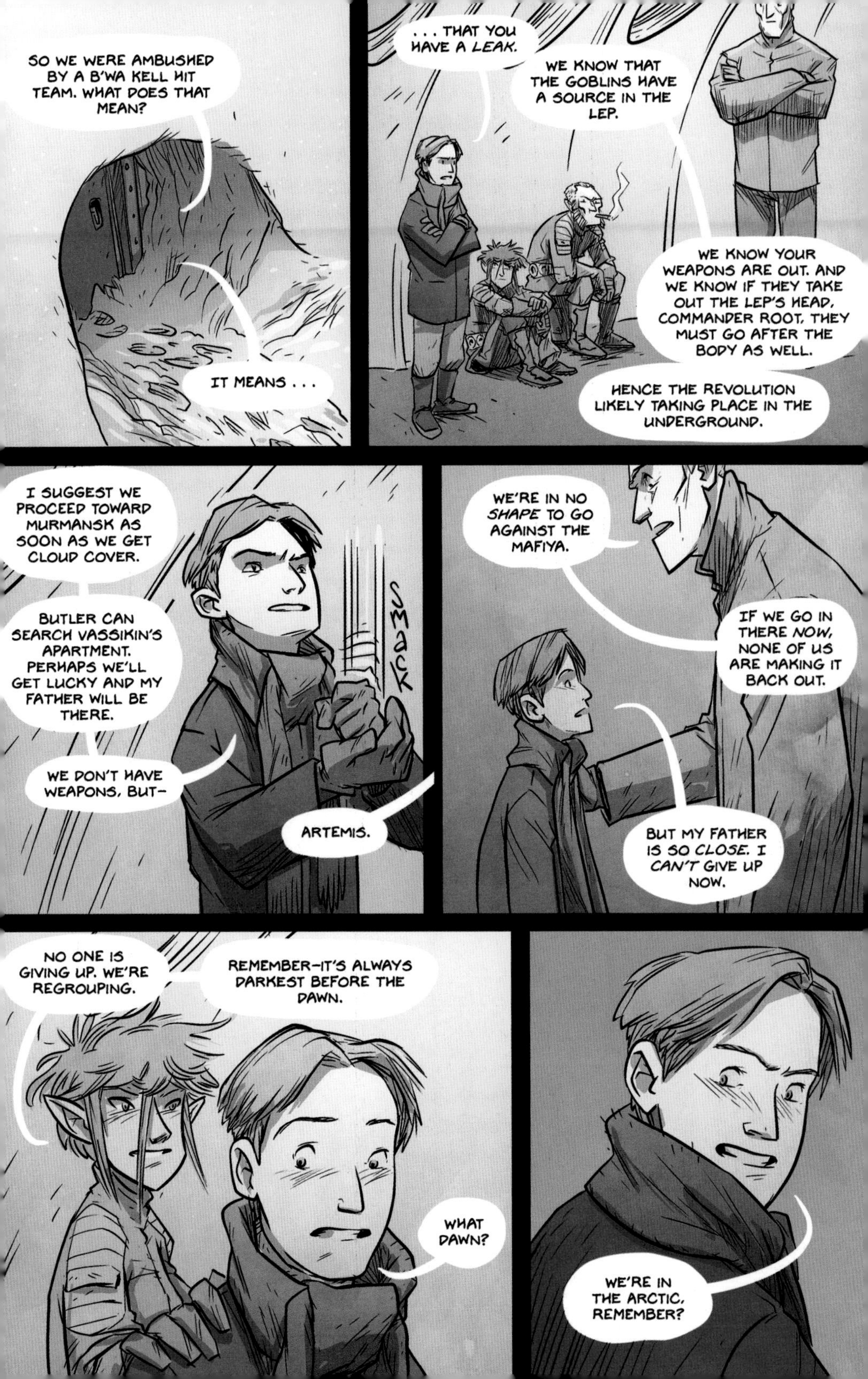
SO WE WERE AMBUSHED BY A B'WA KELL HIT TEAM. WHAT DOES THAT MEAN?
IT MEANS . . .
. . . THAT YOU HAVE A *LEAK.*
WE KNOW THAT THE GOBLINS HAVE A SOURCE IN THE LEP.
WE KNOW YOUR WEAPONS ARE OUT. AND WE KNOW IF THEY TAKE OUT THE LEP'S HEAD, COMMANDER ROOT, THEY MUST GO AFTER THE BODY AS WELL.
HENCE THE REVOLUTION LIKELY TAKING PLACE IN THE UNDERGROUND.
I SUGGEST WE PROCEED TOWARD MURMANSK AS SOON AS WE GET CLOUD COVER.
BUTLER CAN SEARCH VASSIKIN'S APARTMENT. PERHAPS WE'LL GET LUCKY AND MY FATHER WILL BE THERE.
SMACK
WE DON'T HAVE WEAPONS, BUT–
ARTEMIS.
WE'RE IN NO *SHAPE* TO GO AGAINST THE MAFIYA.
IF WE GO IN THERE *NOW,* NONE OF US ARE MAKING IT BACK OUT.
BUT MY FATHER IS SO *CLOSE.* I *CAN'T* GIVE UP NOW.
NO ONE IS GIVING UP. WE'RE REGROUPING.
REMEMBER–IT'S ALWAYS DARKEST BEFORE THE DAWN.
WHAT DAWN?
WE'RE IN THE ARCTIC, REMEMBER?

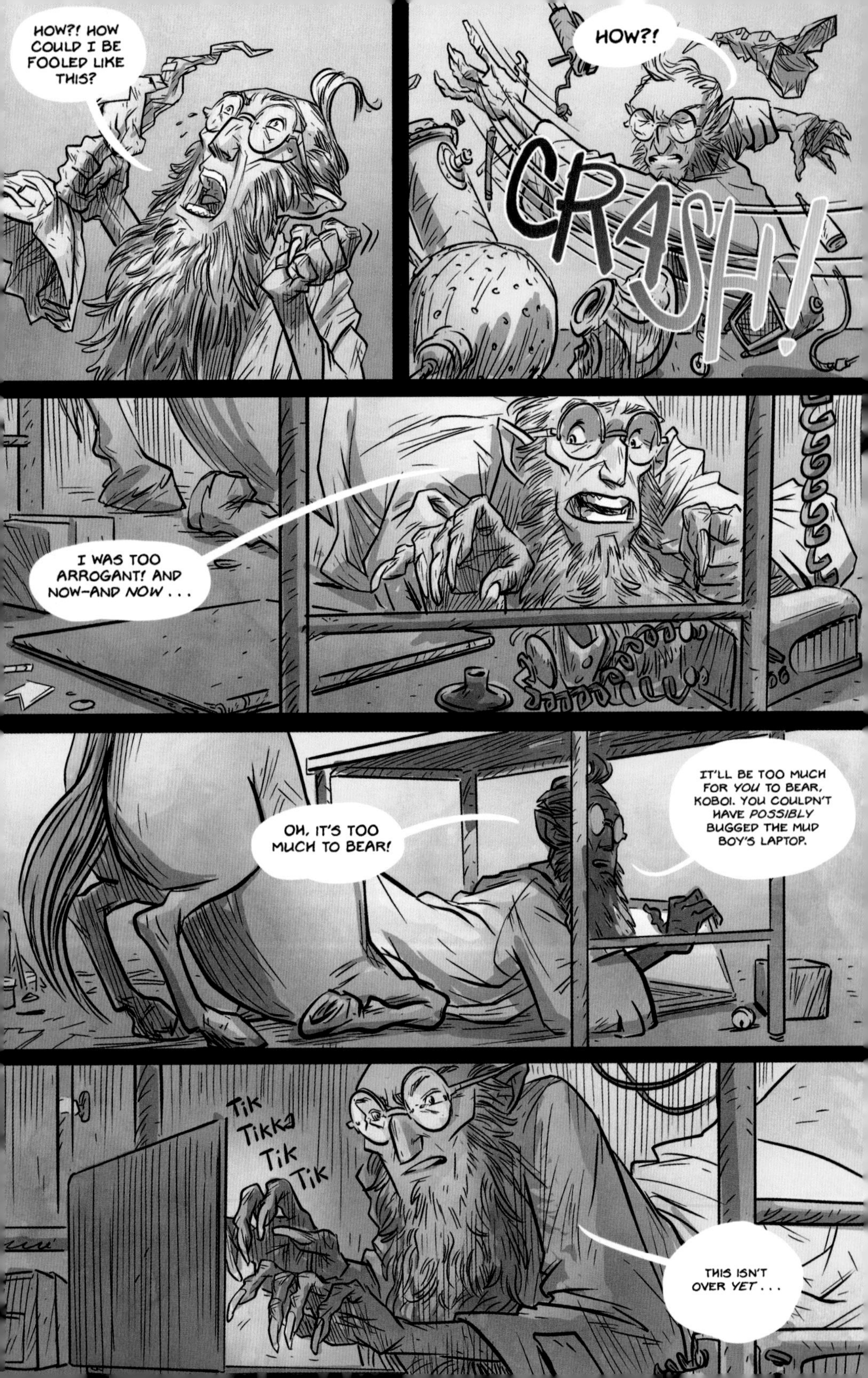
HOW?! HOW COULD I BE FOOLED LIKE THIS?
HOW?!
CRASH!
I WAS TOO ARROGANT! AND NOW—AND NOW . . .
OH, IT'S TOO MUCH TO BEAR!
IT'LL BE TOO MUCH FOR YOU TO BEAR, KOBOI. YOU COULDN'T HAVE POSSIBLY BUGGED THE MUD BOY'S LAPTOP.
Tik Tikka Tik Tik
THIS ISN'T OVER YET . . .

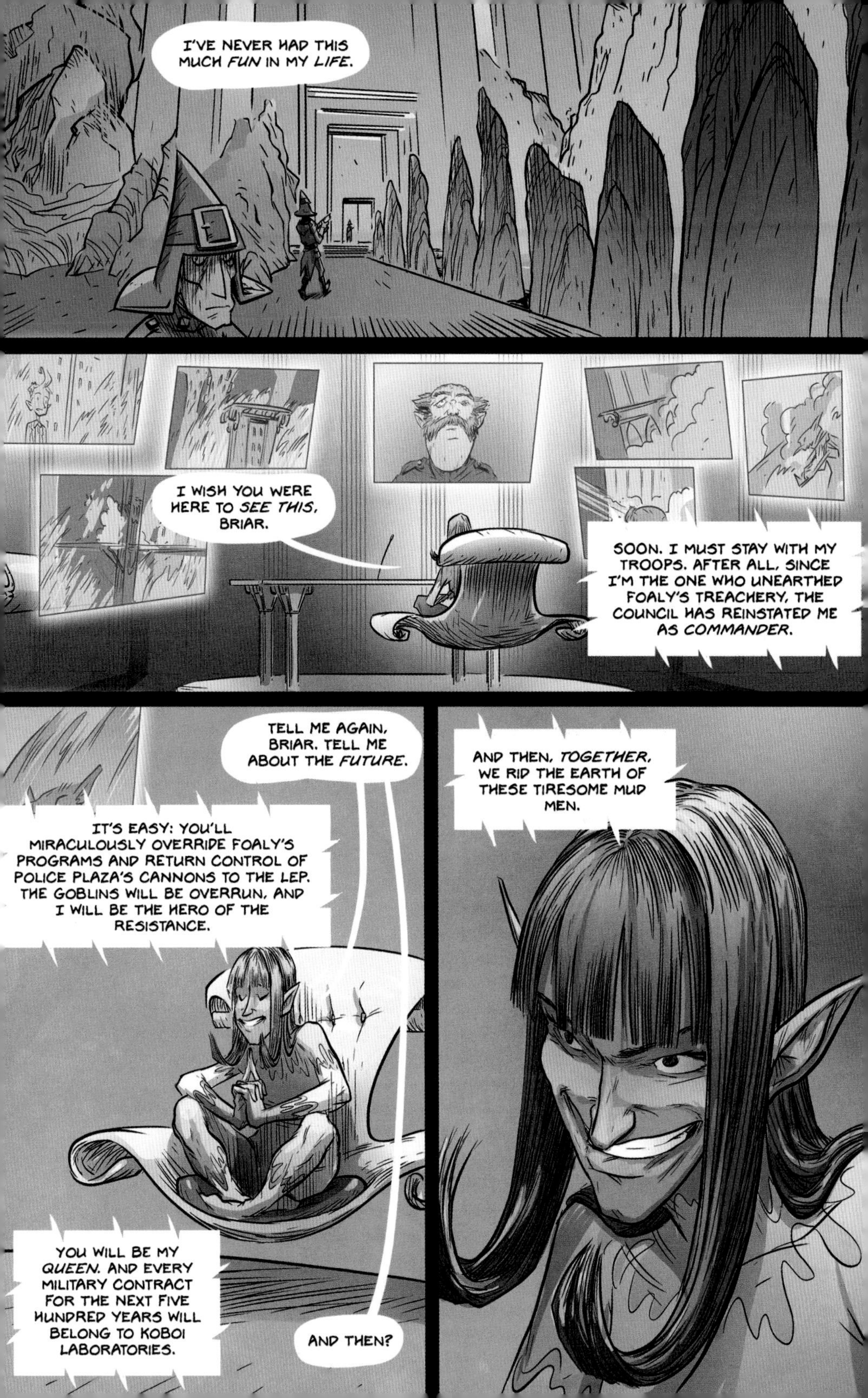
I'VE NEVER HAD THIS MUCH *FUN* IN MY *LIFE*.
I WISH YOU WERE HERE TO *SEE THIS*, BRIAR.
SOON. I MUST STAY WITH MY TROOPS. AFTER ALL, SINCE I'M THE ONE WHO UNEARTHED FOALY'S TREACHERY, THE COUNCIL HAS REINSTATED ME AS *COMMANDER*.
TELL ME AGAIN, BRIAR. TELL ME ABOUT THE *FUTURE*.
IT'S EASY: YOU'LL MIRACULOUSLY OVERRIDE FOALY'S PROGRAMS AND RETURN CONTROL OF POLICE PLAZA'S CANNONS TO THE LEP. THE GOBLINS WILL BE OVERRUN, AND I WILL BE THE HERO OF THE RESISTANCE.
YOU WILL BE MY *QUEEN*. AND EVERY MILITARY CONTRACT FOR THE NEXT FIVE HUNDRED YEARS WILL BELONG TO KOBOI LABORATORIES.
AND THEN?
AND THEN, *TOGETHER*, WE RID THE EARTH OF THESE TIRESOME MUD MEN.

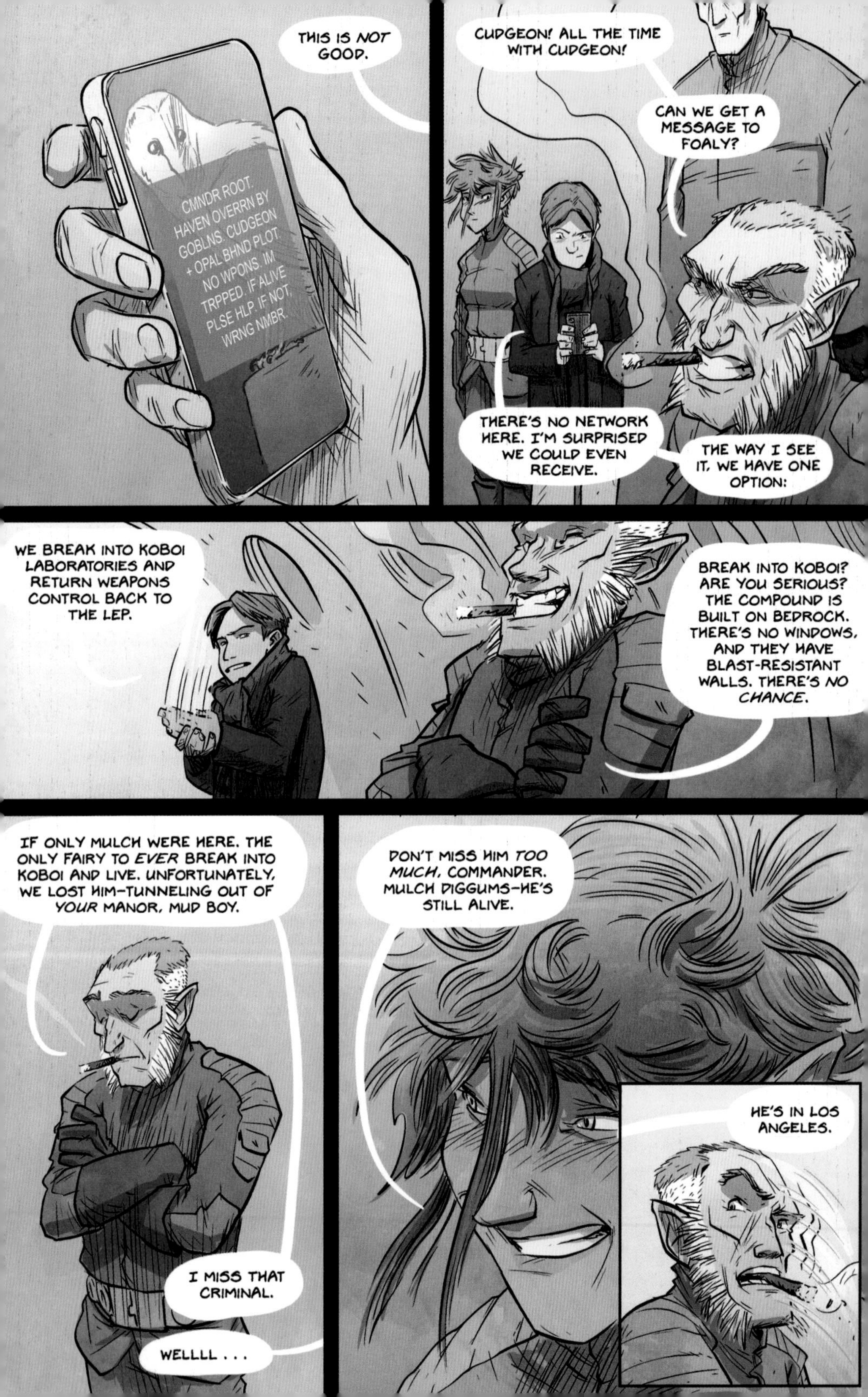
THIS IS NOT GOOD.
CMNDR ROOT. HAVEN OVERRN BY GOBLNS. CUDGEON + OPAL BHND PLOT. NO WPONS. IM TRPPED. IF ALIVE PLSE HLP. IF NOT, WRNG NMBR.
CUDGEON! ALL THE TIME WITH CUDGEON!
CAN WE GET A MESSAGE TO FOALY?
THERE'S NO NETWORK HERE. I'M SURPRISED WE COULD EVEN RECEIVE.
THE WAY I SEE IT, WE HAVE ONE OPTION:
WE BREAK INTO KOBOI LABORATORIES AND RETURN WEAPONS CONTROL BACK TO THE LEP.
BREAK INTO KOBOI? ARE YOU SERIOUS? THE COMPOUND IS BUILT ON BEDROCK. THERE'S NO WINDOWS, AND THEY HAVE BLAST-RESISTANT WALLS. THERE'S NO CHANCE.
IF ONLY MULCH WERE HERE. THE ONLY FAIRY TO EVER BREAK INTO KOBOI AND LIVE. UNFORTUNATELY, WE LOST HIM—TUNNELING OUT OF YOUR MANOR, MUD BOY.
I MISS THAT CRIMINAL.
WELLLL . . .
DON'T MISS HIM TOO MUCH, COMMANDER. MULCH DIGGUMS—HE'S STILL ALIVE.
HE'S IN LOS ANGELES.

CHAPTER ELEVEN

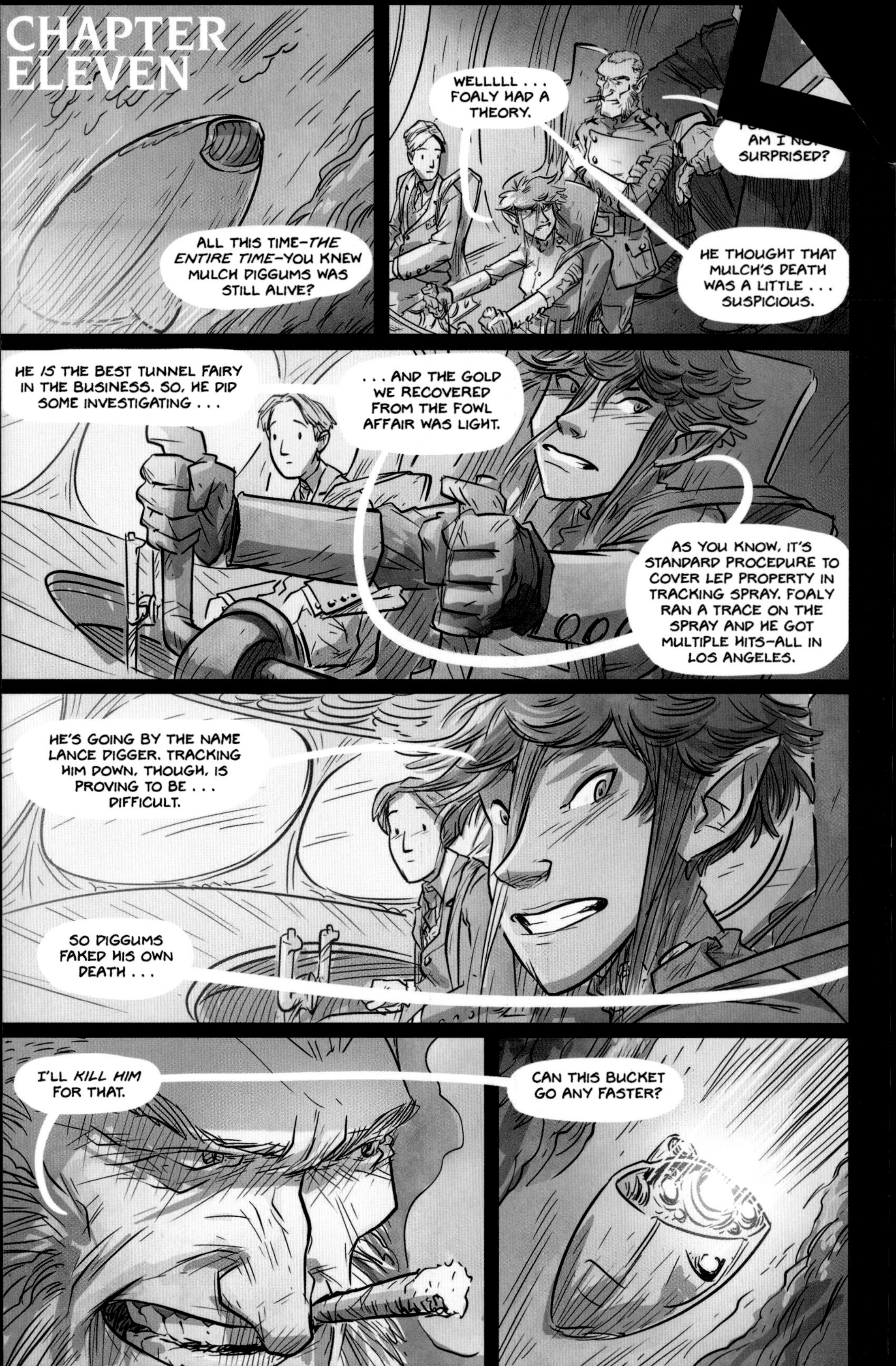

ALL THIS TIME—*THE ENTIRE TIME*—YOU KNEW MULCH DIGGUMS WAS STILL ALIVE?
WELLLLL . . . FOALY HAD A THEORY.
AM I NO SURPRISED?
HE THOUGHT THAT MULCH'S DEATH WAS A LITTLE . . . SUSPICIOUS.
HE *IS* THE BEST TUNNEL FAIRY IN THE BUSINESS. SO, HE DID SOME INVESTIGATING . . .
. . . AND THE GOLD WE RECOVERED FROM THE FOWL AFFAIR WAS LIGHT.
AS YOU KNOW, IT'S STANDARD PROCEDURE TO COVER LEP PROPERTY IN TRACKING SPRAY. FOALY RAN A TRACE ON THE SPRAY AND HE GOT MULTIPLE HITS—ALL IN LOS ANGELES.
HE'S GOING BY THE NAME LANCE DIGGER. TRACKING HIM DOWN, THOUGH, IS PROVING TO BE . . . DIFFICULT.
SO DIGGUMS FAKED HIS OWN DEATH . . .
I'LL *KILL HIM* FOR THAT.
CAN THIS BUCKET GO ANY FASTER?

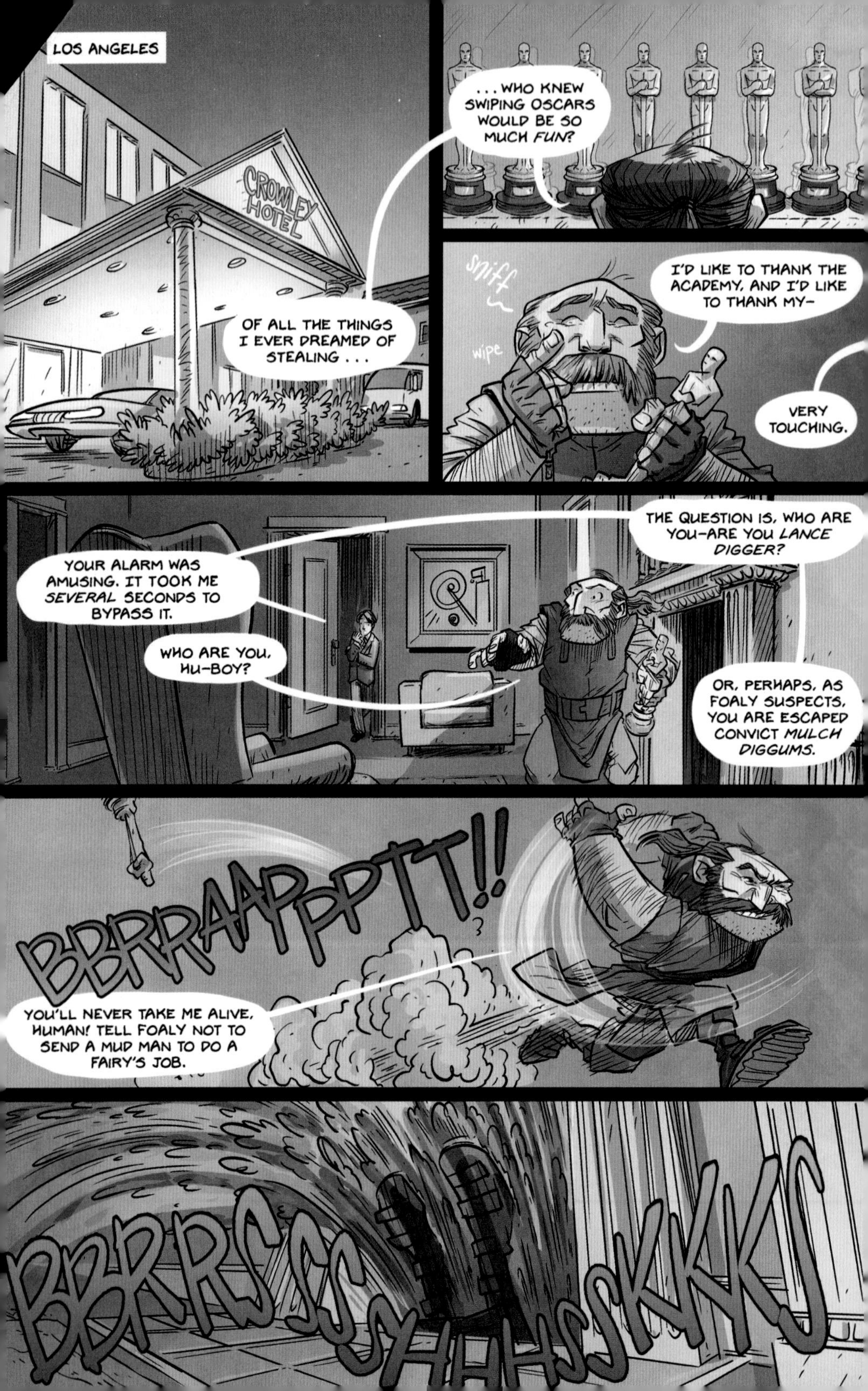
LOS ANGELES
CROWLEY HOTEL
OF ALL THE THINGS I EVER DREAMED OF STEALING . . .
. . . WHO KNEW SWIPING OSCARS WOULD BE SO MUCH *FUN*?
sniff
wipe
I'D LIKE TO THANK THE ACADEMY, AND I'D LIKE TO THANK MY–
VERY TOUCHING.
YOUR ALARM WAS AMUSING. IT TOOK ME *SEVERAL* SECONDS TO BYPASS IT.
WHO ARE YOU, HU-BOY?
THE QUESTION IS, WHO ARE YOU–ARE YOU *LANCE DIGGER*?
OR, PERHAPS, AS FOALY SUSPECTS, YOU ARE ESCAPED CONVICT *MULCH DIGGUMS*.
BBRRAAPPPTT!!
YOU'LL NEVER TAKE ME ALIVE, HUMAN! TELL FOALY NOT TO SEND A MUD MAN TO DO A FAIRY'S JOB.
BBRRSSSSHHHSSKKKS

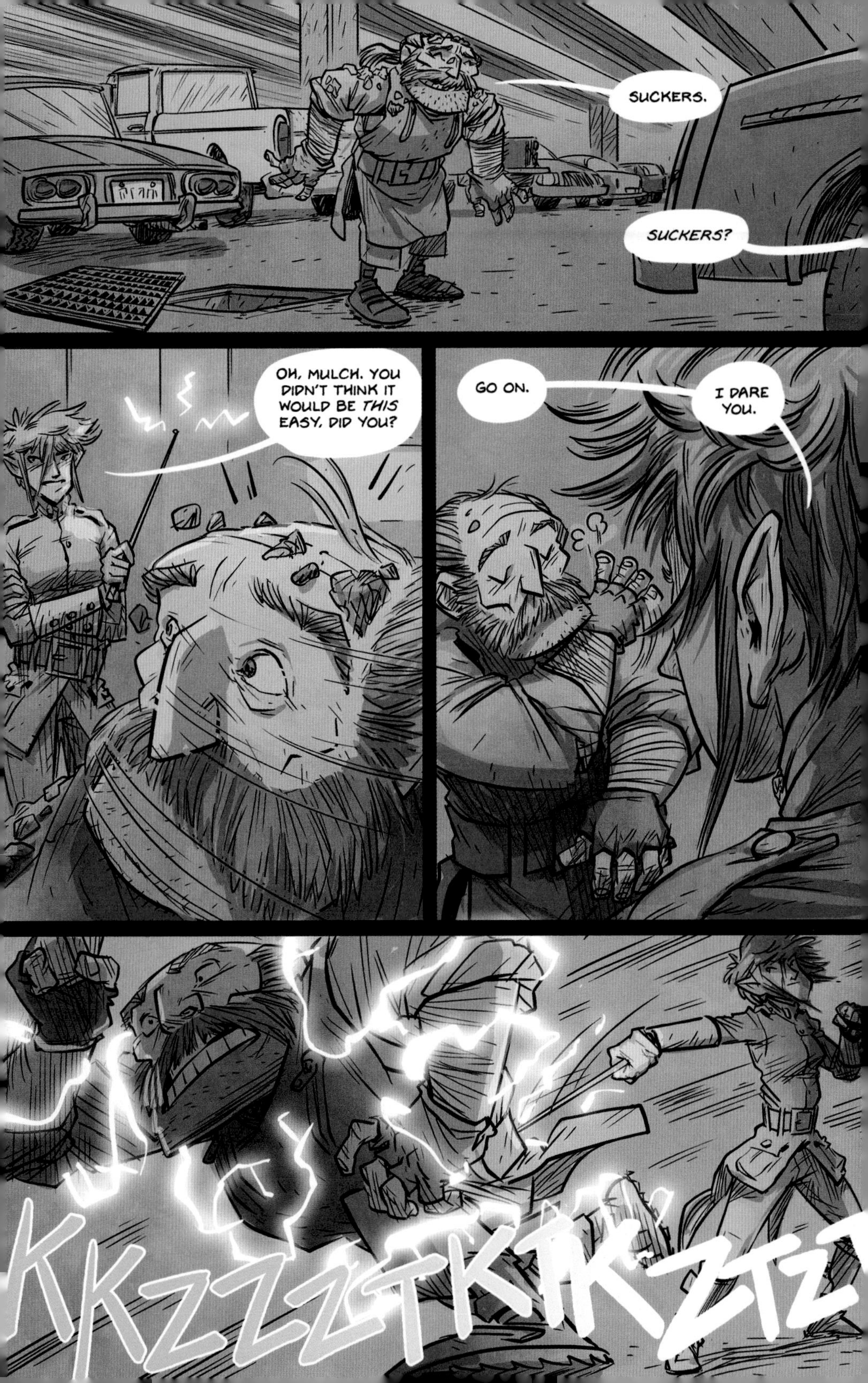
SUCKERS.
SUCKERS?
OH, MULCH. YOU DIDN'T THINK IT WOULD BE *THIS* EASY, DID YOU?
GO ON.
I DARE YOU.
KKZZZZTKTKZTZT

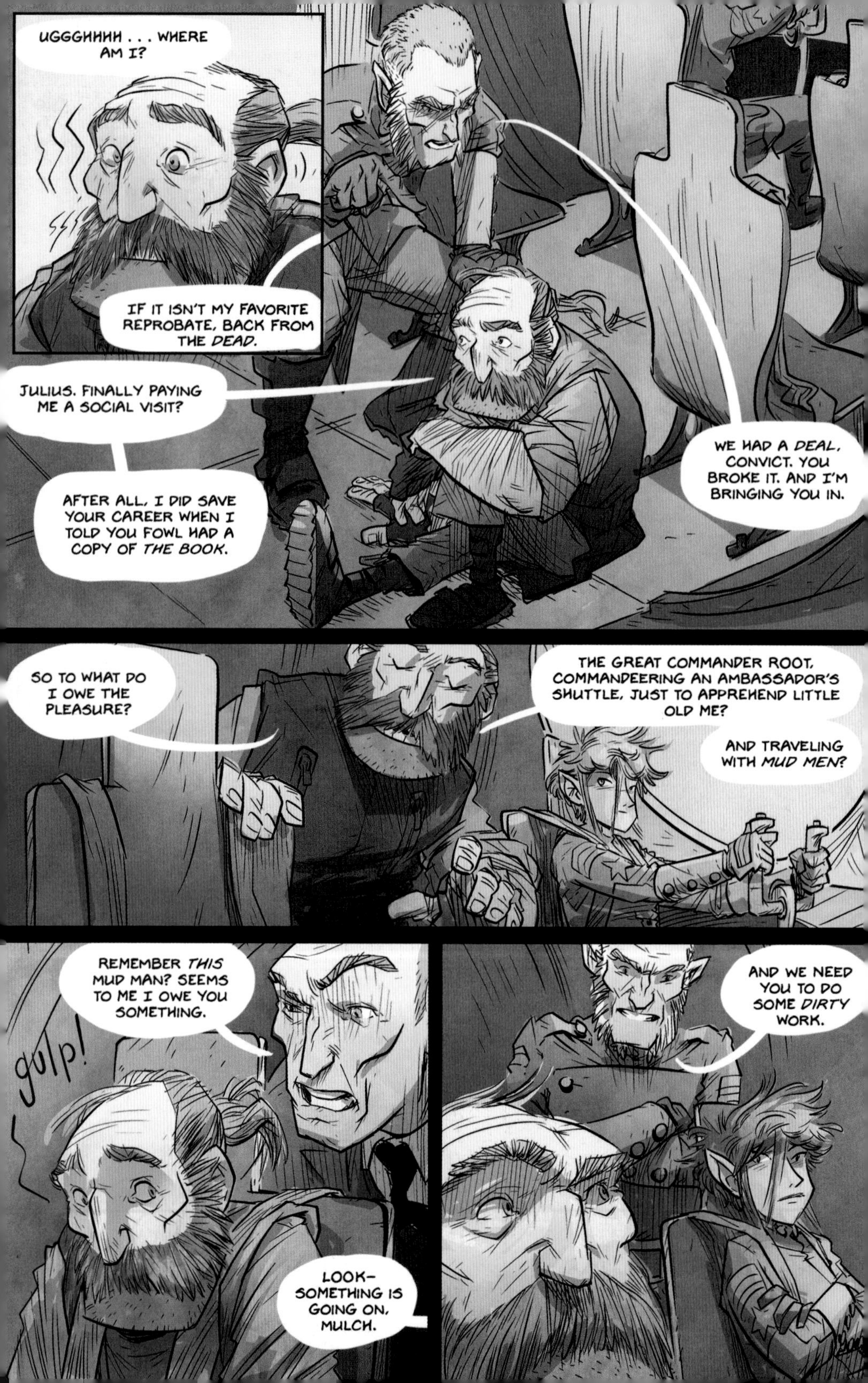
UGGGHHHH . . . WHERE AM I?
IF IT ISN'T MY FAVORITE REPROBATE, BACK FROM THE *DEAD*.
JULIUS. FINALLY PAYING ME A SOCIAL VISIT?
AFTER ALL, I DID SAVE YOUR CAREER WHEN I TOLD YOU FOWL HAD A COPY OF *THE BOOK*.
WE HAD A *DEAL*, CONVICT. YOU BROKE IT. AND I'M BRINGING YOU IN.
SO TO WHAT DO I OWE THE PLEASURE?
THE GREAT COMMANDER ROOT, COMMANDEERING AN AMBASSADOR'S SHUTTLE, JUST TO APPREHEND LITTLE OLD ME?
AND TRAVELING WITH *MUD MEN*?
REMEMBER *THIS* MUD MAN? SEEMS TO ME I OWE YOU SOMETHING.
gulp!
LOOK— SOMETHING IS GOING ON, MULCH.
AND WE NEED YOU TO DO SOME *DIRTY* WORK.

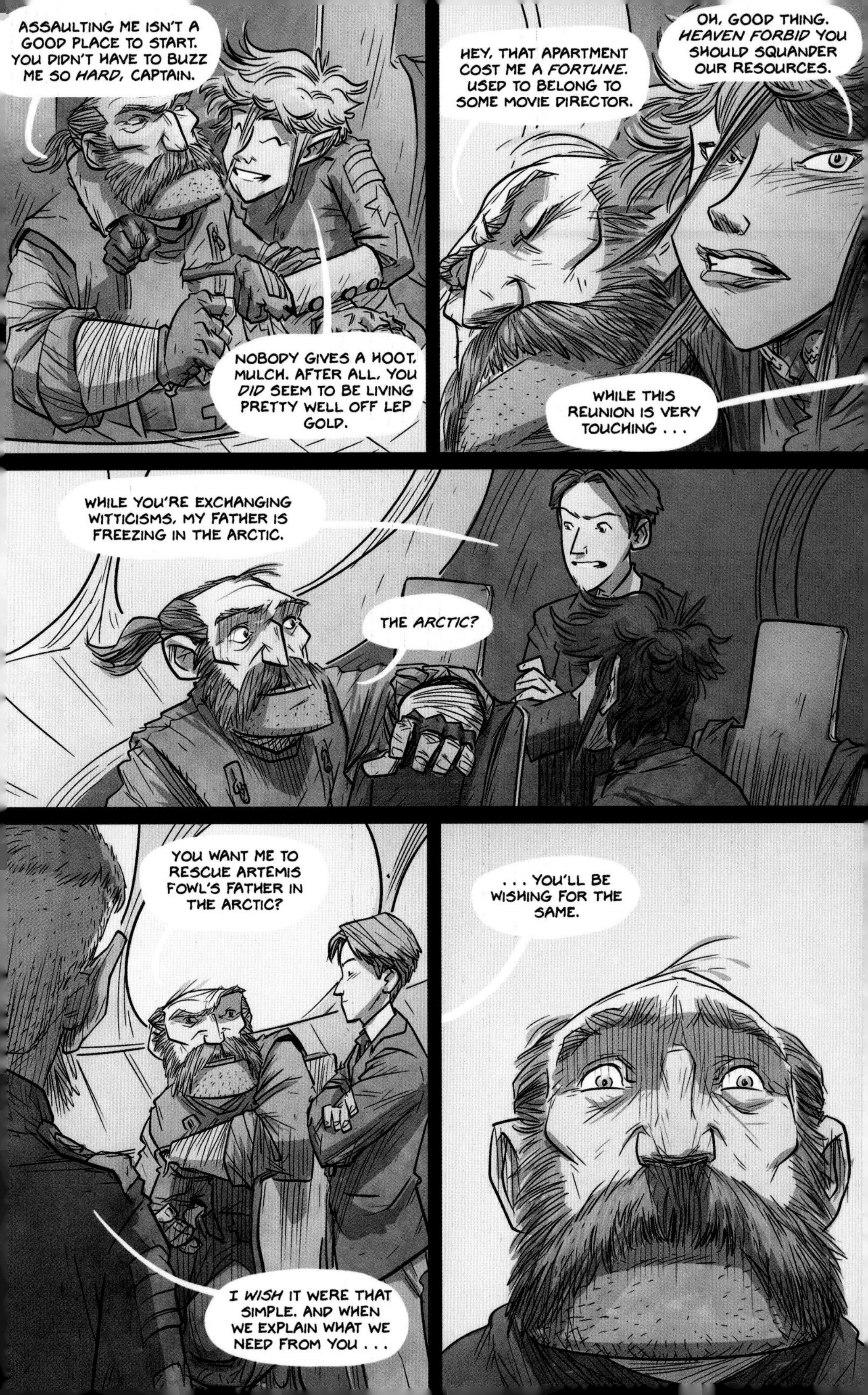
ASSAULTING ME ISN'T A GOOD PLACE TO START. YOU DIDN'T HAVE TO BUZZ ME SO *HARD*, CAPTAIN.
NOBODY GIVES A HOOT, MULCH. AFTER ALL, YOU *DID* SEEM TO BE LIVING PRETTY WELL OFF LEP GOLD.
HEY, THAT APARTMENT COST ME A *FORTUNE*. USED TO BELONG TO SOME MOVIE DIRECTOR.
OH, GOOD THING. *HEAVEN FORBID* YOU SHOULD SQUANDER OUR RESOURCES.
WHILE THIS REUNION IS VERY TOUCHING . . .
WHILE YOU'RE EXCHANGING WITTICISMS, MY FATHER IS FREEZING IN THE ARCTIC.
THE *ARCTIC*?
YOU WANT ME TO RESCUE ARTEMIS FOWL'S FATHER IN THE ARCTIC?
I *WISH* IT WERE THAT SIMPLE. AND WHEN WE EXPLAIN WHAT WE NEED FROM YOU . . .
. . . YOU'LL BE WISHING FOR THE SAME.

CHAPTER TWELVE

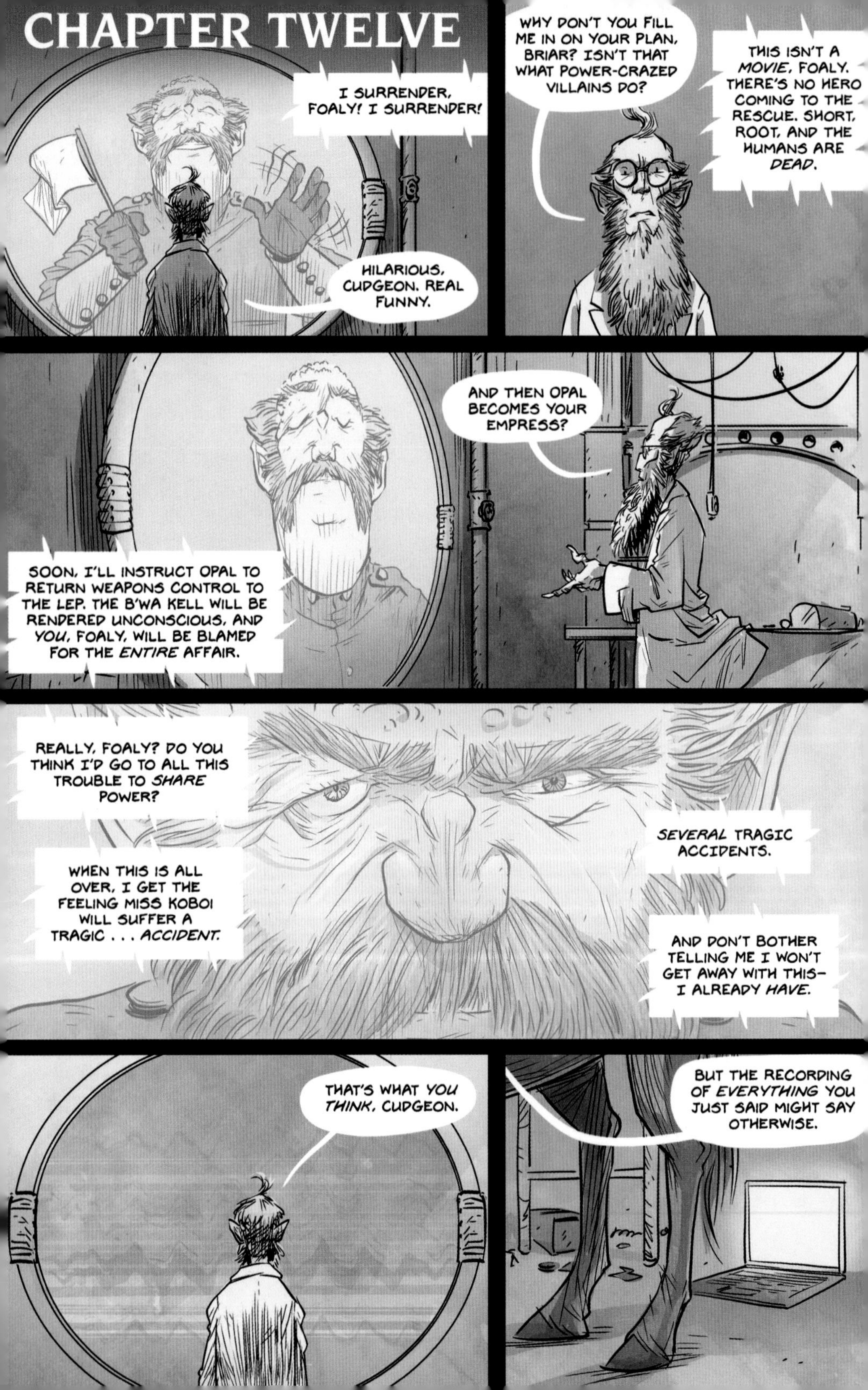
I SURRENDER, FOALY! I SURRENDER!
HILARIOUS, CUDGEON. REAL FUNNY.
WHY DON'T YOU FILL ME IN ON YOUR PLAN, BRIAR? ISN'T THAT WHAT POWER-CRAZED VILLAINS DO?
THIS ISN'T A *MOVIE*, FOALY. THERE'S NO HERO COMING TO THE RESCUE. SHORT, ROOT, AND THE HUMANS ARE *DEAD*.
SOON, I'LL INSTRUCT OPAL TO RETURN WEAPONS CONTROL TO THE LEP. THE B'WA KELL WILL BE RENDERED UNCONSCIOUS, AND *YOU*, FOALY, WILL BE BLAMED FOR THE *ENTIRE* AFFAIR.
AND THEN OPAL BECOMES YOUR EMPRESS?
REALLY, FOALY? DO YOU THINK I'D GO TO ALL THIS TROUBLE TO *SHARE* POWER?
WHEN THIS IS ALL OVER, I GET THE FEELING MISS KOBOI WILL SUFFER A TRAGIC . . . *ACCIDENT*.
SEVERAL TRAGIC ACCIDENTS.
AND DON'T BOTHER TELLING ME I WON'T GET AWAY WITH THIS— I ALREADY *HAVE*.
THAT'S WHAT *YOU THINK*, CUDGEON.
BUT THE RECORDING OF *EVERYTHING* YOU JUST SAID MIGHT SAY OTHERWISE.

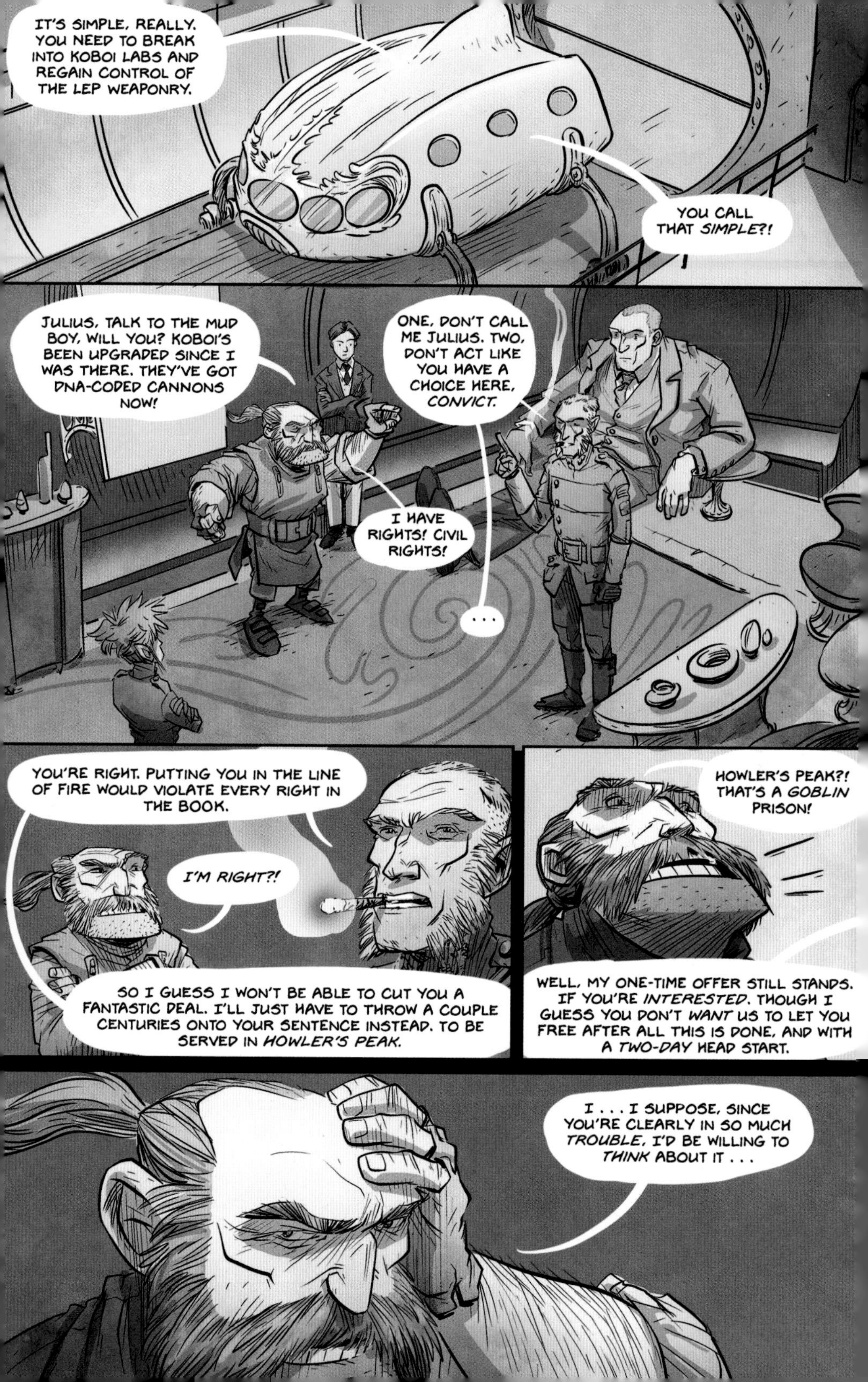
IT'S SIMPLE, REALLY. YOU NEED TO BREAK INTO KOBOI LABS AND REGAIN CONTROL OF THE LEP WEAPONRY.
YOU CALL THAT *SIMPLE?!*
JULIUS, TALK TO THE MUD BOY, WILL YOU? KOBOI'S BEEN UPGRADED SINCE I WAS THERE. THEY'VE GOT DNA-CODED CANNONS NOW!
ONE, DON'T CALL ME JULIUS. TWO, DON'T ACT LIKE YOU HAVE A CHOICE HERE, *CONVICT.*
I HAVE RIGHTS! CIVIL RIGHTS!
. . .
YOU'RE RIGHT. PUTTING YOU IN THE LINE OF FIRE WOULD VIOLATE EVERY RIGHT IN THE BOOK.
I'M RIGHT?!
SO I GUESS I WON'T BE ABLE TO CUT YOU A FANTASTIC DEAL. I'LL JUST HAVE TO THROW A COUPLE CENTURIES ONTO YOUR SENTENCE INSTEAD. TO BE SERVED IN *HOWLER'S PEAK.*
HOWLER'S PEAK?! THAT'S A *GOBLIN* PRISON!
WELL, MY ONE-TIME OFFER STILL STANDS. IF YOU'RE *INTERESTED*. THOUGH I GUESS YOU DON'T *WANT* US TO LET YOU FREE AFTER ALL THIS IS DONE, AND WITH A *TWO-DAY* HEAD START.
I . . . I SUPPOSE, SINCE YOU'RE CLEARLY IN SO MUCH *TROUBLE*, I'D BE WILLING TO *THINK* ABOUT IT . . .

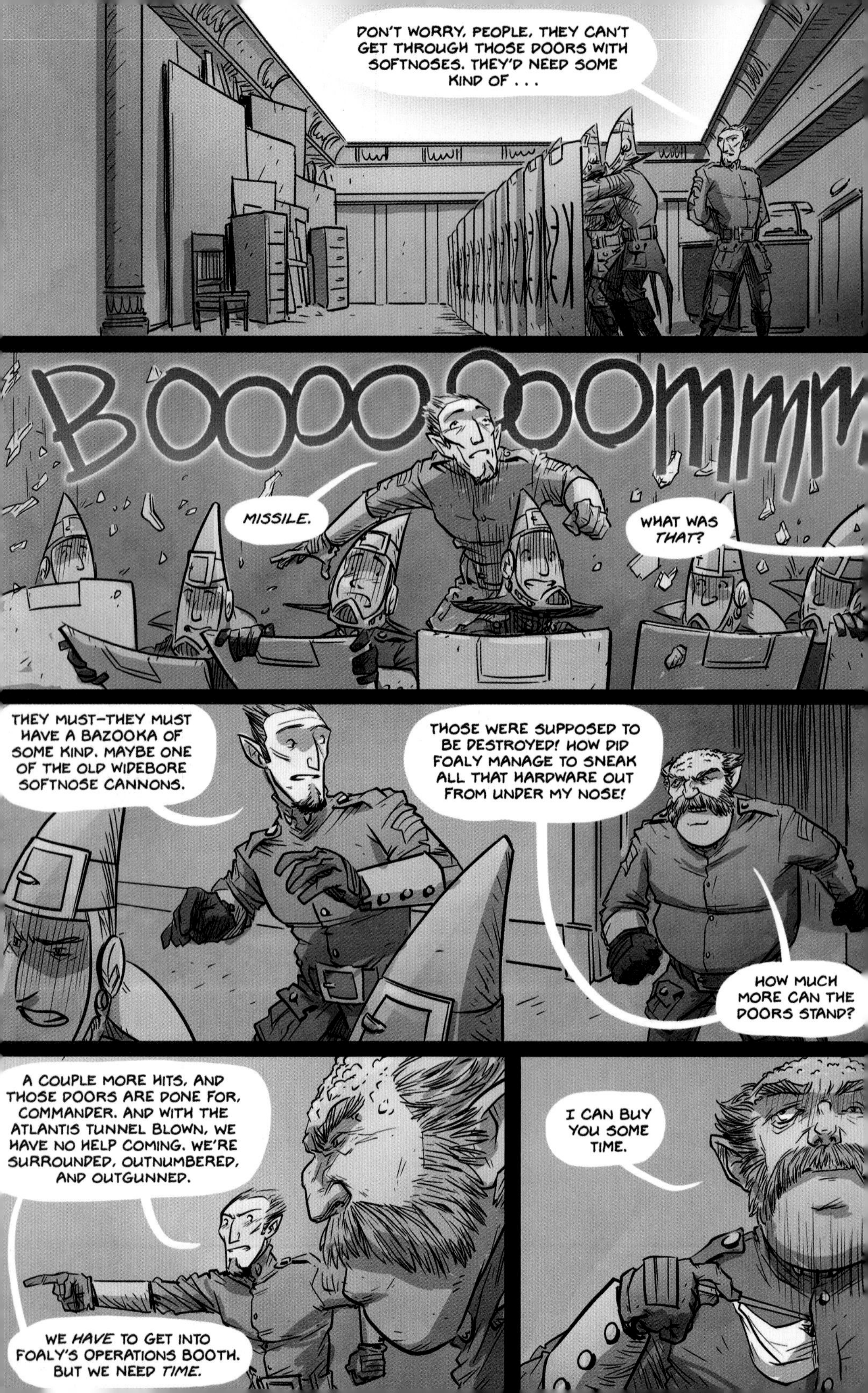
DON'T WORRY, PEOPLE, THEY CAN'T GET THROUGH THOSE DOORS WITH SOFTNOSES. THEY'D NEED SOME KIND OF . . .
BOOOOOOOMMM
MISSILE.
WHAT WAS *THAT*?
THEY MUST—THEY MUST HAVE A BAZOOKA OF SOME KIND. MAYBE ONE OF THE OLD WIDEBORE SOFTNOSE CANNONS.
THOSE WERE SUPPOSED TO BE DESTROYED! HOW DID FOALY MANAGE TO SNEAK ALL THAT HARDWARE OUT FROM UNDER MY NOSE!
HOW MUCH MORE CAN THE DOORS STAND?
A COUPLE MORE HITS, AND THOSE DOORS ARE DONE FOR, COMMANDER. AND WITH THE ATLANTIS TUNNEL BLOWN, WE HAVE NO HELP COMING. WE'RE SURROUNDED, OUTNUMBERED, AND OUTGUNNED.
WE *HAVE* TO GET INTO FOALY'S OPERATIONS BOOTH. BUT WE NEED *TIME*.
I CAN BUY YOU SOME TIME.

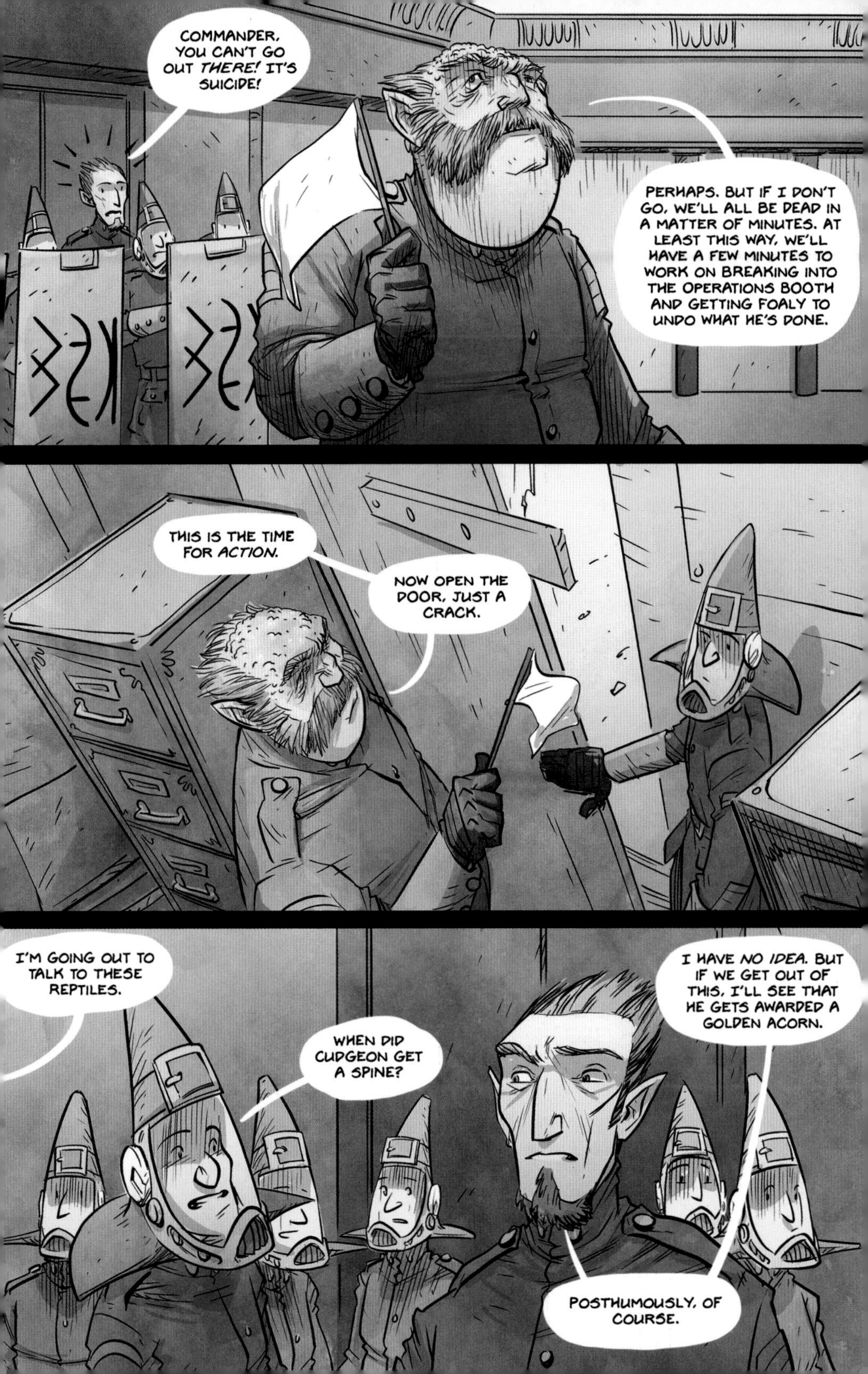
COMMANDER, YOU CAN'T GO OUT *THERE!* IT'S SUICIDE!
PERHAPS. BUT IF I DON'T GO, WE'LL ALL BE DEAD IN A MATTER OF MINUTES. AT LEAST THIS WAY, WE'LL HAVE A FEW MINUTES TO WORK ON BREAKING INTO THE OPERATIONS BOOTH AND GETTING FOALY TO UNDO WHAT HE'S DONE.
THIS IS THE TIME FOR *ACTION*.
NOW OPEN THE DOOR, JUST A CRACK.
I'M GOING OUT TO TALK TO THESE REPTILES.
WHEN DID CUDGEON GET A SPINE?
I HAVE *NO IDEA*. BUT IF WE GET OUT OF THIS, I'LL SEE THAT HE GETS AWARDED A GOLDEN ACORN.
POSTHUMOUSLY, OF COURSE.

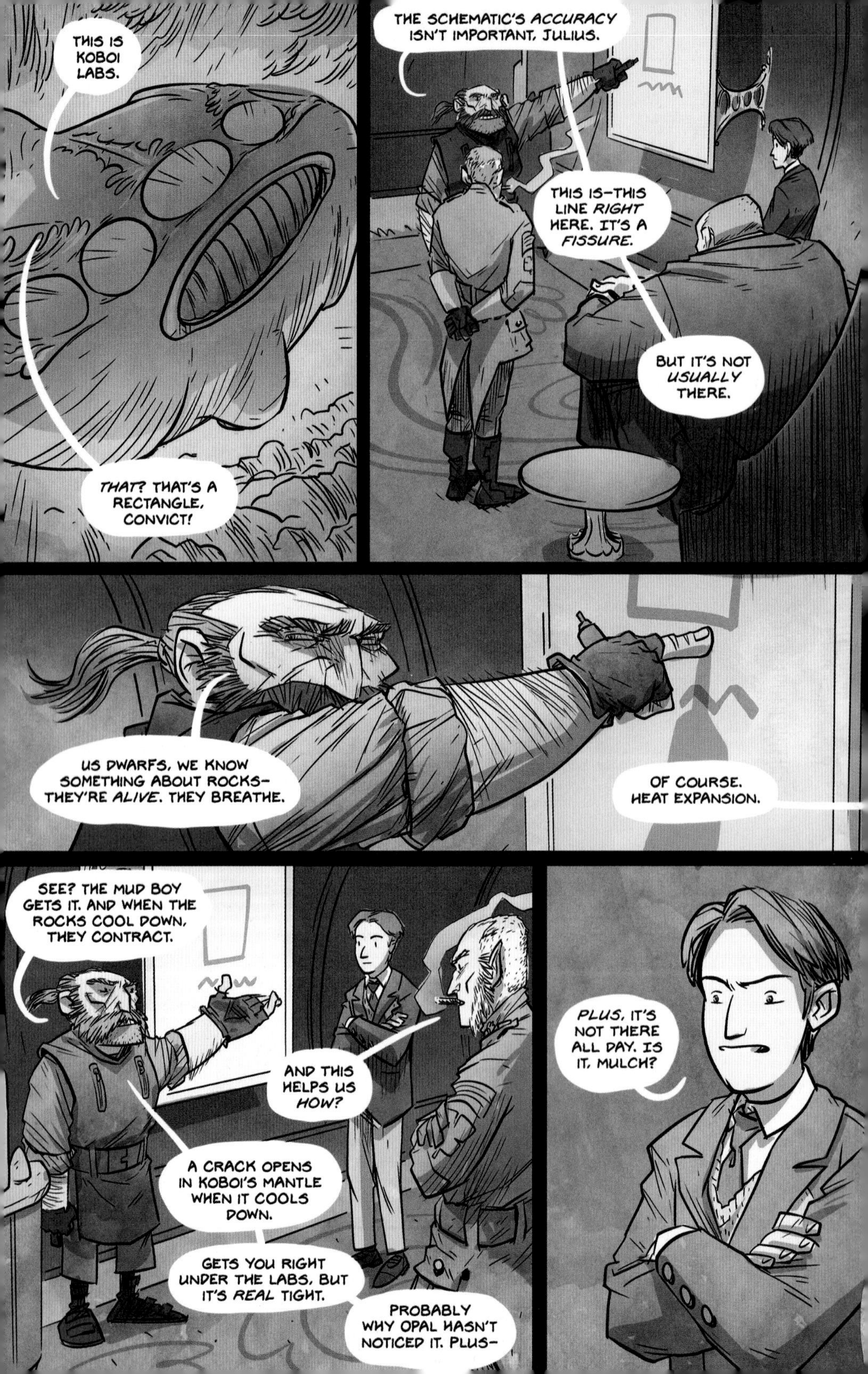

THIS IS KOBOI LABS.
THAT? THAT'S A RECTANGLE, CONVICT!
THE SCHEMATIC'S *ACCURACY* ISN'T IMPORTANT, JULIUS.
THIS IS—THIS LINE *RIGHT* HERE. IT'S A *FISSURE*.
BUT IT'S NOT *USUALLY* THERE.
US DWARFS, WE KNOW SOMETHING ABOUT ROCKS—THEY'RE *ALIVE*. THEY BREATHE.
OF COURSE. HEAT EXPANSION.
SEE? THE MUD BOY GETS IT. AND WHEN THE ROCKS COOL DOWN, THEY CONTRACT.
AND THIS HELPS US *HOW*?
A CRACK OPENS IN KOBOI'S MANTLE WHEN IT COOLS DOWN.
GETS YOU RIGHT UNDER THE LABS, BUT IT'S *REAL* TIGHT.
PROBABLY WHY OPAL HASN'T NOTICED IT. PLUS—
PLUS, IT'S NOT THERE ALL DAY. IS IT, MULCH?

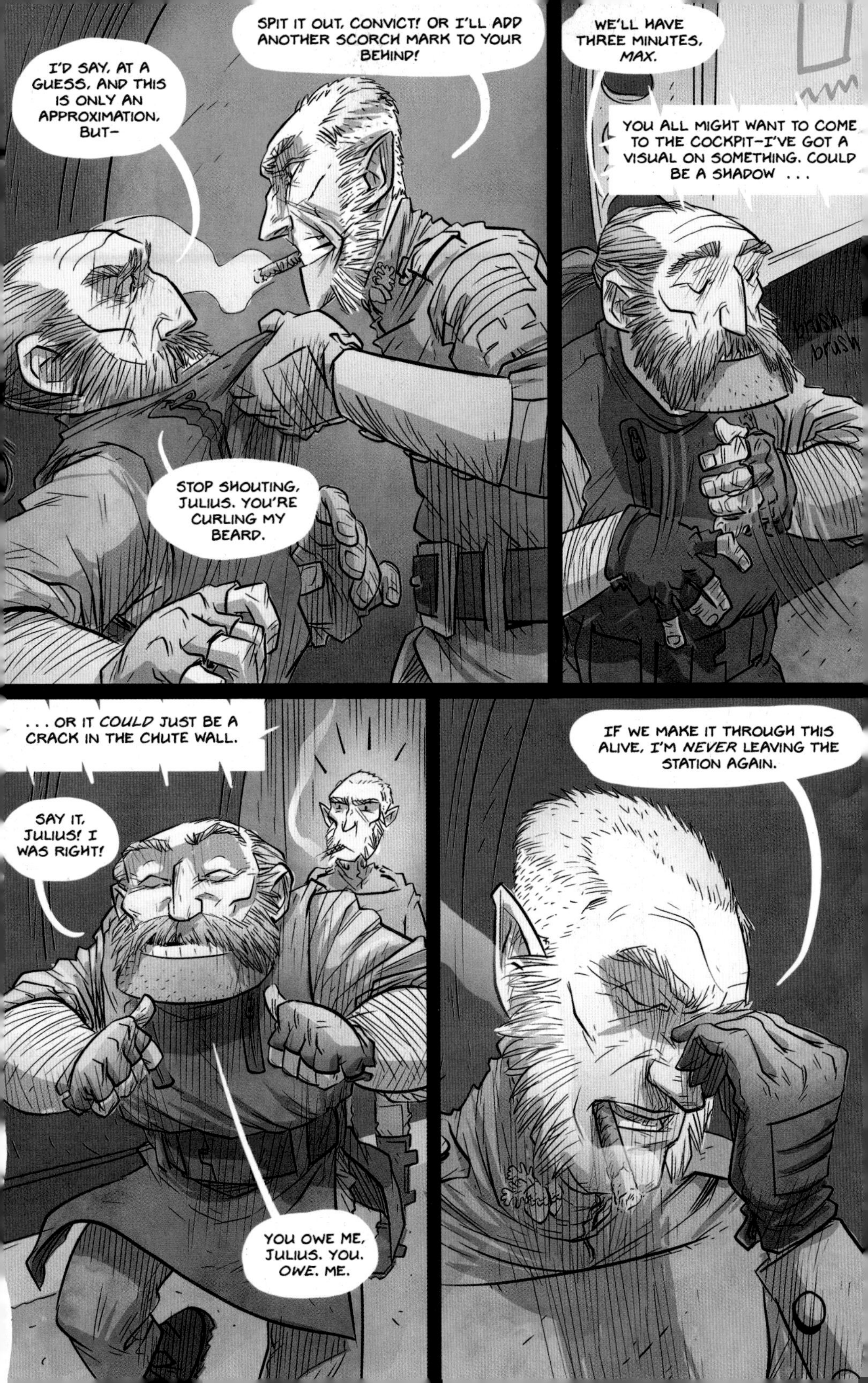
I'D SAY, AT A GUESS, AND THIS IS ONLY AN APPROXIMATION, BUT–
SPIT IT OUT, CONVICT! OR I'LL ADD ANOTHER SCORCH MARK TO YOUR BEHIND!
STOP SHOUTING, JULIUS. YOU'RE CURLING MY BEARD.
WE'LL HAVE THREE MINUTES, *MAX.*
YOU ALL MIGHT WANT TO COME TO THE COCKPIT–I'VE GOT A VISUAL ON SOMETHING. COULD BE A SHADOW . . .
brush brush
. . . OR IT *COULD* JUST BE A CRACK IN THE CHUTE WALL.
SAY IT, JULIUS! I WAS RIGHT!
YOU OWE ME, JULIUS. YOU. *OWE.* ME.
IF WE MAKE IT THROUGH THIS ALIVE, I'M *NEVER* LEAVING THE STATION AGAIN.

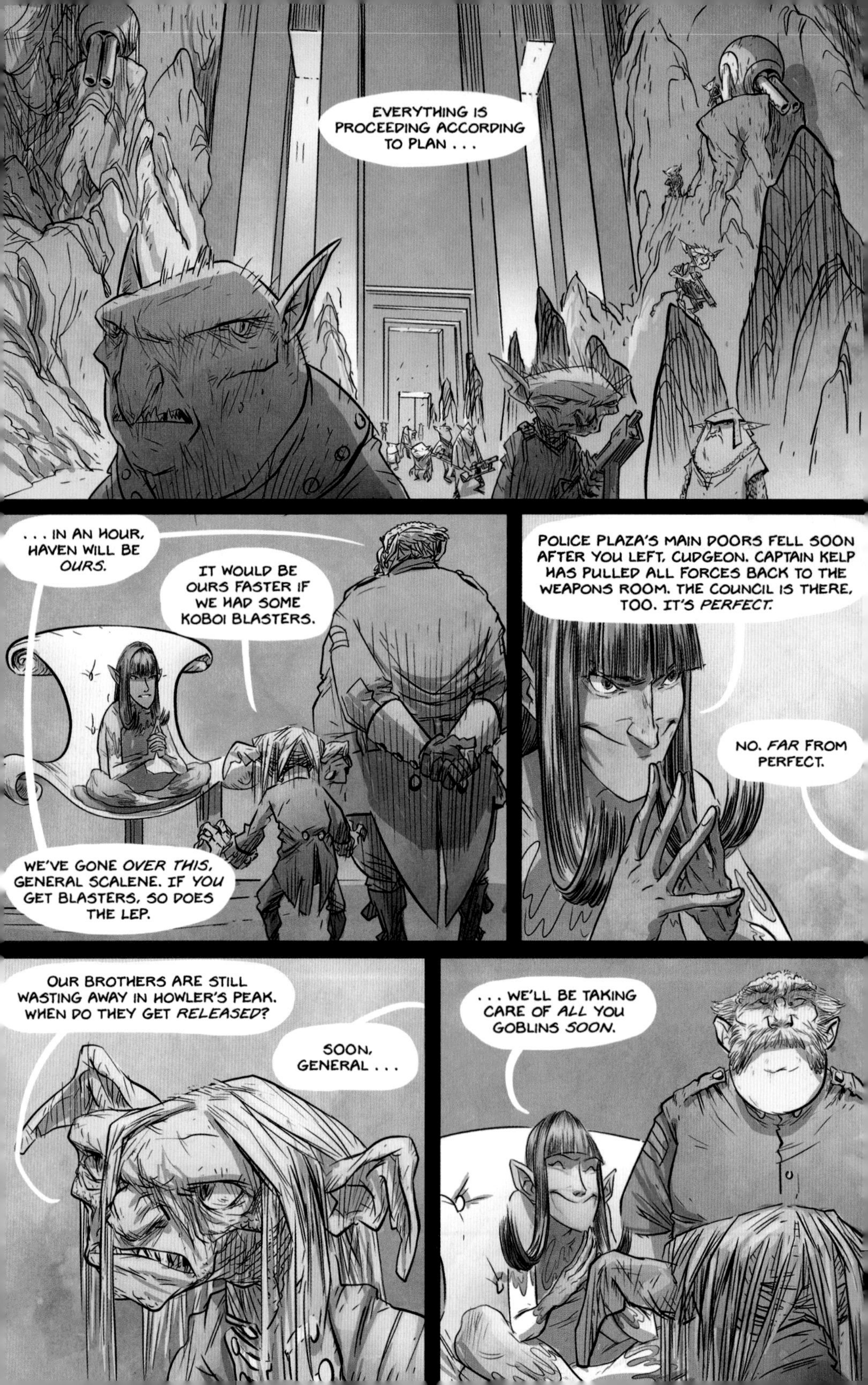
EVERYTHING IS PROCEEDING ACCORDING TO PLAN . . .
. . . IN AN HOUR, HAVEN WILL BE *OURS.*
IT WOULD BE OURS FASTER IF WE HAD SOME KOBOI BLASTERS.
WE'VE GONE *OVER THIS,* GENERAL SCALENE. IF *YOU* GET BLASTERS, SO DOES THE LEP.
POLICE PLAZA'S MAIN DOORS FELL SOON AFTER YOU LEFT, CUDGEON. CAPTAIN KELP HAS PULLED ALL FORCES BACK TO THE WEAPONS ROOM. THE COUNCIL IS THERE, TOO. IT'S *PERFECT.*
NO. *FAR* FROM PERFECT.
OUR BROTHERS ARE STILL WASTING AWAY IN HOWLER'S PEAK. WHEN DO THEY GET *RELEASED?*
SOON, GENERAL . . .
. . . WE'LL BE TAKING CARE OF *ALL* YOU GOBLINS *SOON.*

CHAPTER THIRTEEN

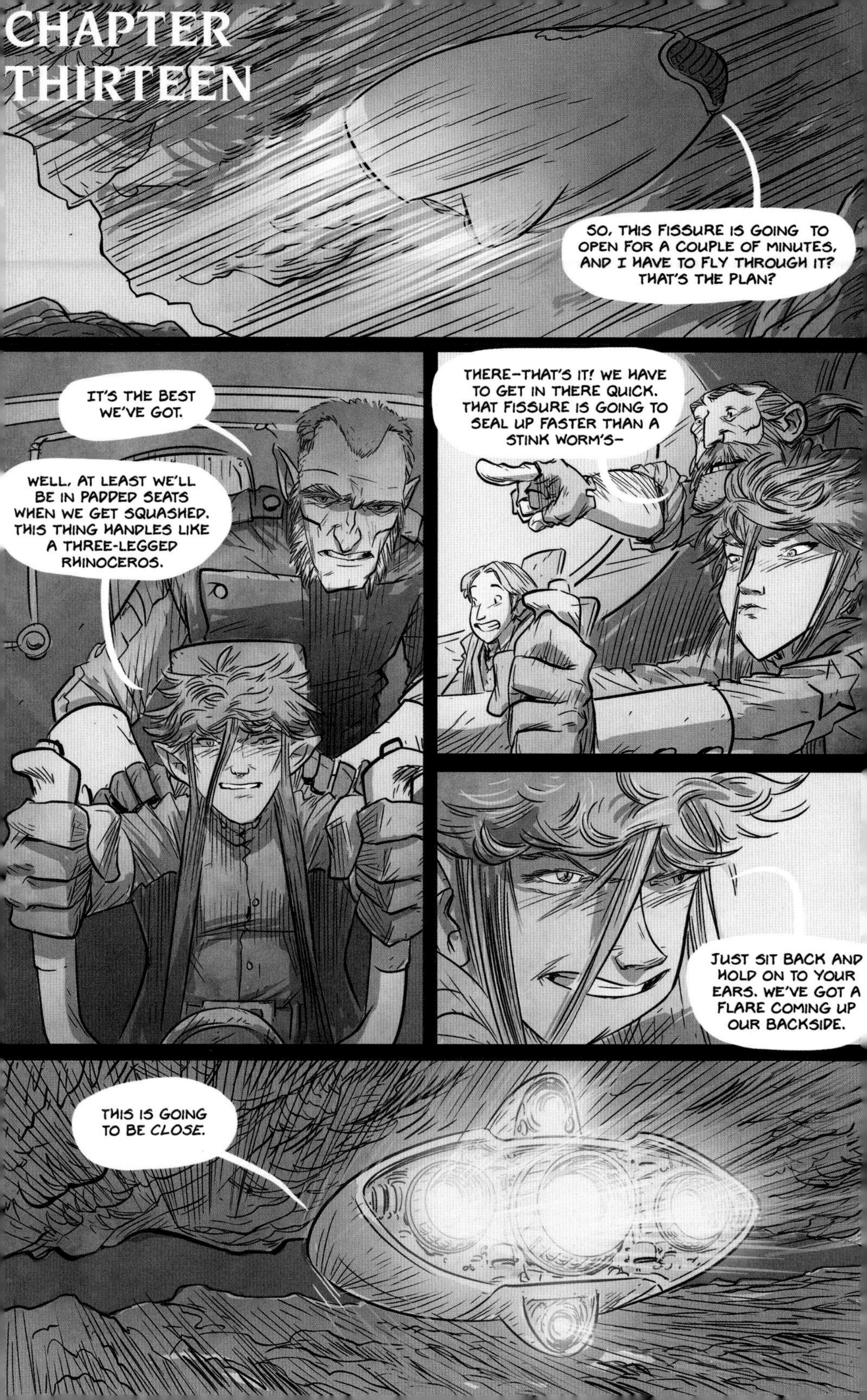
SO, THIS FISSURE IS GOING TO OPEN FOR A COUPLE OF MINUTES, AND I HAVE TO FLY THROUGH IT? THAT'S THE PLAN?
IT'S THE BEST WE'VE GOT.
WELL, AT LEAST WE'LL BE IN PADDED SEATS WHEN WE GET SQUASHED. THIS THING HANDLES LIKE A THREE-LEGGED RHINOCEROS.
THERE—THAT'S IT! WE HAVE TO GET IN THERE QUICK. THAT FISSURE IS GOING TO SEAL UP FASTER THAN A STINK WORM'S—
JUST SIT BACK AND HOLD ON TO YOUR EARS. WE'VE GOT A FLARE COMING UP OUR BACKSIDE.
THIS IS GOING TO BE *CLOSE*.

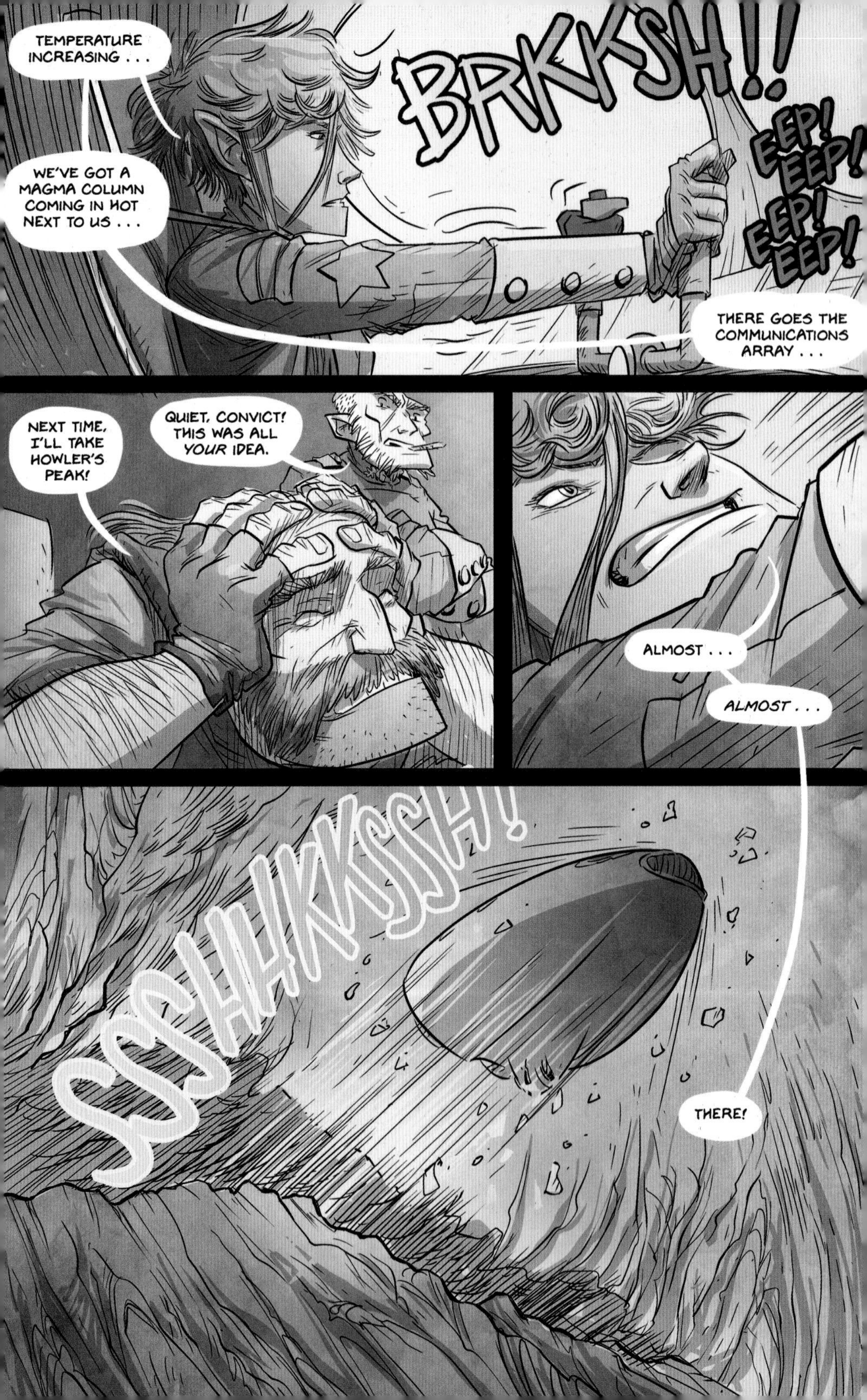
TEMPERATURE INCREASING . . .
BRKKSH!!
EEP! EEP! EEP! EEP!
WE'VE GOT A MAGMA COLUMN COMING IN HOT NEXT TO US . . .
THERE GOES THE COMMUNICATIONS ARRAY . . .
NEXT TIME, I'LL TAKE HOWLER'S PEAK!
QUIET, CONVICT! THIS WAS ALL YOUR IDEA.
ALMOST . . .
ALMOST . . .
SSSHHKKSSH!
THERE!

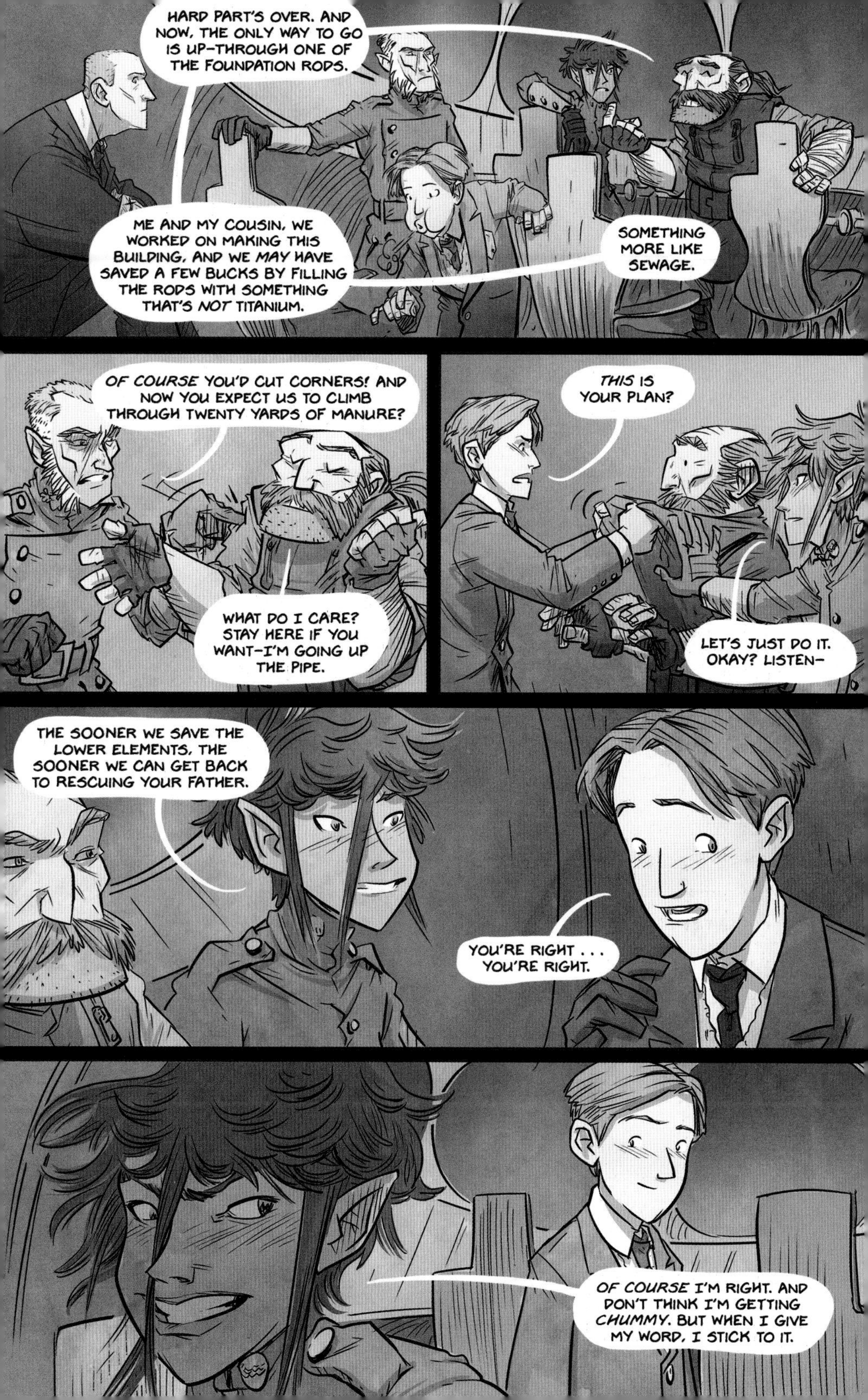
HARD PART'S OVER. AND NOW, THE ONLY WAY TO GO IS UP—THROUGH ONE OF THE FOUNDATION RODS.
ME AND MY COUSIN, WE WORKED ON MAKING THIS BUILDING, AND WE *MAY* HAVE SAVED A FEW BUCKS BY FILLING THE RODS WITH SOMETHING THAT'S *NOT* TITANIUM.
SOMETHING MORE LIKE SEWAGE.
OF COURSE YOU'D CUT CORNERS! AND NOW YOU EXPECT US TO CLIMB THROUGH TWENTY YARDS OF MANURE?
WHAT DO I CARE? STAY HERE IF YOU WANT—I'M GOING UP THE PIPE.
THIS IS YOUR PLAN?
LET'S JUST DO IT. OKAY? LISTEN—
THE SOONER WE SAVE THE LOWER ELEMENTS, THE SOONER WE CAN GET BACK TO RESCUING YOUR FATHER.
YOU'RE RIGHT . . . YOU'RE RIGHT.
OF COURSE I'M RIGHT. AND DON'T THINK I'M GETTING *CHUMMY*. BUT WHEN I GIVE MY WORD, I STICK TO IT.

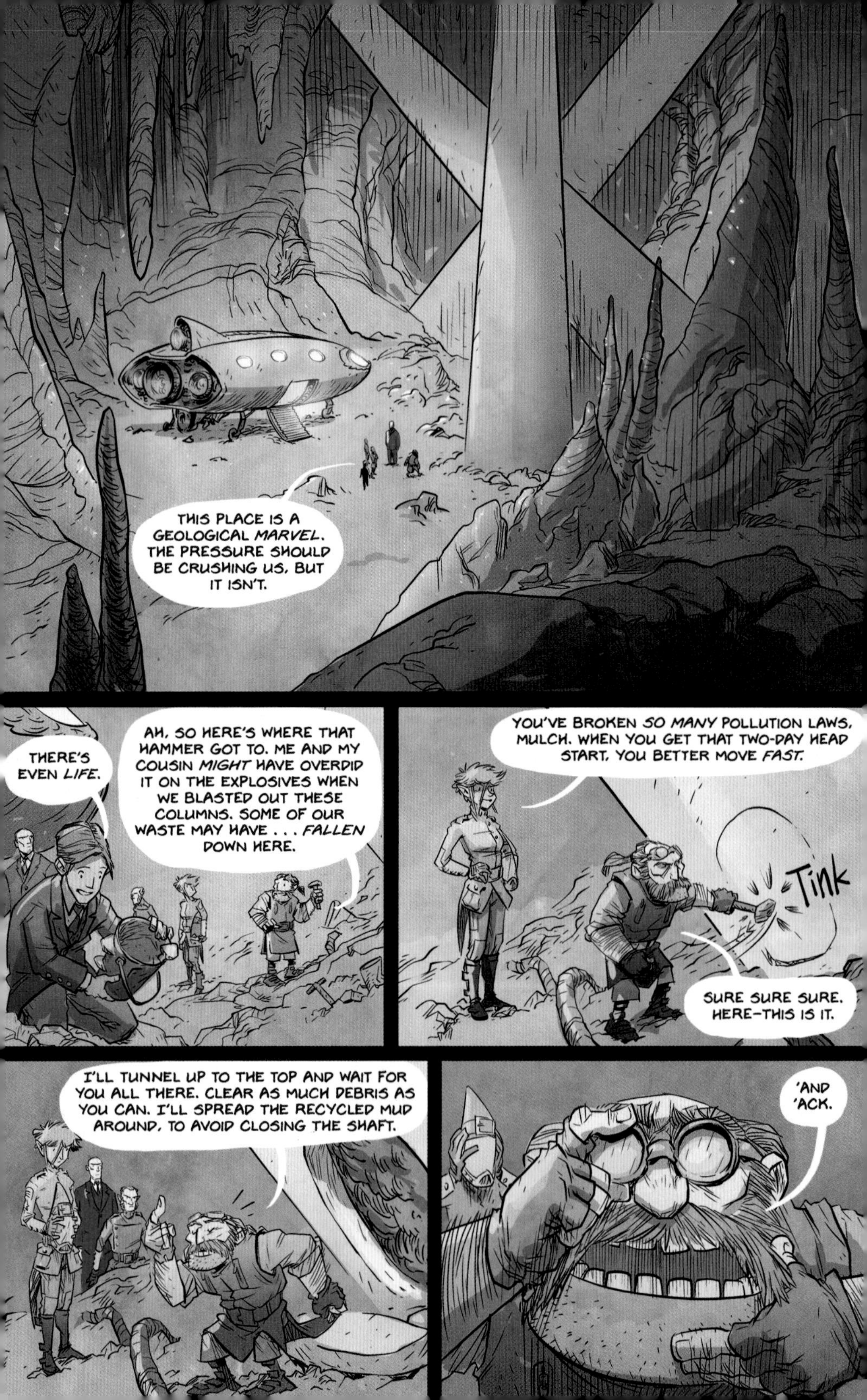
THIS PLACE IS A GEOLOGICAL *MARVEL*. THE PRESSURE SHOULD BE CRUSHING US, BUT IT ISN'T.
THERE'S EVEN *LIFE*.
AH, SO HERE'S WHERE THAT HAMMER GOT TO. ME AND MY COUSIN *MIGHT* HAVE OVERDID IT ON THE EXPLOSIVES WHEN WE BLASTED OUT THESE COLUMNS. SOME OF OUR WASTE MAY HAVE . . . *FALLEN* DOWN HERE.
YOU'VE BROKEN *SO MANY* POLLUTION LAWS, MULCH. WHEN YOU GET THAT TWO-DAY HEAD START, YOU BETTER MOVE *FAST*.
TINK
SURE SURE SURE. HERE—THIS IS IT.
I'LL TUNNEL UP TO THE TOP AND WAIT FOR YOU ALL THERE. CLEAR AS MUCH DEBRIS AS YOU CAN. I'LL SPREAD THE RECYCLED MUD AROUND, TO AVOID CLOSING THE SHAFT.
'AND 'ACK.

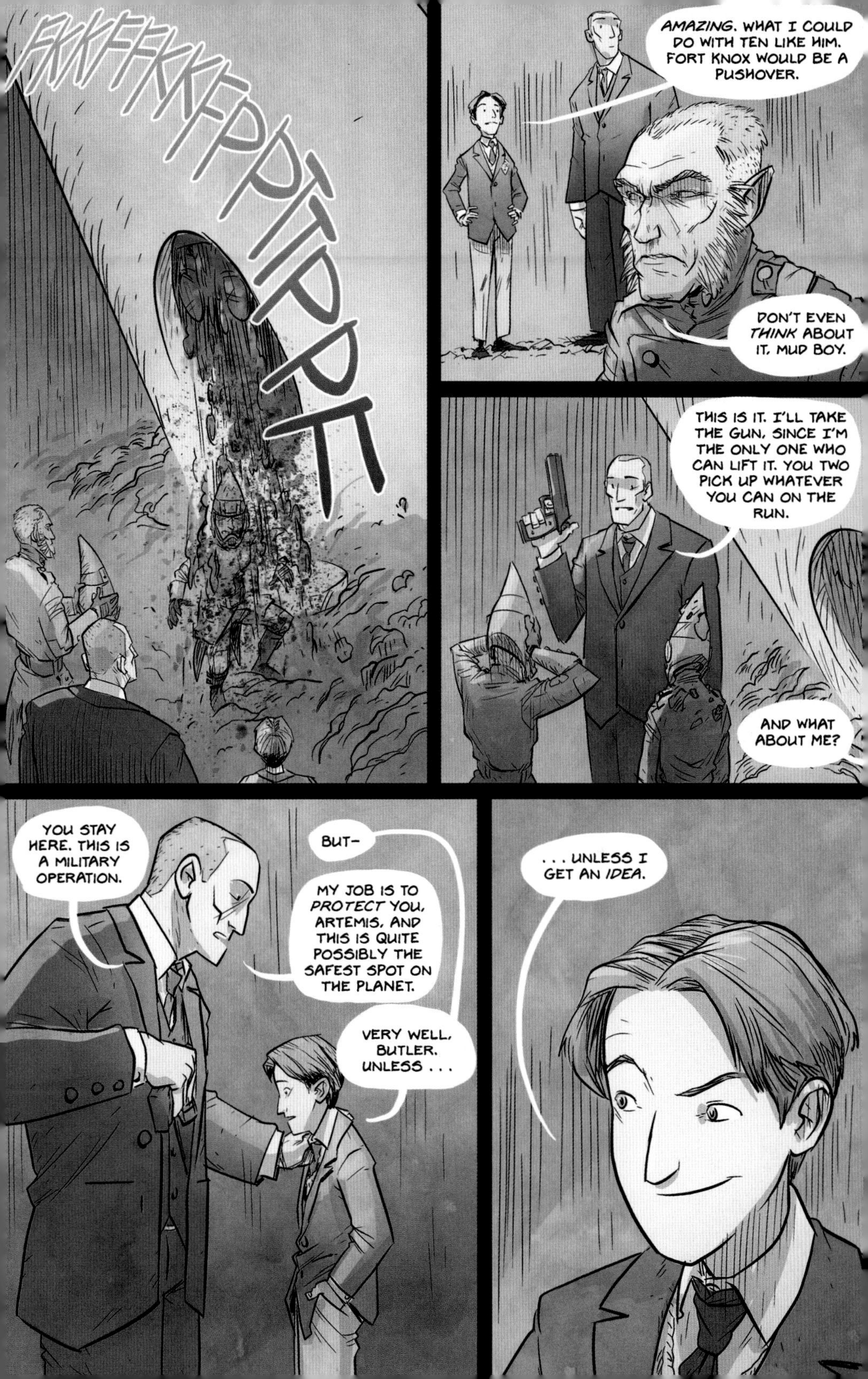
FKKFFKKFFPPTTPPTT
AMAZING. WHAT I COULD DO WITH TEN LIKE HIM. FORT KNOX WOULD BE A PUSHOVER.
DON'T EVEN THINK ABOUT IT, MUD BOY.
THIS IS IT. I'LL TAKE THE GUN, SINCE I'M THE ONLY ONE WHO CAN LIFT IT. YOU TWO PICK UP WHATEVER YOU CAN ON THE RUN.
AND WHAT ABOUT ME?
YOU STAY HERE. THIS IS A MILITARY OPERATION.
BUT–
MY JOB IS TO PROTECT YOU, ARTEMIS, AND THIS IS QUITE POSSIBLY THE SAFEST SPOT ON THE PLANET.
VERY WELL, BUTLER. UNLESS . . .
. . . UNLESS I GET AN IDEA.

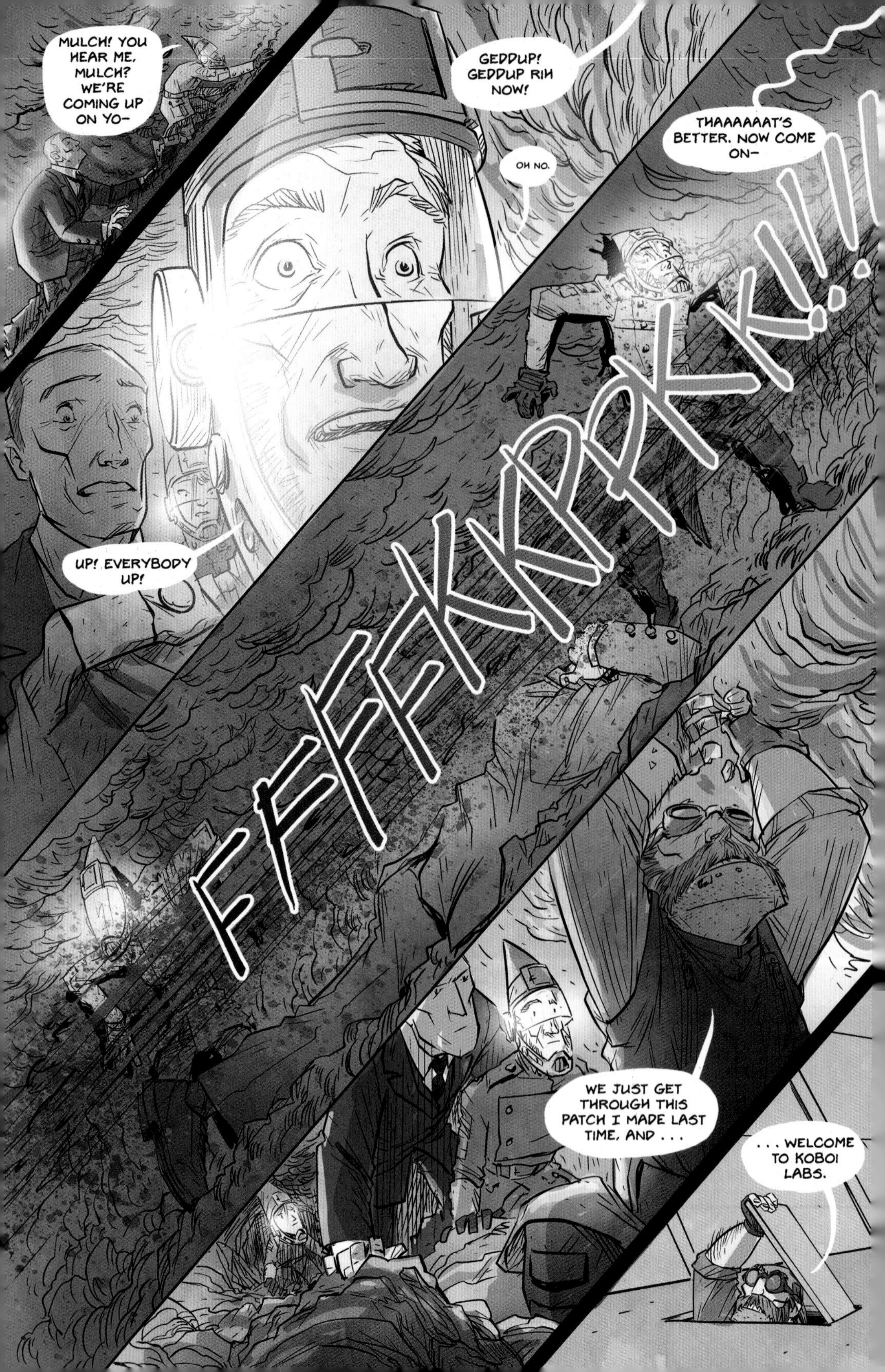
MULCH! YOU HEAR ME, MULCH? WE'RE COMING UP ON YO—
UP! EVERYBODY UP!
GEDDUP! GEDDUP RIH NOW!
OH NO.
THAAAAAAT'S BETTER. NOW COME ON—
FFFFKKRRRKK!!!!
WE JUST GET THROUGH THIS PATCH I MADE LAST TIME, AND . . .
. . . WELCOME TO KOBOI LABS.

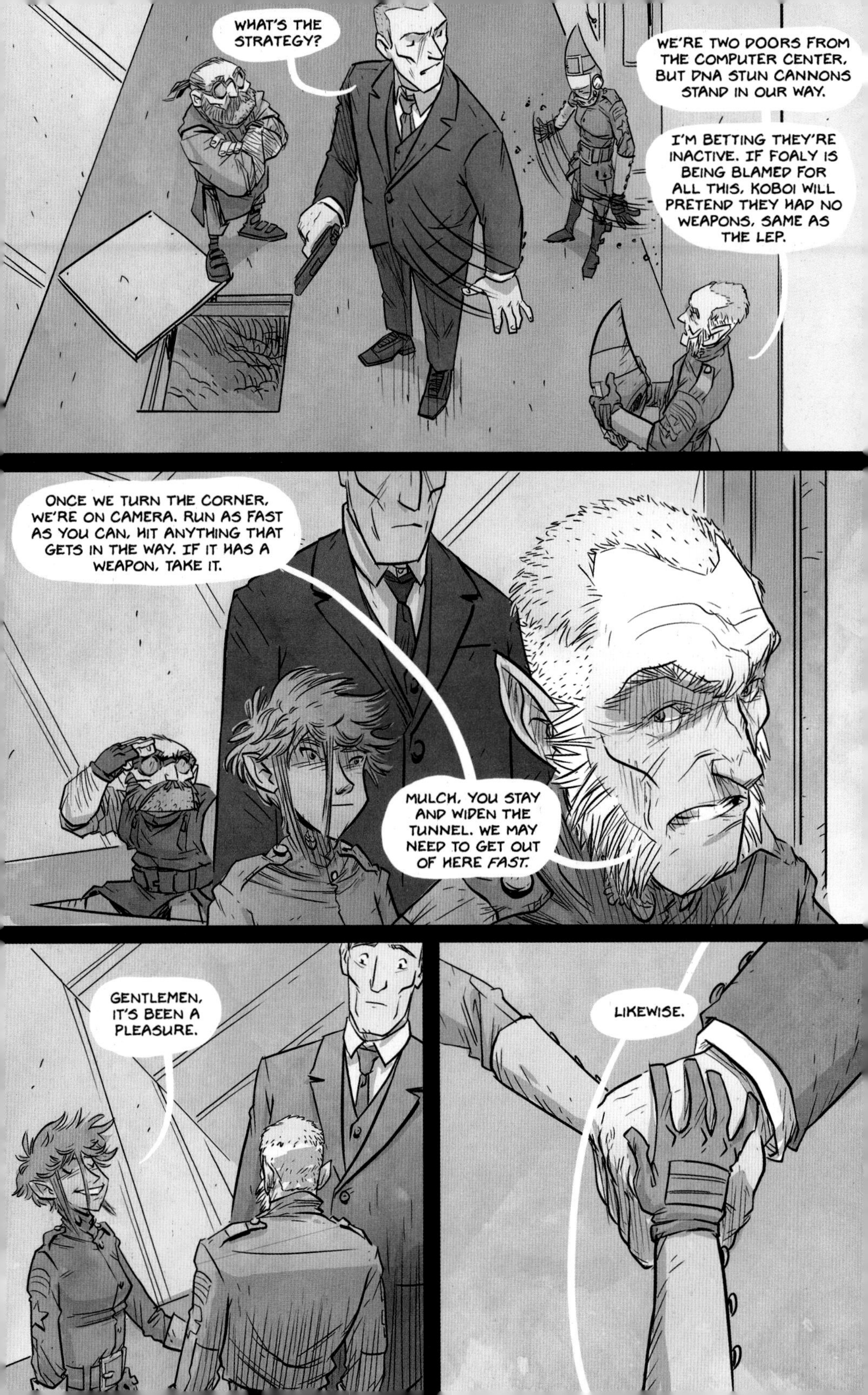
WHAT'S THE STRATEGY?
WE'RE TWO DOORS FROM THE COMPUTER CENTER, BUT DNA STUN CANNONS STAND IN OUR WAY.
I'M BETTING THEY'RE INACTIVE. IF FOALY IS BEING BLAMED FOR ALL THIS, KOBOI WILL PRETEND THEY HAD NO WEAPONS, SAME AS THE LEP.
ONCE WE TURN THE CORNER, WE'RE ON CAMERA. RUN AS FAST AS YOU CAN, HIT ANYTHING THAT GETS IN THE WAY. IF IT HAS A WEAPON, TAKE IT.
MULCH, YOU STAY AND WIDEN THE TUNNEL. WE MAY NEED TO GET OUT OF HERE *FAST.*
GENTLEMEN, IT'S BEEN A PLEASURE.
LIKEWISE.

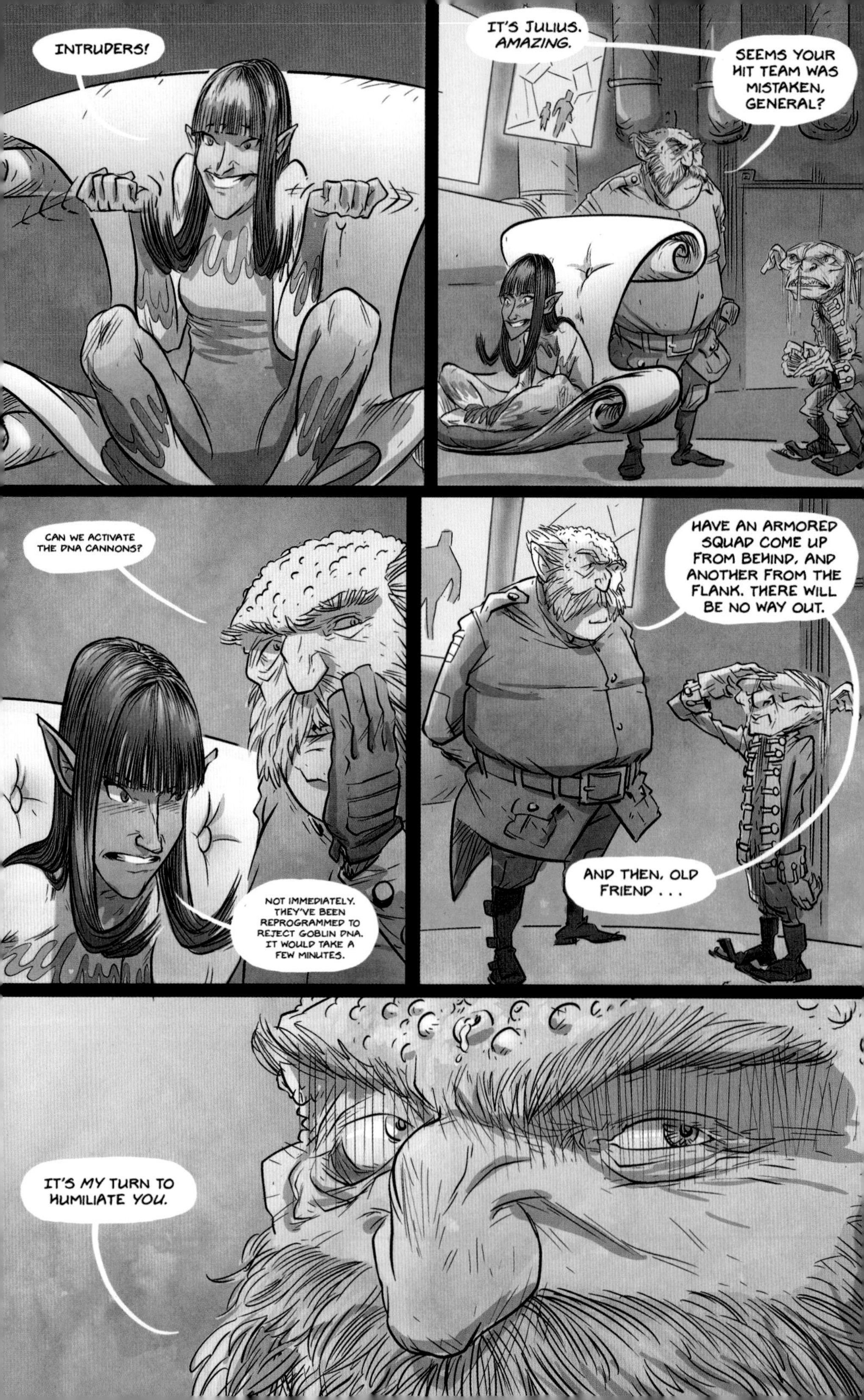
INTRUDERS!
IT'S JULIUS. AMAZING.
SEEMS YOUR HIT TEAM WAS MISTAKEN, GENERAL?
CAN WE ACTIVATE THE DNA CANNONS?
NOT IMMEDIATELY. THEY'VE BEEN REPROGRAMMED TO REJECT GOBLIN DNA. IT WOULD TAKE A FEW MINUTES.
HAVE AN ARMORED SQUAD COME UP FROM BEHIND, AND ANOTHER FROM THE FLANK. THERE WILL BE NO WAY OUT.
AND THEN, OLD FRIEND . . .
IT'S MY TURN TO HUMILIATE YOU.

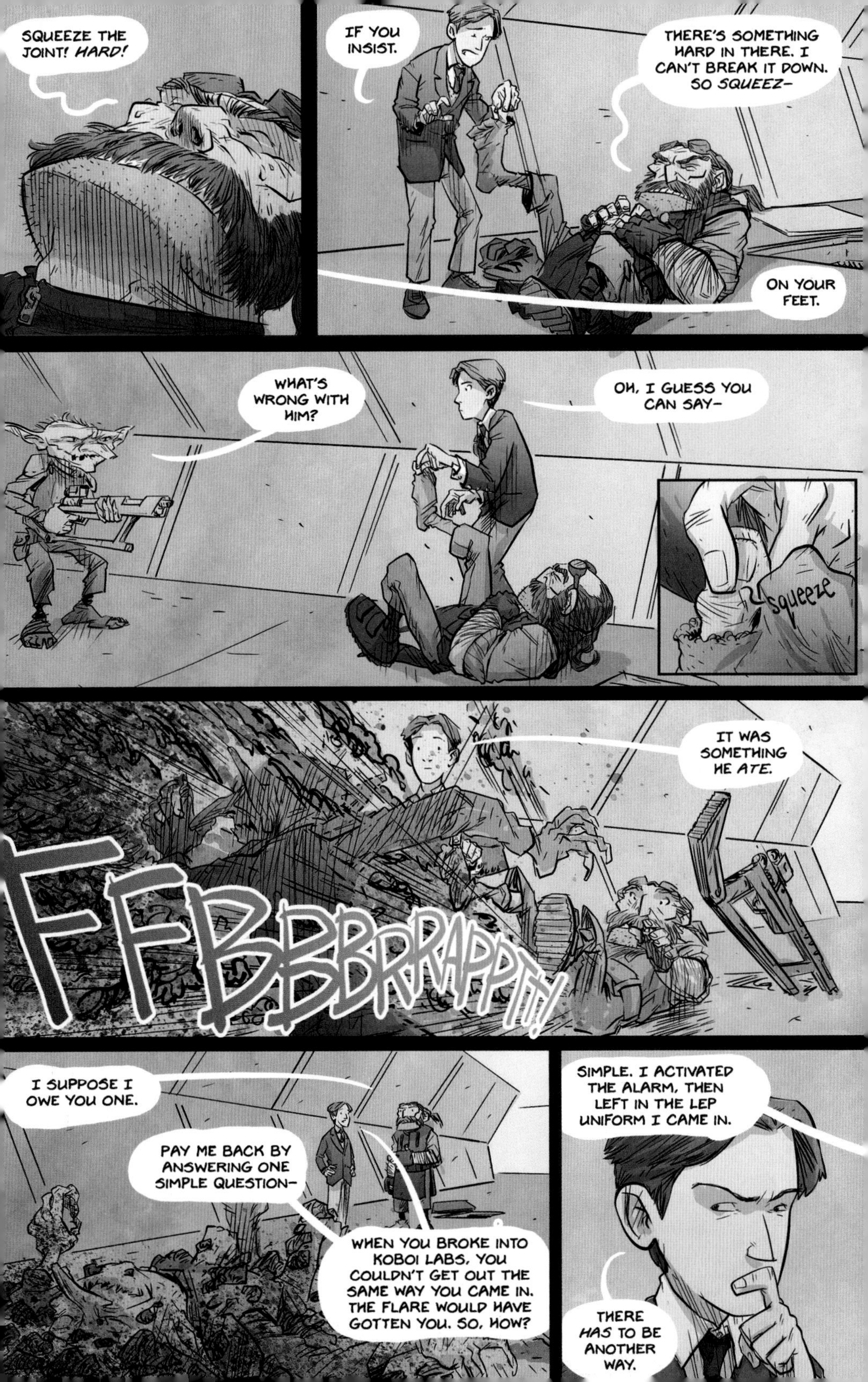
SQUEEZE THE JOINT! HARD!
IF YOU INSIST.
THERE'S SOMETHING HARD IN THERE. I CAN'T BREAK IT DOWN. SO SQUEEZ–
ON YOUR FEET.
WHAT'S WRONG WITH HIM?
OH, I GUESS YOU CAN SAY–
squeeze
FFBBBRRAPPTTT!
IT WAS SOMETHING HE ATE.
I SUPPOSE I OWE YOU ONE.
PAY ME BACK BY ANSWERING ONE SIMPLE QUESTION–
WHEN YOU BROKE INTO KOBOI LABS, YOU COULDN'T GET OUT THE SAME WAY YOU CAME IN. THE FLARE WOULD HAVE GOTTEN YOU. SO, HOW?
SIMPLE. I ACTIVATED THE ALARM, THEN LEFT IN THE LEP UNIFORM I CAME IN.
THERE HAS TO BE ANOTHER WAY.

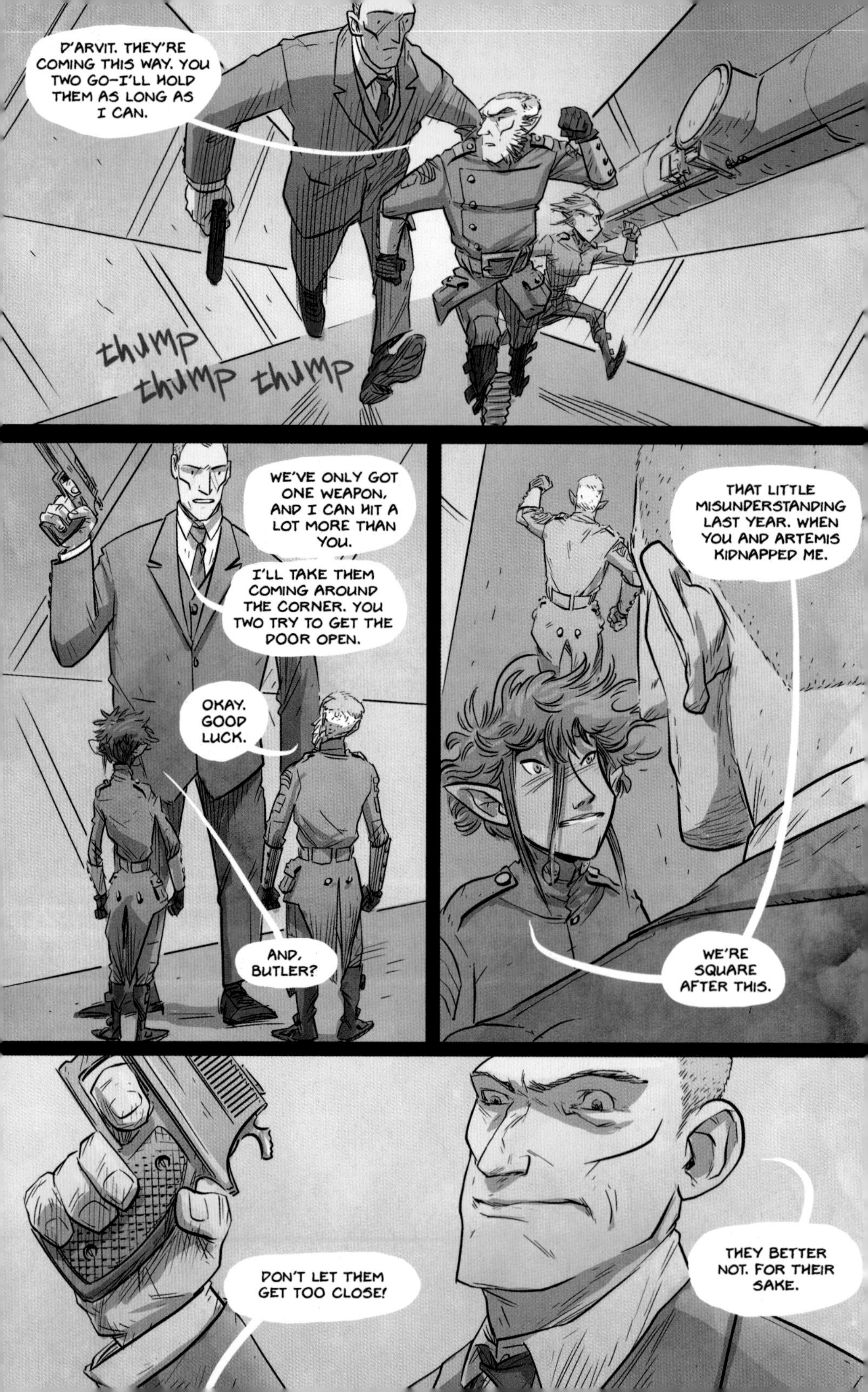
D'ARVIT. THEY'RE COMING THIS WAY. YOU TWO GO—I'LL HOLD THEM AS LONG AS I CAN.
thump thump thump
WE'VE ONLY GOT ONE WEAPON, AND I CAN HIT A LOT MORE THAN YOU.
I'LL TAKE THEM COMING AROUND THE CORNER. YOU TWO TRY TO GET THE DOOR OPEN.
OKAY. GOOD LUCK.
AND, BUTLER?
THAT LITTLE MISUNDERSTANDING LAST YEAR. WHEN YOU AND ARTEMIS KIDNAPPED ME.
WE'RE SQUARE AFTER THIS.
DON'T LET THEM GET TOO CLOSE!
THEY BETTER NOT. FOR THEIR SAKE.

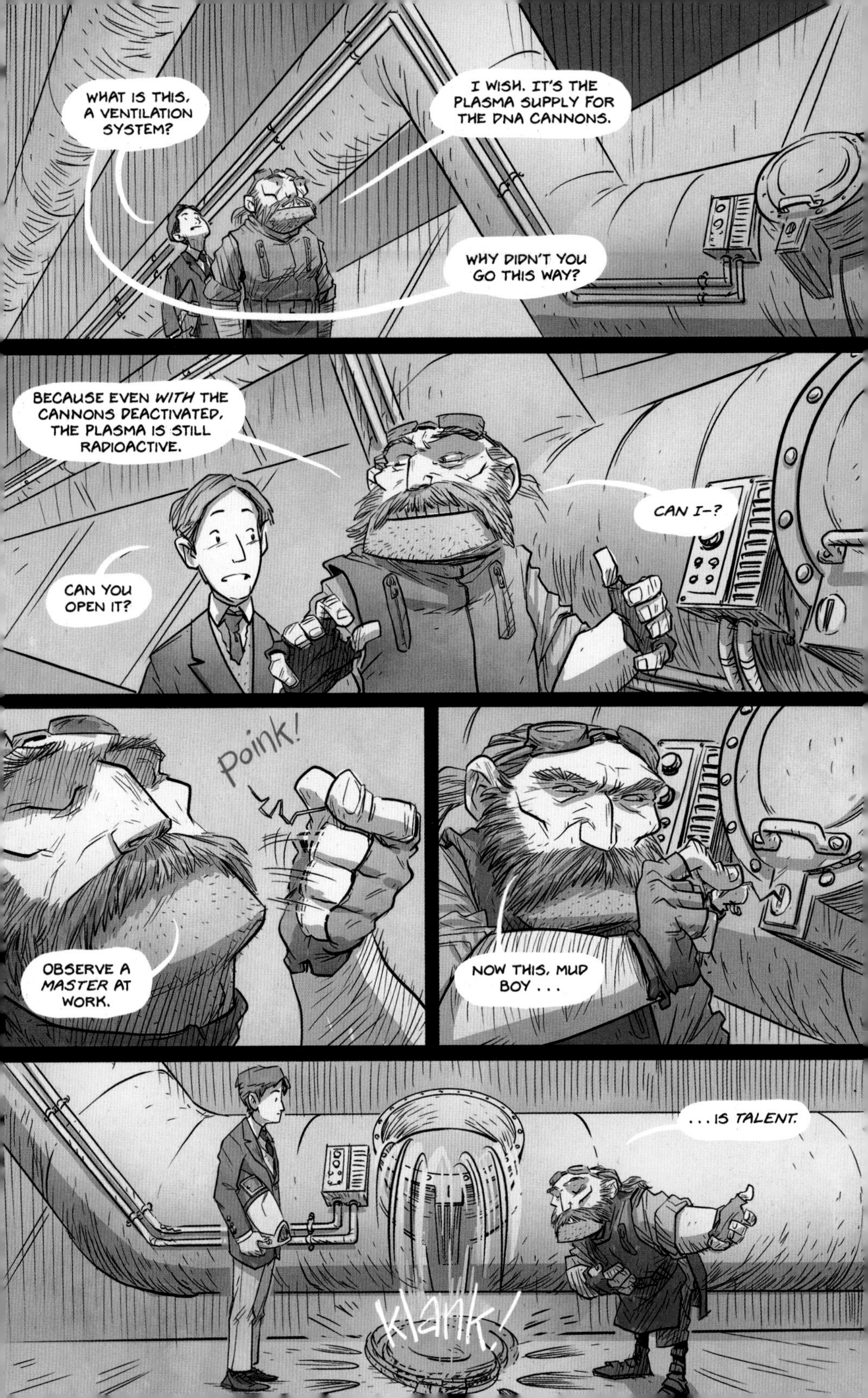
WHAT IS THIS, A VENTILATION SYSTEM?
I WISH. IT'S THE PLASMA SUPPLY FOR THE DNA CANNONS.
WHY DIDN'T YOU GO THIS WAY?
BECAUSE EVEN *WITH* THE CANNONS DEACTIVATED, THE PLASMA IS STILL RADIOACTIVE.
CAN YOU OPEN IT?
CAN I–?
Poink!
OBSERVE A *MASTER* AT WORK.
NOW THIS, MUD BOY . . .
. . . IS *TALENT.*
Klank!

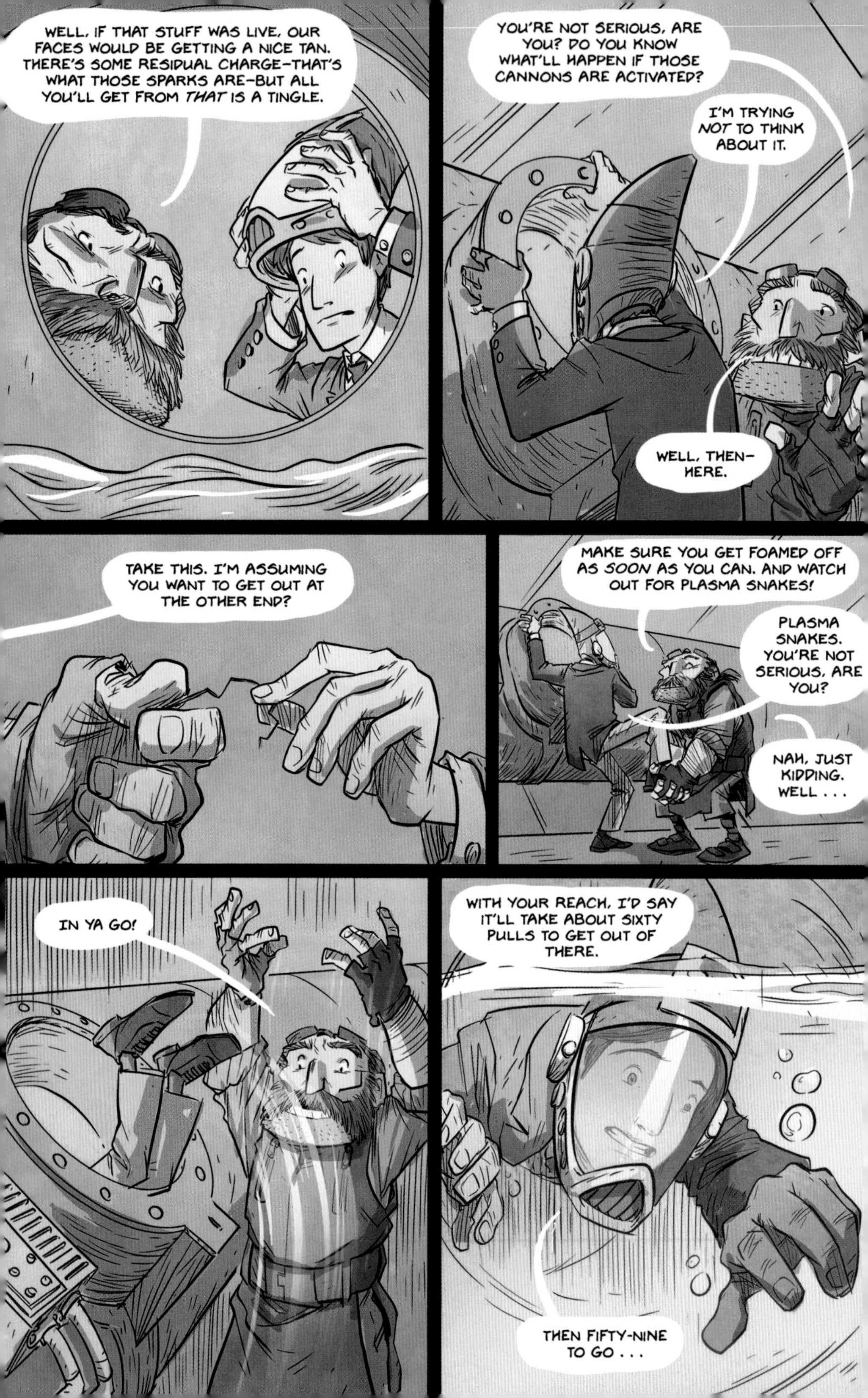

WELL, IF THAT STUFF WAS LIVE, OUR FACES WOULD BE GETTING A NICE TAN. THERE'S SOME RESIDUAL CHARGE—THAT'S WHAT THOSE SPARKS ARE—BUT ALL YOU'LL GET FROM *THAT* IS A TINGLE.
YOU'RE NOT SERIOUS, ARE YOU? DO YOU KNOW WHAT'LL HAPPEN IF THOSE CANNONS ARE ACTIVATED?
I'M TRYING *NOT* TO THINK ABOUT IT.
WELL, THEN— HERE.
TAKE THIS. I'M ASSUMING YOU WANT TO GET OUT AT THE OTHER END?
MAKE SURE YOU GET FOAMED OFF AS *SOON* AS YOU CAN. AND WATCH OUT FOR PLASMA SNAKES!
PLASMA SNAKES. YOU'RE NOT SERIOUS, ARE YOU?
NAH, JUST KIDDING. WELL . . .
IN YA GO!
WITH YOUR REACH, I'D SAY IT'LL TAKE ABOUT SIXTY PULLS TO GET OUT OF THERE.
THEN FIFTY-NINE TO GO . . .

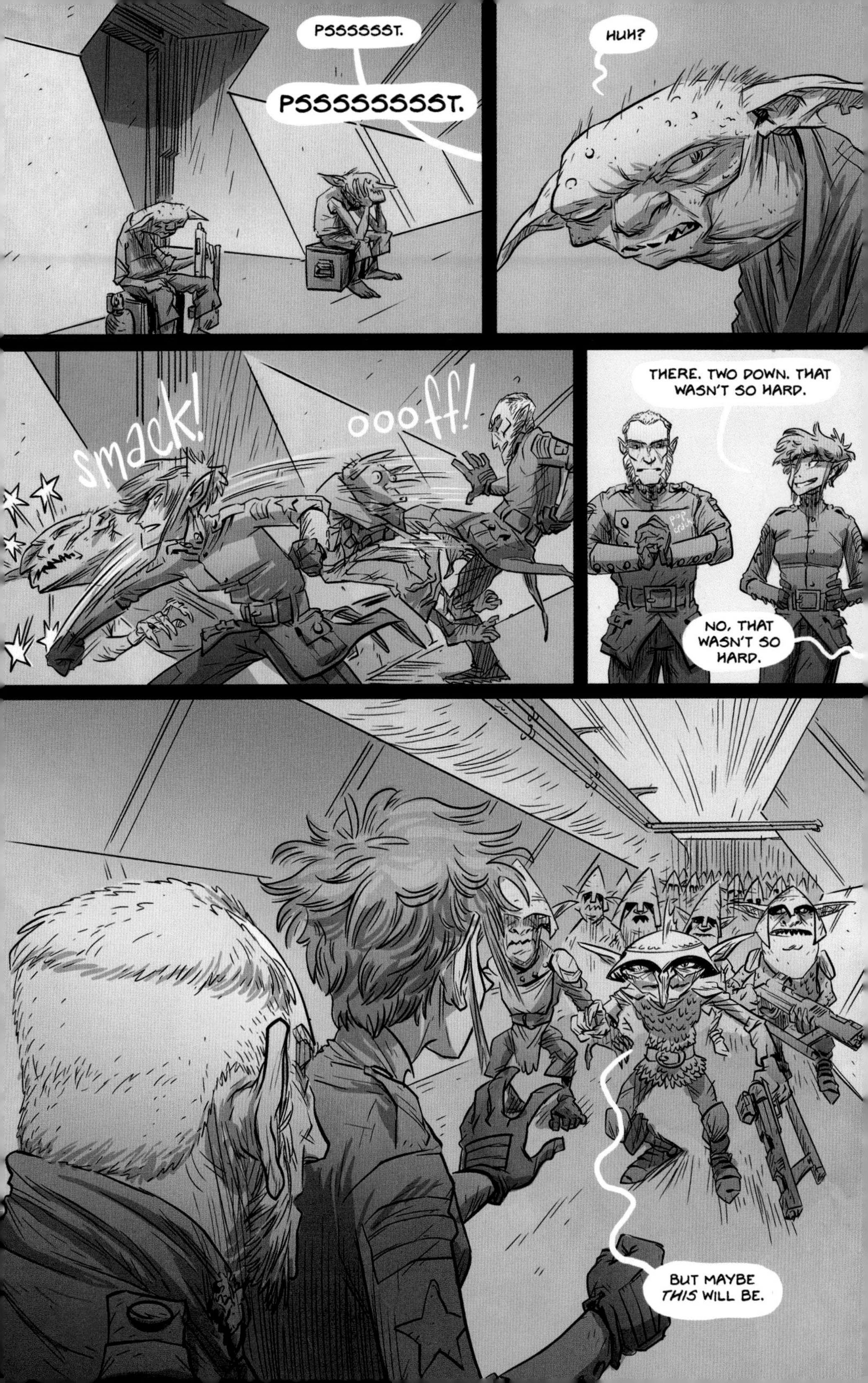
PSSSSSST.
PSSSSSSSST.
HUH?
smack!
oooff!
THERE. TWO DOWN. THAT WASN'T SO HARD.
NO, THAT WASN'T SO HARD.
BUT MAYBE *THIS* WILL BE.

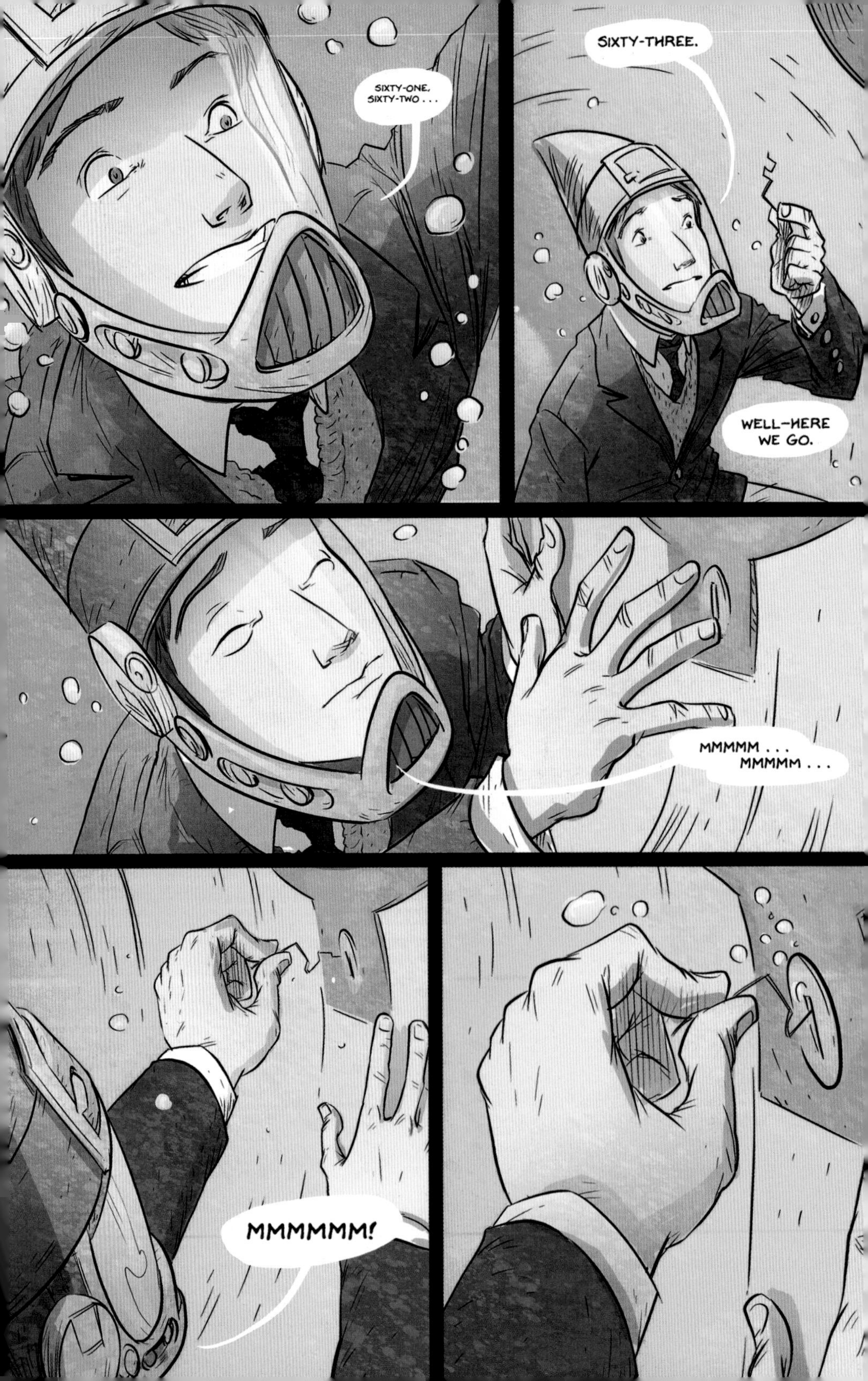
SIXTY-ONE,
SIXTY-TWO . . .
SIXTY-THREE.
WELL—HERE WE GO.
MMMMM . . . MMMMM . . .
MMMMMM!

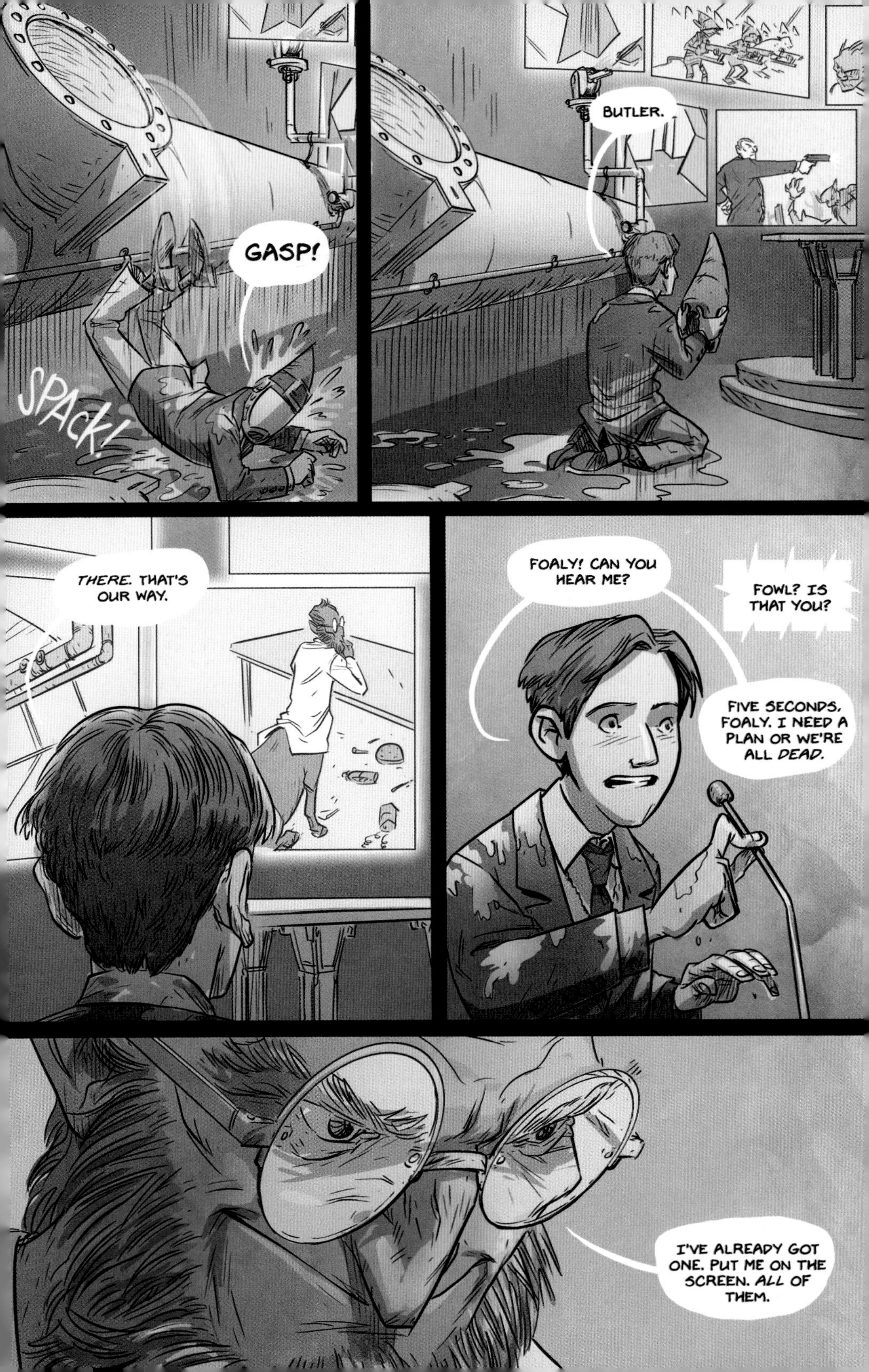
GASP!
SPACK!
BUTLER.
THERE. THAT'S OUR WAY.
FOALY! CAN YOU HEAR ME?
FOWL? IS THAT YOU?
FIVE SECONDS, FOALY. I NEED A PLAN OR WE'RE ALL *DEAD.*
I'VE ALREADY GOT ONE. PUT ME ON THE SCREEN. *ALL* OF THEM.

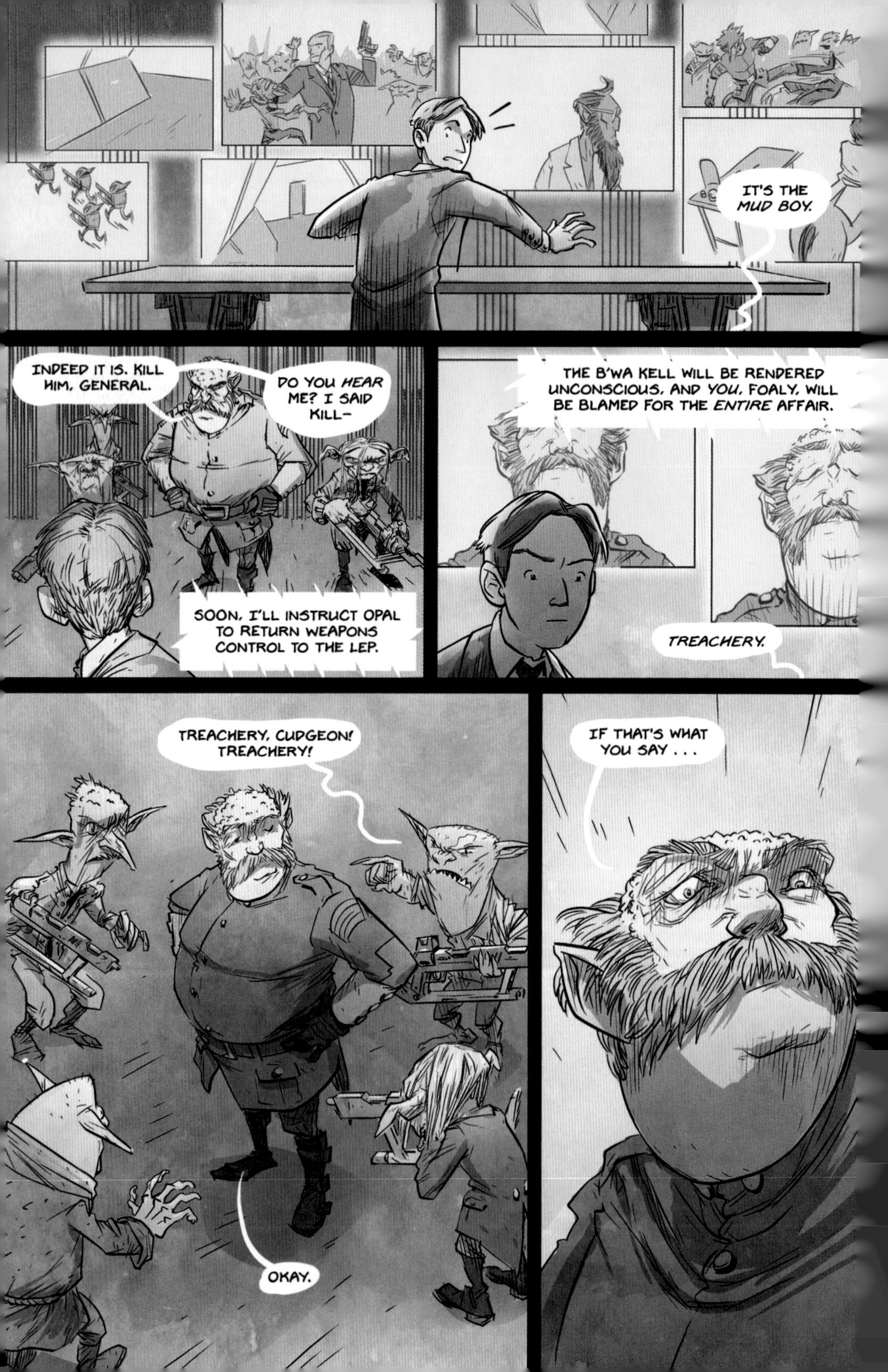
IT'S THE MUD BOY.
INDEED IT IS. KILL HIM, GENERAL.
DO YOU HEAR ME? I SAID KILL–
SOON, I'LL INSTRUCT OPAL TO RETURN WEAPONS CONTROL TO THE LEP.
THE B'WA KELL WILL BE RENDERED UNCONSCIOUS, AND YOU, FOALY, WILL BE BLAMED FOR THE ENTIRE AFFAIR.
TREACHERY.
TREACHERY, CUDGEON! TREACHERY!
OKAY.
IF THAT'S WHAT YOU SAY . . .

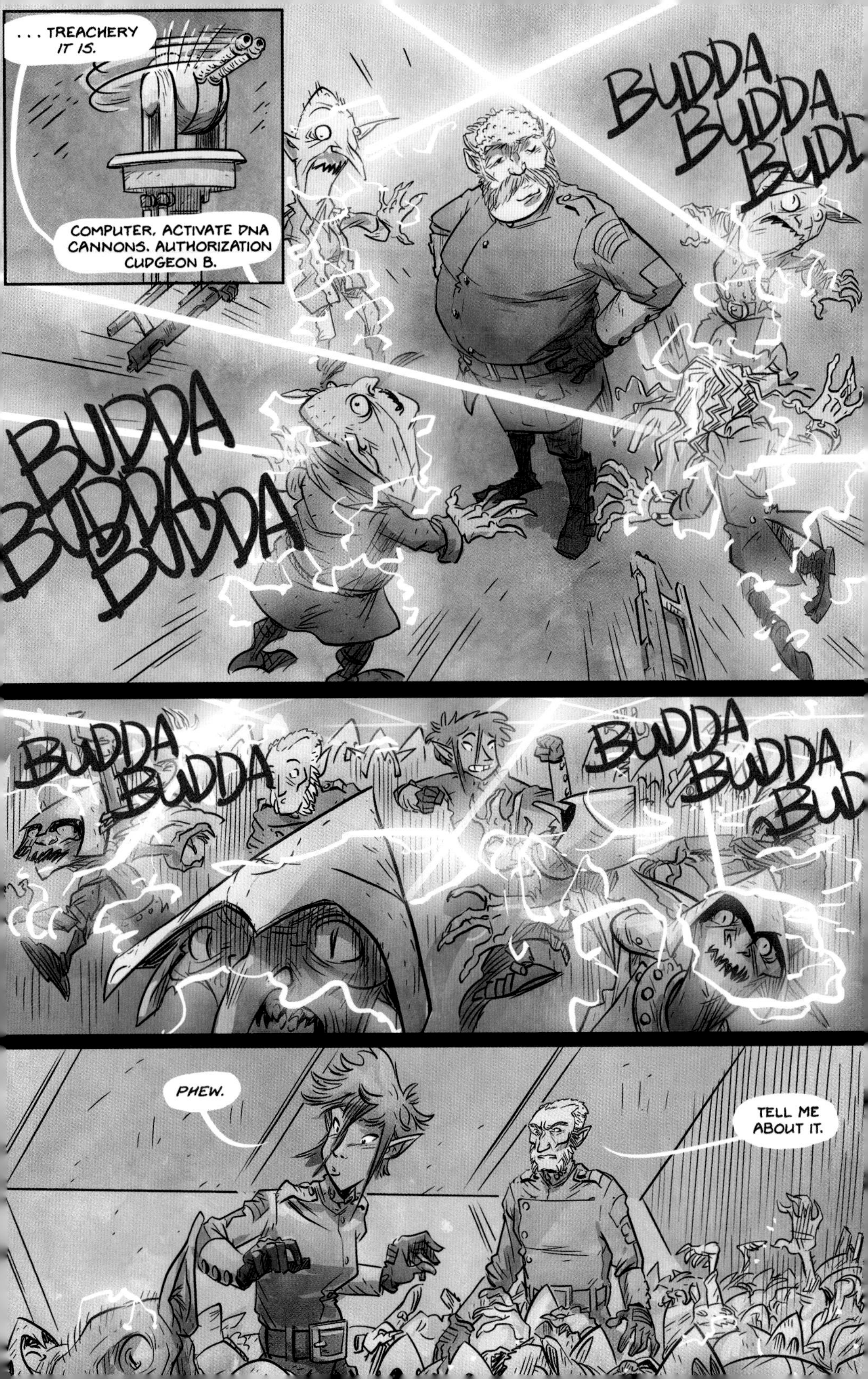
. . . TREACHERY IT IS.
COMPUTER, ACTIVATE DNA CANNONS. AUTHORIZATION CUDGEON B.
BUDDA BUDDA BUDD
BUDDA BUDDA BUDDA
BUDDA BUDDA
BUDDA BUDDA BUD
PHEW.
TELL ME ABOUT IT.

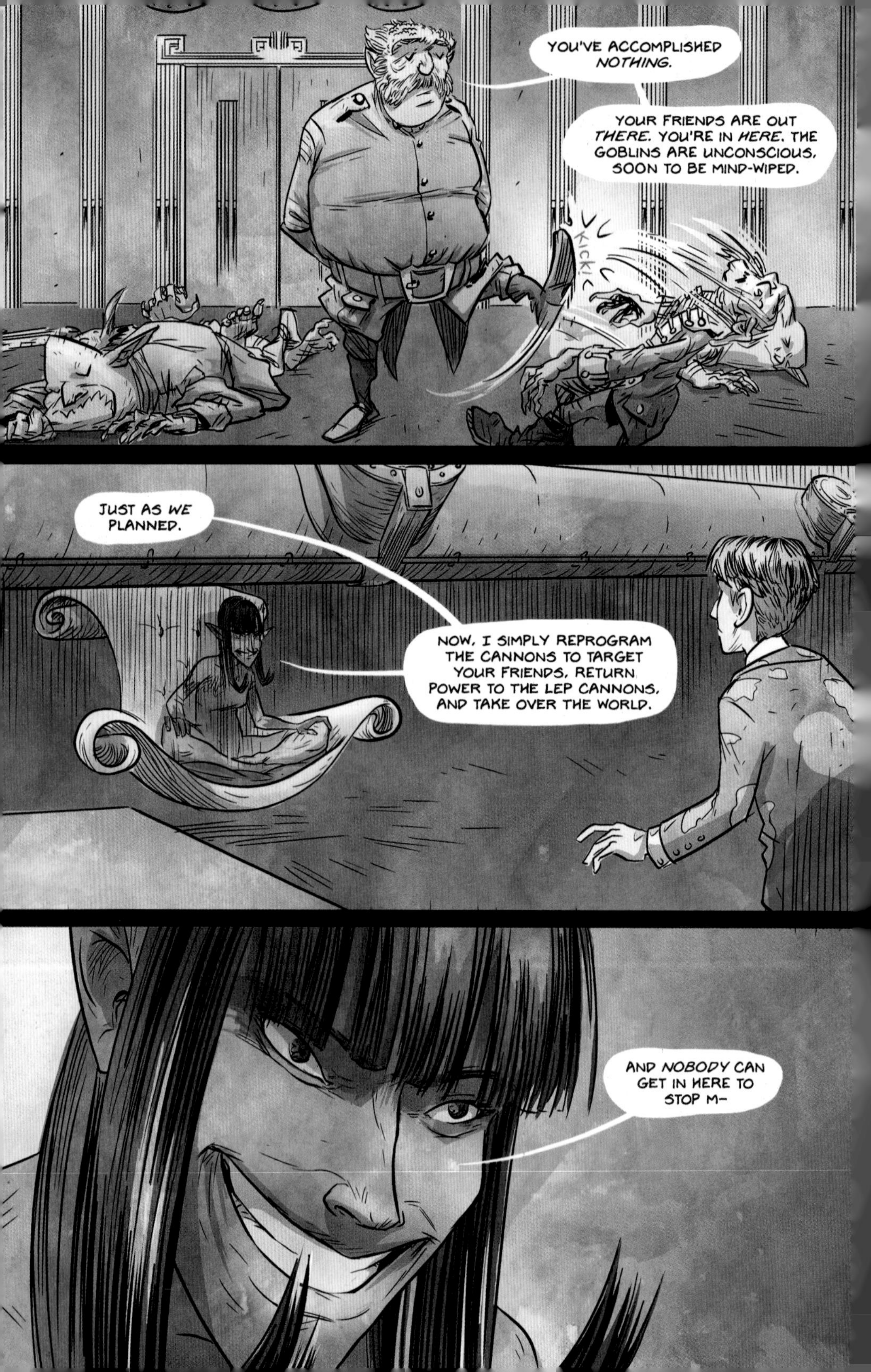
YOU'VE ACCOMPLISHED *NOTHING.*
YOUR FRIENDS ARE OUT *THERE.* YOU'RE IN *HERE.* THE GOBLINS ARE UNCONSCIOUS, SOON TO BE MIND-WIPED.
KICK!
JUST AS *WE* PLANNED.
NOW, I SIMPLY REPROGRAM THE CANNONS TO TARGET YOUR FRIENDS, RETURN POWER TO THE LEP CANNONS, AND TAKE OVER THE WORLD.
AND *NOBODY* CAN GET IN HERE TO STOP M–

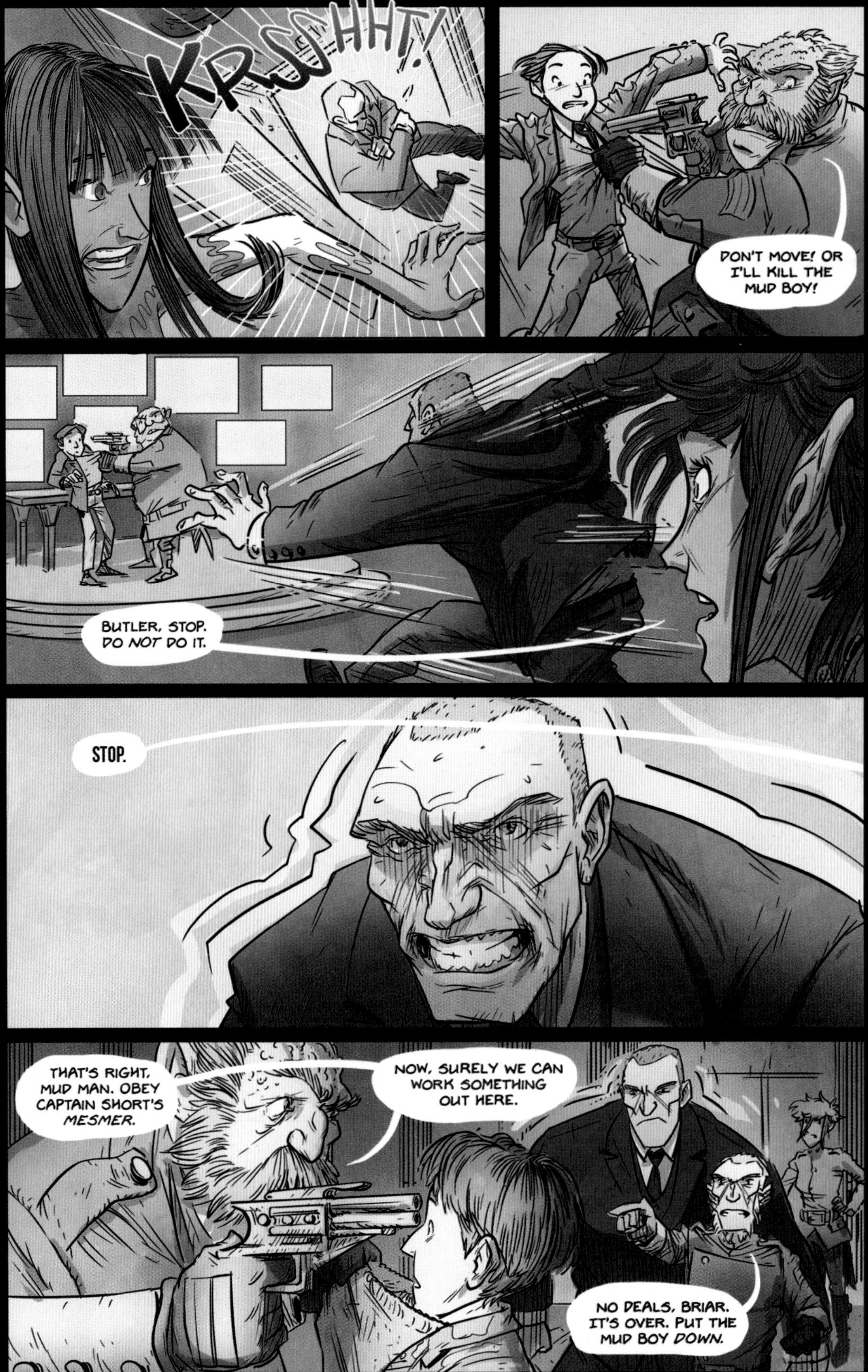
KRSHHT!
DON'T MOVE! OR I'LL KILL THE MUD BOY!
BUTLER, STOP. DO *NOT* DO IT.
STOP.
THAT'S RIGHT, MUD MAN. OBEY CAPTAIN SHORT'S *MESMER*.
NOW, SURELY WE CAN WORK SOMETHING OUT HERE.
NO DEALS, BRIAR. IT'S OVER. PUT THE MUD BOY *DOWN*.

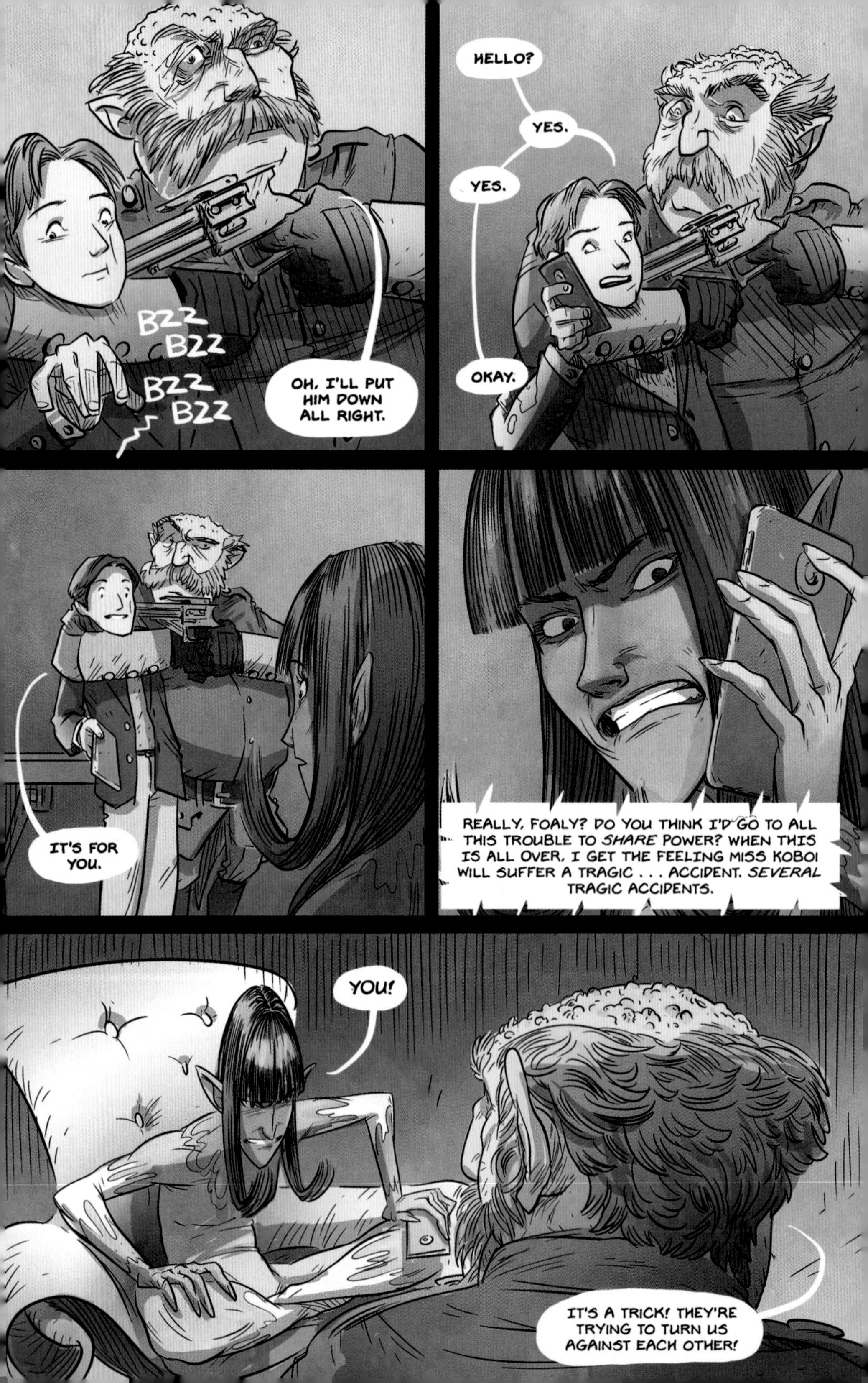
BZZ
BZZ
BZZ
BZZ
OH, I'LL PUT HIM DOWN ALL RIGHT.
HELLO?
YES.
YES.
OKAY.
IT'S FOR YOU.
REALLY, FOALY? DO YOU THINK I'D GO TO ALL THIS TROUBLE TO *SHARE* POWER? WHEN THIS IS ALL OVER, I GET THE FEELING MISS KOBOI WILL SUFFER A TRAGIC . . . ACCIDENT. *SEVERAL* TRAGIC ACCIDENTS.
YOU!
IT'S A TRICK! THEY'RE TRYING TO TURN US AGAINST EACH OTHER!

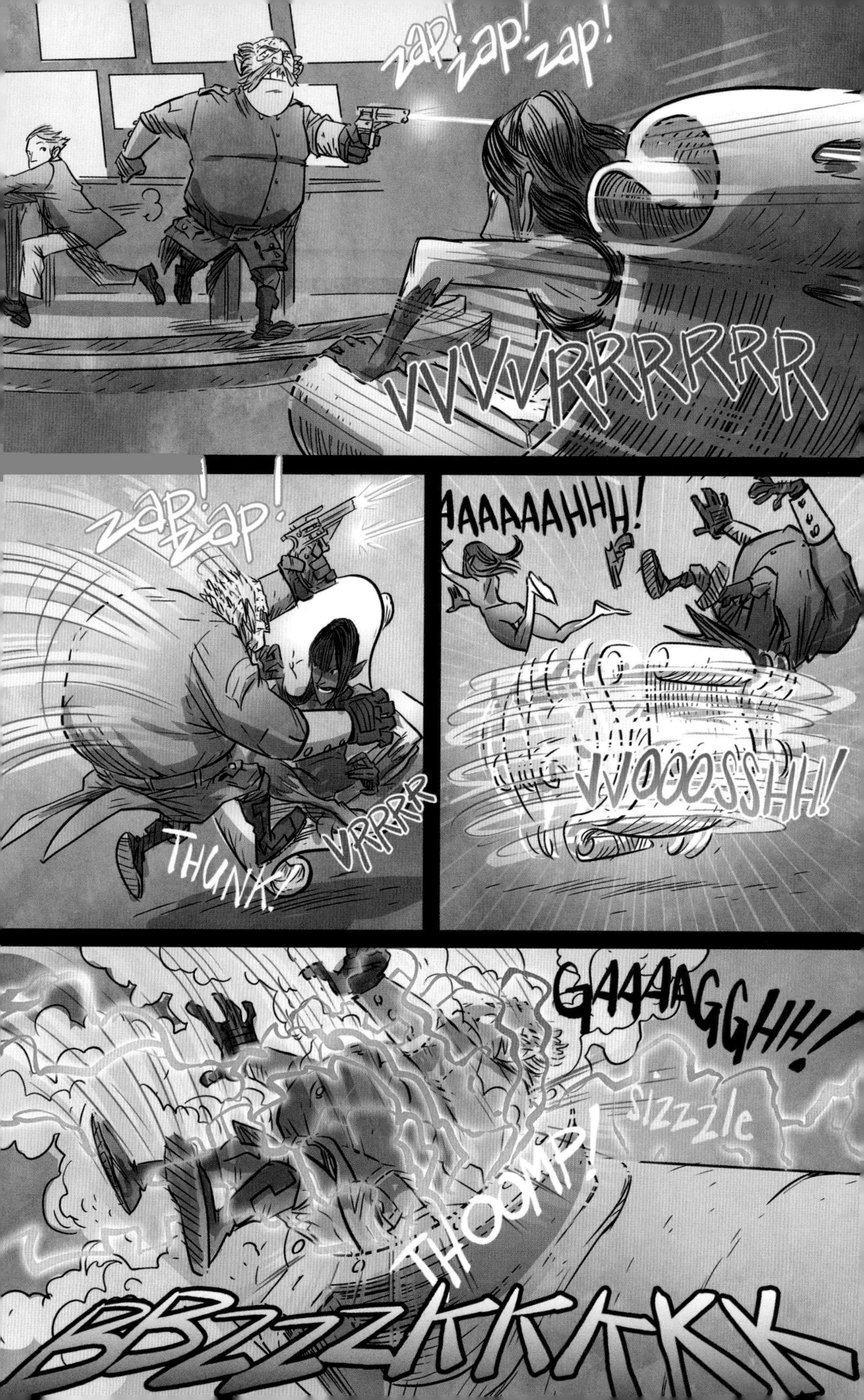
zap! zap! zap!
VVVVRRRRRRR
zap! zap!
THUNK!
VRRRR
AAAAAAHHH!
VVOOOSSHH!
GAAAAGGHH!
sizzzle
THOOMP!
BBZZZKKKKKK

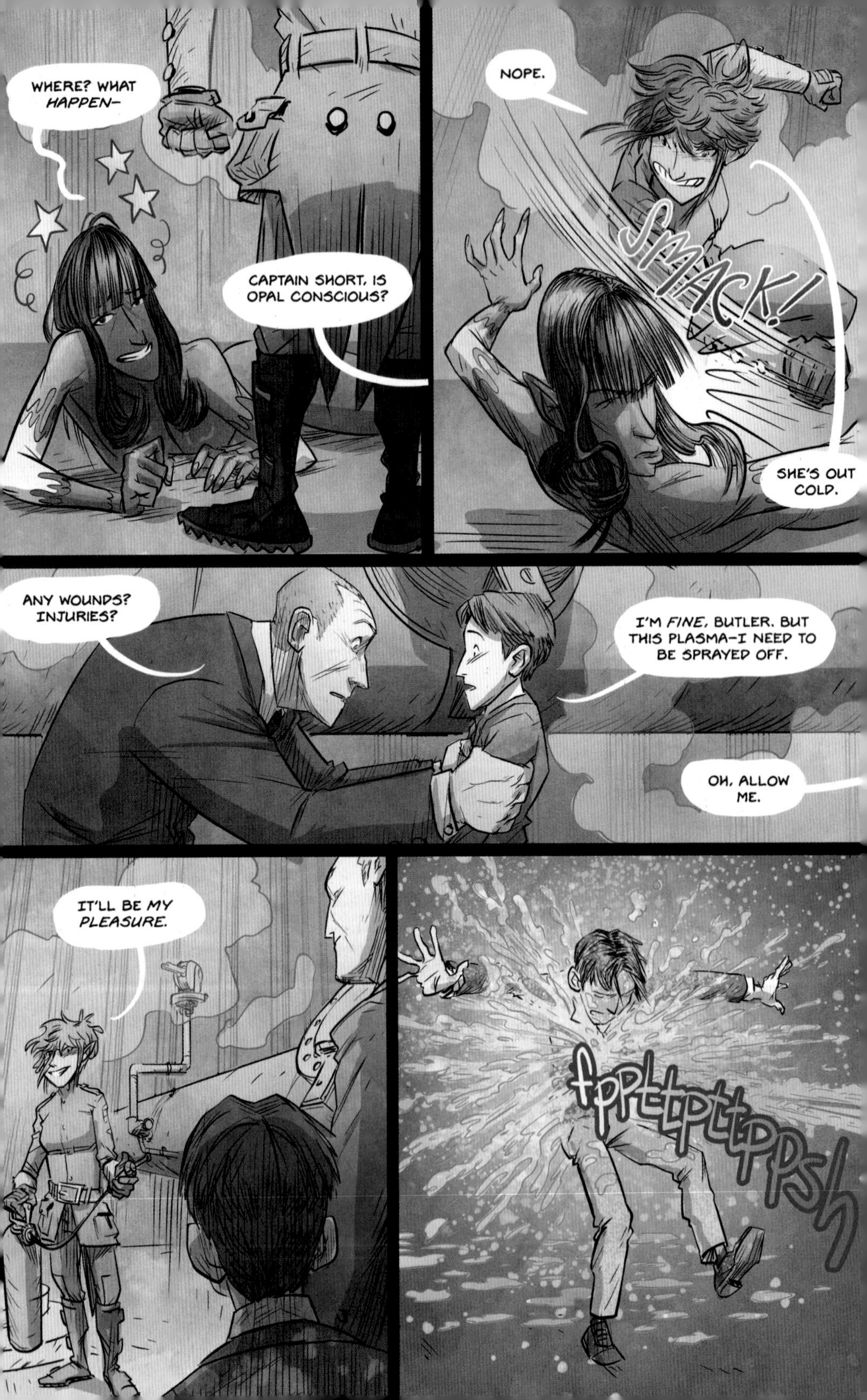
WHERE? WHAT HAPPEN–
CAPTAIN SHORT, IS OPAL CONSCIOUS?
NOPE.
SMACK!
SHE'S OUT COLD.
ANY WOUNDS? INJURIES?
I'M FINE, BUTLER. BUT THIS PLASMA–I NEED TO BE SPRAYED OFF.
OH, ALLOW ME.
IT'LL BE MY PLEASURE.
fpptttptttppsh

CHAPTER FOURTEEN

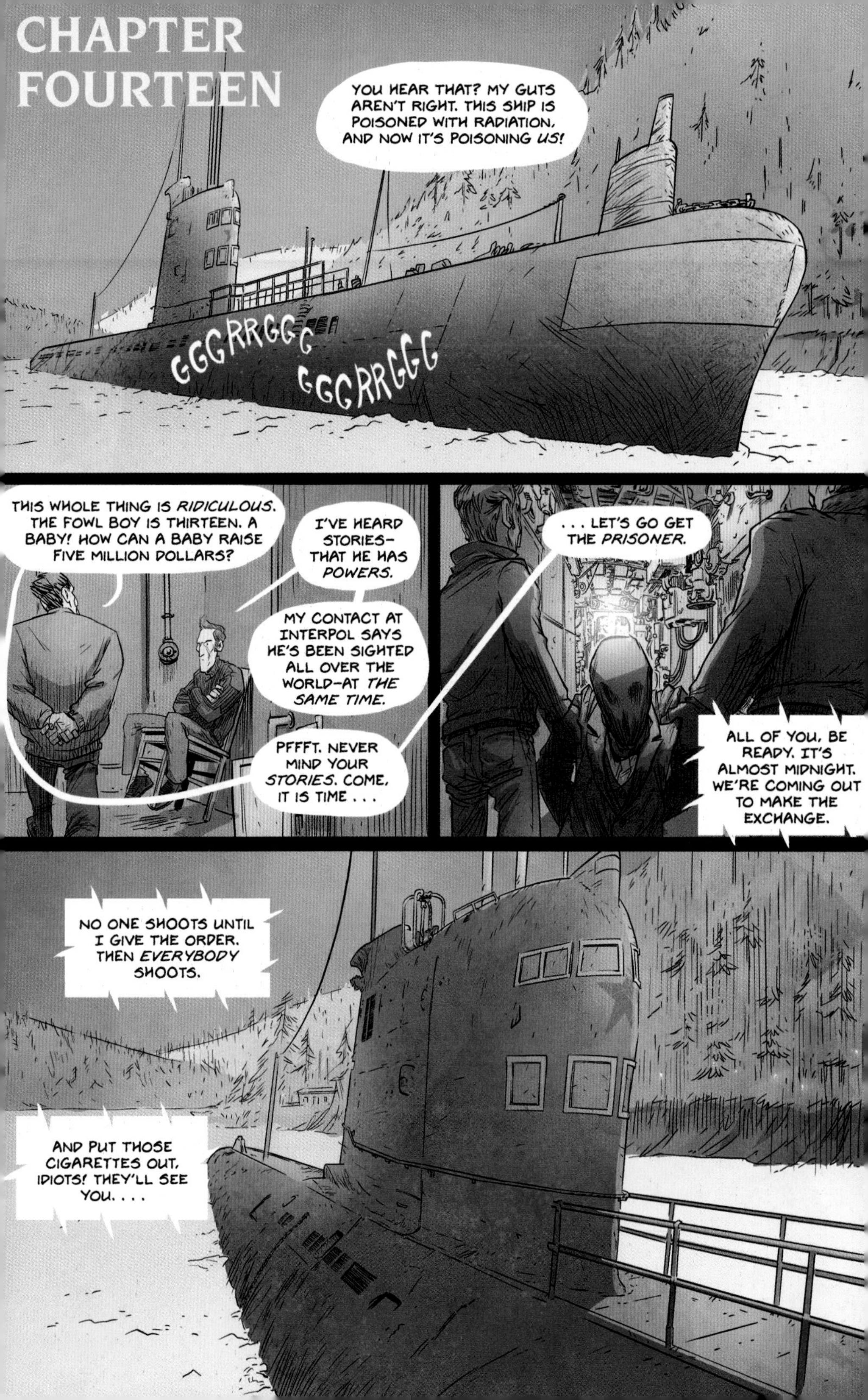

YOU HEAR THAT? MY GUTS AREN'T RIGHT. THIS SHIP IS POISONED WITH RADIATION, AND NOW IT'S POISONING *US*!
GGGRRGGG
GGGRRGGG
THIS WHOLE THING IS *RIDICULOUS*. THE FOWL BOY IS THIRTEEN. A BABY! HOW CAN A BABY RAISE FIVE MILLION DOLLARS?
I'VE HEARD STORIES— THAT HE HAS *POWERS*.
MY CONTACT AT INTERPOL SAYS HE'S BEEN SIGHTED ALL OVER THE WORLD—AT *THE SAME TIME*.
PFFFT. NEVER MIND YOUR *STORIES*. COME, IT IS TIME . . .
. . . LET'S GO GET THE *PRISONER*.
ALL OF YOU, BE READY. IT'S ALMOST MIDNIGHT. WE'RE COMING OUT TO MAKE THE EXCHANGE.
NO ONE SHOOTS UNTIL I GIVE THE ORDER. THEN *EVERYBODY* SHOOTS.
AND PUT THOSE CIGARETTES OUT, IDIOTS! THEY'LL SEE YOU. . . .

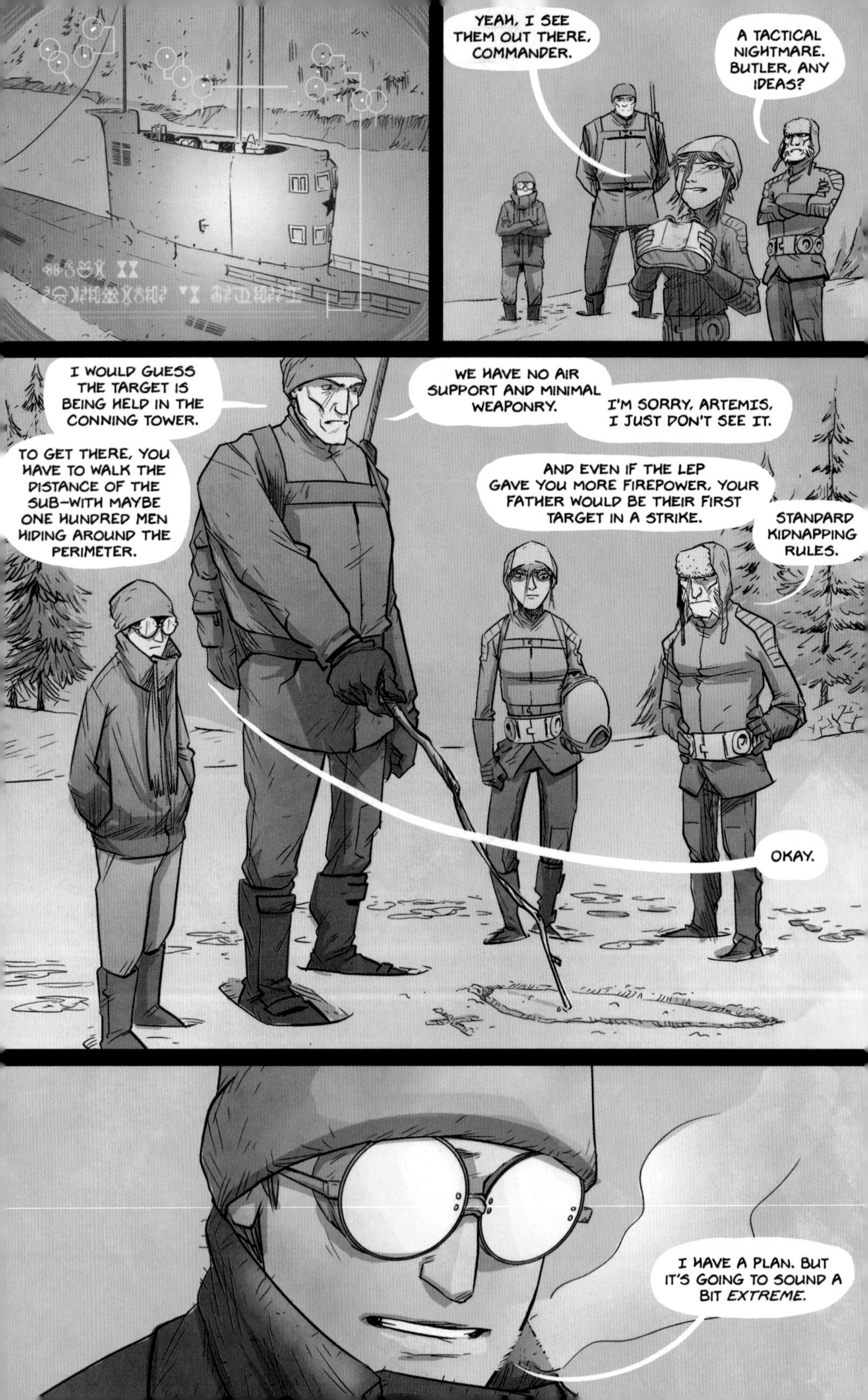
YEAH, I SEE THEM OUT THERE, COMMANDER.
A TACTICAL NIGHTMARE. BUTLER, ANY IDEAS?
I WOULD GUESS THE TARGET IS BEING HELD IN THE CONNING TOWER.
TO GET THERE, YOU HAVE TO WALK THE DISTANCE OF THE SUB—WITH MAYBE ONE HUNDRED MEN HIDING AROUND THE PERIMETER.
WE HAVE NO AIR SUPPORT AND MINIMAL WEAPONRY.
I'M SORRY, ARTEMIS, I JUST DON'T SEE IT.
AND EVEN IF THE LEP GAVE YOU MORE FIREPOWER, YOUR FATHER WOULD BE THEIR FIRST TARGET IN A STRIKE.
STANDARD KIDNAPPING RULES.
OKAY.
I HAVE A PLAN. BUT IT'S GOING TO SOUND A BIT *EXTREME*.

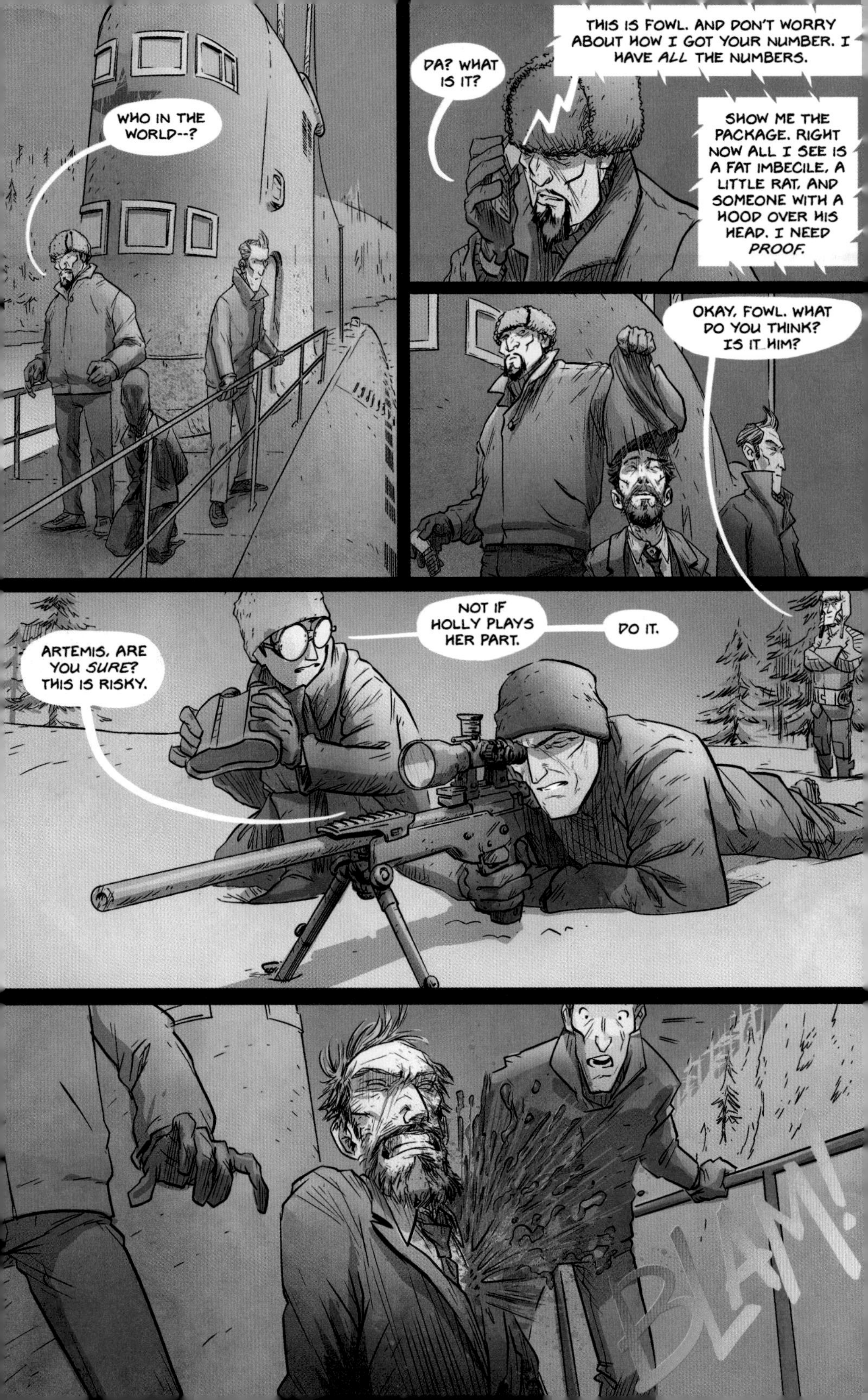
WHO IN THE WORLD--?
DA? WHAT IS IT?
THIS IS FOWL. AND DON'T WORRY ABOUT HOW I GOT YOUR NUMBER. I HAVE *ALL* THE NUMBERS.
SHOW ME THE PACKAGE. RIGHT NOW ALL I SEE IS A FAT IMBECILE, A LITTLE RAT, AND SOMEONE WITH A HOOD OVER HIS HEAD. I NEED *PROOF.*
OKAY, FOWL. WHAT DO YOU THINK? IS IT HIM?
ARTEMIS, ARE YOU *SURE?* THIS IS RISKY.
NOT IF HOLLY PLAYS HER PART.
DO IT.
BLAM!

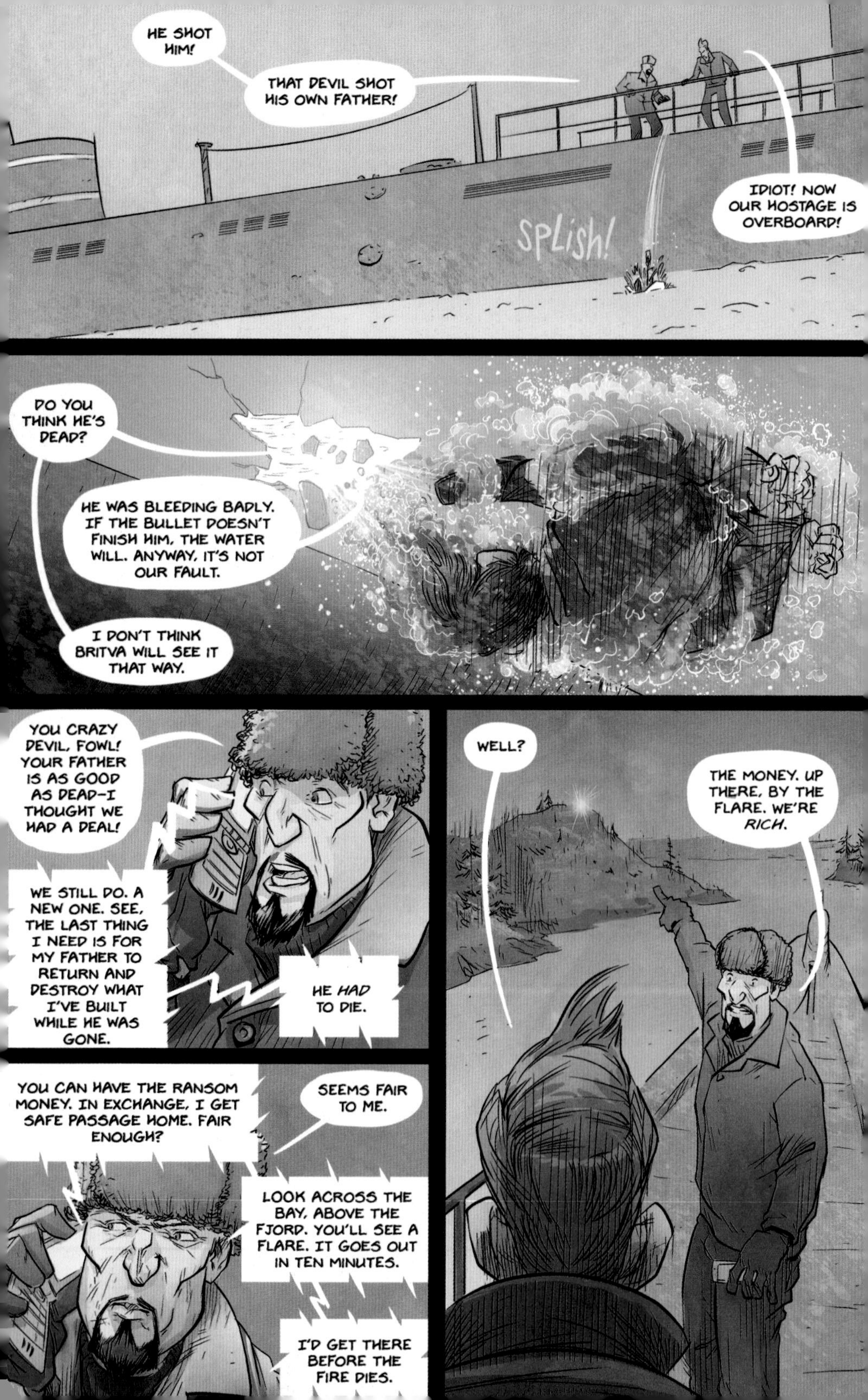
HE SHOT HIM!
THAT DEVIL SHOT HIS OWN FATHER!
IDIOT! NOW OUR HOSTAGE IS OVERBOARD!
SPLISH!
DO YOU THINK HE'S DEAD?
HE WAS BLEEDING BADLY. IF THE BULLET DOESN'T FINISH HIM, THE WATER WILL. ANYWAY, IT'S NOT OUR FAULT.
I DON'T THINK BRITVA WILL SEE IT THAT WAY.
YOU CRAZY DEVIL, FOWL! YOUR FATHER IS AS GOOD AS DEAD—I THOUGHT WE HAD A DEAL!
WE STILL DO. A NEW ONE. SEE, THE LAST THING I NEED IS FOR MY FATHER TO RETURN AND DESTROY WHAT I'VE BUILT WHILE HE WAS GONE.
HE *HAD* TO DIE.
YOU CAN HAVE THE RANSOM MONEY. IN EXCHANGE, I GET SAFE PASSAGE HOME. FAIR ENOUGH?
SEEMS FAIR TO ME.
LOOK ACROSS THE BAY, ABOVE THE FJORD. YOU'LL SEE A FLARE. IT GOES OUT IN TEN MINUTES.
I'D GET THERE BEFORE THE FIRE DIES.
WELL?
THE MONEY. UP THERE, BY THE FLARE. WE'RE *RICH*.

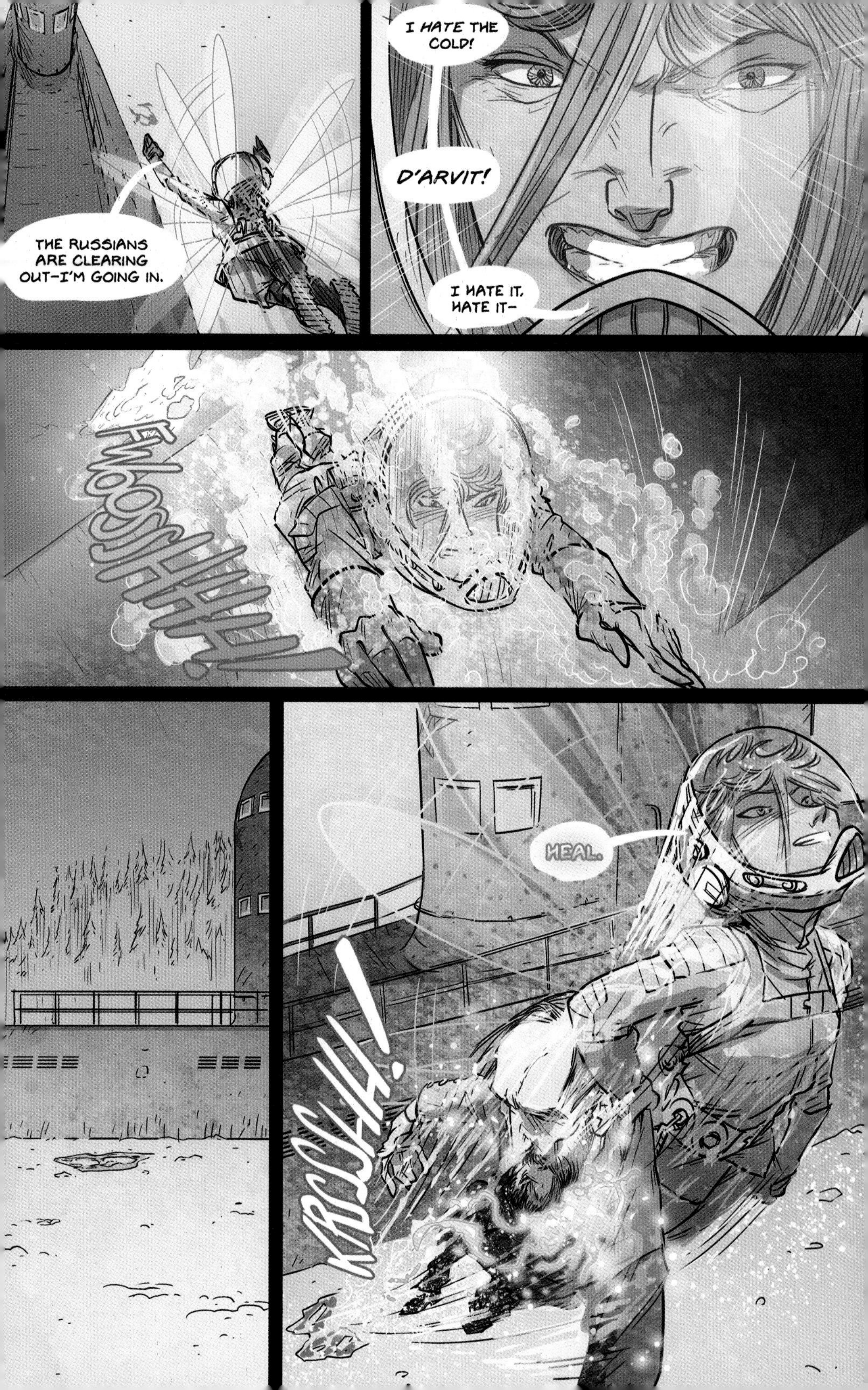
THE RUSSIANS ARE CLEARING OUT–I'M GOING IN.
I HATE THE COLD!
D'ARVIT!
I HATE IT, HATE IT–
FWOOSHHHH!
HEAL.
KRCCHH!

EPILOGUE

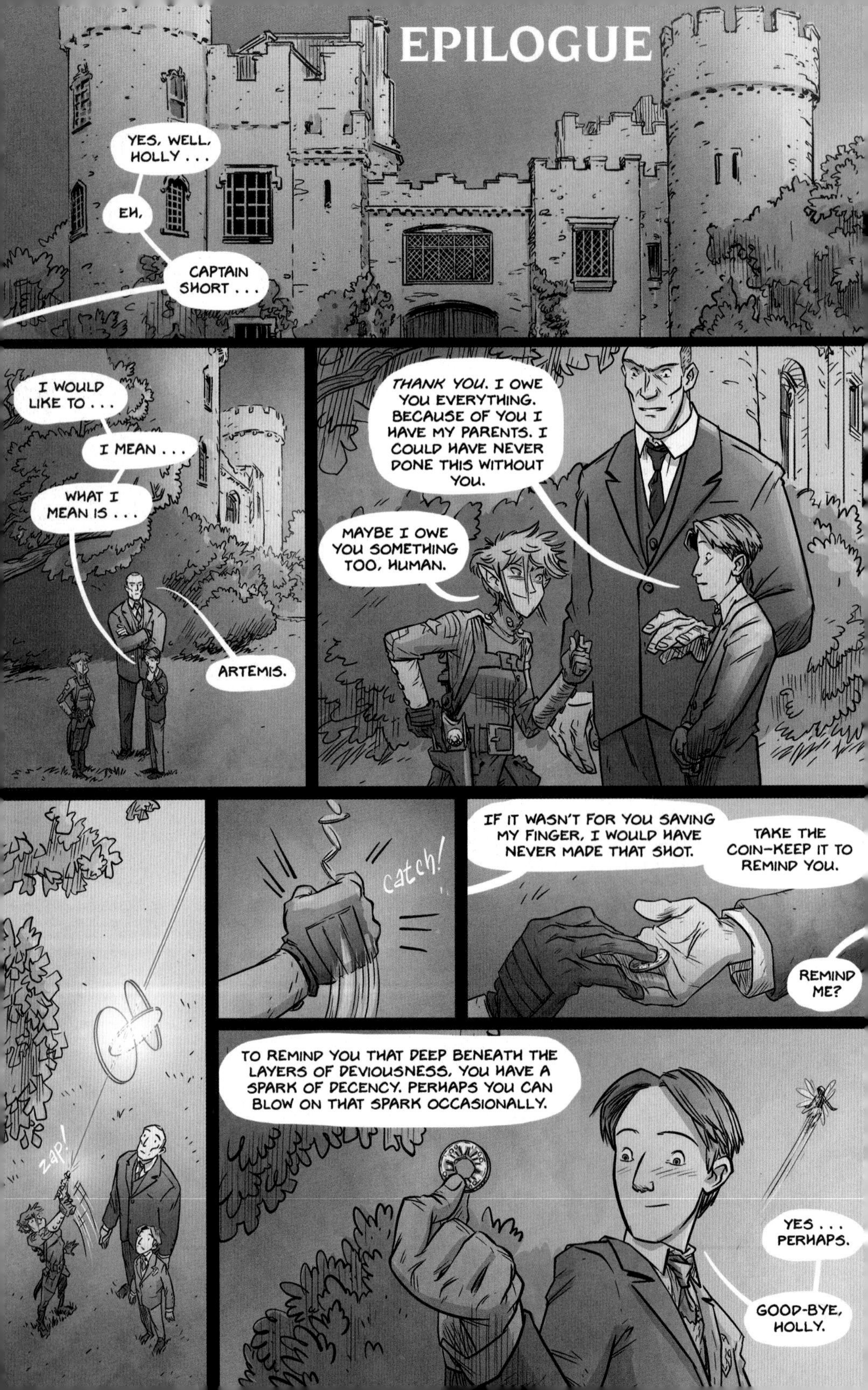
YES, WELL, HOLLY . . .
EH,
CAPTAIN SHORT . . .
I WOULD LIKE TO . . .
I MEAN . . .
WHAT I MEAN IS . . .
ARTEMIS.
THANK YOU. I OWE YOU EVERYTHING. BECAUSE OF YOU I HAVE MY PARENTS. I COULD HAVE NEVER DONE THIS WITHOUT YOU.
MAYBE I OWE YOU SOMETHING TOO, HUMAN.
ZAP!
CATCH!
IF IT WASN'T FOR YOU SAVING MY FINGER, I WOULD HAVE NEVER MADE THAT SHOT.
TAKE THE COIN—KEEP IT TO REMIND YOU.
REMIND ME?
TO REMIND YOU THAT DEEP BENEATH THE LAYERS OF DEVIOUSNESS, YOU HAVE A SPARK OF DECENCY. PERHAPS YOU CAN BLOW ON THAT SPARK OCCASIONALLY.
YES . . . PERHAPS.
GOOD-BYE, HOLLY.

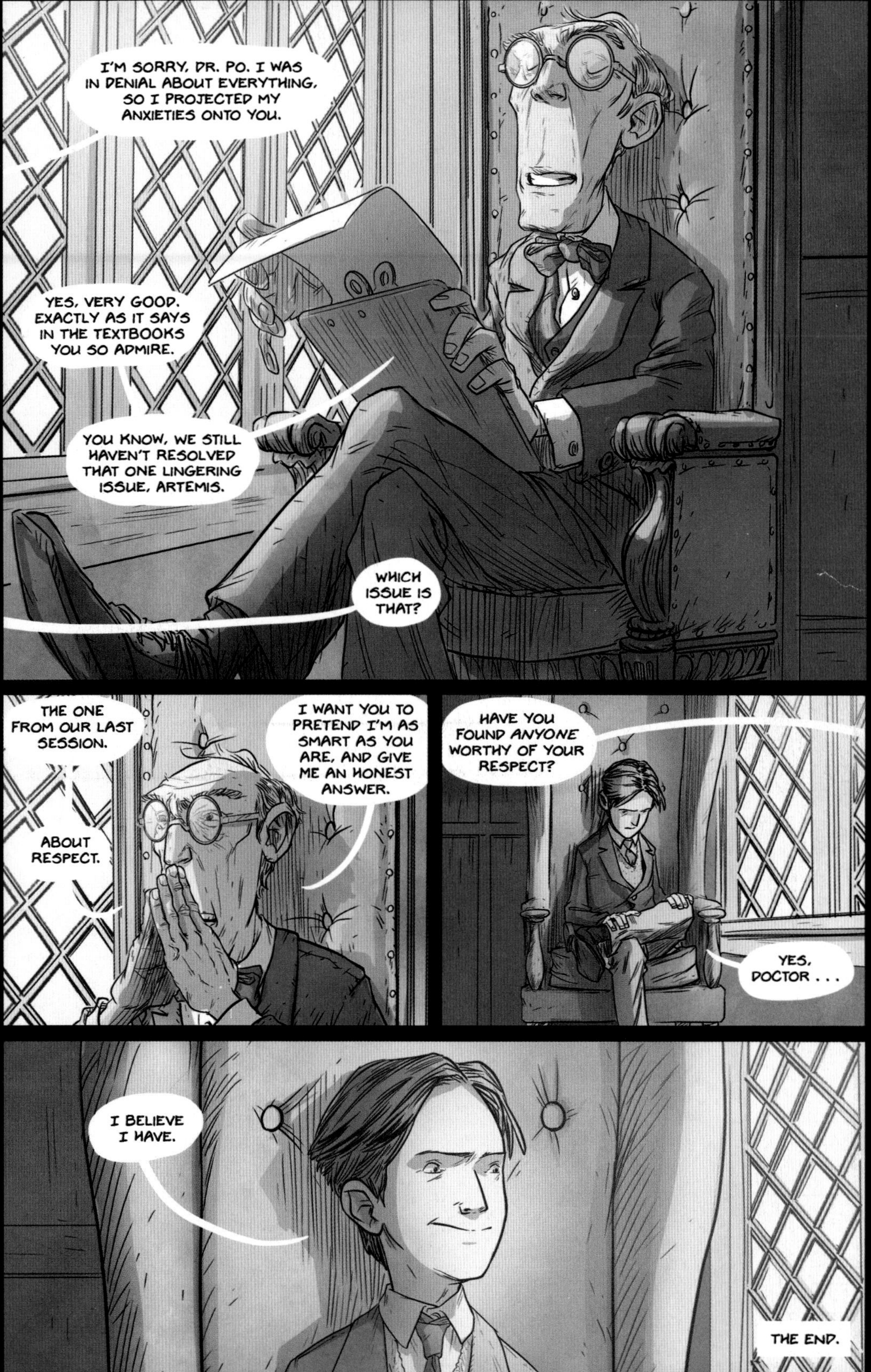
I'M SORRY, DR. PO. I WAS IN DENIAL ABOUT EVERYTHING, SO I PROJECTED MY ANXIETIES ONTO YOU.
YES, VERY GOOD. EXACTLY AS IT SAYS IN THE TEXTBOOKS YOU SO ADMIRE.
YOU KNOW, WE STILL HAVEN'T RESOLVED THAT ONE LINGERING ISSUE, ARTEMIS.
WHICH ISSUE IS THAT?
THE ONE FROM OUR LAST SESSION.
ABOUT RESPECT.
I WANT YOU TO PRETEND I'M AS SMART AS YOU ARE, AND GIVE ME AN HONEST ANSWER.
HAVE YOU FOUND *ANYONE* WORTHY OF YOUR RESPECT?
YES, DOCTOR . . .
I BELIEVE I HAVE.
THE END.